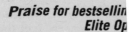

RENEGADE

"Leigh delivers in her latest work. The plot stays on track and the small-town setting serves the story well. Mikayla and Nik are well-developed characters who share a sweet and erotic passion. This is a hot one for the bookshelf!"

—*RT Book Reviews*

"*Renegade* is a wonderful combination of all the right elements—smoldering romance, suspense, and mystery. Add to that the cast of interesting characters—and their pasts—and you have the perfect recipe for one amazing novel."

—*Night Owl Romance* (4.5 stars)

"*Renegade* will have you breathless in places and it gets your blood running hot with the physical attraction between Mikayla and Nik." —*Romance Reviews Today*

BLACK JACK

"Overflowing with escalating danger, while pent-up sexual cravings practically burst into flames." —*Sensual Reads*

"This fourth Elite Ops book has plenty of betrayal, intrigue, and sizzling, undeniable passion." —*Fresh Fiction*

HEAT SEEKER

"Leigh's pages explode with a hot mixture of erotic pleasures." —*Romantic Times BOOKreviews*

"Lora Leigh brings the heat and plenty of intrigue. *Heat Seeker* is aptly named because you'll hear and feel the sizzle every time you turn these pages. Filled with adventure, suspense, action and lots of hot loving, this one's a definite keeper!" —*Night Owl Romance* (Reviewer Top Pick!)

MAVERICK

"A phenomenal read." —*Romance Junkies*

"Scorching-hot sex, deadly secrets, and a determined assassin add up to another addicting Leigh thriller. Leigh's ability to credibly build damaged characters who are both intriguing and intense gives her stories that extra punch." —*Romantic Times BOOKreviews*

"Sex and violence power the satisfying second installment of Leigh's Elite Ops series." —*Publishers Weekly*

"Full of wrenching emotion and self-flagellation by the hero, the new series of Elite Ops promises to be even better than the sexy SEALs at this rate." —*Night Owl Romance*

"With her customary panache for emotionally intense, sensual characters, the author attracts readers into every world she creates. This fabulous follow-up to *Wild Card* is no exception to the rule." —*A Romance Review*

WILD CARD

"Highly emotional and addicting...an intoxicating first installment of a brand-new series." —*Romance Junkies*

"Ferocious passion!" —*Romantic Times BOOKreviews*

...and the novels in her sexy SEALs series

KILLER SECRETS

"A smoldering-hot, new espionage tale. This chapter of Leigh's SEAL saga reverberates with deadly danger."
—*Romantic Times BOOKreviews*

HIDDEN AGENDAS

"Treachery and intrigue combine with blistering-hot sensuality in this chapter of Leigh's SEAL saga. The title of this book is particularly apt, since many of the characters are not what they seem, and betrayal can have deadly consequences. Leigh's books can scorch the ink off the page."
—*Romantic Times BOOKreviews*

"An evocative and captivating read."   —*Romance Junkies*

DANGEROUS GAMES

"A marvelous novel of suspense and raw passion."
—*Romance Junkies*

"Lora Leigh ignites the fire...with steamy heat added to a story that makes you cheer and even tear up."
—*Fallen Angel Reviews*

"Leigh writes...tempting, enchanting romance[s] that readers are certain to devour."   —*Romance Reviews Today*

MIDNIGHT SINS

LORA LEIGH

St. Martin's Paperbacks

This is a work of fiction. All of the characters, organizations, and events portrayed in this novel are either products of the author's imagination or are used fictitiously.

MIDNIGHT SINS

Copyright © 2011 by Lora Leigh.

For information address St. Martin's Press, 175 Fifth Avenue, New York, NY 10010.

ISBN: 978-0-312-38908-6

Printed in the United States of America

St. Martin's Paperbacks edition / August 2011

St. Martin's Paperbacks are published by St. Martin's Press, 175 Fifth Avenue, New York, NY 10010.

10 9 8 7 6 5 4 3 2 1

MIDNIGHT SINS

CHAPTER 1

Cambria at thirteen

It would have been amusing, if it hadn't had the potential to be so dangerous.

Jaymi Flannigan Kramer watched as her younger sister, Cami, sneaked another shy look at Rafer Callahan, one of Corbin County's three bad boys and the man Jaymi's deceased husband had claimed as a blood brother.

He was also the man she was sleeping with, but that wasn't as important as the fact that he was her best friend. And he knew, just as well as she did, that sleeping with him was her attempt to stay close to the husband who was forever gone. He had been Tye's best friend, his blood brother, and the only man she knew who even came close to her soul mate.

She turned her gaze away from Cami and Rafe and let it sweep over the crowd attending the Saturday night social.

Jaymi loved the name of the county's weekly street party and dance that had become a tradition of almost-required attendance. The mayor and city officials pushed the weekend socials the way some towns pushed voting, sports arenas, and political agendas. Wholeheartedly.

Corbin County and its seat, Sweetrock, promoted their drug awareness and "Children First" agenda with the same passion and strength. They had adopted the slogan more than a generation before and made certain everyone knew they meant it.

Friday after school the community center opened and any child enrolled in school from Head Start to college was welcome. BYOSB—Bring Your Own Sleeping Bag—was the rule. But there were so many donated bags that it really wasn't necessary.

City officials, employees, and any and all teachers, from tenured to substitute, were required to give one weekend per month to chaperone the social as well as the community center.

Families donated the food and drinks that were prepared in the community center's kitchen, and parents who didn't stay around to help chaperone were forced to sign a legal release stating that if they left their children, at any time, in the care of the county's volunteers, the parents rescinded all rights or legal abilities to sue in the event of accident.

However all manner of ills could befall anyone who chose not to participate. Permits could get lost or delayed, mail could be misplaced, utility workers could move at a much slower pace, and just forget getting out of that speeding ticket. And that was nothing compared to what local business owners could do.

City Hall had begun the socials, and their commitment to providing something entertaining and supervised for the county's youth had been sustained for over twenty years. It had grown to the point that if that commitment lapsed in any way, then newspapers and radio stations found the phenomenon strange enough to report it.

Corbin County had found that the key to keeping their youth away from delinquency or drugs was to give them something to do. And it was still working.

Parents and teens mingled in the dance area, while the younger children played games or watched supervised videos.

Parents took the few hours' break to dance, socialize, and build not just friendships but also those all-important ties that sustained a community.

But there were undercurrents. Undercurrents existed in any town. It wasn't all sweetness and light. For Corbin County, those undercurrents seemed to swirl most viciously around Rafer Callahan and his cousins, Logan and Crowe. The three disowned grandchildren of Corbin County's founding and most influential families.

Crowe, Logan, and Rafer Callahan were each the son of a reigning princess of one of those founding families and the Callahan brother she had married.

Many said those three unions were born of the murders of the brothers' parents. The couples had died in a suspicious accident on a mountain road. Within days of their deaths the Rafferty, Corbin, and Roberts patriarchs had arrived at the court house with a bill of sale and proof of purchase of the extensive Callahan lands bought by the three men. When their sons Samuel, David, and Benjamin returned from the military to a pittance amount for prime land, they turned their attention to the daughters of these families.

The Callahan brothers had acquired more than they had ever lost when they married those daughters. At least for a few years. Until a freak blizzard had swept through the Colorado mountains. The storm had surprised the three couples who were returning from Denver that night. Slick roads, high winds, and near-zero visibility had sent their SUV careening over a mountain cliff, killing them, as well as a single infant daughter, instantly.

And it had left three orphans whom those influential families had opted to disown and attempt to rob of the inheritances their mothers had left to them. Property, cash, trust funds, and a multitude of stocks and bonds that totaled into the millions. At last rumored count, it was close to $40 million among the three cousins. Funds that were still frozen and in litigation ten years after the death of their parents.

If it hadn't been for Rafe Callahan's uncle Clyde Ramsey, the boys wouldn't have had a chance of surviving or fighting for what was theirs.

But the same city officials and reigning families who sponsored, pushed for, and fought for the weekend attendance at the socials also put just as much energy into ostracizing the Callahan cousins.

And the reasons why just simply didn't make sense.

Why would the Raffertys, Robertses, and Corbins turn on the only heirs their daughters had left? Wouldn't it have made more sense to draw the orphans to their hearts, care for the boys, love them, or at least give them the illusion of love, and steal their inheritance once they were older?

But why turn on them at all? Why try to destroy three kids who simply didn't know what the hell was going on or why their families had disowned them to begin with?

It was a question that Jaymi hadn't really thought much of herself until lately. It was simply accepted. She had accepted it all her life, just as everyone else in the town had.

As their mutual friend Jack Townsend had said the other night when she had asked him about the past, there were just things they had accepted as kids but had learned better than to believe as adults.

But because of his father's demands and a county's blind obedience to the three founding families, Jack had been forced to take his friendship with the Callahans into the shadows. It was either that or watch his parents' garage slowly go bankrupt.

That was how it worked in Corbin County. The county was one of the last holdouts to an archaic community. It was ruled by the financial power of three families whose focus on the destruction of their own flesh and blood was becoming a shadowed, silent feud. That feud had the potential to tear families apart in not too many more years.

Whether the Corbins, Raffertys, and Robertses liked it or not, Corbin County was growing. New blood was coming in. Technology was making the world a much smaller place, and Corbin County would be forced to change with it. Whether any of them liked it or not.

Besides, there were more important things in the world to worry about than these three young men. Men who had been unfortunate enough to have been born to an inheritance their families didn't want them to have.

"Did you hear about Amy Jefferson?" Jaymi heard the question posed several tables over by one of the women who had volunteered to chaperone that weekend.

Amy, the daughter of Colorado's state representative, had been found raped, tortured, and murdered. Another victim of a serial killer's hunger.

"Poor thing," Sara Keane, the wife of the pharmacist Jaymi worked for, said. "They said they found her in her car on the road at the base of Crowe Mountain. She was a mess, too. She had suffered badly the state police reported."

That mountain belonged to Crowe Callahan and it was part of the inheritance he was still fighting the three families over. A mountain that had been in the Corbin family since before the county had first been created that went to the oldest child of the family, and if that child was a daughter, all that was required was that she have a child herself. And all the better if he were a son and carried the "Crowe" name. Bloodline was more important than name to the great-grandmother who had set the trust in motion. Bloodlines, and the family name that originated centuries before.

But the implications of the state representative's daughter dying at the base of the mountain wasn't lost on Jaymi. There were already those more than eager to pin those murders on the Callahan cousins.

She slid a look to Rafe to see him laughing with Logan. Cami had wandered away from the table, as she was prone to do lately, as though she couldn't bear to be around Rafe for long. At the same time, she would catch little glimpses of him as if to be certain he was still there.

Teenage hormones, Jaymi thought sadly, weren't being kind to her sister, and they boded ill for Cami's future. A fascination such as the one she was showing for Rafe would only end up breaking her young heart, one way or the other.

It wasn't as though Cami had a lot to hold on to in her young life. She had Jaymi, and sometimes, if their father wasn't around, Cami had their mother. Unfortunately, their father was around much too often. Cami could do nothing right in his eyes. Just as Jaymi could do nothing wrong. And to preserve the peace in the house, Margaret Flannigan did whatever it took to pacify her confrontational husband. And that meant ignoring her youngest child.

Even the knowledge that his elder daughter was fucking the town's ostracized bad boy wasn't enough to tarnish Jaymi in Mark Flannigan's eyes. As he explained it, grief had overtaken her and Jaymi was temporarily trying to find her husband after his death, in the arms of his best friend. And Rafe Callahan was taking advantage of it. "After all, wasn't that what a Callahan was best known for?" was what her father was prone to say.

Mark wasn't a father to his younger daughter, and that often seared Jaymi with guilt. She didn't understand why, but she suspected. Cami would have been conceived during the year their mother was estranged from her husband. And Jaymi had always wondered.

"Do you think they were involved in it?" Jaymi heard Sara ask, and she knew who "they" were.

"Well, the FBI released their profile on the killer," the other woman stated. "And they *'did'* say they believed it was at least two men acting in accordance. I wouldn't doubt it was three," she concluded with an air of knowing importance.

At that moment, Jaymi's cell phone began vibrating in her jacket pocket, causing her to flinch in fear.

Glancing at Rafe, she saw him and Logan talking to Cami, teasing her as they tried to draw her back to the group.

Pulling the cell phone free, Jaymi glanced at the number before moving a few steps away, then flipping the phone open. She didn't know her caller's identity, but the "unknown" caller was familiar.

"Go to hell!" she hissed into the line as she answered the call.

"My hell is a daily adventure into a torment created by man who is full of infinite cruelty and self-absorbed awareness. A hell created by Callahans. Do you really want me to show you my hell, Jaymi?"

She knew that voice.

Each time he called she tried to keep him talking longer, tried to figure out who he was. Because she knew that voice, had heard it before, and often. But not often enough to place it without seeing his face at the same time.

"Why would you care?" she asked, watching the crowd and trying to spot anyone with a cell phone. Anyone who could be making the call.

She saw no one.

She saw several teenagers texting. The Realtor Dave Stone was laughing into his phone, but he had a high, nasal tone, not a gentle saddened voice that echoed with grief.

"Why do I care?" the caller sighed. "There are so many reasons. I like you, Jaymi. You're different than . . . Well, than most women, who lower themselves to fuck those bastards, I guess." He paused as though he had said more than he intended to. "Don't push me. Get your sister and walk away from him, Jaymi. Cut those ties now, before you force me to cut them for you."

Jaymi glanced over at Rafe again. He, Logan, and Crowe were gently flirting with Cami, as she giggled and watched Rafe with complete female adoration.

"I'll ask you again, why do you care?"

There was a moment of silence.

"Because I have to care," he finally said sadly. "If I don't, who else will? Who else will keep them from destroying families, lives, and morals, if not I?"

"They're just men," she whispered painfully, realizing in that moment what the Callahans had faced all their lives. "Not monsters."

"But they attract the monsters," he said, with grave certainty as though he truly believed monsters existed. "This is your last chance, Jaymi. I won't tell you again. End this illicit relationship or I'll end it for you."

It was what he had said.

"End this illicit relationship."

Who had she heard say that before? It stuck in her mind, the words and that grave, pain-ridden voice.

Who had called her relationship with Rafe illicit?

She swallowed tightly, feeling that knowledge at the very edge of her memory.

The knowledge of who it was was getting closer. She could feel it. And when she remembered she would make damned sure the whole county knew who he was. Moving back to the small group, Jaymi couldn't help but feel a flare of regret for the lives Rafe and his cousins lived. Always aware they were unwanted.

"Jay, you okay?" Rafe slid behind her, his arms going around her waist as she watched her sister from the corners of her eyes.

Jaymi watched as Cami turned away as Rafe came behind Jaymi, Cami's head lowering until Logan drew her attention once again.

Meeting Logan's gaze, Jaymi caught the little wink he directed her way, as well as the compassion she saw in his eyes toward Cami and her obvious affection for Rafe.

She could see Cami's devotion to Rafe also, as well as her tender emotions and the conflict raging inside her. Jaymi knew that Cami loved her. They were as close as mother and daughter at times, but lately, with this crush Cami had on her sister's lover, she found that though the bond wasn't straining, it was changing. That frightened Jaymi for reasons she couldn't explain. She had already lost the man she had called her soul mate since she was thirteen years old. She couldn't lose Cami as well, even in that small way. It would destroy her.

"I'm fine," she told him as he kissed her cheek. "What are you doing flirting with my baby sister? Don't you know she already has a terrible crush on you?"

He was only twenty himself. Hell, she was a cradle robber. She was twenty-five and she should be sleeping with a man her age rather than the young man her husband had called his blood brother. But Rafe had always seemed much older than his age, and far more experienced in life, which he was. It was easy to see why her husband had all but adopted him after meeting him years before.

Tye had been part Native American, raised by his Navajo grandfather, and had been completely loyal to the mocking, sarcastic, often-brooding young man he'd met years before in the middle of the forest while he'd been hunting. Ten years older than Rafe, but infinitely wiser, Jaymi always thought, Tye had taken the young man under his wing and they had formed a bond even death couldn't destroy.

Rafe sighed at her shoulder. "That girl confuses me."

Jaymi knew at that moment that she would be breaking their relationship off soon after all. Very soon. More than likely before the night was over. She couldn't bear to hurt Cami, and this crush she had on Rafe was causing Jaymi to break her young sister's heart.

Jaymi remembered clearly too, the first time she had seen her husband. She had been fourteen and he had been a worldly-wise twenty. Within weeks he'd laughed at her and said the same thing: she confused him. She had told him that was just because he was a boy and she was the girl who loved him.

"And why does she confuse you?" Jaymi asked, though she knew the answer, or a variation of it, that Rafe would give.

"Hell if I know, sweetie," he grunted. "She's got the oddest look in her eyes. Like she's a hundred years old and the secrets she knows break her heart."

Wow. She had expected the hell-if-he-knew part, but she hadn't expected him to acknowledge in even such a small way the fact that Cami was becoming a young woman.

"Perhaps they do," Jaymi said softly. "Her life hasn't exactly been a happy one. And I'm afraid it's about to get worse."

"Your father still hasn't said anything?" Rafe asked her, knowing the plans Mark Flannigan was attempting to put in place. Plans that would destroy Cami.

Jaymi glanced at her sister again. Cami was talking to Crowe about the wolves that roamed Crowe Mountain. He had out his cell phone and was regaling her with the story of the one that came through the dog door of his partially buried home and ate his cat's food before lying in front of the fire for a nap.

Jaymi had seen the pictures herself, but still found it hard to believe. That wolf had acted more like an overgrown pet than a wild animal.

"No, he hasn't said anything," she finally answered. "He's

refusing to even discuss the issue with Mother. It will split them up."

But as far as Jaymi was concerned, her mother should have never returned after leaving years before. This time, however, Jaymi could feel the explosion coming, and when it did she had a feeling it was going to hurt Cami more than anyone.

Mark Flannigan had been offered a promotion at the communications firm he worked at in town. It meant a move to Aspen and he wanted to accept it. The problem was, he didn't want Cami moving with them. He had convinced Jaymi to go with them before she learned he'd asked his brother, Eddy, to take custody of Cami. That betrayal to Cami had broken Jaymi's heart. But the fact that her mother's answer to solving the problem was to up her dosage of Ativan infuriated Jaymi.

"Poor kid," Rafe murmured. "It sucks bad enough when it's other family members, aunts. When it's your parents, it has to slice clear to the soul."

"She doesn't know yet." Jaymi knew her mother was doing her best to avoid the situation while Mark was continuing on with his plan to move.

Jaymi and her mother had managed to protect Cami so far from learning his plans, but that wouldn't last for much longer.

"You can't protect her forever," he said sadly, echoing her own thoughts.

"As long as I'm alive I can."

She lived for Cami. Knowing that Cami would suffer at her father's hands if she was gone, was all that kept Jaymi from joining Tye. From escaping the agony that met her each day in the knowledge that he had been taken from her so quickly.

There were days, nights, that she swore she could hear Tye calling her name. She would turn, expecting him to be there, certain that somehow he had found a way to return to her. If it were possible, Tye would have found a way.

Then, there were the dreams.

"What price would you pay to be with him?" The disembodied voice would whisper through her mind as she watched

Tye doing one of the things he loved best. Playing touch foot-ball with the kids. Laughing, showing them how to play.

"I would pay any price," she always whispered.

"Would you leave her?"

The scene would change then and she would see her sis-ter. Guilt would flay her as she watched Cami crying, sob-bing as though she were in agony as Rafe stood behind her, staring back at Jaymi with a question in his eyes.

"I would leave her." That was always the answer.

"What pain would you endure to be with him again?" The voice would whisper.

"Any pain."

And for a moment, just a moment, she was with him again. Surprise would reflect in his gaze, then regret. He would touch her. "What happened?" he would whisper.

Jaymi would shake her head. She didn't know what had happened, she didn't care, all she wanted, needed, was his kiss, his touch. And for just a moment, she had it again. As though it were real, his lips on hers, his hands pulling her close, the whisper of his voice as he welcomed her into his arms.

She ached for him down to the bottom of her soul. Life no longer held promise, the future no longer appeared excit-ing or bright.

Jaymi had lost her future in a desert a world away when the enemy's bomb had taken out the vehicle he was driving.

Turning her head, she watched Cami again, saw the hurt in her sister's gaze at the sight of Rafe's arms around her, and wanted to sigh at the intensity of emotion she glimpsed in her sister for the man there was no chance of having for a very long time.

Yes, she knew her sister's pain well. And she knew, after tonight, she would never add to it again.

Rafe knew as he pulled the pickup into the parking spot in front of Jaymi's apartment that the relationship was over. He could feel it in the very air, and though there was a sense of regret, there was no anger.

They both knew the reason why they were together.

Jaymi was searching desperately for the husband she had lost, and the closest she could get to him was the man he had called his best friend.

Not that he had cared. Rafe wasn't looking for love, it had no place in his life at the moment. Besides, the day he'd realized Jaymi's sister had a crush on him, Rafe had known this was coming.

The girl was damned confusing, just as he had told Jaymi. She'd managed to slip in beneath his defenses despite the fact he'd been on guard against it. She made him feel protective, made him want to look out for her.

He was aware of the crush she had on him, and was flattered by it. He teased her gently, let her flirt, just as his cousins did, and made damned certain he never let her become hurt by it.

But as Jaymi told her sister gently to go on up to the apartment, Rafe saw that flash of brutal pain in her soft gray eyes before she quickly hid it.

"Night, Rafer." She opened the back door slowly as though reluctant to leave him alone with her sister.

"Night, wildcat." He flashed her a smile and a little wink, pulling a little smile from her as she moved from the car and closed the door behind her.

They watched as the girl moved across the narrow strip of grass to the door of the apartment across from the truck.

She unlocked it quickly before disappearing inside and flipping on the inner lights.

As much as he used to expect it, he never saw her at the curtains spying. She would move through the brightly lit room occasionally but never come close to the windows.

"So, this is it, huh?" he asked Jaymi as he laid his arm over the steering wheel and continued to stare at the window.

He felt her surprise before turning his head to watch her.

Dark blonde lashes swept over her eyes for a second before she met his gaze, regret shimmering in her dark brown eyes.

"I think it's time," she said softly. "Cami needs me right now, Rafe. With the crap Dad is trying to pull on her, and this crush she's picked up for you, she's going to be hurt enough."

A small grin tugged at his lips. "She's lucky to have you, Jaymi."

He'd never resent her for it. Hell, he couldn't even blame her.

"I wish you'd had someone to protect you," she said then, sadness flashing over her delicate expression. "You're too good for the family you have."

He had to chuckle at that. "Of course I am, they're all ass-holes."

He played it off, but he remembered the days, the nights, that he'd agonized over being disowned, wondered what he and his cousins had done wrong that all of them had been turned away by everyone but his mother's uncle.

"Yes, Rafe, they're all assholes," she agreed softly. "And I'm so sorry for the hell they put you through."

"Stop, Jaymi." He gave his head a short shake at the regret that filled her voice. "You have no reason to be sorry for what others did. You're a good friend, and I've always known the reason we were together. You didn't lie to me."

"I didn't tell you though," she whispered. "I should have."

"You told me, sweetheart," he informed her gently. "With the lights out, every time you called me by Tye's name. I knew."

Her lips parted, her eyes filled with tears, and the response assured him that she had never been aware she had cried out for the husband she'd lost each time he was with her.

"Rafe—" Pain filled her voice.

"Jaymi, stop torturing yourself," he told her, his voice hardening at the tear that slipped from her eyes. "Did you know Tye came to me before he went on that last tour?"

"No." Her lips trembled as she shook her head and pushed the long dark blonde bangs back from her face. "Why would he do that?"

"To make certain I knew what he expected from me," he

told her with a small grin, remembering the visit with the same affection he'd felt the day the Navajo warrior had made his appearance at Rafe's uncle's ranch.

"What did he expect?" she whispered, so unconsciously eager for a new experience, a new memory of her husband that she could cherish, that she was now hanging on every word.

Rafe reached out, pushed back the long curl that fell down her face then, noticing, not for the first time, how Jaymi's hair was as curly as her mother's and her father's. Cami's was much straighter, and naturally shot with various shades of caramel, dark golds, and lighter browns amid the heavy strands of dark brown.

"He expected me to stand for him," he told her gently. "And those were his exact words. 'If anything happens to me, Rafe, I give you leave now, to stand for me however my heart needs you to stand'." From the day he had married Jaymi, Tye had called her 'his heart'. "I didn't know what he meant at first," he confessed as he watched her eyes fill with tears again. "He told me if he didn't come home, then he expected me to protect you, to clothe you, to feed you, and if you needed it, he expected me to warm you. Then he looked at me with those black eyes of his eyes and he said 'Rafe, if she needs, turn out the lights and let her pretend it's me. Don't let my heart suffer alone'."

"Oh God." Her hand flew to her lips as they shook, a sob suddenly tearing from her as he reached for her, pulled her into his arms, and held her gently. "Oh God, Rafe. I miss him." Agony pierced her voice. "I miss him so much I don't know if I can bear it."

Holding her, rocking her, Rafe felt his chest tighten with pain as she cried against him, wondering if perhaps he shouldn't have told her.

He and Tye had talked a lot that day, and his friend had told him that the day would come when he might believe it was time to tell Jaymi the request Tye had made of him. Rafe thought it was time, but hell, he'd been wrong before.

"I wouldn't have survived without you," she whispered tearfully against his chest as he rubbed her back, kissed the top of her head gently. "I couldn't have been here for Cami. I couldn't have protected her in the last year, Rafe, if you hadn't done as he'd asked."

She sobbed softly, the never-ending pain he knew she felt filling the air around them.

"I'll always be here for you, Jaymi," he promised her as her head lifted. "For both of you."

Damp eyes stared back at him, filled with misery and loss.

"Thank you, Rafe." She reached up, touched his cheek, then laid her palm against it gently. "One day, someone will love you the way I loved Tye. I know they will."

"I hope not, Jaymi," he whispered, meaning every word of it. "Love like that comes with far too much risk."

And she shook her head, the smile that curved her lips suddenly filled with life, with the memory of love. "I wouldn't have missed it for the world, Rafe. Even if I had known one day he would be gone, I wouldn't have missed it."

And Rafe knew, Tye had felt the same.

His friends had been two parts of a whole, and with Tye's death, there were times Jaymi seemed almost crippled with grief.

But in her eyes, in that moment, he saw another side of it. A side that held no regret. That loved so deeply that the pain was worth it.

And he promised himself, swore to himself, he'd never love that way. He'd never let another person in that deep. He'd never allow himself to be broken by losing them.

Two weeks later

The bronchitis was getting worse.

Jaymi sat beside Cami's bed and read the thermometer worriedly. Her temperature was edging over 102, her sister's face was flushed, her lips dry, and fever glittered in her dove gray eyes.

"But you were getting better," she sighed as Cami stared up at her with overbright eyes.

"Lost my medicine," her sister admitted, struggling for breath as she coughed again, the labored, rough sound worse than it had been when her sister had showed up at her doorstep earlier that day.

Their mother had sent her to the apartment, a good twenty-minute walk from the house that would have taken Cami much longer as she labored for breath.

She glanced at the clock, willing the doctor to call her back about the prescription before it was too late. She worked at the pharmacy, but still, Mr. Keene wouldn't like it if she had to let herself in tonight to fill the prescription.

If he were in town, he would have come in himself and done it, she knew. He liked Cami. Hell, everyone liked Cami, except their father.

"How did you lose your medicine?" Cami's answer perplexed her. Her sister wasn't an irresponsible child. She'd been forced to grow up young, and hadn't had the luxury of being able to forget the simplest things. Mark Flannigan, their father, had little patience for teenage angst or forgetfulness from his youngest child.

Cami shrugged at the question and turned her gaze away to stare at the wall on the other side of the bed.

"Cami?" Jaymi touched her sister's chin gently to turn her gaze back to her. "What happened to your medicine?"

"I don't know." Her dry lips trembled as her eyes filled with tears. "Dad came in the bedroom and he was upset because there were dirty clothes on the floor and the tissues were on my table. I think he threw them away when he started throwing everything in the trash."

Jaymi's lips thinned.

She knew better than to call him, or to appear at the house furious over it. Mark always had a way of making it look as though it were Cami's fault, or even pretending innocence.

While he did, their mother would stare at him in resigned accusation before mumbling about taking her medicine and heading for her bedroom.

She wasn't going to allow this to continue, she decided. Once Cami was better, they would go to the house and pack her things before bringing them to the apartment. Cami was being neglected in the most despicable way. Even worse, Mark was risking her health. He had to have known he had thrown the medicine away. That wasn't something that was done by accident, and she knew Cami wasn't a messy child. She was too neat for her age and Jaymi couldn't believe there had been enough tissues on the bed table for Mark to have missed the bottle of pills and the cough medicine.

She just prayed the doctor was willing to fax the prescription in to the pharmacy before Jaymi broke several different state and federal laws and refilled the prescriptions herself.

She would not allow her sister to suffer more tonight, and the hospital was more than an hour away. After the wreck she'd been in the week before, she was wary about driving the mountain roads.

There shouldn't have been anything wrong with her brakes. There had been no reason they would go out as she started down the mountain, causing her to nearly crash over one of the sheer cliffs that dropped to a boulder-strewn ravine below.

It had been sheer luck that had kept her from going over. That and the fact that a rock slide from the cliff above the road had caused the state to clear a wide area on the other side of the road to make room for debris.

She'd managed to steer her car to the other side and the very fact that she hadn't been going fast had possibly saved her life, Joe Townsend had told her.

But he had acted oddly. He'd refused to look her in the eye, and Joe was the type of man who looked a person in the eye. But when he'd warned her to be careful, and she had taken it as a warning, he'd been more commanding than concerned.

"Jaymi, watch what you're doing," he told her fiercely. *"Don't be taking any chances."*

She hadn't been aware she was taking any chances. At least not in her car.

But the night she and Rafe had stopped seeing each other, another call had come in, and this time, she was certain she knew who it was. Mostly certain of it. There was just enough doubt that she had to see him first, had to look in his eyes as he spoke to her to be certain.

Each time she called him the call went to voice mail. The one time she'd shown up at his office, he had been "unavailable," according to his secretary. But he couldn't hide forever. Sweetrock was a small town, she was going to see him eventually.

The ring of her cell phone had her jerking the device from the table next to the bed and flipping it open.

The prescription had been faxed in. The pharmacy was closed, but the doctor was certain it would be filled before the doors opened the next morning.

So was she. She had the keys to the store and she had the license to work behind the counter and fill prescriptions. She was supposed to have it checked by the pharmacist; she wasn't supposed to fill anything without Martin Keene's presence. But this was an emergency. It was her sister.

Cami fought to cough again, nearly losing her breath as she tried weakly to clear the obstruction in her lungs.

"Cami, I'm going to go get your prescription," she told her as she rose from the chair and grabbed the jacket she'd laid at the end of the bed earlier. "I'll be back in a bit, okay?"

Cami nodded, her eyes drifting closed, her breathing labored as she tried to rest before another bout attacked.

"Get some rest, baby." Leaning down, she kissed her sister on the forehead before grabbing her purse and keys and heading out of the apartment.

It was dark. The street lights glowed weakly in the evening fog, casting sinister shadows along the nearly deserted back streets.

She considered moving to the front of the block, but it was the quieter part of the evening. There wasn't much traffic until Main Street and then heading south toward the interstate.

The pharmacy was only a few blocks from her apartment, which was why she liked the job. She could walk to work and back, and even during the rain and snowstorms, it wasn't a bad walk. It would just be a wet one.

Which was why Cami had bronchitis. Her father had sent

her the eight blocks from their home to the pharmacy to get their mother's prescription rather than waiting for Jaymi to bring it to the house after she locked up.

He had deliberately attempted to get Cami ill, she thought as she tucked her hands into the light jacket she wore and strode faster along the neat, well-lit back street.

Cami was susceptible to bronchitis and pneumonia. If the first stage wasn't treated quickly and aggressively, then Cami could become viciously ill. She'd been hospitalized twice in the past four years, once for pneumonia, the second time for double pneumonia.

Pausing at the street corner, she felt a chill race up her spine and marked it down to the thought that her father might be attempting to kill his youngest child.

If she was his youngest child.

Jaymi had done some counting in the past weeks since her father had revealed his attempt to convince Uncle Eddy and Aunt Ella to keep Cami when they moved to Aspen.

Cami was thirteen. She would be fourteen in three months. Add nine more months to that, and it added up to the time their mother had taken Jaymi and stayed in Denver with Aunt Beth for nearly a year.

Jaymi had been ten, and she remembered, even now, how much happier her mother had been then. She laughed, giggled on the phone. Sometimes, Jaymi would wake up in the middle of the night and thought she heard a man's voice in the bedroom across the hall.

She remembered the man her mother had said was a friend of Beth's. He had worn a uniform. Dark hair, and eyes a soft, soft gray ringed with the same odd blue color Cami's were ringed with.

She walked across the street as realization began to rush through her.

God, why hadn't she made the connection before now?

For years she had watched Mark Flannigan treat Cami like shit, and had agonized over how a father could be so cruel. Why hadn't she remembered the darkly handsome man with the gentle smile and big hands?

Why hadn't she remembered, during that time, the day she had come home from the park with a neighbor to find her mother sobbing as though she were dying? Aunt Beth had been crying as well and Uncle Jonah had been grief-stricken.

She unlocked the pharmacy and stepped in, careful to lock the door behind her, holding her breath as she heard a car easing down the street.

She prayed it wasn't Mr. Keene, or the police. She would hate to have to explain why she was here. Even if she did have the key, she didn't have permission to be in before it was time to open the pharmacy.

Moving quickly to the back, she began to fill the prescription as those memories continued to ease forward from whatever shadowed recess they had been hiding in.

She was still shocked, dismayed that she hadn't remembered that summer so long ago. She should have. Because she remembered her father showing up not long after that and he and Uncle Jonah fighting over something Mark had called a "whoreson" and "wife-stealing brother."

It was beginning to make sense. So much was becoming more clear.

She had been pushing so many memories back over the years, trying to keep the truth at bay. She hadn't wanted to remember, though it was something Cami deserved to know. But that didn't mean it wouldn't destroy her. Cami still had the hope that the day would come that Mark would accept her as a daughter and part of the family.

The fact that he never would wasn't lost on Jaymi, or Jonah, if she could remember the past well enough to recall the screaming match they had gotten into.

Why? Why had she forgotten?

That question tormented her as she finished filling the prescription, capped it, and printed out the label before peeling the paper from it and sticking it onto the bottles.

The antibiotic would take at least twenty-four hours to kick in, but the cough medicine would ease her labored breathing and the horrible coughing.

Did Cami take her susceptibility to bronchitis from her

natural father? Jaymi wondered as she made her way to the back door.

And if her mother had loved this other man so much, why had she taken Mark Flannigan back and allowed him to treat their daughter so dismally?

It was a question she intended to ask him the minute she arrived at the house in the morning. She would make a special trip before work just to throw her knowledge into his face and demand custody of Cami from both her parents.

She'd had enough. She wasn't about to allow Cami to be treated so cruelly, or endangered while ill again.

Re-entering the security code, Jaymi opened the back door to the pharmacy, eased out, and turned back to lock the three locks on the door and reset the code.

The door was almost closed, the keys ready to shove into the lock.

There was no warning.

There was nothing to alert her.

One minute she was filled with righteous indignation over the treatment her sister had received for as long as she could remember, and the next second, everything was black.

The lone dark figure, black mask pulled over his face, his eyes filled with sorrow, looked up to the camera that was almost hidden above the door.

He knew what would be seen later. Rich, sapphire blue eyes.

Picking Jaymi up in his arms, he turned away and laid her carefully in the backseat of the stolen pickup before tying her hands snugly behind her back. Her ankles were secured with another length of rope and gray tape placed over her lips.

He stared down at her, just for a second, before reaching out and pushing her hair back from her face.

He'd tried to warn her, he really had.

She'd pushed too far, though. When she had begun calling his phone, he knew she suspected. He should have known she would catch on quickly, she was really smarter than the others. Smarter, and with the clear advantage of having known him most of her life.

With a last pang of regret he closed the door to the back of the king crew cab pickup before moving to the driver's side and getting into the vehicle.

He stayed on the back streets, easing through them and making his way to the end of town before pulling the mask off and driving the speed limit the rest of the way.

He didn't have far to go. There was a small gravel and dirt road that led to where he'd told the other man to meet him. Once there, he would turn her over to the killer whose lust for blood made him exceptionally easy to use and to control.

The man wasn't good for much else but killing. He'd fried his brain with too many drugs years before, and existed on autopilot until he scored the next fix. Give the man a fix and he obeyed every command given and didn't remember a second of it the next morning.

For the first time since the killing had begun, he knew he wouldn't be participating. He usually took that first taste of them, raping them while they still had some fight to them. But he couldn't, not with Jaymi.

He couldn't hurt her himself.

He couldn't stay and watch her be hurt.

He'd have to trust the drugs to have done the work this time as efficiently as they had the past five times.

Jaymi would be the last nail in the Callahans' coffin. Once her body was found along with another, more significant piece of evidence, the Callahans wouldn't be able to excuse their way out of murder.

There was no way to save her. There would be no way to save the Callahans. And the truth of the events that began this tale twelve years ago would continue to rest in peace along with the bodies of the grandparents that had set the events in motion.

He'd killed them. He'd been forced to kill their sons and their sons wives that snowy day as they returned from Denver. He hadn't wanted to, but he'd had no choice. What they had been doing, and what they had found in that safe deposit box no one had known JR and Eileen Callahan had rented, could have destroyed them all.

Him included.

He couldn't let it happen. He couldn't let them destroy everything he had killed the cousins' parents for.

And it could have ended there.

It should have ended there.

And it would have, if only Jaymi hadn't realized who was calling. And if he wasn't certain she would figure out he was killing as well.

All for the greater good, of course, he told himself as he had been telling himself since that first life had been taken. It was all for the greater good.

But this time, with this woman, he knew the lies were catching up with him.

It wasn't for the greater good.

It wasn't for his own good.

It was for the good of a man that only gave the orders and refused to bloody his hands.

It was for the good of a family that would throw him to the wolves if it meant saving their own asses.

And he had no intentions of taking that fall.

At least, not alone.

CHAPTER 2

Rafe sat in the jail cell, silent, staring unblinking at the stone wall across from him, trying to ignore the blood that stained his clothes nearly two days after Jaymi's death. The sheriff refused to allow them to change clothes or shower. Swabs had been taken for DNA. But despite the tech's request for the clothes, it had been refused. Sheriff Tobias commented that he needed to wear Jaymi's blood a while longer to realize what he had done to her.

He could hear his recruiting officer in the sheriff's office yelling. Ryan Calvert had a strong, booming voice. It carried through the jail and caught attention, but for Rafe, Logan, and Crowe there was very little that could penetrate their shock, even now.

"I know I killed him." Crowe repeated again. "I put that knife straight inside his kidney. It was a kill blow."

At twenty-two Crowe shouldn't even know how to make a kill blow with a hunting knife.

But he had. Unfortunately, the blow had come too late.

They had come too late.

Rafe was yanked back, hours before, to the memory of Jaymi's screams echoing through the forest, jerking the cousins awake as they camped at the side of the lake and sending them crashing through the forest to find her.

They had followed the glow of a fire higher up Crowe

Mountain. Followed her screams which were agonized and enraged. They had rushed into the clearing as her attacker's knife plunged into her side.

Crowe hadn't been able to save her.

After the black-garbed figure had jumped from her, his pants still pushed below his hips his round eyes filled with fear as he ran. Crowe had crashed after him, tackling him to the ground as Rafe ran for Jaymi. He'd been aware of Crowe struggling with Jaymi's attacker. Crowe's knife had gleamed in the moonlight before a high-pitched scream had sounded and the assailant had managed to grip a stone and slam Crowe in the head with it, before escaping.

The knowledge of her death shadowing her gray-blue eyes, Jaymi's last thoughts were of her sister. She was sick. "Take care of Cami," Jaymi begged, crying. As he held her, as her blood soaked into his clothes and Logan made the desperate 911 call.

"Please, Rafe, swear it." The harder she had sobbed, the faster her blood had flowed from her body.

"I swear, Jaymi," he vowed hoarsely knowing she was struggling to hang on. "I swear I'll always watch out for her."

There was no saving her.

Rafe had applied pressure on the wound. He held her. He screamed at her and demanded she live. And still, she had reached up with one hand shaking, touched his cheek and whispered, "She loves you, Rafe. She'll always love you so much, just as I love my Tye. Give her a chance when she grows up." Tears had washed her face as he rocked her, his own cheeks damp as he realized he was losing her forever. "Promise me. Take care of Cami." Then Jaymi had looked over his shoulder and smiled before whispering, "Rafe, it's Tye." Her lips had trembled as such joy flooded her face, her dying gaze. "He's finally come for me, Rafe. Tye finally came for me—"

And she had died. With the greatest joy that Rafe had seen on her face since the day she had married her precious Tye, he watched Jaymi slip from life as he screamed out her name.

But the sheriff hadn't believed the men.

The sheriff and his deputies had arrived ahead of the state police. Immediately he and his cousins had been handcuffed and arrested as Jaymi's murderers. And now they were trying to pin the five other murders that had occurred that summer on Rafe and his cousins.

The black-masked serial killer had been caught on surveillance taking Jaymi outside the pharmacy the night before. Her sister, Cami, had reported Jaymi's disappearance hours later when Jaymi didn't return to the apartment with the medicine she had gone for.

That morning when the pharmacist went to unlock the back door he had found the medicine, Jaymi's key, and the door unlocked.

When he had pulled up the camera footage for the sheriff, they had seen the abduction, which had been taped just hours before Logan made that desperate 911 call. She had been taken at the same time witnesses had seen him and his cousins getting gas in town several blocks away.

Ryan Calvert, the recruiting officer who had taken an unusual interest in him and his cousins, had managed to get a copy of that security footage before the sheriff had gotten to it. Gunnery Sergeant Calvert hadn't rushed to the jail to bail them out, or to hire the nearest lawyer. The minute he'd heard the report over his radio and remembered seeing the Callahan cousins in town as he drove to his hotel, he rushed to the combined truck stop/gas station and restaurant and made nice with the manager, Missy Derringer.

Thankfully, Missy was a friend. Perhaps not a friend that publicly claimed the Callahans, but a friend nonetheless. They did have a few, sometimes.

Being the owner's daughter had helped. She'd quickly copied the security footage before her father could order otherwise and gladly gave it to the brooding Marine demanding it.

It hadn't helped.

They were still sitting there in a damn jail cell two days later wondering how the hell it had happened.

And Rafe couldn't get the memory of it out of his head.

The sight of that smile, so filled with love as she whispered Tye had come for her. It sent a chill up his spine, even now. The sense that she had only been waiting, always been watching for him to come for her had swept over him.

Jaymi had made Rafe swear he would protect Cami. She was sick, alone in Jaymi's apartment, according to Jaymi's friend and neighbor. Cami cried continually. She was begging for Jaymi, and Cami's aunt and uncle were considering having her hospitalized due to the severity of the bronchitis.

Rafe could still hear Ryan screaming about a vagrant who had been found with Crowe's knife in his side, his pants undone, and Jaymi's blood on him.

Ryan was yelling furiously about taking his own samples to a Denver lawyer and having them analyzed. He was demanding the sheriff release his nephews now, by God, before he sued the county for an illegal arrest. "That fucking security tape is all you dumb shits need," he raged. "Now let them the hell out now."

Rafe shook his head.

He and his cousins knew Ryan Calvert was a Callahan, but no one else had, until now. Their grandparents had given Ryan up for adoption, when they couldn't afford to feed their children any longer, long before Samuel, Benjamin, and David had really been old enough to understand their baby brother was gone.

Rafe didn't know the whole story; he'd only just learned that the recruiter who had come to Sweetrock was actually the youngest Callahan son. Ryan's search for his birth family had spanned more than ten years. His commitment to his nephews only grew stronger with the knowledge that his parents, as well as his brothers, were gone.

When his brothers returned, it was learned the child their parents had had so late in life, was dead, or so they believed, and their ranch supposedly sold and split between the Corbins, Raffertys, and Robertses. Their entire lives had been torn apart and all anyone cared about was convincing them to leave Corbin County and accept the losses.

And now that Callahan son was back and raising hell.

Ryan was screaming something about DNA, vagrants, serial murders, and alibis, and Rafe was wondering why he gave a damn.

Standing up, Rafe moved to the door, his hands shoved in the pockets of his jeans, his gaze focused on the night Jaymi died rather than at the stone wall across from him.

How was Cami? He had promised Jaymi he would look after her.

But how was he supposed to take care of her? He'd promised, but he had signed up for the Marines last week. He, Logan, and Crowe. They'd had enough of Corbin County for a while, they'd decided. Like their fathers before them, they thought the military seemed the best option.

For the same reason, perhaps. Because they were tired of the bullshit.

And it all went back to the three families who ruled Corbin County like their own personal little fiefdom.

Generations before, James Randal Callahan had acquired eight hundred acres of prime ranch land from the government as had his three partners James Corbin the First, Andrew Roberts, and Jason Rafferty.

At the time, the four men had been the best of friends as well as business partners. They had acquired the land they needed, the cattle and the horses, then they'd found wives.

They'd settled the land tucked between the rising mountains and proceeded to build a dynasty. But somewhere in those first years, something had happened to change those friendships and the wealth that first James Randal Callahan had brought with him. While the others had thrived, the Callahan family had slowly begun to wither away until Rafe's grandfather had nearly died of some lung infection.

Hospitalized, weak and fighting for his life, he hadn't even been aware that the world believed his youngest son was dead. In fact, his wife, Eileen Callahan had contacted acquaintances that she had known were desperate for a child. She'd sold her baby for the money needed to save the rest of her family and the ranch that amounted to everything they possessed.

Until the morning of their deaths, they had been worth a fortune. For some reason, that morning they had withdrawn every cent they had at the bank, and accepted a paltry couple of hundred thousand for a ranch that was worth three times as much in stock alone.

That night, they had been racing toward Colorado Springs along the curving mountain road with its sheer drops and spectacular cliffs. Somehow, JR Callahan, the great-great-grandson of James Randal Callahan, had lost control of the truck and plunged down one of those cliffs.

Their vehicle had exploded on impact with such force that the explosion had been heard across the mountains. It was the next day, though, before anyone had seen the faint tendrils of smoke rising from the canyon below.

And how strange that years later, their three sons and the women they had married had died in the same manner when their SUV had gone over a cliff as they drove from Denver. The coincidence was simply too great. The deaths too similar.

"Ryan's stopped blasting their eardrums," Logan stated quietly as he and Crowe stood up from the cots they had been sitting on.

When the metal doors at the other end of the cell area opened, Gunnery Sgt. Ryan Callahan Calvert, of the Boston, Massachusetts, Calverts, strode in, followed by two military police personnel and the lawyer he'd brought from Denver the day before.

Ryan was scowling. His strong, weathered face was stone hard, his blue eyes like chips of ice, as he followed the sheriff, Randal Tobias, to the cell Rafe and his cousins had been confined in.

The fact that Ryan wasn't happy was only eclipsed by the fact that Sheriff Tobias was glaring at the cousins with pure, vicious hatred.

"The little bastards fucking well better keep their asses in the county." He shoved the key in each cell door, twisted it furiously, and slammed the iron doors open. "Fuck up and I'll put a bullet in your heads myself."

Rafe sneered. "Only if the barons give you permission,"

he drawled, using the mocking nickname given to the patriarchs of the three families.

In the next second, Tobias buried his fist in Rafe's ribs, stealing Rafe's breath for a second and shoving him into the metal bars. Fury surged through Rafe in the next instant, pounding through his veins and throwing him forward after the sheriff, when Logan, Crowe, and Ryan suddenly grabbed him.

"Let it go, son," Ryan snarled in his ear. "You should have kept your mouth shut or prepared for it."

He was right. Rafe knew he was right. But still, Rafe wanted to take the bastard apart with his bare hands.

The sheriff sneered back at him.

Funny, Rafe thought distantly, the sheriff's son, Archer, seemed to have a streak of honor and had been one of the few people in the county to come forward and object to the treatment Rafe and his cousins had suffered in the past few days. That was one of the reasons Tobias was so furious now. Having his son defend the three cousins couldn't have gone over well with the barons who told Tobias when to breathe, when to fuck, and when to piss.

Rafe let his lip curl in the sheriff's direction. "That's okay, sir," Rafe drawled. "You're right: I should have been prepared. But I think the sheriff is very well aware of the price he's paying for the orders he follows."

He'd lost his son. Archer Tobias had stood in his father's face the day before and told the other man he couldn't believe they were related and that he prayed stupidity wasn't hereditary.

"You little fucker," Tobias snarled. "You'll be back. When you do Archer will see you for the murdering fuck you are."

Rafe shook his head. "Naw, he'll see you and the barons for the manipulative monsters you are. That's too bad, too, because I think Archer is tired of defending your eagerness to jump when they tell you to jump."

"Get him out of here, Calvert," the sheriff ordered. "Before I save the county the money to prosecute him and shoot him myself."

Two military police laid their hands purposely on the butts of their weapons. The action didn't go unnoticed.

"Let's go," Ryan ordered. "You all have a meeting with your lawyer, then you're going to settle in somewhere until we can take care of this."

"I have to take care of something else," Rafe stated as they headed for the door.

"The hell you do," Ryan growled as he followed close behind Rafe. "Don't argue with me, Rafe. Not here."

Rafe waited until they were outside. Turning back to his uncle, Rafe stared the other man in the eye, determination tightening his body and burning through his veins. "I promised Jaymi." His fists clenched at the thought of what he had to do. "I'll meet you wherever you need me to, but I have to take care of something first."

"And what the hell could be more important than your freedom?" Ryan snarled as he gripped Rafe's arm and pulled him around again.

"A promise," Rafe snapped as he jerked his arm back. "And I don't break my fucking promises."

Cami was sick; Jack and Archer both had told Rafe she was alone at Jaymi's apartment, and she hadn't gotten her medicine. It was confiscated as evidence when it was found outside the pharmacy, and Rafe didn't know if anyone had even cared to check on her.

He'd never imagined his life could come to this. At twenty, he thought he had the world by the tail, and despite the problems he and his cousins had faced in Corbin County, he'd believed it would all right itself in the end.

He couldn't have imagine this could happen, not even in his worst nightmares.

That Jaymi could die in his arms. That he could have been arrested for her murder when he'd done everything he could to save her.

And as he stepped out into the bright summer light to the sight of nearly two dozen of Sweetrock's residents glaring at him in accusation, he thought that perhaps he should have expected it.

Moving through the crowd was Clyde Ramsey, Rafe's uncle on his mother's side. A hard scowl covered Clyde's face as he strode the distance in a bowlegged walk that be-spoke his years on the little ranch he owned between Sweet-rock and Aspen, Colorado, well away from the family his sister had married into.

Clyde had raised Rafe and his cousins when no one else would have them. Would he disown them now as well?

"Well, let's go," he growled as he stopped in front of them. "I have cattle to feed and horse stalls to clean. I don't have time to waste."

He'd come for them. When everyone else stood glaring at them, as usual, Clyde was there to protect them in his own gruff way.

"I have to make a stop first," Rafe said quietly.

Clyde's scowl deepened as he blew out a hard breath. "Course you do," he harrumphed. "Let's get it done so we can get home and figure this one out." He shook his graying head. "Saving the three of you is turning into a mission in life, Rafe. And I'm an old man. Find a way to fix this."

He didn't give them time to answer. He turned on his heel and strode to his truck, expecting them to follow.

"Go on; we'll be behind you," Ryan told him. "And hurry with that stop you have to make. We have a long day ahead of us if we're going to figure this out, as you say."

They had more than a hard day ahead of them, Rafe thought. There would also be a hard life because he, Logan and Crowe would be back. He knew his cousins, he knew himself, and he knew there wasn't a chance in hell he was going to let the barons get rid of him this easy.

There wasn't a doubt in his mind that the security footage would be enough to prove their innocence. They were never stupid, and they never let anyone know their plans. They'd learned better than that as young teenagers when they were accused of stealing cars, cash, and a variety of other items.

No one, not even Clyde, had known they were camping out at the lake that weekend. Most weekends they spent alone at the ranch after the ranch hands left, working on fences or equipment.

Killing Jaymi that close to their campsite was a clear attempt to frame them. Rafe was beginning to wonder if the murders the FBI had put down to a serial killer weren't an attempt to frame the Callahan cousins instead.

"Here. The keys to the street and trail." Logan stepped in front of him as they neared the vehicles parked on the other side of the town square. "You're going to check on Cami, aren't you?"

He gave a brief nod.

"We'll follow behind you. Listen to me, Rafe," he snarled as Rafe moved to shake his hand. "This town is crazy right now, man, and you know it. Let me call Jack and Tobias. They'll come get her and make sure someone takes care of her. You can't protect her right now. It's going to take all we can do to protect ourselves."

And he was right. Too damned right.

"Give me a few minutes to make sure she's in the apartment," Rafe told him. "If she's not there, then she's at her parents'. I just want to be sure."

After stopping behind the apartments long enough to quickly change into the fresh jeans and T-shirt his uncle had thought to bring him, Rafe headed upstairs to Jaymi's apartment.

He still had the key. She had never asked for it back. Unlocking the door, he stepped inside before closing it securely behind him and staring around silently.

If he hadn't known Jaymi was dead, then he would have expected it the minute he entered the apartment. Her presence had always been there when she was alive.

It was gone now, replaced with the heavy weight of grief that wrapped around him and seemed to permeate the entire room.

He had hoped Cami would be at her parents'. That was where he had expected her to be. He damned sure didn't expect her to be there alone. As he stepped to the open bedroom door, he saw how wrong he was. She was here alone, huddled in the bed, exhaustion marking her sleeping face.

But at least she had her medicine and beside the bed was a glass of chilled water. Someone had been checking up on her at least.

Breathing out roughly, he sat on the side of the bed and tucked her blanket around her shoulders gently.

Instantly, feather-soft lashes lifted, and soft, blue-ringed dove gray eyes filled with an overload of tears.

"Rafe." Her breathing hitched as the tears overflowed.

"Come here, Cami-girl." He opened his arms to her, his throat tightening as she threw herself against his chest, the sobs tearing from her as he closed his eyes and fought against his own pain.

"Go ahead and cry, sweetheart," he whispered gently as he laid his cheek against the top of her head and ignored the trail of liquid warmth he felt ease from his eyes. "Cry for both of us."

He'd lost his best friend, and he was damned if he knew how to handle it. He hadn't been able to protect her as he'd sworn to Tye he would do. He had broken the only promise the man who had called him brother had ever asked of him.

As he held Cami, rocked her, and felt the grief that tore through her, he wondered why Jaymi had thought to entrust him with her sister's protection when he'd just failed to protect Jaymi.

How could he even trust himself now to protect this little waif who had managed to worm her way into his heart?

He'd promised. He'd find a way to do it.

Jaymi couldn't have known what she was asking. She had no idea he and his cousins were signed to go into the military. They'd all chosen the Marines. And who did that leave to look after Cami?

"Oh my God!"

The frightened squeak had his head jerking around to see Ella Flannigan, Cami's father's sister-in-law as she stood poised just inside the doorway.

She looked like she was ready to run screaming.

"Rafer Callahan, you just scared the shit out of me." Her expression turned chastising rather than terrified as she noticed the way her niece held on to him as though he were a lifeline.

Compassion and sorrow filled her eyes.

"I promised Jaymi." He swallowed tightly as Cami's sobs began to ease as exhaustion seemed to tax her weakened body. "I promised to look after her."

She blinked quickly before nodding. "I'll be in the living room with Eddy."

Her husband hadn't been here when Rafe entered the apartment and he hadn't heard anyone come in. Ella looked as though she had just woken up, so he sincerely doubted her husband was here. But he would be here quickly enough considering their small house was only blocks away.

He nodded, his hand stroking down the back of Cami's head as he felt her relaxing marginally.

She would be asleep in a minute, he thought. The bronchitis medication was obviously keeping her sedated enough to allow her to rest.

"I miss her, Rafe," she whispered, her weary and tear-thickened voice slicing across his heart.

"So do I, sweetheart," he whispered. "Go to sleep now. Get better for me, okay?"

He couldn't leave while she was still ill, and the second he and his cousins were cleared, he was out of there. For a while.

"Don't leave me, Rafe." Misery filled her voice. "Please, don't you leave me, too."

"I'll be here, Cami," he promised. "For as long as possible, I'll be here."

He wouldn't upset her more by telling her he would have to leave soon.

It eased her enough to allow her to drift back into sleep, though, and when he laid her back in the bed and pulled the covers over her, he wiped his hand down his face tiredly.

He wondered if he would ever sleep again. If there was any way in the world to sleep at all after Jaymi's death.

Moving to the living room to face her aunt and the smart-assed sarcasm her uncle Eddy had in abundance, Rafe found himself unwilling to listen to any further insults.

Mark and Eddy hadn't been outside the jail when they were released, despite the fact that he had more than expected Mark Flannigan to cause a public scene.

For once, Eddy Flannigan was quiet when Rafe walked into the room.

Ella stood next to the kitchen, leaning against the door frame while Eddy stood looking through the large picture window.

"Jaymi's lease is paid through the next three months," Ella said heavily. "Her father wants her to stay away for a while. And her mother isn't doing well."

Eddy turned around, and he and his wife shared a look that had Rafe's gaze narrowing. "They don't want their own daughter now, after losing their eldest."

Eddy's expression was tight and hard as Ella's eyes filled with tears again.

"It's a complicated situation, Rafe," Ella finally stated. "But we'll take care of Cami the best we can."

"Let me know if she needs anything," he bit out roughly. "I'll take care of it."

"She's not your responsibility," Eddy growled then. "We will take care of her."

"Let me know," he repeated softly, watching as Ella slowly nodded. "I have to leave now, but if you don't mind, after—" He swallowed, the movement tight and mixed with fury and pain. "Once we're cleared, we have to leave."

"Surprise," Eddy grunted.

Rafe ignored him as his wife sliced a disapproving look his way.

"We'll take care of her, Rafe, and if she needs anything we can't provide, we'll contact you," Ella promised.

It was far more than he had imagined he would get from the two.

"Thank you, Ella."

There was nothing more he could do, and no other way to look after Cami as he'd promised her sister he would do.

He left the apartment without saying anything more, and as he closed the door behind him, he could have sworn he heard Cami cry out his name.

Rather than turning back, he forced himself to walk down the hall and down the steps to the lobby before exiting the building at the back once again.

His cousins, two uncles, and the two military police personnel were still waiting on him. Moving to the motorbike, he kicked the ignition and hit the gas the minute the motor throbbed to life. Tearing from the driveway, he headed out of town and toward the Ramsey ranch he had been raised on.

They would be cleared. He knew they would be, but this town would never admit they hadn't committed the crimes. At least a large majority of it wouldn't.

That didn't mean he would stay away. It didn't mean he had any intentions of giving up the battle to claim the inheritance that was still locked in litigation, or the land that was rightfully his, Logan's, and Crowe's.

On the contrary. He would only fight harder.

Cambria at twenty-one

She slipped out of the hotel, her heart racing out of control, pain and regret tearing through her in equal measure. It had taken every particle of strength she possessed to ease from his arms, ease from the big bed, and hurriedly dress. Leaving the hotel room had been even harder.

Her body ached in her most personal places, her nipples were tender, her clit still throbbed with lazy satisfaction, and she could still feel the warmth where his palm had spanked her lightly as he thrust into her from behind.

The sun was barely peeking over the horizon, the blizzard that had grounded the planes in Denver having lifted several hours before. The forecast was for cold and only partly cloudy skies. The text on her phone said her plane would depart in two more hours, taking her home.

Rafer was once again leaving Corbin County and heading back to wherever the Marines needed him.

He had changed in the past seven years, but some things about her hadn't changed. Rafer still took her breath away. He still made her feel things she didn't understand and had no idea how to control. But, unlike seven years ago, those feelings were stronger, hotter, and more mature. With that maturity there was the arousal, the lust and hunger that she couldn't fight.

Rafer's smile, the hunger in his sapphire-blue eyes, the sensuality that filled his expression. Thick, black lashes that were much too long to fairly belong to a man. His hair wasn't as long as it once was. Rather than falling to his shoulders, it was almost military short and gave his face a more savage, forbidden cast.

But did she have the good sense to fear what he was capable of doing to her? What she knew he was capable of making her feel?

Of course she didn't.

Cami?

She lifted her head from the book she was reading, more bored with the story than anything else, but the nearly deserted airport wasn't providing entertainment of any sort either.

But that voice—

She heard that voice in her dreams so often.

Her gaze rose to meet his brilliant gaze.

"Rafer." She hadn't realized his name would slip past her lips so easily until it did.

It was a whisper, and even she recognized the husky need in her own voice.

Her heart began to race at an almost brutal pace, thumping against her breasts erratically as she took a shaky breath.

"Stranded?" His head tilted to the side as he stood before her, a heavy duffel hanging from his hand as though it weighed nothing.

He hadn't changed. Other than the maturity in his face, the experience in his expression, and the male hunger that gleamed in his sapphire eyes.

He was dressed in street clothes. Jeans and T-shirt, leather coat and boots. His broad shoulders looked a mile wide. His thighs powerful, his legs long and strong.

The moment her gaze traveled over him she could feel her pussy creaming, her clit throbbing, her nipples tightening and hardening, and her entire body sensitizing.

She knew arousal. She had been thirteen the first time she'd felt that breathlessness. At fourteen she'd become aware of her body when she saw him. Rafer, Logan, and Crowe had come home for a week because of yet another lawsuit the Corbins, Raffertys, and Robertses had lodged against their inheritances. When he had, he'd made sure to find a few moments to say hello.

The summer she turned fifteen, they were back again. That year, Rafe had danced with her at the Spring Fling Social. He had entered the festivities, walked straight to her in his black evening suit, and asked her to dance.

He'd asked her how she was doing, how school was. He'd asked her about her parents, about her aunt and uncle. He'd asked her if she needed anything and she'd wanted to cry because all she could think of was how much she had missed him and the fact that it felt so nice to be in his arms. She wanted to be there forever.

The next four years were variations of the same theme, except with each year, with each phase of her own sexual maturity, Cami had come to recognize the signs of arousal, of need, of awakening sensuality whenever she saw him. Over the years she'd seen him several times, and as she matured, those meetings had become even more heated, then explosive, until it had finally flamed out of control.

Until he had stood on the other side of the table at an airport that had nearly been deserted, for once, chance working in the favor of the travelers to provide the majority with accommodations in the nearby hotels. Unfortunately she hadn't been part of the majority.

"Stranded, Cami?" he repeated the question, his gaze somber but lit with an inner glow of hunger. That glow had been there since the summer she had turned eighteen and slipped out to a street dance in Denver the night she and her aunt had stayed over.

It was there between them, like a live current, pulsing beneath their flesh. He kissed her that night and nothing had been the same since.

"Yes," she whispered, breathless. She was always breathless around him. Always filled with anticipation and need.

He held out his hand.

A strong, broad palm, his fingers looking powerful, capable, and God help her all she could think about was how it would feel if they were stroking between her thighs, parting the lips of her pussy, rimming the juice-saturated slit of her entrance.

The need for it was so strong, so striking, she was forced to press her thighs together, wishing there was some way to ease the sudden, unbidden throbbing of her clit.

But nothing could have kept her from taking his hand and letting him pull her from the hard plastic stool she had been sitting on.

Their gazes locked, hunger rushing through her body, the need to touch him clamoring through her senses. The feel of his palm, calloused and warm surrounding hers, sent a spike of sensation shooting straight to her womb.

A sensitivity she had never felt before, a need, rose inside her, dark and so sexual, so overriding she could barely keep from begging him to take her at that moment.

"Such hungry eyes," he whispered. "Every year they're darker, more mysterious, and always filled with that hunger. Tell me, Cami, how much darker and hungrier could they get?"

Like a switch flipping on, a breaker sending electricity surging through her body, Cami felt the arousal heightening uncontrollably.

She could barely breathe. Getting enough oxygen simply wasn't going to happen. She had waited so long for the in-

*tensity of the hunger she saw in his eyes now. She had en-
dured three years, three hard kisses that had grown in
intensity. The awareness that his control was stronger than
his need for her, and the knowledge that her body refused to
accept any other man.*

*"Have you made me wait long enough?" she asked him
then, realizing in that moment the delicate dance they had
been weaving with each other since the summer she turned
eighteen was now beginning to whirl out of control.*

*His gaze slid slowly to her lips as he took a single step to
her. As he held her hand with one of his, the other slid into
her hair, all the while his eyes holding hers captive, mesmerizing her, drawing her into a vortex of sensation that
laid waste to any objections she could have thought of. Not
that she had intentions of thinking of any.*

*His head lowered as he cupped her cheek, held her still,
then brushed his lips over hers.*

*She was a virgin, but she wasn't completely ignorant of
her own body, her needs, or the arousal that just the thought
of Rafe could inspire inside her.*

*There, in the middle of a nearly deserted coffee shop, his
lips slowly pressed against hers, his tongue parting her lips
licking against them. He must have dropped the duffel bag,
because she felt his arm curve around her hips and pull her
closer as the kiss began to deepen.*

*It was exploratory and knowing. It was rife with demand
and acquisition. Rafer demanded and Cami had no choice
but to submit. The effect he had on her wouldn't have allowed her to turn away. The pleasure he gave her, the heat
that rushed through her senses and swept over her body,
was simply too addictive to deny.*

It seemed more a dream than reality.

*On the drive from the airport to Rafer's hotel in the four-
wheel drive he'd had waiting for him, the blizzard raged
around them, at times so heavy it seemed to surround them
in their own little world.*

Once they reached his room—

Cami's breath caught in sharp remembrance. Sensation

tore through her, clenching in the depths of her newly awakened flesh, her clit throbbing.

Tearing herself away from him had been all but impossible. As she flagged down a cab and stepped inside, she still couldn't believe she had actually managed to do it.

He had to have been exhausted.

No, that wasn't it.

With a heavy heart she admitted the truth.

He'd pretended to sleep and he'd allowed her to slip away.

And she was too big a coward to even guess why.

Rafe watched Cami slide into the cab, saw her gaze lift to the window where he stood carefully behind the curtain and narrowed his eyes on her thoughtfully.

He'd let her leave. Everything inside his soul had demanded he hold on to her, that he tighten his arms around her and fuck her until she was too damned tired to try to slip from him while she thought he slept.

But what was the point? If not now, she would have slipped out later. While he showered. Perhaps while he met with Logan and Crowe at the lawyer's office. There was no way to hold Cami if she didn't want to be held, and Rafe knew it.

And she was simply too damned scared of what had happened between them not to run.

Blowing out a hard breath, he looked around the hotel room, then finally focused on the incriminating stain on the sheets.

Cami had been a virgin.

His throat tightened at the proof of her innocence, at the knowledge that he had been the first to touch her so intimately. That he had been first to possess the liquid heat and fist-tight depths of her pussy.

The first to hear her cries of completion.

Instantly, furiously, his dick was spike hard, the head throbbing in renewed hunger. Perhaps it was a good thing she had slipped out so early, because fucking her into complete screaming submission had been all he could have thought of.

Logan and Crowe would have had to drag him from the room.

All these years, along with his cousins, he had fought to hold on to what was his. Not just the property their parents had left to them but also the cash that had been frozen in their accounts since the day the Callahan brothers and their wives had been killed.

Fourteen years. He and his cousins had been fighting for their inheritance for twelve years and there were times he swore it was a battle that wouldn't be won until the Corbins, Robertses, and Raffertys were dead.

But, as imperative as this appointment was, as crucial to their case as it was, still, he didn't know if he could have forced himself away from Cami long enough to have made it on time. She did something to his brain. He couldn't help it. She managed to get under his skin and made it damned impossible to think of anything but touching her once she had stood up from that table and he'd seen all the hunger filling her eyes.

He'd fought it. God knew, he'd been fighting it at least for the past three years. Each time he'd seen her since she had turned eighteen, once a year, it had ended in a kiss. A kiss that had nearly flamed out of control last year. She was like this fire he couldn't resist because when he was with her, he found the cold that usually encased him becoming heated and warm.

Admitting to it now was a moot point. It was there like a fire in the night, like a temptation no man could be expected to resist. That was Cami. His own personal temptation. The one woman he couldn't turn away from no matter how hard he tried.

Rafe was being driven insane by the need to have her again already. She hadn't been gone five minutes and the need throbbing through his body was like a vicious hunger, impossible to deny.

Pushing his fingers through his hair, Rafe blew out a hard breath before heading toward the shower.

He had things to do. Things that didn't include pacing the floors because Cami had slipped out of his bed.

And it sure as hell didn't include chasing after her, no matter how desperately he wanted to.

Two months later

Fate conspired against her. It laughed at her. The playful bitch did its best to destroy her, Cami thought as she stared out the window of the apartment her sister had once lived in. The one Cami now lived in herself.

She couldn't seem to stop crying, sobbing actually. It had been two months, eight weeks to the day since she had run into Rafe while in Denver for educational training. It was the third year they had run into each other and shared a night of passion.

Her palm was pressed flat against her abdomen, the realization of the emptiness that existed there tearing through her again as her breathing hitched and she cried with all the rage and lost hope that filled her.

She was aware of her aunt in the kitchen behind her. Ella had brought Cami from the hospital that morning and had stayed with her throughout the day. She had listened to Cami's sobs silently, and a few times she thought she had caught her aunt crying as well.

Cami's mother wasn't here.

Margaret Flannigan hadn't come to the hospital. She hadn't called or come to the apartment. Cami's father had answered the phone when she had called, though.

"Your mother's busy," he'd informed her when she asked to speak with Margaret.

"Please, Dad," Cami remembered whispering tearfully. "Please let her know I need to talk to her."

"So you can cry over losing that little bastard he gave you?" Cami's father had rasped furiously. "Your sister is turning over in her grave, Cami. Your mother's heart is broken. How could you allow the monster that stole your sister from us to touch you? Are you so desperate to take everything your sister had that you have to take the lover that killed her? The child she couldn't have? Maybe we'll all get lucky and he'll kill you next rather than some innocent, helpless girl."

Then he'd hung up on her.

Cami had listened numbly to the dial tone in her ear for long moments before placing the phone back in its cradle slowly.

At least, for a while, he had made her stop crying. Shock had driven every emotion she could have felt so deep inside her that it had taken hours for her to make sense of what he had said, what he had meant.

"Cami." Ella stepped to the window seat as Cami continued to stare onto the street below. "Come to the house, baby. Eddy's beside himself worrying about you, and I don't want to leave you here alone."

"I'll be fine," she said.

She was lying. She would never be fine again. As long as she lived, she would never be fine again.

She had lost her baby. The baby she and Rafer had created the night they had come together two months before.

It hadn't been a blizzard. She told herself it had been a coincidence, nothing more. Just as she told herself every year and managed to convince herself of it. There was no way he could have known where she would be and when. There was no way he could have been heading to the airport on the same day, at the same time, to the same city, every year. It couldn't be coincidence; that was simply stretching the explanation further than she could believe.

But what else could it be?

The only other explanation was more than she could imagine. That it was by design.

"Are you going to call him, Cami?" Ella asked gently.

Cami shook her head, sobbing again as she turned her head from her aunt.

Cami ached. Inside, out. To the depths of her soul, to the last particle of her spirit, she ached until she wondered if it were possible to die of it.

"He would want to know."

Ella eased down beside her niece, her heart breaking for the girl. It was all Ella could do to hold back her own tears. To keep from sobbing with Cami.

God, how could her mother leave her alone now? How could Margaret have left this precious, beautiful child to fend for herself against the cruelties her father waged against her?

Did Margaret even know the many, many times Mark had separated them? Had her sister-in-law even realized, in the Valium haze she existed within, that her daughter was being tormented by the man who had sworn to protect her?

"Cami," Ella whispered as she laid her hand on the girl's knee. "You don't have to go through this alone. He would want to know."

She shook her head again.

"Why?"

Cami turned back to her, the gray of her eyes like storm clouds, swirling with pain, with anger and desperation. "Hasn't he had enough taken from him?" she asked painfully. "I can't tell him, Ella. I can't do that to him."

No matter how much she needed him.

"Don't tell him." Cami suddenly gripped Ella's arm, as though she knew the thoughts that hadn't yet fully formed in her mind. "Please, Aunt Ella. Don't do that to me. Don't let me be someone else that's hurt him. Please." The last was a sob as more tears fell from her eyes, joining those that already had soaked her face.

Ella nodded hesitantly. She didn't like it. She hated it. But this was Cami's choice, and she chose to bear the burden alone rather than allow that young man to know that he had lost something so precious as the child he had created with Cami. She clearly remembered how he had come to her after getting out of jail, accused of Jaymi's murder, his own eyes wet with tears as he comforted Cami then. He would have come for her now as well.

Could she blame her niece? Wouldn't she have protected Eddy if the situation were the same though? Would she have done anything different? She knew she wouldn't have.

Ella sighed heavily. "How much more are you going to carry alone, Cami?"

Cami shook her head, those tear-drenched eyes breaking Ella's heart. "Don't," Cami whispered. "Just let it go. Just let *me* go, Ella. Please. I can't talk right now."

Ella let her go and understood the request. Cami had whispered those words to her the first time, nine years ago, when her sister had been laid in the ground.

The funeral had been over and everyone had left. Ella and Eddy had been unable to find Cami until the funeral director had called.

Cami had stayed at the gravesite, and she was silently watching as they buried her sister's coffin. He was terrified if someone didn't come for her, then they might be laying her beside Jaymi soon.

Ella had rushed to Cami's side, trying to convince her to return to the house.

"Let me go, Aunt Ella," her voice had echoed with such pure, deep agony that even Eddy had grimaced, forced to turn his head away to fight his tears. *"Let me go, before I hurt you, too."*

Cami had just drifted away then. Ella had watched her eyes lose emotion, her expression become distant despite the tears that rained down her face. Emotionally and spiritually, Cami had drifted away from them.

That was what she was doing now. Turning back to the window, she stared out onto the street, and Ella wondered what Cami saw there. Where did Cami go when she sat there and stared onto the sun-drenched street that seemed quieter and more peaceful than it ever had, as though the world itself were holding its breath and grieving with her?

Ella wasn't able to leave Cami. She couldn't walk away from her. That was exactly what her mother had done. Ella refused to do it.

She stayed in the background, watched until Cami finally fell asleep, her small, fragile body curled into the window seat, her arms wrapped around her self as though there was no other way to feel the warmth of human touch.

And for a moment, for the briefest second, Ella nearly broke her word to Cami and called Rafe. She actually turned to go into the kitchen to retrieve her cell phone.

Because Ella knew he would come to Cami the minute he could, and she knew he would make Cami come back to them. But Cami carried enough guilt. Ella couldn't imagine heaping more on her delicate shoulders.

Instead, Ella laid her head on the kitchen table and silently allowed her own tears to fall for the girl who deserved so much more.

Three years later, Cami at twenty-four

Coincidence.

Cami simply didn't believe in it.

At least, not to the extent that it seemed someone wanted everyone in Corbin County, Colorado, to believe in it.

She stood on the edge of the small crowd, toward the back, as the Reverend Mayer said the final prayer over Clyde Ramsey's coffin.

Rafer Callahan's uncle and the only member of the family who hadn't disowned him when his parents had died was laid to rest on a sunny summer day. Twenty-two years to the day that the Callahan brothers and their wives had gone over a mountain cliff, Clyde Ramsey had fallen from his horse and broken his neck.

The coincidence was simply too strong, especially considering that the so-called accident had come only days after he had filed papers with the courthouse that gave his nephew possession of the 450-acre ranch Clyde owned.

A ranch that Cami knew he had had several resort investors contact him over selling or at least leasing part of the property.

She was certain she had heard the sonic boom the second the three barons had received the news.

Now Clyde Ramsey was dead, and the ranch the three powerful families had been trying to buy was about to become the center of yet another court battle for Clyde's heir, Rafer Callahan.

The battles begun twenty-two years ago after his parents' death still hadn't been resolved either. As of six months ago, the inheritance Rafe and his cousins had been entitled to was still frozen as part of the litigation the families of their mothers had brought against it.

Those families were still attempting to deprive their grandsons of everything their mothers had left to them on their deaths. Especially the property, left in trust that had been bought from Rafer, Logan, and Crowe's grandparents JR and Eileen Callahan. A transaction that their sons, Rafer, Logan, and Crowe's fathers had sworn their parents would have never signed.

To deflect suspicion, the vast amount of property had been placed in trust for the youngest daughters in each family. That inheritance went to each child on her thirtieth birthday. Those daughters, as fate would have it, had married the Callahan sons whose parents had supposedly sold it. Those three daughters had turned thirty only days before their deaths.

Coincidence.

Cami hated that word.

Corbin County and its three powerful families were haunted by the coincidences of blood and death when it came to those who opposed them or possessed something they coveted. So far, the Callahan cousins had managed to evade the repercussions of that opposition. Evaded it . . . or perhaps the powerful barons hadn't yet managed to overcome their consciences to outright murder their own grandsons.

Of course, this was all supposition on Cami's part. Or her paranoia as her mother liked to say while smiling back at Cami indulgently, if a little absently.

How her mother had changed. Even before Jaymi's death, Margaret Flannigan had been prone to depression and had lived in a Valium haze. In the ten years since Jaymi's death, her depression had deepened, especially after her parents had moved to Aspen two years ago. Four years later than they had planned, as Cami understood it.

Her parents had been making plans to move the year
Jaymi had died and had been trying to convince her to move
as well.

The big day would have come the summer Cami graduated from high school. But no one had mentioned the move
to her. Her parents' way of silently emphasizing the fact that
she wasn't welcome, Cami thought mockingly.

How different families could be.

Her parents rarely acknowledged her presence, and even
when her mother did seem to notice Cami, it was with loving surprise. She never doubted her mother's affection for
her, simply Margaret's ability to deal with the world with
her husband in it. On the other hand, Cami's uncle Eddy and
Aunt Ella and had treated Cami like the daughter they never
had. They had always been there for her.

They had bought her senior prom dress for her, despite the
fact that Cami hadn't wanted to go. Thankfully, her friend
Jack Townsend had had a friend willing to escort her, Archer
Tobias, the son of the former sheriff. Archer was now Corbin
County's sheriff. Which surprised her considering the fact the
barons had not backed his election.

Her aunt and uncle had helped her get her a loan for college,
and when Cami had lost her best friend that last week of college, it had been her aunt and uncle who had dried her tears.

But even more important, when she had lost the one thing
she had wanted above anything else in the world it had been
Eddy and Ella who had rescued her. They had forced her to
move out of her apartment and had brought her into their
own home.

Now Cami stood watching another friend being buried.

As the Reverend Mayer drew the prayer to a close and the
small crowd began drifting away, Cami made her way to the
gravesite and the three men gathered there.

"Rafer." She stood in front of him, feeling just as vulnerable, just as weak and hungry, in the face of the powerful
dominant male she faced, as she ever had.

"Hey there, kitten." He greeted her softly, the dark rem-
nants of arousal in his voice sending heat flashing through her.

She couldn't avoid the arms that wrapped around her. She tried. She tried to make herself step back and then tried to make herself stiffen in his arms. She told herself she couldn't feel this, couldn't allow it, and she definitely couldn't have him.

It didn't work.

She felt herself soften against him involuntarily, and felt her arms go around his shoulders. Her face pressed against his powerful chest as she relished the subtle heat and powerful warmth that eased the chill inside her soul. She drew in the scent of him. Uniquely male, hinting at the dominance, at the sheer male strength that filled his body. Cami could feel her senses coming alive. The dormant warmth and sensuality flaring to life inside her, and reminding her of the pleasure she had once found in his arms.

She let herself relish those seconds in his arms. Let herself revel in them and told herself she wasn't going to allow anything more.

She couldn't allow anything more. She had nearly lost her will to survive when she lost their child. She couldn't risk that again.

"You're as beautiful as ever, Cami," he whispered against her ear. "And you make me just as damned hungry."

And he was hard.

His cock pressed against her lower belly and she felt his hunger for her begin to burn. As well as her own. Heat built between her thighs as her clit awakened with a vengeance. Her womb clenched, sending a rush of breathlessness through her as she felt the liquid response to his touch dampen her pussy.

She couldn't, wouldn't, allow herself to give in to it.

Drawing back was even harder than slipping from his embrace and his hotel room three years before.

"I'm sorry about your uncle," she said, stepping back. "He was a good man."

"He was as unbending as steel and just as rigid." Rafe was smiling, though, his blue eyes amused at the description.

"But he loved the three of you," she reminded Rafe softly.

"He tolerated us anyway," he tried to tease her.

She could see the knowledge in his gaze, though, that she wasn't returning the warmth, the teasing, where she had always teased back before. She was drawing away from him because she had no idea how to be close to him without wanting him, needing him; without taking everything she knew he would be willing to give her. All she had to do was reach out for it. Reach out for him.

Oh God, it hurt so bad to pull away from the warmth of his arms, to see that flash of hurt and anger brighten his eyes. It was like tearing a chunk of her soul out of her body. And here she thought she had already lost her soul.

She hated how weak she was, and she hated that she had no idea how to take that risk again and survive it. She had lost too many people, too many things in her life that she had loved. Her mother, her father, or rather accepting he had no desire to be her father. And her child.

The thought of allowing herself to weaken that far, to allow his touch again terrified her. The chances of losing Rafe were incredibly high. The chance of standing and watching as his body was lowered into the ground increased every day that he was in Corbin County.

So she stepped back. Her fingers clutched the edge of her purse as she gazed up at him in regret.

"I just wanted to say hello," she said softly. "And to tell you how sorry I am."

His expression closed, when he saw her deliberately put distance between them. His eyes burned with anger.

"You shouldn't have wasted your time, Cami," he drawled. "Run on home now, before I show you exactly how I make little girls like yourself admit that you know me a hell of a better than you're pretending."

"I've never pretended Rafe," she told him, refusing to hide, refusing to back down. "I've simply learned how to accept reality."

"Whose reality?" he snorted. "The truth or the reality the barons attempt to force feed everyone?"

It was better that he was angry, she told herself. So much better that he hate her. Because any other emotion would just cause her to break the promise she had made to herself. The promise that she would never risk her soul again to the extent that simply surviving seemed an insurmountable obstacle.

And the vow that he would never know what they had both lost. That he would never, ever know exactly how it had destroyed her.

"Good-bye, Rafer," she said softly. "Take care."

He didn't speak as she turned and walked away, but she could feel his gaze on her back. It was like a caress. A dominant, fiery stroke of his hand along her body. A phantom reminder of everything she couldn't have. Of everything she now denied herself.

CHAPTER 3

Eighteen months later

It was colder than a witch's tit. The temperature hovered just below zero with the windchill and a hard western wind blew across the mountains with a banshee's moan. The blizzard had become a whiteout, with the rapidly falling fluff piling fast and hard against the house in heavy pristine drifts.

The weatherman said to expect a blizzard, and he hadn't been far off track. Problem was, this looked like *blizzards* combined. The previous year's mild winter was cashing in interest during this late-season storm.

He was snowed in on a Saturday night watching the snow pile up and wondering what the hell he was doing back in Corbin County. And he was doing it just after yet another funeral. Just after the death of another man who tried to stand against his grandfather, Marshall Roberts, and his two business partners. The group everyone called the barons. He was half-drunk, damned morose, and fighting nightmares from a past he couldn't seem to shake. And son of a bitch if he wasn't so fucking horny for one damned woman that he could barely stand it. His dick was iron hard, his balls throbbed. They were so tight and the need to touch her was almost torture.

So it wasn't exactly hard for Rafer Callahan to convince

himself that the woman standing on his doorstep couldn't be real.

Could she?

After all, why would this particular part of his past show up now, of all times? Hadn't she already shown him that there wasn't a chance in hell of ever having her again?

Which was the reason he just went ahead and convinced himself that she was the vision of his most explicit, his naughtiest, his nastiest fantasies.

Sometimes, a man just needed something to hold on to, and she was it for him.

"Hello, Rafer."

Rafer stared hard at the young woman standing on his porch, watching him expectantly.

He lifted his gaze, checked the position of the moon, and gave a mental nod.

Yep, it was midnight.

Now all he had to decide was if this lovely, too-alluring vision was a figment of his fantasies coming to life or if fate was standing behind the lovely Cami Flannigan, laughing her ass off while he stood there with a hard dick.

Hell, he could always take his chances. After all, he'd made a huge gamble returning once again to the small town that had spawned him, hadn't he? What was that if it wasn't the dumbest decision of his life? This one couldn't be any worse, now could it?

"You're not naked," he drawled, deciding to go with the fantasy idea. And boy, did he have enough fantasies where Cami Flannigan was concerned.

Black lace, candlelight, slick, wet flesh, and hungry-feminine-moaning type fantasies that he couldn't manage to shake. He'd only had her three times in the past five years and the last time was three years ago. It wasn't hardly enough.

The vision of creamy flesh and blue-ringed velvet gray eyes blinked back at him before narrowing in feminine offense. "I have to be naked to knock on your door?"

There was a sudden snap to her tone that had a smile wanting to curl his lips. Damn, he surely did love that tone in her

voice. It just made his dick harder, just made all his little per-
verted fantasies push to the forefront of his mind. But it also
made him doubt that it was possible this was a fantasy. Only
the real version of Cami spoke to him with that snap in her
voice.

Yes she was acting less and less like a figment of a fantasy by the second. Especially when she propped a slender
hand on her cocked hip and glared back at him as though he
had crawled from beneath a rock. When had Cami begun
looking at him like that?

A sigh of resignation escaped his chest. A man could
dream, couldn't he?

"It depends on why you're here," he still answered her,
though, and he still kept to the program.

Fantasy. Erotic. Hard dick.

That little frown brewing between perfectly arched—
plucked or waxed? he wondered—dark brows tightened.

Was her pussy still waxed? The first time he'd glimpsed
those perfectly bare folds he'd nearly come in the sheets
rather than her snug little pussy.

"I can't imagine the reason why it would matter. Did one
of those bulls you breed butt your head a little too hard or
something? I'm stuck in the snow, Rafer. Why else would I
be standing in the middle of a blizzard on your front porch?"

For his hard dick?

The words almost slipped past his lips.

"What did you say?" She blinked back at him in outraged
amazement.

Oops, maybe he hadn't meant to say that out loud.

He smiled back at her, still not certain. "I said something?"

He arched a brow. He'd learned early that the gesture
tended to throw most people off and he used it shamelessly.

Hell, maybe he'd just drunk too much damned whisky.
That was always a possibility.

Suspicion filled her eyes, narrowed them, and thinned her
lips. "I'm pretty certain you did," she informed him between
clenched teeth. "And I'm really certain it was uncalled for."

Well, he didn't know how uncalled for it was. It was honest. A man could hope.

"I might be drunk." He cleared his throat as she continued to stare, anger beginning to shadow her gray eyes. "Can I blame it on the booze?"

Hell, she did have pretty eyes. They looked like the finest dark gray velvet with a narrow ring of dark blue. He'd always said Cami Flannigan had the prettiest eyes. Anyone could just ask his cousins, Logan and Crowe, they'd tell it; Rafe said it often. So often sometimes that they told him to shut the fuck up.

"'Might' hardly describes the situation," she snorted with ladylike charm. "You reek of booze, Rafer."

Cami called him Rafer sometimes, rather than the shortened version, Rafe, that most people used. He liked the sound of it on her lips. Especially when she was moaning it. She wasn't moaning right now.

"That could be possible." He nodded as his gaze raked over her shivering body. "It just seemed the night for it, I guess."

He'd only just realized she was shivering, hard. Her hand had dropped from her hip and she was once again huddled against herself. She was obviously cold, dressed in nothing but jeans, boots, and a heavy hooded sweatshirt that proclaimed: *Teachers Rock*.

He wondered if she would let him warm her. He knew exactly how to do it. How to touch her so her eyes darkened in passion, how to make the juices slicken the delicate tissue of her tight pussy.

"Stop undressing me with your eyes, Rafer," she ordered. "Could you at least let me in where it's warm? Or perhaps drive me home? My car is stuck in the snow out by the main road." She waved her hand toward the drive, now covered in nearly a foot of snow in less than an hour. "Surely you still have a four-by-four?"

All his fantasies came crashing down on him. No fantasy. She wasn't there for his hard dick, candlelight, or black lace. She was there because her car was stuck in the snow.

Lifting his gaze again, he stared into the blizzard. The whiteout conditions were only increasing. Travel would be impossible, let alone getting the car out of wherever it was stuck.

So this wasn't the erotic fourth chance of a lifetime standing on his doorstep. The first three chances hadn't been nearly enough to satisfy him, let alone to sate the hunger he had for her.

"Rafer, are you all right?" Suspicion laced her voice. "Are you smoking something you shouldn't be as well as drinking too much whisky tonight?"

He snorted at that as his gaze dropped back to her. Short, sassy layered strands of dark brown hair framed almost kittenish features as big gray eyes blinked back at him. Suspicious gray eyes. She thought he was high?

He wasn't that lucky.

"I told you, I might be a little drunk." He sighed, glancing at the snow again. "But not too drunk to know we're not going anywhere in this storm." He turned back to her, arched his brow, smiled. "Looks like you're stuck here with me, Cami-girl. Unless you want to take your chances in the snow?" He nodded toward the storm outside the porch. "Personally, I'm not willing to take that risk with my truck or my life." And especially not with her life.

Rafe watched her still for the briefest second before turning to look out at the storm herself.

Her shoulders seemed to slump, as though whatever weight she carried was too much for her. He wished he could see her face, look in her eyes and read her thoughts as he had when she was younger. But hell, it seemed those days were gone. When she turned back to him, all he saw in her face, or in her eyes, was weariness—weariness and resignation.

That look made his chest ache. Son of a bitch, Cami should never have such a look in her eyes.

"Come on in; I'll make coffee." Hell, he might as well sober up. A man had to learn to keep his wits about him when dealing with a Flannigan. Especially this one.

"I can't stay, Rafer." Pure tempered steel filled her voice

as well as her expression as she stared back to him, the quiet, even tone at odds with the conflict he could see in her eyes.

What the hell had happened to the sweet, loving Cami he had once known?

"Afraid temptation will get the best of you?" Letting his gaze drift over her, Rafe made damned certain she remembered everything he knew she wanted to forget.

She flushed. Her gray eyes darkened in both arousal as well as anger. Temptation was the least of her worries. It wasn't the temptation that was going to get her back into his bed. It was the memories that would accomplish that. The memories of pleasure so hot, so intense it had sent her running in fear when she thought he had finally gone to sleep. Oh yeah, he had her now and there would be no escape. At least, not until someone managed to dig the snow out of his road.

His cock throbbed, pulsing in memory of the sweetest pleasure he had ever known, buried in the ultratight, fiery hot grip of her pussy. For a second, the remembered sound of her shattered cries, the feel of her going wild atop him, riding his dick until they both exploded in a release he swore marked something inside him. It was definitely a memory that tortured him with a hunger no other could slake. The memory of it had the power to keep him awake at night. And it made him ache.

Five years. For five years he had been tormented with that memory, unable to find that release with any other woman, and ache for the pleasure and the woman who caused it, until at times he swore even his back teeth hurt from the need.

"Stop, Rafer." She shivered hard as the wind whipped around them and the memories heated them. "We agreed—"

"We didn't agree to a damn thing; you fucking decided to pretend it didn't happen without so much as consulting me. And I've had enough of the cold. I'm going inside."

He turned and slammed inside the house, entering the warmth of the kitchen. Furious now, his drunk wearing off, Rafe stalked to the counter and the coffeemaker he prepped for morning.

Flipping the switch, he stood, waiting until the dark liquid began streaming into the pot. Behind him, the door opened, then closed again softly, bringing with it the sweet, clean scent of the blizzard and the woman he hadn't been able to even try to forget.

He stared at the wall, anger churning along with the lust and creating a searing heat in his gut.

She still wore that familiar spicy scent he remembered. It tugged at a man's memory making him think of summer, sex, and pleasure. The scent of her perfume became a little deeper, a little more evocative, and hot when she melted beneath him.

"What the hell are you doing out in a blizzard anyway?" he asked, keeping his back to her as he pulled two mugs from the cabinet over the coffeemaker.

"I was visiting my parents in Aspen." There was no sense of reluctance or hesitation in her voice as there had been the last time she had spoken to him at that damned funeral. But it also wasn't as husky and sexy as it had been the last time he'd had her. Or the first time.

His balls tightened in agony.

Son of a bitch, forgetting the pleasure he found in her was like trying to forget the sweetest paradise ever experienced after being thrown from it.

"And how are your parents?" It was a social nicety and one he had to force past his lips.

How she could stomach even acknowledging her parents, he had never been able to figure out. Neither her mother nor her father had been supportive of her. They hadn't even pretended to care about her.

"I was there to help Dad settle Mother into a rest home. She never recovered from the stroke she had in the summer." There was a poignant sadness in Cami's voice. He couldn't imagine it was because either parent had tried to make her feel accepted, let alone loved.

No, it had been her aunt and uncle who protected her after her sister had been killed, it had been her aunt and uncle, Ella and Eddy, who had celebrated all the successes and failures, both big and small, with her.

Rafe's jaw clenched as he turned back to Cami, forcibly pushing those memories aside. "I'm sorry about your mother, Cami," he said sincerely. For her and for her parents. They'd made her life hell and they both knew it. Cami's compassion and the love she'd always felt for her parents had been apparent, though. It was a damn shame they hadn't cared nearly as much for her as she had for them.

"Thank you for that, Rafer." Cami nodded as she remained poised at the back door. "And thank you for meaning it."

His lips thinned. He wasn't going to broach the subject of her parents any further. To do so would only invite the destruction of the fragile truce he could feel settling between them. Though why one would be needed, he wasn't quite certain. What the hell had he done to make Cami hate him? Or had she too simply given into the hatreds that rose from his past?

That past was a bitter, poisonous brew best left untasted, unremembered, and unvisited.

"I saw your father in town just after I returned home," he told her.

He'd been back since early fall, and she hadn't even called. Not that he had expected to hear from her. He'd never imagined she *would* call. But still, he'd watched his cell phone. He'd watched the driveway, and he'd watched for her in town. He hadn't given up on her, even if he was certain she had never even considered attempting to find out what it was that lit such a spark between them and had them blazing out of control so quickly.

"I heard Logan and Crowe had returned as well." There was an edge of worry in her voice now, and he wondered if she even realized it.

His cousins, Logan and Crowe Callahan, along with himself, were considered the scourge of Sweetrock, Colorado, and the citizens most likely to kill everyone else in their sleep, he thought sarcastically.

"They have," he agreed. "Crowe went back to the cabin his mother left him in the mountains for a while and Logan has moved into the house in town. We finally managed to win the property that was left to us when our parents died. We're fighting over everything else now."

She bit at her lip as he turned from her and poured the coffee. Yeah, they were all home now. If everyone didn't know it by now, then the good citizens of Sweetrock weren't as diligent in their gossip as they used to be.

Turning back, he set the coffee in front of her and watched as Cami wrapped her fingers around the cup and stared into the contents.

"It's not poisoned," he promised as he sipped at his coffee to prove it was safe.

"I never imagined it was." That frown edged between her brows again. "Stop reading something into everything I do and say. I never imagined for a minute you would hurt me Rafe. Since when did you begin believing something so asinine?"

"And you're being too sensitive yourself," he told her. "That wasn't what I mean by it, Cami. I was being facetious."

"You're never facetious." She shook her head in denial. "I take you at face value, because that's how you are."

He had always tried to be, but there had been times over the years that he had wished he wasn't so damned honest. That trait could be decidedly inconvenient when the rest of the world just loved a good lie.

He sipped his coffee, refusing to comment or to refute her statement.

"I really need to get home," she finally sighed as she lifted the cup to her lips again.

Rafe let her take a sip, gave it time to hit her system, then sat back in his chair and watched her with lazy amusement.

"It's not happening, sweet pea," he told her lightly. "Even I'm not crazy enough to try to drive in that particular blizzard. We wouldn't even make it out of the drive to the main road."

She brushed back the long fringe of bangs that fell over her forehead. Rafe realized then that her fingers were shaking.

Glancing at the vein throbbing at her throat, he saw the hard, quick pulse as it thundered beneath her flesh.

Excitement or fear?

There wasn't a chance it was fear. She was aroused. Hot. Horny. She was ready to fuck. At least her body was. And he could just imagine how sweet and tight her pussy was.

"I'm going to fuck you before you leave here," he told her carefully, leaning forward against the table as he braced his forearms on the top and stared into her shocked face. "I'm going to have the sweetest treat right here on this table when I bury my lips in your pussy and lap at the sweetest cream in the world. Then, I'm going to watch, Cami. While those pretty, pink lips stretch around my dick, I'm going to watch while I sink every inch of it up your hot little pussy."

Her lips parted, eyes widening, her face flushed a becoming peach, almost the color of her pussy in full arousal.

"Tell me, do you still moan and cry when you come? Do you make your lovers growl like an animal when they come inside you because it's so fucking good they could die in that moment and never regret it?"

"Stop." She stumbled from the table, heading for the door as Rafe jumped from the chair, uncaring as it crashed to the floor, and caught her around her waist. In the next heartbeat he had her front pressed against the wall, his harder, taller body pressing against her back.

"Don't say stop, damn you," he said his head bent, his lips touching the delicate shell of her ear. "Say no. Go ahead, Cami, fucking say it. Tell me you don't fantasize about having me inside you. Fucking you like I'm dying for you." Tell me that you don't touch yourself, whisper my name, and masturbate to the memory of my dick stretching you to the point where you didn't know if it was pleasure or pain. Go ahead. Tell me, damn you, that you don't want my dick buried inside you so bad it's all you can do to breathe for it."

A whimper, a fragile, soft little cry, was his only answer as he watched her fingers curl into a fist against the wall, felt her body tense as she fought against the hunger.

"I dare you." He breathed out against her ear. "I dare you to tell me 'no.'"

He had braced one hand against the wall, and pushed the other beneath her sweatshirt, immediately finding silky, heated, naked flesh.

He flattened his hand against her stomach, feeling the muscles clench and ripple in response. His fingers moved to the snap of her jeans.

"Rafer, please!" A beseeching little whimper slipped past her lips. As though she wanted to. She wanted to tell him no. She wanted to deny it, refuse the pleasure.

He knew it, and a part of him hated her for it.

"Don't do this to us," she whispered, her voice hoarse despite the softening of her body as the snap of her jeans released and his fingers gripped the tab of the zipper. "You'll destroy us both Rafer."

One hand jerked to his wrist, her delicate fingers gripping it as he slid the zipper down.

"And this hunger isn't already destroying us?" His fingers were almost shaking as he pushed them into the opening he'd made in the jeans, her fingers uncurling but still lying against his forearm. "Tell me, Cami, how could it be worse?"

He prayed he didn't give her a chance to answer, because he knew it could get worse. He had seen it worse.

But this, this was paradise. This was a healing balm to the pain that often racked his soul. This was Cami, and God help him, he needed her.

His fingers found the folds of her pussy, so slick and naked to the touch. He had to clench his teeth to hold back the groan rising in his chest.

"You still wax," he whispered as her legs shifted, parting farther for him rather than closing against his touch. "I love the feel of your bare pussy, Cami. Feeling it against my fingers." He licked the shell of her ear as he fought to breathe. "Against my tongue," he said with rising hunger. "I'm going to fuck you with my tongue, baby. Fuck you and taste your come as you orgasm. I'm going to lick every sweet drop of it from your pussy."

He stroked his fingers around her clit as he spoke, plumping it, exciting it as he felt it throb and swell beneath his fingers.

"Why?" she whispered. "Why do you have to do this to me?"

He slid his fingers lower, parting the plump, swollen flesh and finding the clenched entrance of her cunt.

"Why?" Was the anger churning with the hunger inside her as it was for him? "Because you ran from me. Not just once or twice, Cami. Three times. You ran from me as though you were too ashamed to face the fact you had let a Callahan touch you. Because you left before I even awoke, and thought I'd take it."

Two fingers. With two fingers he pushed inside with a determined, hard stroke as the silky juices gathered around his them and aided the penetration. Her snug flesh was liquid-hot, her too-tight pussy clenching and rippling around the impalement.

She was still virgin tight, reminding him how long it had taken him to work his cock inside her untouched flesh that first time. And the two years after. He'd known each time he took her that there had been no other lovers. No other man had touched what he had been the first to claim.

"We could be stuck here for days," he groaned as she cried out against the penetration. "Just think of how many ways I could fuck you, Cami. And if you're as brave as you were five years ago, I'll end up sinking my dick up that sweet ass of yours before you leave."

Pressing her hips closer, he ground his jeans-covered dick against her rear at the thought. She would be a virgin there as well as untouched. The extremity of the pleasure he could give her was unknown. The thought of the uncontrolled violence of her pleasure—a pleasure only he would give her—had him desperate for her now.

And it was no less intense for her. He could hear it in the low cadence of her moans, feel it in the clench of her ass against him, and her pussy gripping his fingers. Her juices spilled slick and hot around him with each thrust of his fingers, each slow grind of her hips.

"Rafer." The sound of his name on her lips had the power to make his dick harder, thicker. And he would have thought that was impossible.

He wanted inside her. So deep inside her that he couldn't tell where he ended and she began. So deep that when it was over it would be like ripping her heart from her chest to deny him, because that was what it was like for him. Like killing himself.

"Please—" Her hips churned moving against his thrusting fingers with jerky, desperate movements, as her sex clenched and milked his fingers hungrily.

"You want me inside you, don't you, Cami?" he said. "You want me to fuck you, don't you, baby? Deeper and harder than before. Fuck you until you can't live without my cock sliding inside you any more than I could live without your sweet pussy milking the come from my balls."

He pushed his hand up her torso, his palm finding a bare, unrestrained breast and he cupped the swollen mound with hungry desperation.

Her nipple was spike hard against his touch and responsive beneath the rasp of his thumb as he caressed her. It tightened further beneath his touch, the mound of breast becoming more swollen.

"Rafer. God, yes," she cried out as he found that spot in her pussy that had her jerking against him as his thumb stroked the berry-hard tip of her breast. "Oh God, it's been so long," she moaned.

She was beginning to lose herself to pleasure. Her pussy spasmed around his fingers as her hips shifted and ground into the penetration. The ripple of her inner muscles around each thrust was heaven and hell. The need biting at his cock, aching in his balls, was nearly more than he could stand.

This was what being with Cami was. Sensations so rich, so striking, it was all a man could do to survive it.

"Tell me, Cami," he demanded his lips against her ear, his need to hear her acceptance tearing at him. "Are you brave enough, Cami girl? Tell me what you want. Are you hungry enough to ask for what you want now?"

Her head tipped back to rest against his shoulder. Each breath that passed her lips was a little moan as she fucked his fingers back. Her hips moved hard and fast. The warning ripples of her release began to tighten around his fingers as her body lifted and strained against him.

"Tell me, or I'll stop." He wouldn't stop. He didn't dare. His fingers were moving inside her. The need to feel her release becoming more desperate by the second.

Quick, hard strokes buried inside her flesh. His fingertips stroked the walls of her pussy. Each caress found nerve endings so sensitive that she was crying out begging with each whimper that left her throat.

"Please." Her hands gripped his wrists, holding on to him as she began to pant for air. Her lashes feathered against her cheek. Her eyes closed, as her lips parted, and her expression began to tighten with her impending release. "Please, Rafer. Fuck me," she pleaded breathlessly. "Fuck me until I come for you."

He nearly spilled his seed in his jeans with no more than the sound of her voice begging for his touch, his fingers, his possession.

He increased the strokes, driving inside her harder, faster, as he began to work her into the release she begged so prettily for.

"Let me feel you come on my fingers first, baby. First my fingers, then I'll fuck your sweet pussy with my tongue until you're begging to come on it, too."

He was too far gone, too far enmeshed in the hunger tearing through him to stop now. The need to pleasure her was suddenly deeper, more driving than his own need for release. Nothing else mattered, nothing else was as important as giving Cami the pleasure, the sheer ecstasy she deserved.

The long, ragged wail that left her lips was barely audible. As though the violence of the spiraling sensations had stolen the last breath she possessed as she suddenly tensed and began shuddering violently in his arms.

Her pussy flexed, tightening until he was forced to bury his fingers inside her and simply stroke the over excited flesh with his fingertips rather than risk hurting her with hard thrusts. The orgasm that tore through her and rippled around him, tightening her flesh around them had her juices rushing across his fingers.

So tight, the thought of having his cock buried in her as she came so violently made him insane to fuck her.

He existed purely for this pleasure.

In the back of his mind, Rafer knew he had been born to possess this one woman. That he could easily find himself living simply for the chance to touch her, to feel her coming for him, to hear his name as a gasping plea on her lips.

And if he wasn't very very careful, she would destroy him when she slipped away from him again.

When Cami collapsed against him, her breathing harsh, heavy, Rafe lowered his head to her ear once more.

"Now, it's my turn," he said as she trembled against him. "Are you ready for me, baby? Because I'm damned sure ready for you."

CHAPTER 4

She couldn't do this.

As they tore off each other's clothing, dropping shirts, jeans, and in her case silk panties, Cami kept telling herself she couldn't allow this to happen.

This was Rafer Callahan. She had fought him, fought this hunger, this attraction for him for as long as she could remember. She had fought the emotional ties she had felt tugging at her. Well, not always. Not until Jaymi had been killed and she suspected her sister had died because of her friendship with Rafe, rather than because of a serial killer choosing her. She had realized what those emotional ties could cause. Losing Jaymi had nearly destroyed her world. She wouldn't survive losing Rafe.

As he tore her panties from her hips his lips were on hers, his hands lifting her as her knees lifted and gripped his hard, lean flanks. Her body refused to obey the demands of her common sense. Her lips refused to say "no."

The stiff, furiously engorged flesh of his cock was trapped between them, throbbing and pressing against the swollen, sensitive bud of her clit. Every nerve ending was sensitized. Hunger was tearing at her with furious demand.

He stumbled across the room as her hands buried in his hair, pulling free the strip of leather that held his long, thick black hair back from his savagely hewn face.

Gripping the thick strands, she tried to lift herself closer, to bury herself deeper in the kiss that stoked the flames burning in her pussy.

Her womb clenched, her body became hot and flushed despite the perspiration that gathered on her flesh.

This was what tormented her long into the night.

This was that unnamed hunger that gnawed at her and kept her searching restlessly for ease.

It was Rafer. His touch, his kiss, the steady, fiery demand of the hunger he poured into her.

This was what she hungered for.

For his lips moving over hers as she felt her naked buttocks settle on the heavy kitchen table.

The coffee cups were raked aside, the heavy plastic crashing on the floor.

Was this one of the fantasies he'd once told her he had about her?

Nothing could be as explicit as her fantasies for him.

"No," the desperate command burst from her lips as his lips lifted, from hers his head pulling back as he stared down at her. Deep sapphire-blue eyes narrowed on her as they gleamed with naked, furious lust.

"I told you, I'm going to fuck your pussy with my tongue," he told her. "I have every intention of tasting every bit of flesh I bury into."

Her lips parted on a shocked exclamation. A totally involuntary sound as her hands dug deeper into his hair. Her neck arched as his lips ran along her jaw, then the column of sensitive flesh as her head fell back weakly to allow him access.

Broad hands flattened on her back as he kept her close to him, despite her perched position on the table. Angling his body between her knees, he pressed her thighs apart as he nipped at her neck. Then he licked the light abrasion, his tongue rasping over the sensitive flesh with erotic roughness.

Another moan slipped past her lips. That part of her that lived in fear of losing someone else she loved was screaming out in agony. Begging her to deny him.

What was it about his touch? What made Rafer Callahan so different from the other men she had dated? So different that as he lowered her along the table, her back meeting the cool wood, she would try to arch closer in eager anticipation. So different that the voice of agony was slowly silenced. She needed this. Needed him, his touch, his kiss, like the land needed sunlight and rain.

His thumbs found her nipples as her back arched.

The exciting abrasion of his calloused thumbs against the sensitive tips had her arching, twisting to get closer.

"Suck them, Rafe," she moaned. "Oh God, I need your mouth on my nipples again. Just one more time hard like you did before."

She could have been shocked that the words slipped out so easily, the demand in her voice as explicit as the words themselves.

Her fingers curled, tightening in his hair.

She couldn't stand to breathe. She wanted no other need, no other impulse, no matter how life sustaining, to distract her from his lips as they painted a trail of sizzling electric pleasure over her flesh.

The shaft of his cock pressed against the wet folds of her pussy, the grinding shift of his hips forcing her swollen folds to part and rasping at the tiny bud.

She wanted. She wanted him so badly that she could barely hold back a scream of reaction as the iron hot shaft moved against the tender bud, stroking it.

Not that she had the breath to scream. She could barely breathe.

Her eyes fluttered open, her gaze on his lips as he placed small, nipping kisses along the mounds of her breasts. His eyes glittered with wicked promise, with teasing sensuality. As she watched, his lips moved closer, then pulled back from the aching nipples.

Her nipples ached.

Licking her lips to ease the dryness there, she could watch, ache for more. As she watched his lips draw closer, closer.

"I love your lips, your tongue," she breathed out. "I love it when you suck my nipples, Rafe. I dream of you sucking my nipples."

Oh God.

Keening and low, shattered and weak, a moan burst from her as his lips covered an agonizing hard tip. It was like pure liquid heat surrounding it. His tongue rubbed, licked. Heated and moist, he flicked it over her nipple before he began sucking it with fiery abrasions. He drew on it with erotic hunger, sucking it, sending jagged fingers of intense sensation rushing to her womb, her clit.

"Rafer." She was delirious with pleasure. "Yes. Suck it. Suck it hard."

She needed more. She couldn't get a hard-enough caress, a deep-enough touch.

At her trembling plea his lips tightened around the nerve-laden center, suckling it deeper, his cheeks hollowing, his tongue flicking against it, rasping the nerve endings as flares of brilliant flames began to ignite across her body.

"Rafer," she cried out his name. Her fingers clenched in his hair, moved to his shoulders. Her fingers restless, desperate to experience the feel of his body just one more time.

One more time. That was all she wanted; it was all she ached for, fantasized for. She would survive if she could have him just one more time.

His lips moved from one breast to the other, copying the harder sucking motions of his mouth and the caress of his tongue. Each rasp to her nipple, each hungry draw of his mouth, deepened the hunger rising inside her once again.

"So good." Her voice trembled. Need was tearing through her like wildfire. "Rafer. It's so good."

And it was.

Her hips ground against the wide shaft pressing into her folds, stroking her clit and the sensations higher as his lips, teeth, and tongue tormented her nipples.

The flares of sensation, fingers of electric pleasure that tore through her, increased the desperation growing in her womb. As though she hadn't just come for his fingers moments before.

Lust burned through her veins as her blood thundered, rushing through her. It spiked her arousal with adrenaline and pushed her closer to a hunger she may never escape again. He had never taken her like this. He had never used such deliberate seduction and fiery caresses before.

Then his lips began moving lower. His hands gripped her hips, holding her still, steady, as she levered her upper body up on her elbows, panting, watching as intense, burning blue eyes stared up at her. He kissed his way to the moisture gleaming on her sex, his tongue licking a heated trail to her bare flesh.

His hands slid to her thighs as he moved farther down her body, slowly easing to the chair he jerked to him. He pushed his hands between her thighs and parted her legs as he lowered his head further.

Gripping her ankle, he bent her knee, pushing it back until he could place her foot on the edge of the table. The other he placed on the back of the chair still pushed beneath the edge.

She was fully open to him, the juices easing from her vagina, sliding along the crease of her rear, and heating the small, hidden entrance to her body lower.

She was too aware of each point of her body that he had paid such special attention to in the years before. His touch had that effect on her. Affected her as no other pleasure had, before or after.

Her pussy rippled with anticipation; her clit throbbed with the need for release.

"Touch your nipples," he growled, his voice demanding and rough as he breathed the words over her clit.

Almost involuntarily she slid one hand along her stomach, moving up to the tight bud mound of her breast as his lips reached her lower belly. His fingers clenched at her hips, a groan rumbling in his throat as she found her nipple with her fingers, pinched it, rolling it delicately as several panting cries left her lips.

His lips brushed against a hip bone, went lower, moved in

closer, until they were poised over the straining bud of her clit. Glistening with moisture, swollen, peeking past the folds of her pussy, the little bundle of nerves begged for his touch.

Cami could only watch.

Just watch. And wait in agonized anticipation for the touch of his wicked mouth.

His tongue licked over the slick, bare flesh of her pussy. If they ever had a next time, then she would pay him back for the weakness invading her limbs and the lack of control she had over the hunger tormenting her.

"What are you waiting for?" She moaned, prepared to beg if that was what he wanted, demanded that she do.

"What do you want?" His tongue peeked out, touched his bottom lip, then retreated back inside his mouth teasingly. It was his tongue, his lips, his hungry suckling mouth on her clit that she was dying for.

"Your tongue." He knew exactly what she wanted. "Your lips," she all but begged. "Your tongue. Suck my pussy, Rafer." Her free hand was in his hair and she had no idea how it made it there. "Lick it all over like you promised."

Her fingers buried themselves in the hair at the back of his head, her hips shifting, tilting as she pressed him to her. She all but tried to drag his lips to her flesh.

Her lips parted, the erotic, hungry impulses surging through her turning her into the woman she had glimpsed only three other times. Every time Rafe had touched her. Every time he had taken her.

"Lick my pussy, Rafer," she all but begged. "Fuck it. I want to feel your tongue—" She arched, the breath leaving her lungs in a rush of pleasure and excitement as his head lowered and his lips surrounded her clit.

Every muscle tightened in her body as pleasure screamed through her senses.

His tongue licked around it, sensation curling, burning around the small knot of nerves as her thighs widened, further, her hips tilting higher.

Oh, yes. She needed this. She dreamed of this and she ached for it. Every night since she had been old enough to understand the effect Rafe had on her, she had dreamed of his touch.

She couldn't remember a time that she hadn't wanted him in one way or the other.

"Yes," she breathed out roughly, involuntarily as electric pleasure crashed through her system.

His tongue rubbed along the over-sensitive nubbin as she watched, his lips pursing over it and giving it a firm, burning kiss.

Sensation flashed through her, surging from that caress to torment her body and pull a desperate moan from her lips.

He kissed her again, pursing his lips over her clit, drawing it to him, sucking it into the heat of his mouth as Cami felt the need, the burning tension, tightening with sensual agony.

Another broken moan left her lips as she felt the slick presence of her juices spilling from her cunt in a heated rush.

This time, his fingers were there to catch the slick essence, to ease it lower. His tongue began licking, stroking, moving steadily to the flexing entrance of her pussy as she arched, her hips writhing against the kiss.

She could feel the imperative need beginning to tighten between them.

He had been like this before, she thought. They both had. Fighting for patience, fighting to make it last, because they both knew it couldn't last forever. Because Cami knew it wasn't something she could keep.

Patience was eroded by the need building between them with furious demand.

As his tongue reached the vulnerable entrance to her vagina, she felt him lose the fine edge of his patience. Rather than licking and teasing, his tongue suddenly plunged inside her, into the violently sensitive flesh with hungry sensual strokes. Each hard licking thrust. Each plunge of his tongue triggered a flash fire. Each penetration sent pulses of sizzling pleasure surging across her nerve endings as the explosions of release began tearing through her system pumping.

"Rafer!" She screamed hoarsely. Suddenly flung into a

vortex of sensation so incredible, so intense, she knew she'd lost another part of herself to him.

Her upper body jerked, quivering as she flung her head back and clenched her hands in his hair. She felt his tongue rubbing the sensitive tissue. Each stroke, each caress prolonging the explosions rippling through the sensitive flesh of her pussy. Pleasure swirled through her, the explosion still vibrating, echoing through her pussy.

Then it was gone. His tongue pulled back, licked her clit, his lips surrounding it and sucking it hard and deep into his mouth as he forced her to lie back, pressing his hand between her breasts firmly.

Her knees tightened at his shoulders, her hips surging beneath the caress of his mouth.

Her hips lifted, rolled, a groan filling the room as his fingers went to her nipples again, pinching and pulling at the tender buds as he whipped the sensations through her clit hard and fast as she felt the sizzling, burning explosion ripping through her again.

This time, it went deeper, harder.

As the fiery tension began rushing through her again he pushed two fingers into the depths of her pussy, stretching her again, sending her senses rushing into that realm of agony and ecstasy. The detonation of ecstasy began spreading through her, overtaking her senses.

He didn't give her body a chance to adjust to the impalement. With the first hard, inward stroke he pulled back, pushed in again, pumping his fingers into her sex with quick destructive jerks as he sucked and licked at her clit with deliberately sensual strokes.

She couldn't bear it. She couldn't hold on. The sensations were too extreme, blazing through her, building immediately from the last orgasm and building the next with each lick, suck, touch.

She felt her eyes roll back as it hit her again, the pleasure surging so deep, so filled with a sense of agonizing rapture that there was no resisting. There was no denying it. The tension stringing tight and blazing hot inside her exploded with a suddenness she couldn't have prepared herself for.

She came to his lips again, jerking against him, a sob tearing from her lips as she let the pleasure surrounded her, racing through her with an implosion so forceful she felt her womb contract, as her pussy began to spasm and clench violently.

She was flying, hurtling through a place of such ecstasy that she couldn't force herself down. She couldn't ease back; and she couldn't dim the impact of the sensations she had only felt with Rafer.

The vibrations of ecstasy hadn't eased. They hadn't even begun to ease when he jerked to his feet, gripped his cock, and pressed it into the swollen, flushed folds of her saturated pussy.

She watched again, panting, still trembling and shuddering with each aftershock of pleasure bombarding her.

"Yes," she breathed out roughly at the burning heat beginning to spread through the entrance. "Oh, Rafer, yes. Fuck me. Fuck me hard and deep." She was almost sobbing, hips lifting as he began working his cock inside her. "I dream of it, Rafer," she sobbed desperately. "I dream of every touch."

"Oh yeah, baby, milk my dick," he whispered down at her. "Milk it good, sweetheart. Pull my cock right into that tight little pussy."

The erotic, explicit words stroked the flames higher. Her pussy clenched tighter, doing just as he asked, milking the broad head of his erection as he worked it inside her, stretched her. The snug, hungry flesh surrounded it, and rippled around the crest.

The pleasure was violent. Sharp spears of electric sensation tore through her. Each pulsing surge of sizzling pleasure surged across her nerve endings, rushing across her nerve ending, and jerking her hips up in sharp, tight movements.

She couldn't stay still.

She couldn't just lie beneath him and accept the pleasure. Her hips twisted and ground into each thrust, her cries broken and ragged, breathless rather than loud as she felt the furious pleasure ripping across her nerve endings.

She was going to come again. So soon. The rapidly building sensations throwing her toward release began building inside her again with each heavy thrust inside the clenched sensitized tissue.

Fluttering wings of sensation beat at her womb while each rake of his pelvis against her clit stroked the furious ache centered there ever higher.

Her nails bit into his biceps as she held on, her knees gripping his hips, tightening with each lunge of his cock inside her.

The flared, thickly swollen head of his cock pierced her with each impalement, exciting and rasping against exposed nerve endings. The pleasure was exceeding. Exacting.

It was hotter, stronger, than it had been five years before. It was a flame growing in the pit of her belly and spreading outward, encompassing her clit, filling her cunt until the explosion tore through her with such voracity that it totally consumed her.

She jerked in his hold, her eyes opening wide, dazed, blurred as she felt the implosion tearing through her. The muscles of her pussy tightened on his shuttling cock, locking down on the stiff, exciting shaft and throbbing around it furiously as she gasped his name and she felt his release spurting hot and hard inside her.

Each heated ejaculation inside her, each flex of her pussy, sent repeated ecstasy rushing through her. A conflagration of sensations and rapture that whipped through her senses and finally left her limp and exhausted in his arms.

The past week had been heartrending for her; the pain of dealing with her mother's condition and her father's grief and heartache had sapped at Cami's strength.

Lying beneath him, Cami realized with a flash of sudden insight that she had deliberately dared take that turn that brought her past Rafer's. She knew the sky had darkened with snow. She had known there was a chance of being stranded.

She had taken the risk because she had known she could make it as far as Rafer's ranch.

Feeling the heavy shudders that wracked both their bodies, she realized it wasn't the pleasure she had been fighting, and it hadn't really been Rafer she had fought through the years. It had been this—what she could feel at this very moment building inside her.

Those emotional ties tightening inside her, tying knots in her heart that she wouldn't have a chance of unraveling.

Jaymi had done that. She had let Tye wrap so many chains around her soul that when she lost him, she lost a part of herself.

Losing herself in such a way terrified Cami.

What would happen to her if Rafer was gone? If the dark danger that swirled around him decided to tighten and strike out with the same murderous intent she suspected it had struck out to destroy the rest of the Callahan family?

It wasn't the danger to her that terrified her. It was the danger to Rafer. The danger to her soul if anything happened to him.

That was what she fought. That was what she continued to run from. Because she knew once she gave her heart to him fully, then if anything happened to him, it would destroy her as well.

The pain of Jaymi's death had scarred her soul, but when she had lost Rafer's child, she had never lost her will to live. The agony that had gripped her, the sheer depth of the pain that had held her in its grip had seemed never-ending.

It had followed her every second of her life, and even now, two years later, the realization of the life she had lost burned inside her continually.

It was another loss that had driven her when she had sensed the snowstorm coming. The days spent getting her mother settled into the rest home, feeling her father's pain, his devotion to her mother, and the sense that his hatred for her had only grown.

She'd needed Rafer. She'd needed him to pull her out of

the memories of the little girl who had begged her father to love her. The woman who had knelt before her mother and sobbed against her knee when she'd lost her own child.

Margaret Flannigan had lifted Cami's chin and stared down at her with sudden, lucid sobriety and whispered, "Trust me, Cami, losing that child was the best thing that could have happened for the baby. Or for you."

Cami had felt something inside her that had struggled to survive over the years simply fade away. Perhaps it was the love she should have known for her parents. Perhaps it was the compassion for their weaknesses that had seemed to hobble her all her life.

Whatever it was, it had just faded away inside her as though it had never existed.

She should have used her common sense rather than her emotions tonight. Her emotions were about to get her into more trouble than she wanted to deal with.

As Rafe lifted himself from her, Cami deliberately kept her eyes closed, her breathing even. She refused to leave that halfway place where the past the didn't matter and the future hadn't yet arrived. God knew she didn't think she could handle any more upheaval inside her or around her. She wanted to stay right where she was, safe and warm inside. While the realizations and realities she faced remained at a distance.

Rather than forcing her from that place, Rafer slid his arms beneath her and carried her slowly up the huge staircase and into his bedroom. He didn't speak or force her to speak. He simply took care of her.

She didn't want to face what she had just done, what she had known she would end up doing the second she had stepped from her car after it slid into the snowdrift at the side of the main road.

Cami didn't want to face the fact that she had complicated her life more than ever and ensured that she likely would see no peace for quite a while.

Rafer was like a dog with a bone; no, he was worse than that. Five years ago he had given her a clue exactly how serious he was about being her lover.

She couldn't handle it then, and she couldn't handle it now. There was too much between the two of them, as well as between him and the townsfolk of Sweetrock.

Her gaze fluttered open long seconds later, though, as she felt him parting her legs. As she watched, he ran a damp, warm cloth between her thighs and along the slick, wet folds of her pussy as he wiped the excess of both their releases from her body.

He had done this every time they were together. Pushing aside his own need to luxuriate in the satiation, or in his own release, he had instead cleaned her and ensured her comfort.

She couldn't fault Rafer there. The three times they had been together he had taken excellent care of her. The first time, just after she'd turned twenty, she'd been shocked by it. She'd never heard her friends bragging of their lovers doing such a thing.

"This can't last, Rafer," she whispered as he drew back, her gaze caught by the dark sapphire of his eyes and the lazy, satisfied expression on his face.

"I never said it could, Cami." He shrugged.

But wasn't exactly agreeing with her either.

"Just for tonight," she reaffirmed as he drew a dry towel between and over her thighs. "Then we forget it happened."

And just as it had five years before, something seemed to explode in her chest at the very thought of it. She could feel the dark, forceful contradiction screaming inside her and couldn't understand why.

"Until the storm is over, and the roads are clear enough for travel."

He was hard again.

Kneeling with one knee on the bed, the furiously flushed, wide shaft of his cock pointed out at her, the flared crest dark and throbbing as she dampened her dry lips with a sudden hungry thought.

She could have him.

Dawn's arrival didn't mean discovery and there was no way she could run from whatever it was he made her feel. It just meant more snow as the system just edging in continued to dump the white stuff across the mountains.

Twenty-four to thirty inches within the first twenty-four hours based on the winds and the amount of precipitation coming through. They could be there for days. She could get the hunger and the need out of her system, and maybe, once it was over, she could find a way to live without the memory of Rafer Callahan tormenting her.

She reached out, her fingers curving beneath the heavy weight, her lips parting, her tongue reaching out to touch the furiously swollen flesh. Slightly salty, tinged with a hint of storm. The subtle tastes and male power sent a heavy fist to clench her womb, her suddenly aching pussy.

Shards of sizzling sensation raced from her scalp to her nipples, her clit, the inner muscles of her sex as his fingers clenched in her hair and tugged.

She licked, circled the silk-over-iron flesh, and tasted the pre-come that eased from the slit at the tip. Her fingers moved lower, cupped his balls, held them, tested their weight as well, and with a hungry cry she sucked the thickened crest deep into her mouth.

"Ah hell, Cami," he groaned. "There you go, suck my dick, sweetheart."

His thighs were rock hard.

His hands controlled her head, moving it back and forth, fucking her mouth with slow, shallow thrusts.

Her lips burned. Her tongue flicked against the sensitive underside, tasting him, the freshness of soap where he had washed moments before, and the heat of his hunger.

As though they hadn't just had each other, as though the pleasure hadn't burned out of control, within seconds the need was once again raging.

"Come here," Rafe growled as he pulled her head back, staring into the dark gray of her slitted gaze as he pulled his dick from her mouth.

Her tongue licked over her lips drawing the last taste of him to her tongue. The sight of it had his balls tightening furiously as adrenaline rushed through his system.

"Turn around, on your knees," he ordered, his jaw tightened as she moved, the pretty curves of her ass tempting him as she lowered her shoulders to the bed and spread her thighs.

Juice gleamed once again on the flushed folds of her pussy. Then he watched as her hand moved beneath her body, her fingers, slender and graceful, parting the intimate lips, as she rubbed at the entrance in invitation. Then he watched, groaning in hunger and need as she pressed that finger slowly into the saturated entrance before easing back.

He gripped the shaft of his cock, moved to the bed on his knees, and over her.

The second the sensitive head met the fiery portal of her cunt, he nearly came instantly.

What was it about Cami? He'd never been able to control his lusts with her as he had with other women. Since the summer she turned eighteen, she had been his greatest weakness.

Easing forward, Rafe felt the slick, hot entrance begin to stretch and flare around his crest. One hand gripped her hip as he fought to hold back, to control the blazing hunger to fill her pussy with his come. To blast inside her and mark her forever with his semen.

Only Cami did this to him.

Only Cami had the power to make him want to beg her for just one more night, just to see if was better than the time before, only to learn that the time before hadn't even compared. There was nothing so pleasurable as burying his cock in the sweet mindless ecstasy to be found inside the gripping depths of her fiery pussy. To feel it milking him in, rippling over his cock.

It was like having the tightest fist gripping his dick and pulling him to paradise. His balls clenched with painful need and his heart began to pound harder in his chest. Excitement and adrenaline poured through his system as her hips moved with him, her slender back arching, the shaggy cut of her hair feathering below her neck as she moaned his name.

He could feel her masturbating, her delicate fingers

stroking her clit, and that knowledge had an animal lust pouring through him.

She knew what she wanted from him. She knew how to pleasure him, but she also knew how to pleasure herself. With Cami, it was simply about pleasuring and pleasing each other as they took for themselves as well.

Perhaps that was why he couldn't forget the night he had her innocence. That despite her virginity, she had touched him with such hunger and with such need that there had been no hesitation or coy games.

Gripping her hips with his fingers, Rafe held on tight as he began to fuck her deeper. He slammed his cock into the flexing, ever-tightening depths of her cunt. The world narrowed to the steady hum of pleasure beginning to vibrate between them, and the need for release tearing through them.

Husky sensual cries fell from her lips as he glimpsed the fingers of one hand clenching in the sheets beneath her. Her back cushioned his chest as he let his lips move to her shoulder. There, he delivered a rough, sucking kiss that marred the flesh with a reddened love bite.

No one else might ever see it, but she would. If nothing else, she would be forced to acknowledge that for at least a brief period of time she had belonged to him.

At this moment in time, she was his. The tight, hot depths of her sex, the pebble-hard nipple his fingers found, the gasping, breathless little moans that fell from her lips.

God yes, she was his.

"I feel you stroking your clit," he growled at her ear. "I'm going to get you some toys, Cami. A nice, thick dildo, one that vibrates in that pretty pussy of yours, and I'll watch you use it. Then I'll watch you stroke your hard little clit. I'll watch you pleasure yourself, see the way your quick little fingers move against the swollen little knot."

She was whimpering, her cheek pressed to the comforter. Her fingers moving faster against her clit. Her pussy was clenching, fisting.

"And one night, I'll show you exactly how much I love your pretty ass," he promised, the thought of it causing his cock to throb harder, to feel thicker, hotter, the need for release more imperative.

"I'll stretch you there so sweet, Cami. I'll watch as you take my fingers, then a select toy or two, and when the need for that pleasure, so close to the most erotic pain you'll ever know, overwhelms you, then I'll push my dick up that tight little ass and listen to you scream for me."

Harder. He was gasping for air himself as his hips began pounding into her ass, pushing his dick as deep as possible, feeling her pussy began to convulse, to spasm around the rapidly throbbing cock head until they both began to come. Simultaneously, his head buried against her neck as he groaned her name, his seed pumping inside her, filling her, marking her.

He'd never given another woman the intimacy of coming inside her, of feeling his seed spurting hot and hard in the blistering heat of her vagina.

Not until Cami. He trusted her that first time when she had said she was protected. But even more, Rafe knew if she wasn't, if she conceived his child, then it would only bind her to him. It would ensure she never ran from him again. That she never left him again.

Buried as deep inside her as possible. Holding her as close to him as possible, he felt a steady glow radiate in the pit of his stomach that he'd only felt with Cami.

CHAPTER 5

She slept peacefully, deeply, her head resting against his heart as her deep, even breaths feathered over the light dusting of hair on his chest.

Rafe kept his arm curled around her shoulders, kept her as close to his body as he could get her, allowing his fingers to stroke the silk of her hair every so often.

He'd waited years to get her here, and now that she was, rather than sleeping as peacefully as he had that first time with her, Rafe was left staring into the darkness of the bedroom.

He was damned wary about going to sleep and he fully admitted why. Every time he had done so, he had wakened to a missing Cami and an empty bed. Not even so much as a letter or a short *good-bye* written in lipstick on the hotel mirror.

If she ran out on him again in such a way, he'd end up doing more than busting a hole in a hotel wall with his fist. Rafe would go looking for her, and that might be the worst idea he'd had in years. He could just imagine the shock, the fear, and the suspicion that would fill her neighbors' faces if he did such a thing.

She would probably have every male within three blocks in front of her home within minutes, and every one of them would be armed. Every one of them would have murder in his heart and hatred in his gaze, and Rafe had never fully understood that. Because it had begun long before the year six young women had died at the hands of a brutal rapist and torturing murderer.

Cami's older sister, Jaymi, had been one of the victims.

For a second, he heard her screams as clearly as he, Logan, and Crowe had heard them that hot summer night they had been quietly fishing on the bank of Sweetrock Lake, in the densely covered forest outside of town.

He didn't want to remember that night. He'd spent too many years trying to forget it. But the facts were that the Callahans had been ostracized far sooner than that year. They'd been ostracized decades before that, and there had been no explanation why.

There had only been that barely disguised distrust and wariness, as well the thinly veiled dislike.

There had been days Rafer had existed in such a state of rage during his teenage years that even his Uncle Clyde had been wary of him. Hell, even his cousins had steered a wide path around him in those days.

He reminded himself that he hadn't allowed their opinions to bother him since then though and he wouldn't allow them to matter now. Never again would he allow such destructive fury to rise inside of him because of such pettiness and never again would he run from it.

But it would matter to Cami and he couldn't even blame her for it. There were times when he had been able to view the situation logically. Had he believed a man responsible for such heinous crimes, he then too would have gone out of his way to make his life hell.

And even before the murders, the years he and his cousins had endured the scorn of the citizens of Corbin County, he'd understood, sort of, why they had done so.

The barons of Corbin County were a powerful force in not just the county, but also in the state of Colorado. Their anger could have far-reaching consequences.

No doubt Cami knew exactly what those consequences could be. She had seen the many jobs her sister had gone through and knew what Rafe had only suspected, that Jaymi had lost those jobs because of him.

She was a teacher; her job depended on the goodwill of the other teachers, the school board, and the parents. No parent in Sweetrock would want a teacher instructing their children who was sleeping with the man suspected of having murdered her sister twelve years ago. A man suspected of conspiring with his two cousins to rape, torture, and murder five other young women between Sweetrock and Aspen, Colorado, during that same time period as well.

Rafe had learned years before not to worry about what the good people of Sweetrock might believe. His mind was invariably set on shocking and scaring any adult who dared to offend him. Hell, they didn't have to offend him. He was ready to shock, piss off, or frighten any adult who found the courage to confront him in any manner. The inheritance left to him by his mother might have still been tied up in the court system, but the interest from it was not. He was financially secure enough that he didn't need the barons' goodwill to survive. Hell, he didn't even need their ignorance of his existence to make it in Corbin County. All he needed was the military check he received and the considerable interest payment he received each month. After that he could piss off or nearly frighten anyone who attempted to foolishly confront him.

And he didn't care a bit to do so.

There were even times he had even gained a hint of morbid satisfaction in doing so.

He couldn't do it to Cami, though. It wasn't her fault the school board was filled with the high-minded, panty-starched little prudes. The bastards had seemed to actually enjoy each punishment they had dealt out to him during the few years he had attended the high school.

But he'd seen in the shamed, regretful gazes of a few of them that they hadn't agreed with it. He could find no respect for them, but there was a part of him that could understand it.

Thankfully, he'd managed to graduate early. By the first semester of the final year he had had the credits needed to bypass attendance for the rest of the year.

The school board had been more than willing to allow him to simply return home until the end of the school year. What they hadn't told him? Unless he was in attendance a required number of days he would lose that year and the credits he had accumulated. Had it not been for the recruiting officer who'd been shadowing Rafe during those last months of high school, then he would have never managed to graduate. He would have been forced to get a GED rather than the diploma he had busted his ass for and had suffered at the local high school to attain.

He'd been determined to have that diploma, even if getting it had been hell. It had been a fight that both he, and the soldier who had befriended him, grew frustrated with.

But Rafe had learned why that soldier had been there. Why he had befriended the three outcast cousins and drawn them into the armed forces, and away from Corbin County. Because he, too, was a Callahan. Given up for adoption by his parents when he was barely six months old, the only knowledge he had of his birth family was what his adopted parents had given him.

When he'd arrived in Corbin County, first during Rafe's final year of high school and again six months before Jaymi had been killed, he had seen the hell his nephews had endured. It had been on that trip to see them that he had convinced them to join the Marines.

Rafe looked down at the woman in his arms and felt that familiar dark anger from his youth rising inside him. He knew that any moment she could bolt and run, then she would be gone. And the thought of it infuriated him.

He was too damned restless to sleep now. It was one of the reasons he had been drinking himself into a drunk when she showed up on his doorstep. So he could sleep. So he could escape the restlessness and the wary sense of foreboding that had haunted most of his life. Well, at least that part of his life spent in Corbin County. Twelve years in the Marines and eight of those years spent as a sniper, and not once had he felt that same dark foreboding mission. Step his ass into Corbin County with the intent to stay, though, and once again it became a near daily companion.

Easing from the bed, he felt his heart clench at her disappointed little murmur when his warmth eased away from her. She shifted on the bed, searching for him for a moment before settling back to sleep with an unconscious little pout to her lips.

She would walk away, he warned himself again. As easily as, perhaps more easily than, she had walked into his life once again.

It was better that neither one of them grew used to sleeping with the other. Better that he simply let her go. If he could. He had a feeling that letting her go again would be impossible.

Moving to the dresser on the other side of the room, Rafe pulled on jeans and a heavy flannel shirt before sliding his feet into a pair of comfortable sneakers. He collected one of the slim, fragrant cigars he preferred, a lighter, and moved to the balcony doors.

Slipping quietly onto the balcony and easing the door closed Rafe let the night settle around him.

The acrid, spicy sweet taste mixed with the smoke had the immediate effect of easing the worse of the tension that had begun to fill him.

This wasn't the same warning, or foreboding as his recruiting officer had called it, that had served Rafe so well in the Marines. This was something he had only felt when heading into the most dangerous of the missions he'd undertaken. This wasn't just a foreboding, it was a straight-up fucking warning.

From the moment Cami's firm little knock had sounded on his door, those inner sirens had begun going off. And now, staring into the night, he wondered at the sense of danger he could feel edging closer.

He had hoped he could return home, slip in without too much of a ripple, keep to himself, and find the life he'd searched for around the world.

And God knew he'd searched for that place in the world where he could, at the very least, be content. He wasn't asking for happiness. He'd learned long ago that was far too much to ask for. Contentment, though, hadn't seemed too high a price to charge for the years he had spent defending his country. After all, he'd also been defending this little corner of America that had decided he and his cousins had no place in their midst.

Or perhaps those other places just weren't the place whose proud mountains sustained them. That place where their fathers, their grandfather, and his father before him had planted Callahan roots. Those other "places" hadn't been home.

Logan and Crowe too had found that contentment eluding them. Crowe had actually resigned from the Marines the year before Rafe and Logan had and spent those months alone searching for a place he could call home. Crowe had traveled around for a while, but as he'd written in his last e-mail before they'd returned, evidently there really was no place like home.

For Crowe no place like the cabin his mother had left him that overlooked the sheltered valley below. For Rafe it was the small ranch his Uncle Clyde had owned. The one that his grandmother had been raised on before marrying JR Callahan.

For Logan it had been the house his mother had owned before her death. The one she and his father had lived on. The one he had been born in. It was flat in the middle of Sweetrock. A two-story traditional American with a wide porch surrounding all sides. In the back was the roomy yard he and his cousins had played in as toddlers. Next to it was the garage where his father had allowed him to "help" work on the family car.

The house was surrounded by other similar houses. Once, long, long ago, before his mother had given in and married the father of her child, Logan had played with the neighborhood children there. He had been accepted, and had known a childhood happiness that Rafe only barely remembered while Logan refused to discuss. And none of them could pinpoint why it had changed. Why had their grandfathers, their entire families, turned on the children left behind? What had made them suddenly hate and despise the sons that cherished daughters had given birth to? And why didn't anyone seem to have the answers to those questions?

Rafe puffed on the cigar again, frowning into the swirling snow and listening to the moan of the wind. Rafe knew it had begun with the daughters marrying the Callahan brothers. Still though, that animosity hadn't grown against their children until after their deaths.

A grimace tightened his face as he forced himself away from the maze he was beginning to step into. Questions without answers, they could pile up into a mess inside his brain if he let them. There was simply no way to figure out why the families that he and his cousins should have been able to turn to had turned their backs on them instead.

They were the sons of the daughters those three men were known to have once cherished and adored, until the night they had eloped with the three brothers. Three brothers who had spent every day since their return from the military accusing the barons of having murdered their parents, JR and Eileen Callahan.

After twenty-two years of asking "Why"? and of all but begging the good people of Corbin County to just explain what sin they felt their parents had committed, Rafe, Logan, and Crowe had simply stopped caring.

They'd had enough of it the three days they'd sat in that tiny jail cell, frozen with shock and horror, accused of killing a woman all three of them considered their best friend.

It had taken three days for Uncle Calvert, a Marine recruiter, and the lawyer he had hired, to get their release.

Then for another three days Rafe and his cousins had lived in silent shock beneath the care of the man who had raised them and the uncle they hadn't known still lived.

If it hadn't been for Ryan, they would have rotted in prison. If they had lived that long. Before Ryan had made it to the jail with the lawyer, all three of them had been beaten so badly by the sheriff and his deputies that it had taken all they had to walk out of the jail.

The evidence at the scene of the crime had been conclusive, the judge had decided. The DNA testing on the blood indicating an older male had gone along with the FBI's profile of the serial murderer. A profile the FBI stated the Callahans in no way matched. The judge had further concluded that as much as he would love to see Rafe, Logan, and Crowe Callahan locked up for the rest of their natural-born days, he couldn't in all conscience bring them to trial for a crime he was certain they hadn't committed.

A man who didn't know them and hadn't taken the time to learn anything about them would have loved to see the three of them locked up for the rest of their natural-born days.

Son of a bitch, that memory still had the power to amaze him, and never failed to confuse him.

Leaning against the balcony railing, Rafe flicked the cigar ash over the edge of the railing and narrowed his eyes against the snow.

Their fathers hadn't been scions of society, but neither had they been the dregs of humanity. And for not the first time in Rafe's life he was beginning to wonder exactly what three cherished daughters could have done to their families to ricochet back on those daughters' children? And once again he was asking questions he couldn't answer.

Now, here Rafe was, right back where he had started, and wondering what the fuck he had come back for. What had made him, Logan, and Crowe hunger for this particular little place in the world?

Because insanity must run on the Callahan side of their genetics, he decided as he puffed the cigar once again and relished the aromatic burn that filled his senses.

He'd be damned if he knew where to go from here, though. He could rebuild the ranch; it had been damned profitable before Clyde Ramsey had died.

Rafe, Logan, and Crowe had had plans for the ranch. They'd been certain the climate would have to be different when they returned and living there wouldn't be the hardship it had once been. He'd be damned but they couldn't have been more wrong.

The quiet musings and his enjoyment of the cigar were disrupted by the sound of a powerful snowmobile motor cutting its way through the heavy windswept snow falling from the sky as well as that layered on the ground.

Strong LED lights cut through the white walls of fluff falling around them and traversed at least two feet of heavy, wet snow as the powerful machine made the precarious turn between snow-hidden fences.

Logan or Crowe. The new snowmobiles were unmistakable, and only they were insane enough to be riding through a blizzard for whatever it was they wanted. It could be as simple as sharing a cup of coffee or as complicated as heading back out for whatever wild-assed idea one of them had.

They were bored. He'd sensed it weeks before. And things could get dangerous, especially for Rafe, when Logan and Crowe were bored.

There were times Rafe felt as though he was the adult and his cousins were no more than wayward overgrown children. Very dark, very cynical, but nonetheless as wild as hell and without the normal cautious attitudes most adults displayed at their age. Hell, their time in the Marines as snipers should have fucking matured them. At least by a few more years than it appeared it had.

Sighing heavily, he turned, tamped the cigar out in the small ashtray kept on a ledge by the door, then slipped back into the bedroom.

Cami was still sleeping peacefully, sprawled out on her stomach, her pretty rounded ass emphasized by the silk sheet lying over it.

He pulled the comforter over her body then tucked it to her shoulders before moving for the door. Opening it he headed to the kitchen his steps quick and silent as he moved down the wood stairs.

He'd forgotten about the clothing left tossed on the floor until he stepped into the brightly lit kitchen to see Logan twirling a pair of tiny violet panties on one finger while he held up a matching lace and silk bra with the other. He looked from one to the other with curious moss-green eyes.

As though trying to determine exactly what it was or why it was there.

Glancing at Rafe, he dropped the lingerie on the table, then picked up the sweatshirt and read the front of it. Rafe watched as his cousin visibly tensed before turning the sweat shirt and reading the back.

Flannigan #12, Corbin Co. Teachers Softball League.

"Cami Flannigan," Logan mused softly as Rafe began picking up the clothes, folding them haphazardly, and laying them on the counter. "Did you lose your mind sometime between the agreement we made about Corbin County beauties and whenever you picked her up at?"

The agreement? They weren't to fuck any woman within a hundred miles of Sweetrock.

"Don't start, Logan," Rafe warned him quietly, unwilling to start an argument with Logan that could end up waking Cami.

"You don't think her father caused us enough trouble after Jaymi was killed? Come on, Rafe, he bombarded your commanding officer with e-mails about us for years. Even Clyde wasn't safe from Mark Flannigan's vindictiveness. Do you really want to give him another shot at us? What the hell do you think he's going to do when he learns you're fucking his baby girl?"

Mark Flannigan wouldn't give a damn one way or the other Rafe knew. From what Rafe had learned over the years, Cami's relationship with her father had only grown colder. The only reason Cami's father would even pretend to care would be if he could destroy the Callahan cousins with it.

"What I think is that this is my business," Rafe informed him as he moved to the other side of the kitchen and began making more coffee. "Now, tell me why the hell you're here in the middle of a blizzard rather than sitting in front of a fire in the house?" Rafe shot him a disgruntled look. "Didn't we just spend three days opening the house and moving you in?"

And it had sucked, too. Every day neighbors had glared at them from porches or through their windows. Old men had shot them the finger while teenage boys steered a wide path around them. It was more than apparent they weren't welcome and they sure as hell weren't wanted.

"I was bored." Logan shrugged, his expression smoothing out to cool disregard.

"Try again," Rafe snorted. "Why are you here?"

Sure, he was bored, but his cousin had ridden over thirty miles in a blizzard on a snowmobile. The fact that Crowe had tinkered enough with the engine to make the vehicle capable of it didn't mean it wasn't still a damned dumb decision.

Logan leaned back against the inside of the bar counter, crossed his arms over his chest, and stared back at Rafe quietly. Behind him, the darkened living room reflected the fiery red glow of the coals in the fireplace and the large oil portrait of Rafe and his mother when he had been three, standing at her knee.

With long blond hair, dark blue eyes, and porcelain, delicate skin his mother had been Corbin County's homecoming queen her senior year in high school, voted most likely to succeed, and was considered one of the most beautiful young women in the county.

Her father had commissioned the portrait when she was eighteen. It had taken three years for the artist to get to it. When she'd insisted on including her son, he'd refused to complete payment. Her mother's older brother Clyde had paid for it instead and hung it over the fireplace.

As she was elegant, considerate, and compassionate, it was often hard to imagine she was actually a part of the cutthroat, icy-eyed Roberts clan. Sometimes, Rafe had heard his father joke, he believed his mother-in-law must have had a lover who fathered Ann Roberts Callahan, because there was no way in hell the heartless Marshal Roberts could have fathered a child so beautiful and warm-hearted. But Rafe had always heard how Marshal had spoiled and adored his daughter. And how he'd fallen into a drunken rage the night she eloped with Sam Callahan.

Logan shifted, drawing Rafe's attention back to him. "I tried to call, but the phones aren't getting reception and the land lines are down somewhere between here and town. I thought I'd head out and check on you." He made it sound as though he had done Rafe a favor.

"In a blizzard?" Rafe arched his brow quizzically. That wasn't like his cousin. "What happened Logan?"

Rafe could feel the suspicion building inside him stronger now. He knew Logan, and he knew that was bullshit.

"You heard from Crowe lately?" his cousin asked rather than answering the question.

"This morning. He met me out at one of the line shacks to check the condition of it. He seemed fine and didn't mention any problems. Do we have any problems?" They sure as hell didn't need any.

Logan shook his head. "Probably just my paranoia," he finally sighed. "Or the fact I'm the one in town and easier to access."

"No doubt it's 'not' your paranoia," Rafe growled. "What was it?"

He grimaced. "Someone was in the house while I was out at the grocery this morning. When I returned, the tape placed at the top of the door had been moved and replaced and the strand of hair in the lock was gone."

"That doesn't sound like paranoia to me, Logan," Rafe growled. "What makes you think it could be?"

Logan's lips thinned. "Because nothing was on the security camera but the neighbor kid knocking. If he was messing with my locks at the same time, I might have to kill him."

Rafe hid a smile. The boy, Logan's neighbor's brother, had decided to torment Logan however possible.

"Maybe he's bored," Rafe suggested with mocking sobriety.

"Yeah, fucking bored," Logan grunted with a roll of his eyes. "Or maybe he has a death wish I could accommodate."

Rafe stilled his laughter as he watched the irritation that settled in his cousin's expression.

"Do you have any idea what he wanted?" Rafe asked as he fixed his cousin's coffee and slid it across the counter.

"No, to aggravate the hell out of me, maybe? Neighbors

are damned sassy, though. All but the kid's sister that lives next to me. Fucking night owl." Logan almost grinned.

Evidently that fucking night owl had managed to entertain his cousin in some way.

"Why would the kid care enough to try to pick your lock?"

"For the hell of it? Because he's a damned teenager?" Logan grunted after sipping at the coffee, then turned and moved to the table.

Before sitting down, Logan stared at the wood table top for a long, thoughtful moment. "You fucked her on the table, didn't you, cuz?" There was an edge of irritated resignation that Rafe sensed stemmed from the neighbor kid's sister.

Rafe merely lifted his cup and sipped at his second cup of strong coffee that night. If this kept up, then he was going to start drinking decaf. No wonder his chest was tight with a sense of foreboding.

"Drink your coffee, Logan." Rafe almost allowed himself to grin. "You can sleep in the downstairs guest room tonight. We'll check out the house in the morning." Hell, he'd hoped to get out of letting Cami know about the snowmobile.

Logan stared back at him mockingly. "Storm is supposed to last three days, with a healthy helping of four to maybe six more feet before it's over, and up to three days to dig out if the temperature stays in the teens as they're predicting. You really want to lose your houseguest that soon?" Logan's smile was knowing as he continued.

"I'm fairly certain she doesn't know about your snowmobile, or she wouldn't be upstairs in your bed. You'd be on the road trying to navigate the storm and your lust."

Sucked when someone knew you as well as he and his cousins knew each other.

Rafe sipped at his coffee again, refusing to comment as Logan sat back in his chair and watched him with silent amusement.

"What are you getting yourself into, Rafe?" he finally asked him again the amusement dissipating. "Have you thought about this? Have you thought about how old she is? The same age as Jaymi—"

"Enough, Logan." He glared back at his cousin. "I won't think about Jaymi. Not tonight."

Logan rubbed his hand over his face wearily. "She's the wrong woman," he finally growled. "Her father will come after you shooting when he finds out. Are you going to shoot back? Could you shoot back if she were watching?"

"There will be no shooting," Rafe promised him. "Her father's in Aspen and he doesn't come back to Sweetrock very often. Her mother's health isn't that good any longer."

Not that Mark Flannigan had ever taken much interest in his younger daughter. It had been Jaymi that he had shown his love to, and only Jaymi.

Logan shook his head. He was aware of the lack of concern Mark had always shown Cami, especially the summer Jaymi had died. "If she were my daughter, there's no way in hell I'd sit still while she was in possible danger. Flannigan could end up fooling us."

"Yeah, and I believe in fairy tales, too," Rafe drawled cynically. "Trust me, Flannigan's not going to go to the trouble."

"And I'm telling you, fucking her is going to rain hell down on you."

Logan warned him. "For God's sake, Rafe—"

"Let it go, Logan. As you said, once the storm is over she'll be gone and she'll pretend it never happened, just as she has every other time."

"And the next time the two of you have five minutes alone you're ripping each other's clothes off and fucking like minks on top of the kitchen table," Logan reminded him. "Does that tell you anything?"

"I was too drunk to ignore my hard dick?" Rafe shot back.

"Or too damned stupid to ignore it." Logan finished his coffee before rising to his feet. Moving to the heavy winter wear he'd taken off after entering the house he told Rafe, "I'm heading to Crowe's. I doubt very seriously he has a woman in his bed tonight. It would surprise the hell out of me to even learn he'd stayed in the county. That boy ain't happy to be back. And here he's the one that talked us into coming back."

"Why did we come back?" Rafe asked, refusing to stand, knowing how Logan could be. He could get ready to leave fifty times before ever making it out of the door. Knowing Logan as well as Rafe did how and much colder the mountains were as one moved higher into them, he knew damned good and well Logan had probably regretted heading out no sooner than he passed the city limits. Logan was hell for doing his job, no matter how hot or how cold. He was a one-man tracking/killing machine. But he liked his creature comforts and didn't leave them unless he simply didn't have a choice.

In his mind, he'd had no choice. He couldn't reach Rafe by phone and he was determined to ensure his safety. But now he knew his cousin was safe, he'd be damned slow about leaving.

"Why don't you drop the damned coat and stay here tonight," Rafe growled as Logan looked outside at the snow and gave a heavy sigh. "If Cami sees you or the snowmobile, then just tell her you're on your way to Crowe's and not heading back to town until everything melts enough to drive in."

That would keep her here without her anger affecting Rafe's pleasure. And he did intend to have his pleasure until he couldn't keep her there another second longer.

"That will work." Logan dropped the coat, but he wasn't making a move to leave the kitchen.

"What now?" Rafe asked him.

Logan stared back at him, his eyes so hard, so cold, that Rafe wondered if his cousin ever felt warm inside anymore. He definitely didn't act as though he did.

"You in love with her?" Logan finally asked before giving his head a hard negative jerk as he grimaced. "Yeah, you are," he answered his own question. "You have been since that first night you spent with her."

Rafe rose from his chair, finished his coffee, then moved to the sink and set the cup inside it.

"I'm not in love with her." He turned back to his cousin, confident he wasn't in love, he couldn't be in love, he refused to feel anything as futile as love for Cambria Flannigan. She'd run out on him one time too many for him to allow himself to touch that particular fairy tale.

"She's just a fuck then?"

Rafe's jaw tightened at the description, some furious, unknown denial raging inside him, demanding he voice the refusal. He held it inside, convincing himself it was simply the too-explicit description his cousin used that bothered him.

"Keep convincing yourself of that," Logan stated with a mocking smile as he collected his coat, boots, and cold-weather paraphernalia and moved for the living room entrance. "You keep convincing yourself, I'll keep reminding you, and maybe, when she helps the fine folks of Corbin County decide to try to bury us six feet under and then some, you won't find that part of your soul shattered."

As he had before, Rafe wondered as he watched his cousin move through the darkened living room and into the hall that led to the downstairs guest room. Rafe and Crowe had discussed their cousin often, wondering what had happened the year Logan had disappeared from contact completely during a mission he'd been sent on.

Marine snipers were often sent to hotspots that had them out of contact for months at a time. For a year, Logan had been sent on a mission that neither Crowe nor Rafe had been given any information on. Only their uncle and commanding officer, Ryan Calvert, had been aware of what was going on and whether Logan was alive or dead.

When he had returned, he hadn't been the same man who had left. Logan had been so hard and so cold that for a while Rafe had wondered if his cousin had returned or only his ghost.

Giving his head a hard shake, Rafe checked the locks, checked the lower part of the house, the windows, the latches to the iron window covers, and then moved back upstairs where he repeated the lock check.

Satisfied the house was secure and the alarm system operating fully, he moved back to the bedroom and the woman sleeping in his bed.

She hadn't moved other than to gather his pillow closer beneath her as though searching for him.

No, she wasn't searching for him, he told himself. He couldn't let himself think it or believe it. She was going to walk out of his life the minute the roads were open to afford her escape. And once she left, she wouldn't return unless she simply had no other choice, as she had had no choice tonight.

Shedding his clothes, Rafe slid back into the bed, eased his pillow away from her, then in surprise felt her moving against him until she settled over his chest once again.

Her head rested on his shoulder, her arm was thrown over his abdomen, one slender, silky warm leg tucked between his, she whispered a discontented little sigh and nudged against him once again.

Pulling the blankets carefully around them, Rafe wrapped his arms around her and held her snug against him. Her next sigh was one of satisfaction, of contentment.

What had he gotten himself into here? he wondered, because holding her felt as natural as breathing and just as imperative. But hell, every time they had come together it had felt like finding home. In his life, nothing had ever felt as warm or as natural as her body against him or the warmth of her sinking into him.

Would she try to leave without waking him if he somehow managed to sleep deep enough to miss her slipping from the bed? In all the years since his training in the military, nothing had ever slipped by him in his sleep as easily as Cami had slipped from his bed that first night.

He'd awakened before she'd finished dressing that morning. For a while he had watched her from beneath his lashes as she hurried and dressed. And he'd let her leave. He had refused to hold her to him and he'd refused to confront her.

It wasn't a mistake he would make again.

He stared down at her for long moments.

Hell, there was no way he could be certain that he would even awaken this time. It had been three years since the last time she had slipped out of the bed on him. She'd almost been gone before he'd missed her warmth.

Rafe hoped, in the past five years his senses had grown sharper, stronger, and he would know when and if she tried to do it again.

To be sure, he set that mental alarm he'd developed. One hour. He'd check on her in one hour. An hour in this kind of weather wouldn't get her far; he'd at least have a chance of catching up with her before she froze to death.

And if she did try to leave?

Well then, he'd paddle her ass, before he fucked it until she swore, until she knew, believed, and had cemented in her head forever the idea that she would never, ever, run from him again.

CHAPTER 6

It was overcast, bitterly freezing cold, and as white outside as Cami was certain she had ever seen it.

Even dressed, she wrapped her arms around herself, and a shiver still raced through her at the sight of it. Jeans, wool socks, and fur-lined boots simply weren't enough covering for more than a few minutes in weather such as what she was facing now.

Standing on Rafer's porch and staring into the heavy, dark clouds still bearing down as they swept around the mountain, she couldn't help but breathe out roughly.

The blizzard was only waiting to hit with its second round of downy snow to catch the unwary as they foolishly left the warmth of their homes.

She'd listened to the weather after awakening and watched the reports on the satellite before the gathering clouds had completely obliterated the line of sight between satellite and dish.

It may not have been snowing furiously at the ranch at the moment, but it was hitting Aspen and spitting on Sweetrock with a vengence.

And from the looks of it, it would be dumping on the Rafe's ranch once again as well.

Cami didn't dare move from the porch. The drifts were

piled high around it, on it, and against it as though there were simply no other place to store the icy fluff.

For the first time in her life, she found the snow to be an inconvenience and she was wishing it away with everything inside her. The longer she stayed here, the more likely destruction was apt to build around her.

What had possessed her to ever take this much longer route home? To ever risk something like this happening?

Just to see if she could glimpse signs of life in the Ramsey ranch house. To see if the rumors that Clyde Ramsey's nephew, Rafer Callahan, had returned were true.

She hadn't expected it to begin snowing. When it had begun just after she made the turn from Aspen, she had convinced herself it was nothing. It would flurry awhile, then go away just as it had done several times in the past weeks.

By the time her car had slid into an icy drift at the mouth of his driveway she was certain fate was laughing its ass off at her. This was what she got for tempting it, for all those dark, lonely nights that she had wished things were different and she was in his arms rather than sleeping alone.

How silly she had been to have slipped away from him the few nights they'd had together. She should have just stayed with him while he was in and gotten the hunger out of her system rather than running. Leaving as she had, had left so many things unanswered and incomplete. And it had left so many desires still raging inside her, tempting her, tormenting her—

She rubbed at the chill in her arms as a wave of inner heat swept through her womb to settle in her pussy and wrap around her clit.

She was growing wet again, but she was also wishing, remembering—wishing things had been different and remembering the fantasies, not so much of sex or the wild, impossibly heated pleasure that could flare between them. It was the dreams that slipped into her mind once she slept that really tore at her.

The dreams of his arms around her, his laughter at her ear.

The sound of his voice, low, deep, as he just whispered her name. The sound of something more—she pushed the thought away. It was those thoughts, those dreams, that slipped up on her and weakened her. That created moments like now. When the nightmares slipped out as well and threatened the fragile peace she had found.

She couldn't have him and she knew it.

There was too much Rafe was unaware of, and too much pain tearing at her to allow it.

Too much pain, fear, and the knowledge of what would happen to her soul if she lost him to death. If somehow, someone decided to try to harm him, and, God forbid, succeeded.

And still she was torn in her needs and in her anger. She fought not just herself and her own needs but also his desires and the return of reality.

A reality that could destroy her and her own needs.

This wasn't a good thing. She couldn't be stuck here until the roads were cleared. Once her car was found, then the first place state workers would search for her was at the ranch. Her uncle Eddy Flannigan worked on the state road crew. She couldn't imagine the worry, and possibly the fear that she was about to repeat the past, if he found her there. Especially if he realized where she had slept.

In Rafer Callahan's bed and in his arms. Of course he wouldn't have to realize anything. He knew her and he would know where she had slept.

She leaned against the support post and stared at the ground where more than four feet of snow had fallen, and the drifts against the house were even higher. In places, they were at least five feet deep or more. The news said to expect two or more feet as well, coming that day or into the evening, and possibly another six to twelve inches before dawn.

It was the blizzard that had threatened to roll across the mountains all winter.

There wasn't a chance of escaping the icy sanctuary she had found or the emotional abyss she was beginning to stare into.

There was a reason she had run from Rafe each time they

had spent the night together. Slipping from his hotel room before he awoke and catching a ride to the nearest airport or car rental.

She had run because sleeping with him had opened something inside her that she hadn't been able to face. It had thrown her back into the past with a suddenness that had left her crying for days. The memories were going to destroy her. She could feel it coming. They were right there, fighting to rush in and destroy her control, and there wasn't a lot of control left some days. Some days the unnamed restless pain that never seemed to dissipate seemed to grow. To overtake that part of her with a hunger that threatened to destroy her.

The first time she had seen him the summer she had turned thirteen, she had sworn she had fallen in love with the man her sister called her best friend, Rafer Callahan. The man Cami had known instinctively that her sister was sleeping with.

Cami had loved his name. She had loved his fierce blue eyes, the laughter in them, the way he walked with such cocky confidence, and the way he had smiled at her.

For months she had haunted her sister's apartment, even though he had moved out. Cami had watched for him, searched for him. He had never been far from her mind on any given day.

She had promised herself she wouldn't do this again. Irritation and frustration were rising inside her now. She had sworn she wouldn't allow herself to ever come this close to losing her soul as she had the last time she and Rafer had been together. Yet here she was doing just that. She was losing the control it took to keep him at arm's length and to control the emotions that swirled inside her like a violent storm.

Turning, Cami moved back into the warmth of the kitchen, watching as Rafe cleaned up the dishes from the simple dinner of pork roast, red potatoes, gravy, and rolls she had prepared from the supplies he had on hand.

He'd watched her cook as though no one had ever cooked for him. Silently, his sapphire gaze had tracked every move she made, hunger gleaming in his eyes.

"Coffee?" He looked at her expectantly, one black brow arching quizzically.

He was too damned good-looking for her peace of mind. Six feet, three inches, broad, muscular—if there was an ounce of fat on his flesh, then she hadn't found it yet.

His thick, silky black hair fell around his face, giving the savage features a sexy, sensuous cast that immediately drew female eyes. It always looked a bit mussed, as though a woman had just run her fingers through it and enjoyed the soft, cool feel of it.

Dressed in jeans, sneakers and a flannel shirt, the long sleeves rolled to his elbows, he looked like a lazy tiger prowling his lair. Biding his time before he took his mate.

She almost didn't control the jerk of shock that hit her at the thought. She wasn't a mate; she wasn't a lover. This was where she invariably managed to get herself in trouble when it came to Rafer.

Rafe, she reminded herself. She was going to have to begin calling him Rafe, or she would draw more attention to herself than she wanted. Everyone called him Rafe. No one ever called him Rafer except her. And she just couldn't seem to break the habit.

"Daydreaming or fantasizing, Cambria?" That silky drawl, so wicked in its sensuality, had her gaze jerking from his chest to his face.

"Excuse me?" She blinked back at him, wondering if he could see into those fantasies and daydreams.

He gave a light chuckle as he moved to the coffeepot. "Have a seat; I'll make the coffee."

She stepped warily to the table, only just barely controlling her flush of embarrassment at what had taken place on that table the night before.

His head between her thighs, his tongue dancing wickedly over and inside her pussy. His hands on her breasts, her nipples. Her own hands there—

She clasped her hands in her lap tightly and pressed her thighs together with a firm admonishment that she was not going to get wet. She would not get wet. She wasn't wearing panties and she simply couldn't afford to have her juices gathering and easing—

Her teeth clenched in anger at herself.

There it was. The slow, easy glide of her juices from her vagina. At this rate, her jeans were going to be wet and she didn't have anything else to wear.

"You slept deep last night." He spoke quietly as he set the coffee in front of her. "I think we could have had a bomb going off outside the bedroom and it wouldn't have shaken you."

His smile was a slight quirk.

How long had it been since he had smiled?

Had he gotten over Jaymi's death? Did he even think of the death of his lover in his arms as anything other than the event that had nearly destroyed his life?

"I need to make a few phone calls," she said. Rather than asking the questions raging through her, she went for something more mundane, something simple. She needed to get in touch with her aunt and uncle and let them know she was safe. No doubt Aunt Ella was beside herself, pacing the floors by now.

"Phones are down; cell-phone reception is lousy at best," he told her. "There's a chance you'll get a text out if you stand on the balcony outside the bedroom."

Her aunt and uncle were no doubt worried to death.

"There was about a forty-minute lag time on mine to Crowe," he told her. "He's in the cabin." He nodded toward the mountains rising behind the house.

Crowe Callahan's cabin was so far up that mountain that when the cousins had disappeared after the judge released them twelve years before, it had taken days for the sheriff to find them again when he'd been forced to return their belongings.

She nodded. If she was lucky, her aunt and uncle would at least know she was safe and warm until the storm was over. She'd simply stated she was with a friend. Would they suspect who that friend was, she wondered? Perhaps not at first, but her aunt's intuition could be amazingly precise.

Sliding the cup of coffee across the table minutes later, Rafe took the opposite chair and lounged back in it lazily.

"So what's your story?" he asked.

Her cup halfway to her lips, Cami looked up at him slowly, knowing exactly what he was talking about simply from the hint of underlying anger in his voice.

What would her excuse be for being at the Triple R Ranch during a blizzard with Rafer Callahan? And in his eyes she could see a demand for a reason why she would need an excuse.

"The truth usually works." She sighed. "The car slid into a snowdrift and I had to stay here."

"And where did you sleep?" The hard curve of his lips didn't even resemble a smile. "I need to know what to say when the good folks of Sweetrock decide to decimate me again because I slept with one of their favorite daughters."

"Like I tell the kids at school, don't borrow trouble and you won't have as many problems," she told him. "If they ask, do what you've always done before and shoot them that arrogant look before turning and walking away. Change the way you act and you give them more to talk about."

And what the hell was *she* going to say? The question was bound to come up. Any woman seen in the company of a Callahan eventually faced the third degree. Then, there was always the series of lectures, and enough harassment that they'd walk away from the Callahan simply out of frustration.

But it was rumored Rafe never really gave a damn. If a lady left before he did, then *oh well,* was the attitude he seemed to take. That was the impression he had always given, but Cami remembered Jaymi's comment once that Tye had told her about the times Rafer had often retreated within himself afterwards. Tye had sworn that those rejections and opposition were destroying Rafe. Cami couldn't imagine that he had endured them without serious internal scars.

"So, we're on the sly here then." He gave a slow nod. "Did I give up my bed for you? Or was I my normal cruel self and forced you to sleep on the couch?"

"Don't, Rafe." Cami wrapped her hands around the cup

as she stared back at him directly. "Things can't be any different and you know it. What happened to Jaymi changed everything."

He snorted. "You were only thirteen then, Cami. I had no thoughts at all of you, sexually. But later—" He shook his head. "You want me until it's all you can do to sit still in that damned chair and you'll still deny it, won't you?"

He leaned forward, pushing the cup slowly out of his way as he braced his arms on the table and glared back at her. "Tell me, Cami, when will it stop mattering to you what the people think?"

"When my job no longer depends on it?" she suggested, feeling his tension, his anger, licking at her now. "When my parents don't stare at my sister's picture with such grief and my mother isn't sobbing because she lost her daughter and the men she believes killed her have gone unpunished."

Her lips thinned as she breathed out roughly.

Cami's hand jerked up, covered her lips.

God, she hadn't wanted to say that; She hadn't wanted to hurt either of them with the truth he should know by now couldn't be avoided.

His eyes narrowed back at her as mockery filled his expression. "Yeah, that was real dumb," he drawled. "We both know there's no way the Callahan cousins can defend themselves against what the good people of Sweetrock think." He gave a short bark of laughter at the thought. "Or should I say, what the barons tell them to think?"

Cami could only shake her head at the comment. "You know how they are, Rafe. The barons, for whatever reason, want the three of you out of Sweetrock forever. You've had twelve years to try to convince everyone differently and you haven't even made the attempt. You return home every so often, stare down your nose at them, and pretend they don't matter. When you know that if you want to stay here, then it does matter."

"What matters, Cami? Their opinion?" Rafe smirked. "When I was ten and my parents had just died, one of the fine teachers of Sweetrock informed me I was better off without

them and while the principal lectured me because I had gotten into a fight with a boy that called my mother a Callahan
whore." By the time he finished he was leaning across the
table, almost nose to nose with her, the fury that filled his
sapphire eyes frightening in its intensity. "Tell me, why the
fuck *should* I care?"

She hadn't known about that but she didn't doubt it in the
slightest either.

She knew his life in Sweetrock had never been easy, but she
hadn't known that it had been that terrible when he had been
so young. No more than his parents' lives had been easy. As
though there were those determined to make the orphans pay
for their fathers' supposed crimes since their fathers weren't
there to pay themselves.

"I'm sorry," she whispered.

Pulling back, he shot her a disgusted look before picking
up his coffee cup and moving to the sink. It was set in the
sink gently, despite the tension raging through him. She had
expected him to throw it. She would have.

"Fuck your 'sorry,'" he grunted. "Your parents for all their
love for each other and for Jaymi, they never gave a damn
about you. And they had no compassion, and they sure as hell
had no sympathy, for three little boys suddenly orphaned and
about as alone in the world as they could get. When our parents died every damned one of them turned on us and the few
that didn't ignored it," he accused. "Tell me, Cami, do you
even know why the hell the fine citizens of Sweetrock hated
my father and uncles more than they hated any others? What
the hell did they do to inspire such fucking animosity toward
their children as well?"

Cami could only shake her head. She'd had this discus-
sion with her Aunt, and Ella Flannigan hadn't been willing
to supply the answers.

There had been excuses. There had been embarrassment.
But, there hadn't been an explanation that made sense other
than the fact that the barons had set the rules on their treatment and everyone seemed to follow.

Even among the teachers Cami had been friends with

most of her life seemed unwilling to discuss the Callahan cousins.

She'd always felt as though her parents and their friends were unwilling to face whatever had happened in the past. They were definitely unwilling to discuss their own reasons for so blindly following the cousins' families in that regard.

Sweetrock was a very small town. A church, a courthouse and sheriff's office, a single grocer, and several feed and supply stores were all they could boast of. There were fewer than a thousand citizens; the last census counted 605 within the city limits.

"So you're just going to lie about your little adventure with Rafer Callahan." He strode back to the table and leaned over, his palms flattening against the tabletop.

"There's no lie. It was snowing, my car was stuck, and I'm staying here until I can get the car out." She had to force the words past her lips as she stared into the depths of his burning gaze.

There was anger there. A male fury that burned clear to his soul. But there was also betrayal, and she couldn't blame him for feeling it or for hating her and everyone else in the county for it.

"If I could get you out of here now, right this minute, I would." His lips pulled back from his teeth in a snarl. "I'll be damned if I even want you here."

She rose slowly to her feet, watching as he straightened as well, his chest rising and falling harshly, those blue, blue eyes glaring at her with something akin to hatred.

"I can leave," she stated.

It shouldn't be too bad. If she could make it to her car before the storm began again.

If she could get through the freezing drifts before the cold got to her.

But here wasn't a good place to be if—

Her eyes narrowed.

"Like hell," she snapped back at him. "You had your chance to get me out of here and you blew it, big boy. It looks like you're damned sure stuck with me until the storm lets up or someone can bulldoze their way through the snow to get to me."

"Stuck with you?" he bit out harshly. "Oh, baby, the very last thing I am is stuck with you. Haven't you heard the fucking rumors in this fine county? I kill women for a fucking hobby." His voice rose on that last note, the incredulity she knew he felt lying just beneath the fury.

"You wouldn't hurt a woman! You sure as hell wouldn't hurt me!" she yelled back at him, suddenly incensed that he would even dare to use such a threat against her. "You would make one want to kill you instead. What the hell does it matter to you that the whole world doesn't know we were fucking while I was stuck here? Do I have to spread my business around town to satisfy your male pride?"

Her hands went to her hips, indignation and anger surging through her so hard that her heart was pounding furiously kicking her senses into overdrive.

"My male pride doesn't have a damned thing to do with it," he snarled back. "But tell me this, Miss Flannigan, once someone rescues your tight little ass, will you even recognize me on the street?"

"I've never ignored you, Rafer Callahan," she burst out, "and don't you even pretend I have." She jabbed him in the chest with her finger, shaking in admonishment as his gaze flicked to it with arrogant disregard.

"And when have you seen me on the street since I was arrested for Jaymi's murder?" He stepped closer. The sound of Cami's sisters' name on his lips sent a rush of pain sweeping through her.

"I didn't do that to you," she said hoarsely, her throat tightening at the dark emotions that tightened his face. "I never thought you had anything to do with that."

"How far does your belief in me go then?" he asked her roughly, the sound of his voice, scraping against emotions-raw and pulsing with a hunger that she didn't understand. "Tell me, Cambria. Does it extend to going to dinner with me? To waking up next to me when there's no storm to excuse your presence in my home? Tell me, does that belief extend to being my lover or just being my occasional fuck?"

Before she could stop it her hand flew out, cracking against his cheek with a suddenness that drew a gasp from her, and a sneer from him as she jerked her hand back. The red imprint stood out on his face. Rafe curled his lip in the insulting disregard for it, his eyes blazing as he reached out, grabbed her wrist, and yanked her against him.

"You get to pay for that little blow," he growled, that hunger that had mystified her seconds before now glowing in his eyes like neon lights. A sexual, overpowering hunger so filled with demand that it nearly stole her breath. "If you're just my occasional fuck, then I'm claiming another of my occasions right now, by God."

CHAPTER 7

Cami wanted to protest. She wanted to smack him again, to hurt him as he had hurt her. She wanted to rail as much against fate and the past as against him and what he had said.

She wasn't an occasional fuck, and she wasn't afraid of the people of Sweetrock. She was afraid of doing as her sister had done, as she had nearly done three years before. Cami was terrified of giving him everything and losing it all if something happened to him. If the sins of the past were to strike out with deadly accurate fury, leaving her alone. So totally alone she would never recover.

That was it, she assured herself as his lips covered hers and stole her ability to scream or to rail at anything or anyone. As the hunger, a dark, bitter storm inside her began to rage.

She bit at his lips as they moved over hers, only narrowly missing as her teeth snapped together. A snarl grated from her throat.

"How bad do you want it, Rafer?" she snapped furiously as she struggled in his arms, her teeth snapping back at him again.

"Oh, I don't think so, sweetheart," he growled, one arm holding her locked to him as the other gripped her jaw. He exerted just enough to control her, just enough pressure to keep her from biting as his lips possessed hers.

Possessed her kiss, possessed each response he wanted, and sent a wave of fiery hunger, need, and anger slamming through Cami. Waves of cataclysmic sensation began tearing through her, mixing with the anger, the hunger, the overwhelming need for this one man. A need she was determined she would not allow to destroy her.

She pushed against his tongue as it thrust past her lips, tangled with it, and fought him for every second of the possession he was claiming. With each stroke of his lips, each arrogant thrust of his tongue, she was enraged anew at him. Enraged and desperate for every caress every touch. So hungry for him that her blood boiled with it, her flesh sensitizing for him.

The pure dominance was more than she could resist. There was something about him, something so wild and untethered, that she couldn't help but be drawn by him. To hunger for him with a strength that made little sense.

Like a moth to a flame. The pleasure that rose between them was that irresistible and that incredibly bright. Like nothing she had known, like every fantasy and every dream she had ever imagined.

It would be her destruction, but resisting that destruction was beyond her ability. Resisting Rafer had always been impossible and she had sensed it, known it. But a part of her was too aware of every obstacle standing between them.

A moan tore from her throat as his tongue pumped into her mouth, licking at hers, then pulling back to nip at her lips before licking over the erotic little pain.

Her hands were in his hair, mussing it. His hands pushed beneath the layers of her sweatshirt and T-shirt. There he found her needy flesh, stroking her sides and stomach with firm, calloused fingertips as she arched into his touch. The sensations building between them were beginning to burn out of control. The power of their lust overtaking any objections she might have had.

Cami could feel intense burning with a blinding heat blazing as his lust tore through her; resisting him was impossible. Her body was clamoring for more, each touch stroking the flames of lust higher, she moaned into his kiss, his taste; Each stroke of his tongue an aphrodisiac to her senses. Each touch of his body against hers a flame she couldn't deny.

It had to just be lust.

She could control it. She promised herself she would control any emotions that threatened to rise in that darkened corner of her soul that she'd always ignored. Ignored yet protected with every breath. Until Rafe stole her breath and slipped right past those defenses.

The emotions threatened to build as she gave in to the kiss and returned it with the same ferocity, the same hunger, which it was given. Focusing on the pleasure alone was all she could do. If she let herself feel, if she allowed that dark corner inside her, where Rafer always dominated, to open then she could be lost forever.

The sensual, dominant, and forceful plundering of her mouth was only the precursor to the pleasure, and she knew it. She could feel what was coming. She could feel the flames building, the sensations becoming stronger, piercing deeper than they ever had before. As though the primal anger, the rage that burned so deep inside her, had only this outlet to find freedom.

His hands pushed beneath the shirts, moving to her back to unclip her bra, and dragging a hungry moan from her throat. A wild, feverish heat burned through her womb. It spreading to her pussy, to the swollen bud of her clitoris, and made her drunk on the need.

The lace and silk cups of her bra loosened, rasping over the tender nipples as his hands moved to cup the swollen mounds.

His fingers found the tender tips, gripping them firmly, sending a furious burst of pleasured pain through them as his fingers worked them sensually. Milking them. Sending fingers of fiery, agonizing pleasure tearing through them straight to her womb.

She could feel her juices gathering. Liquid hot, sensitizing her pussy further.

She should be furious. She should be fighting him tooth and nail. She should never give in to the dominant, forceful taking of her senses.

But this was Rafer.

He *was* dominant.

He *was* forceful.

His head jerked back, but only because he was quickly pulling the sweatshirt and T-shirt over her head.

He tossed them to the floor before pulling the straps of her bra over her arms and throwing it aside.

She had a chance to fight; to escape. Instead, she pulled at his shirt, buttons popping, scattering heedlessly to the floor as she tried to tear it from his shoulders. Nothing mattered but touching him. She needed to feel his flesh against hers. She ached for it. Her body pulsed with the overwhelming hunger for it.

"Damn you," she cried out furious with him, with herself, because once he'd touched her, she'd been lost. She was lost. His lips moved to her neck, raking over the sensitive nerve endings as the pleasure pouring through her rocked her senses. "I won't let you do this to me." But she let her head fall back, trembled at the feel of his tongue licking over it. "I won't let you—" She wasn't going to let him steal her heart, too.

"Who's asking your permission?" he growled. "Shut the hell up and give me your kiss. Damn you, you'll fucking be the death of me."

His lips came over hers again, hungry, seeking, his tongue meeting hers and creating a wave of powerful sensuality that that threatened to overpower them.

Cami was only barely aware they were moving, gravitating to the living room. There was no time to make it to the bedroom. There was no patience to find the nearest bed.

There was no way she could have navigated the stairs. There wasn't a chance in hell she wanted to hold back to make it up the hall.

She wanted him now, just as quickly as possible, and she wanted all of him.

Nothing mattered now but the blazing, agonizing need consuming her, tearing through her. It was like being forced on a wild, rapidly spinning merry-go-round that refused to stop. Her senses were spinning with each touch, with each lash of sensation whipping through her.

As she was backed into the living room the fiery, biting kisses that ate so hungrily at her lips moved to her neck. His hands went to the snap and zipper of her jeans as the need for flesh on flesh whipped through her senses.

She was pulling at his shirt, one hand beneath it to feel the warmth of his skin, touching his flesh, the other jerking at the loosened edges and fighting to push the material over his shoulders.

Desperate hands, hers and his, tore at metal tabs, at zippers at buttons moored to fragile cloth. Their clothes and her boots were jerked off, cast aside, leaving them blissfully naked. Their hands hungry for bare skin stroked and caressed as Rafe tugged her to the heavy, thick rug before the warmth of the blazing fire.

As they went to their knees, Cami became the aggressor.

She remembered that first night, five years before, much too well. Remembered each sensation of controlling the heavily engorged flesh of his erection, working it inside her and crying out at the pleasure. Moving over him, her thighs had straddled his hips, the sensation of controlling his hunger had made her drunk on the pleasure.

She had controlled each thrust. She had controlled each sensation, and the power had been heady. The remembered ecstasy, the sheer rapture found at the end of that wild, impulsive ride was too much to resist.

"Let me," she whispered desperately as he moved to force her back to the rug. "Let me ride you Rafer. Let me have it again. Oh God, I might die if I don't have it again."

If she didn't have the pleasure and exquisite sensation of controlling a wild sexual beast as she moved above him.

Her hands pushed at his shoulders, her lips moving to his

chest, to the flat, hard male nipples. His hands dug into her hair as her teeth scraped the tips, rasping over them, licking them as the salty male taste intoxicated her senses.

Reclining on the rug as she pressed him down, Cami followed, a wild, feral need flowing through her. It pounded in her veins, clenched her pussy, and rippled through her womb.

Staring down at him, watching the corded strength rippling through her body, Cami felt a moan rising inside her chest. The wicked sensuality gleamed in the intense blue of his eyes as his hand lowered. His fingers curled around the heavy width of his cock.

Long, powerful fingers began a slow, deliberately teasing rhythm along the thick shaft.

"Take it, Cami," he dared her, his hand stroking up the length of his cock, squeezing the wide, engorged crest as it throbbed imperatively. "Come on, baby, show me how bad you want to fuck me, or do you just want to talk about it?"

It was a dare that hadn't been required. A challenge she had intended to meet whether it was issued or not.

"You talk about it," she ordered, feeling powerfully erotic, sensual. "Come, Rafer, tell me what you want. Tell me if you're enjoying it."

Swinging her leg over his thighs as he reached down to grip the shaft of his cock, Cami swore she could hear a sob echoing around her.

Her sob.

It was a sound rife with a need that went far beyond the lust she had promised herself she would stop. It sliced straight through her senses, and she swore she could feel the pleasure straight to her soul.

"Ah yes, Cami-girl," he groaned. "Take it. Show me how much you want my dick."

Sensation ricocheted through her senses as the blunt, widened crest of his cock slid through the thick, heavy juices coating her cunt. The heated, blunt crest grazed the hard, nerve-laden bud of her clit, circled it, then slid back down to tuck against the clenched entrance of her pussy.

She hadn't had sex since the night he had given her a child.

She had tried, God knew she had tried, to replace his memory with another man. She had dated; she had even gotten close. A few times, she had even enjoyed the kisses and the touch of several of those men. But it had simply been enjoyment. There had been nothing wild, nothing that even came close to the pleasure she'd found with Rafer. No other man had ever tempted her to rush her heart and her sanity as he did.

Rolling her hips, she felt the crest parting her entrance further, already beginning that slow, pleasure-pain-edged sensation that left her feeling drugged, high on building ecstasy.

Rafer gripped her hips with one hand as he paused, waiting, his gaze narrowed as he watched her.

The world seemed suspended, poised on this moment as she stared down at him. The thick head of his cock just barely breaching at the entrance to her sex. Almost penetrating her, heating her, making her so hungry for him, so desperate to fuck him that her fingers curled against his chest into fists as she fought to hold back.

She trembled.

Shuddered.

"Rafer," she whispered his name, wishing she could convince herself it was a dream. That she could live the dream, awaken when morning came with no more repercussions than a dream would bring. "Don't let it end," she begged, still poised above him and taking only the very tip of the throbbing flesh.

"I have you, love," he promised, the guttural, raw sound of his voice whispering across her senses. "Let it last, Cami. Don't rush it, baby; ease into it all you want."

She didn't want ease. She wanted it all. The powerful burn, the agonizing pleasure. But there was no way to let that last. No way to make that heat last forever.

"I need you," she sighed, her lashes fluttering as her hips shifted, pressing down, taking him at the first sensation of heavy pressure parting the clenched entrance. "Oh God, Rafer, how I've needed you."

Was that her voice, so ragged and filled with aching hunger as she began to roll her hips? As she worked the engorged head past the snug, narrow entrance to her pussy.

Flares of wild, agonizing pleasure shot through her clit and ricocheted to her womb.

She could hear herself whimpering, pleasure whipping through her with a painful edge.

She needed him. She needed the pleasure mixed with that flash of pain. The intensity, the binding ecstasy that seemed to wrap around her senses and sink into her soul.

Her lashes fluttered, pleasure suffusing her face as Rafe felt the involuntary jerk of his hips. The pleasure took over, the hunger racing through both of them. She felt the head of his dick pierce the hot entrance to her pussy, pressing inside and stretching her erotically.

A low moan of pleasure whispered in the air around them. Cami lifted against him, then with a hard shift of her hips buried the head of his cock in the torturously tight, ecstatically hot muscles of her pussy.

Rafe's teeth clenched until his jaw hurt. His hands gripped her hips, possibly too hard, as her nails dug into his chest. Her head tilted back, her breasts pushing as her nipples stood out explicitly. Desperate pleasure twisted her features, her pleasure amplifying his and driving through his senses sharply.

Silky, slick, and fist-tight. The ripple of her flesh around the sensitive head of his cock was almost too much to bear. Satiny, her juices slid along his flesh, easing the penetration, Rafe felt the pinch of her tight pussy opening for him before clenching tight again.

Her pussy milked the engorged width of his cock-head. Her muscles rippled around it as his balls drew tight and he fought to hold back his release. The thick flesh, pulsed warningly. God help him, he didn't know if he could hold on, didn't know if he could hold back.

"Rafer," she gasped his name her voice hoarse as her hips shifted, rolling, pressing, tilting lower as she began to work herself on the iron-hard shaft. "Yes. Fuck me Rafer. So good," she moaned ecstatically. "Please fuck me harder." Let me fuck you."

Slick, easing his way, the slide of her heated cream along his shaft to his balls tore a groan from his chest.

Rafe forced himself to hold back, to hold himself still as she moved over him and above him. Her hips circled and moved over him, rising, falling on the hard shaft.

"Ah, Cami," he groaned. "That's it, baby. Work your pussy on me. Take my dick, sweetheart." His teeth gritted with the burning pleasure of it. "Take every fucking inch of my dick."

Only the head was buried inside her, throbbing in pleasure as the need for release pulsed in his scrotum.

She was moving so slow, a sensual, erotic vision of sexual hunger and feminine lust as she began to ride him. Her hands pressed into his chest, bracing herself against him as she began rocking above him, taking him inch by inch, her expression transforming to sublime rapture.

Each inch worked inside her was a flash of sizzling electric heat raging through his senses. Each rapid-fire jerk of her hips, burying his flesh ever deeper inside her pussy, tore a groan from his lips.

His hands slid from her hips to her breasts, feeling the firm, pleasure-swollen mounds as he cupped them. He palmed the tight flesh as he fingered the tight, stiff tips and watched her expression at each touch. The pleasure on her face, pleasure he gave her, which she found while working his dick inside her, had an impossible pride racing through him. Her expression was nearing ecstasy. Her teeth dug into her lower lip; her nails bit into his chest. Nothing existed in her world at the moment but him and the hard dick he gave her.

He was giving her this pleasure. Working her into a frenzy of ecstasy when he'd already heard the rumors that Cami Flannigan never gave out. But Rafe knew she did give out. She gave out to him. With every kiss, with every touch, she gave to him.

Perspiration gleamed on her body, beaded on her creamy breasts. She was giving in, taking every inch of him, and loving every second of it. Loving every inch of his cock as she fucked him.

Cami swayed above him, taking him to the hilt with hard, fierce downward glides of her hips. She ground her clit against his pelvis, rocked them with jerky desperate movements as her pussy milked his shaft with erotic spasms.

Small, whimpering moans fell from her lips, tiny erotic cries that sent heat flooding his senses. God, she made him crazy. She made his senses explode just from the hunger, the sheer overriding demand that he touch, taste, that he fuck her as hard and as fast as possible. That he mark her clear to her soul. That he possess—own. Oh God, fill every part of her until she couldn't survive without him.

She swayed above him, taking him to the hilt with hard, fierce downward glides of her hips. She ground her clit against him again, whispered his name, and—damn her straight to hell—made his fucking arms ache to just hold her.

"Fuck me, damn you," he snarled his hands tightening on her hips as the lazy movements worked his lust higher. The hunger tore through him in ways he couldn't explain. It would take more strength than he ever possessed to be able to tear himself away from her at this point.

"Rafer." Her lashes parted, the soft gray of her eyes darker, the dark blue ring around the dove-gray color nearly black, her face flushed, as she stared down at him, then she licked her lips with a lazy, sensual flick of her little tongue.

Desperation whipped at his control as he slid his fingers from her breasts, down her thighs, and around to her buttocks. "Fuck yes," he gritted out. "Work that tight little pussy on my dick. Give it to me, Cami."

Her cry was sharper. Her hips moved faster, lifting and falling in tight, imperative strokes he knew he couldn't bear for long, as he gave the explicit order.

His fingers slid along the crease of her ass, firm, determined caresses that suddenly had her senses heightening further. Her breathing becoming harder, more labored.

He gripped the rounded little mounds, spread them apart, then delved inside to find the sweet tight little rosebud hidden there.

Her movements became jerkier, tighter. Her eyes flashed open, locked with his.

"I love your ass," he whispered hoarsely. "So sweet and rounded. So tempting. I'm going to fuck that ass, Cami. I'm going to watch my cock pierce it, stretch it."

"Rafer?" The confused pleasure that tightened her face had his hips arching, taking over the hard strokes, pushing them both closer to release "So fucking sweet and hot," he growled, his fingertip working against that forbidden little entrance. "Being buried in your tight little pussy is pure paradise."

Cami couldn't stem the pleasure. She couldn't hold back the sensations or make him stop. The sound of his rough, guttural tone talking dirty to her, the words piercing her pleasure-hazed senses, stoked the flames higher.

As her hips rolled against him, his fingers slid to the heavy layer of juices. With two fingers he eased the slick moisture back, lubricating the tiny entrance, preparing her, wishing, gritting his teeth at the demand that he flip her over and work his cock up that tight little hole. The ultimate possession. It would be the ultimate trust, given to him. It would be pure, sweet, fucking bliss.

"I can make the hurt so good, Cami," he groaned, and damned if he had ever talked to another woman quite this way. "I can make it so good that you beg for more. That you ache for it. Scream for it."

Cami felt the erotic pinch of heat as he worked his fingertip inside the virgin entrance, bringing her to an abrupt stop. Her hips stilled instantly. Despite the demand to move. The pleasure pounding through her. Staring down at him, panting for air, she bit her lip and tried to decide if she wanted this new touch, if she could handle it.

But Rafer wasn't giving her a chance to decide. Wrapping his free arm high around her back, he pulled her down, nearly bringing her to his chest before she jerked back, a little whimper escaping unbidden from her lips.

"Rafer, I don't know—" if she could handle the sensations. If she could handle the emotions.

She could feel the unknown looming before her as he continued to work his finger gently against the opening.

He tugged her down again, this time his hold firmer, her attempt to jerk back halted by the strength in his powerful arm.

"Scared, baby?" The amusement in his voice was a challenge and a dare. "Are you finally realizing you may not be able to handle me as easily as you think you can?"

He was daring her and he knew it. Pushing her, making the challenge impossible to resist. He knew his Cami. He knew that hidden core of competitiveness, that vein of fierce determination inside her.

The sound of it had her pausing. The pause, the weakening in her resistance, was all it took.

Before she could consider how to resist, how to adapt to the different sensations, his arm tightened around her, two fingers pressing firmly against the tight, too-sensitive, nerve-laden entrance that had never been touched before.

"What are you doing to me?" There were too many sensations, the pleasure and the pain building, the fiery intensity beginning to bloom from her rear through her pussy, her clit, raking through her womb.

His hips rolled beneath her, grinding his pelvis against her oversensitive clit as he thrust just enough, just hard enough, stroking violently sensitive inner nerve endings as his fingers stretched, worked, burned the sensitive ring of tissue that protected the inner flesh of her rear.

She could feel a fury of flames beginning to burn inside her. Wicked, intense, and violently erotic. The heat began to build, to focus inward, blazing through her womb as she felt it begin to convulse.

Her body tightened, the muscles of her pussy, her anus, clamping down on the dual penetration, throwing her into ecstasy.

The implosion blinded her. Pleasure began tearing through her. It rippled and surged through her system as she tightened convulsively crying out and shuddering violently as his name tore past her lips in an agony of pure, burning rapture. She felt the hard, fiery blast of his semen pulsing inside her. Felt his fingers scissoring in her rear, extending the sensations. His free arm held her close to him, and a muted, broken male groan sounded at her ear.

Ecstasy exploded again, tearing through her and pulling a desperate cry from her lips as she heard him whisper her name. His free hand moved up, locked in her hair, and turned her head to him, his lips catching hers, kissing her, devouring her cries and her pleasure as it tore through her.

Torturously intense shudders of rapture raced through her flesh as she swore she could feel Rafer not just inside her body but also under her skin. He was invading parts of her she hadn't realized he could ever breach.

Lying against him, waves of heat sinking deeper and deeper inside her, Cami fought and failed to keep that inner part of her closed against him.

She could feel, hear, his heartbeat against her breast as her throat tightened with tears. Tears she couldn't, wouldn't, allow herself to shed.

Tears that didn't make sense to her, because she had known, even before he touched her that first time seven years before, that between them there could never be anything more.

Rafe lay silently, petting Cami's body gently as the shudders of her release began to slowly ease. The incredibly tense, violent vibrations of her orgasm had taken him by surprise. As though the pleasure had been pulled straight from some inner part of her feminine core and raced through her repeatedly before releasing.

It took long minutes for her body to slowly relax, for the

tremors to ease and the heavy, satisfied lassitude to move in and do its work.

To keep her in place. To hold her to him while he tried to find a way to figure out exactly what had just happened.

What had begun out of arrogant male pride and a lust he had no idea how to combat had turned into something more, into something he wasn't certain he knew how to control.

There was something about Cami that slid right past his defenses and locked inside a part of him that he simply wasn't familiar with. A dark, dominant, primal part of his psyche that only awakened when he was with her.

And he had no idea what the hell he was supposed to do about it or how to rid himself of it.

"What's going on between us, Rafer?" Her voice was quiet, wary, as she asked the question. "How do you do this to me?"

In that soft, cautious tone she expressed the same conflicting feelings he could feel roiling inside himself.

"Hell if I know," he breathed out roughly after several long moments. "Whatever it is, it's damned good, though."

It was a pleasure he would be loathe to lose after the storm was over and Cami left. He couldn't imagine letting her go when the time came. Hell, he couldn't imagine her walking away from him. Surely there was a way to convince her to stay, just for a little while. Just long enough to explore the pleasure, the dark, sensual need that drew them together.

"It's snowing again," she said rather than taking the current conversation any further.

Cami made all those dark hungers swirling inside him, so thick and heavy that it obliterated good common sense.

He stroked his hand slowly down her back, relishing the feel of her satiny flesh, the warmth of her skin, the feel of her heartbeat against his own.

"How long do you think we can stay apart this time without tearing into each other like love-starved teenagers the first time we see each other again?" That was what he was often reminded of since she had shown up on his doorstop the night before. "Do you really think you can escape this addiction another three years?"

She tensed in his arms and for a moment, the briefest weakening moment, he wished he had kept his damned mouth shut.

But the more realistic, logical part of his brain assured him it was a valid question and one she needed to be prepared to answer when they saw each other again. Reality sucked bad enough and there were times he'd give almost anything to escape it, but the truth was, there was no escaping. It. Better he face it now, and deal with it, than to have it surprise him later.

"This can't happen again, Rafer," she said softly, pulling out of his arms to sit up in front of the fire. She gazed into the flickering flames.

Her expression was somber, resigned, as she wiped a hand over her face and breathed in roughly. "We aren't teenagers. And we're going to have to simply accept that it can't go anywhere and let it die as it should."

With her legs bent, her arms wrapped around them, as her chin rested at the top of her knees, she looked like a little lost girl. Especially with that short mop of hair framing her delicate face. She was a woman, though, and she was talking about walking away from something neither of them had been able to deny each time they had been face-to-face with each other.

Her ability to fool herself, to weave daydreams and to believe them, simply amazed him.

"You don't really think that's going to happen anytime soon, do you, Cami?" he said mockingly.

No, she didn't but she knew what was best for her heart, and allowing herself to fall once more into the emotional abyss that awaited her, if she allowed this to continue, was not what was best for her heart.

Turning her head, she stared back at him. He was so comfortable in his nudity, so confident in it that she could only envy him.

"Is this because of your parents?" he asked as he curled

one arm behind his head and appeared as relaxed and comfortable as any finely muscled, highly sexual male animal.

God, the man made her breathless only seconds after an orgasm so violent she'd nearly lost her mind. As that thought hit her, so did his question. She stared back at him with a frown. "What? Is what because of my parents?" Genuine confusion filled her.

"Your refusal to admit there's something between us," he growled, a disgruntled frown tightening his brow.

"There's nothing between us," she agreed. God, she didn't want to do this right now.

His expression tightened. She could see the male calculation that filled his gaze as well as the determination, and she knew what she had done.

"I'm not a challenge or a dare, Rafer, so don't start attempting to see me as one. I have no intention of falling into some kind of love-trap with you and losing my soul."

"Love-trap?" A black brow arched with deliberate arrogance. "What exactly is a love-trap, Cami?"

Her lips thinned. Twisting around, she searched for her clothes before gritting her teeth in frustration. Hell, she had left them in the kitchen. Actually they were scattered from the kitchen to where they were now. She grabbed Rafer's shirt instead and pushed her arms into the sleeves before pulling the material around her.

"I'm not getting into this with you, Rafer," she informed him as she moved to rise to her feet.

"The hell you're not."

Before she could avoid him, his fingers circled her wrist and pulled her back to him. Caught off balance, Cami found herself sprawled across his chest, staring back at him in surprise.

"And what is this going to accomplish, Rafer?" she questioned him, struggling to keep calm, to refuse to allow the past between them to overwhelm her.

"Tell me, Cami, do you know what everyone in town says when they talk about you?"

He let her push away, but only far enough to sit up again.

Cami turned her gaze away from him to stare into the flames flickering in the fireplace. "Do I want to know?" Wrapping her arms around her knees, she refused to stare back at him.

"Cambria Flannigan doesn't give up," he mocked out. "She's a hell of a friend. Honest as hell. She's even a cheap date. But she's frigid as hell, no doubt a virgin, and refuses to let a man get even as far as first base."

"Well, then, evidently 'everyone' is wrong." Turning back to him, she wished she had kept her eyes averted.

"You've not been with another man other than me, Cami."

"Maybe my lovers just know how to keep their mouths shut," she retorted with a blatant lie. "And maybe, Rafe, I simply don't want the emotional ties that go with a 'relationship'," she bit out sarcastically. "There are those of us who aren't all about that commitment that goes with sleeping with certain men."

She tried to rise to her feet again only to have him pull her back.

"What the hell are you doing, Rafer?" she burst out at the dominance in his refusal to allow her to move away from him.

"I'm getting fucking answers," he snapped, his voice rising just marginally as his head lifted, his gaze flashing in anger.

"Answers to what, Rafer? Why I refuse to fuck around or fuck men who would just love to advertise it? What business is it of yours?"

"Liar!" His lips drew back as the word rasped from his lips. "You've been running from me for six years now, Cami. Sneaking out of the bed like a damned thief when the sun rises and avoiding me like the plague for the past three years. And I want to know why."

"Well, it sucks to be you, Rafer," she announced archly as she fought the anger she could feel rising more sharply inside her now.

"And what the hell do you mean by that?" he growled back at her, the muscles of his jaw flexing tightly.

"Exactly what I said." Shrugging, her lips pursing to hold back the anger, she jerked her arm out of his grip before rolling quickly away from him and to her feet. "I need a shower. Do me a favor and stop listening to gossip. You should know yourself exactly how destructive it can be."

She stalked from the living room, all but running from the living room and the questions she knew were getting ready to come from him.

Why had she begun ignoring him?

Why had she stopped making the trips to Denver that allowed him to waylay her for those few hours that allowed her to slip away at dawn? And why did she refuse to even question why they couldn't resist that sexual pull that kept bringing them together?

And they were questions she simply refused to answer. There was too much pain, too many emotions she had no choice but to keep buried inside her.

"Things are going to go your way and be done your way, no matter what. Right?"

"Pretty much," he agreed.

She so didn't think so.

Rather than stating the obvious, she turned and stalked to the shower, slamming and locking the door behind her.

He should have followed her. It was his bathroom, his damned house. And by God, she was his damned woman. That was a decision he'd made six years ago, when she was more than eighteen years old. When he left the Marines, when he came back to stay, Cami would be his.

He'd kept track of her. The few contacts he still had in Corbin let him know if she was dating anyone, if it was getting serious, what she was doing, and if she needed anything. He'd taken the decision he'd made very damned seriously.

Cami was his, and he figured it was time he let her know that little fact.

She would fight him. He wasn't certain why she would fight him, but it was more than apparent that that was exactly what she had in mind.

He hadn't expected a challenge from her, but he wasn't

about to turn away from one either. It would only make her surrender sweeter, he thought. One of the reasons he'd looked forward to this return was the chance to finally claim Cami once and for all. He might not have that romantic, sweet idea of Prince Charming that she might think she wanted, but he knew how to keep her warm when the nights were cold.

He knew how to please her.

He knew how to protect her.

Now if he could just convince "her" of those few, though no doubt important, facts.

CHAPTER 8

"Has he lost his fucking mind?" Crowe Callahan asked Logan the next morning, speaking through the voice-activated link to his cousin's communications set. Crowe sat on the winter-white snowmobile, the winter camo protective gear he wore insulating him against the freezing wind as he held the matching binoculars to the eye slit of the thermal full-face ski mask.

Staring from his position on the snow-covered mountainside, he couldn't believe Rafe was actually standing out in the freezing cold and smoking yet another of the cigars Crowe and Logan kept trying to convince him to throw away.

"Told you," Logan said as he leaned back, ignoring Crowe's intense, questioning look.

Dressed in identical snow gear, Logan rested casually against the pack strapped to the back half of the seat as the now gently falling snow, the final edge of the blizzard, collected on the protective face mask and shaded goggles he wore. "What's he doing this time?"

The lazy, unconcerned drawl of his voice was distinctly at odds with the worry Crowe had seen earlier in his cousin's face.

Shaking his head, Crowe turned back, lifted the military-issue binoculars back to his eyes, and watched as his cousin leaned against the support post of the sheltered porch below, the cigar clenched between his teeth, tension radiating in the stiff set of his shoulders and the dark glower on his face.

"He didn't close the curtains to the living room," Crowe mused as Cami Flannigan pulled the man's long-sleeved white shirt over her naked body after rising from the bed of pillows, feather comforters, and quilts that Rafe had obviously made the night before.

Like an animal creating a nest for his mate. Soft, warm, comforting, and protective. The aura of intimacy was so heavy it made Crowe's back teeth ache in frustrated anger. His baby cousin was making nests, getting intimate, and staring into the stark snowscape furiously. Just before his little lover stalked from the room. Then, Rafe just had to follow the girl.

"Really?" Logan rose from his reclined position. "Let me see."

Crowe snorted. "Pervert. She's left the room now."

"And you got to see her naked?" Logan chuckled. "Hell, man, what made you get so lucky and not me? Can I tell Rafe you got to see his lady naked?"

Crowe shook his head in amusement as he lowered the device once again. "That boy's going to get himself in trouble." He sighed. "Cami Flannigan is the last woman he should be screwing, especially under the current circumstances."

Especially considering the past and the circumstances of her sister's death. As the sister of Jaymi Flannigan Kramer, the last in a series of serial rapes and murders twelve years before, Cami was a problem waiting to happen. Crowe and his cousins had nearly gone to prison for it at the time. Because of that, Cambria was the last woman in the world Rafe should even be in the same vicinity with let alone in the same bed.

"Hey, I didn't notice a lot of choice when I was there with him," Logan pointed out with a hint of laughter. "And I'm sorry, man, but if I was stuck in a blizzard with Cami Flannigan I'd be all about fucking her too."

"Fucking her, not making yourself crazy over her." Crowe

sighed in resignation. You can fuck your women, Logan, without letting your heart get tangled up with your dicks."

"My dick's untangled just fine, thank you very much, cousin," Logan informed him with a hint of heavy amusement in his voice. "Matter of fact, it's about as untangled as a dick can get."

Untangled, Crowe's ass. Just give it time. Logan was all but hogtied and just didn't know it yet. Dammit. How the hell was he supposed to protect his cousins' asses without their help?

Crowe stared back at his younger cousin as Logan's green eyes twinkled back at him. the laughter in his gaze made the dark green depths seem to shimmer.

"Really?" Crowe drawled mockingly. "And that little neighbor of yours isn't putting a kink in it at all, right?" He couldn't see the frown that pulled at Logan's brow because of the cold weather mask, but Crowe saw the flash of ire in his cousin's gaze.

"Shut up," he muttered, his voice muffled by the face mask he wore.

Crowe breathed out roughly in resignation before turning back. He lifted the binoculars back to his eyes, and staring down at the two-story ranch house Clyde Ramsey had willed to his nephew, Rafer Callahan, along with the ranch.

As Crowe swept over the valley with the binoculars, it didn't take him long to find the road crew slowly working its way up the mountain toward the ranch.

No one might know where Cambria Flannigan was yet, but it wouldn't be long before her uncle Eddy Flannigan would be the first to figure it out. Shit was going to hit the fan when that happened, and Rafe would be stuck in the thick of it with no way out. Because there was no denying she had spent the duration of the blizzard there. It would be the perfect opportunity for Cami to try for a little revenge where her sister Jaymi was concerned. After all, the rest of her family believed the Callahans had killed her sister; over time, there was the possibility Cami could have been convinced.

It would be too damned easy for her to accuse him of raping her, kidnapping her, or performing any other illegal act that could possibly get him thrown into prison.

This was just what the hell the cousins needed.

Not that the Cami he had known eleven years ago could have done such a thing. But that was eleven years ago and this was now. Who knew how she had changed? And Crowe was a suspicious bastard.

They had to returned to Corbin County to find that "something" missing, not to help Rafe find his way into prison.

"Did you check out the car?" Crowe asked as he watched Rafe move through the house, the light curtains on the windows giving a clear view into his home. It appeared Rafe had followed Cami for some sort of confrontation.

Crowe could have sworn he'd taught Rafe better than that at some point. You never confront a possibly enemy face to face, especially if that potential enemy was female.

"I checked out the car," Logan affirmed. "I couldn't see anything that suggests the accident was anything but an accident, but the drifts are piled high around it, and digging it out enough to get under it wasn't high on my list of priorities."

He was wearing military-issue cold-weather gear that would have kept him toasty warm for up to forty-eight hours in the coldest spot in the world and he couldn't dig through a few feet of snow to check the tires.

After the deaths of their parents, Rafe's uncle, and other suspected enemies of the barons on the treacherous Corbin County roads, Crowe no longer believed in accidents or coincidences.

"What is high on your list of priorities, Logan?" Crowe asked absently. He wondered if Logan even understood what direction he was headed in. Or if he had any idea about the woman he was heading in that direction with. Sometimes, that worried Crowe more than the fear that Logan would care about the wrong person too much. His cousin was doing more than simply caring too much. He was on the verge of becoming too involved. Even more so than Rafe.

"Tying my dick in knots, unraveling it, then tying it again?" Logan chuckled. "Whatever it takes to stay footloose and fancy-free, Crowe, while having all kinds of fun. What about you?"

There were very few things Logan allowed himself to possess or to care about. His home had been in Crowe's name for years. It was an attempt to keep Logan from giving it the hell away and Rafe had insisted on it.

The Harley was in Rafe's name; the black Denali SUV was in Crowe's name. The only thing Logan owned, sort of, was the snowmobile, and it was simply in all their names.

Logan had a serious problem where owning things were involved. Even he didn't know why he didn't want to own anything, and Crowe also hadn't yet figured out why.

"I didn't hear an answer there, Crowe," Logan said as he leaned forward, dislodging the snow that had gathered on his shoulders.

"Footloose and fancy-free sounds fine to me." Crowe shrugged. "Seems to me that as long as we're in Corbin County, footloose and fancy-free is all we have."

It wasn't as though a future were going to happen with any of the fine ladies in Sweetrock or at the outlying ranches. Too many people knew their pasts. There were too many of the fine citizens of Corbin County willing to follow any and every order the barons gave.

The barons. His grandfather, James Corbin Rafer, Marshal Roberts, and Logan's grandfather Saul Rafferty. The three largest ranch owners and three of the most powerful financial families to reside in Colorado. Their ranches were the size of small countries. Each ranch resided in a different county, but strangely something tied the three patriarchs of these families together. A loyalty and friendship that spanned decades, fluctuating riches, and the temperaments of three power-hungry men.

Logan sighed. "There's always Aspen. Lots of pretty ladies there. Who says we have to pick from Corbin County anyway? Hell, we might get tired of footloose and fancy-free."

There was an edge of regret in Logan's voice, as though he'd actually had someone in mind. Someone he knew he couldn't have. Hell, Crowe just hoped it wasn't who he thought it was. That was just going to turn into a mess if it was.

"What about your neighbor?" Crowe looked back at Logan, restraining the knowing mockery in his tone. "She's not from Sweetrock."

Logan's eyes widened in shock and male outrage. "That O'Brien girl? Hell no! I watched her tear that builder Ken Stiles' ass up one side and back down the other a few days ago. Accused him for ten minutes of milking hours on that back porch he was building for her. She was right in his face, that little finger shaking like a weapon, and she was ready to use it." He gave a mock shudder. "I think I prefer something a little softer. A little less temperamental."

Crowe snorted. "You mean a little less able to kick your ass when you're acting like an ass?"

Who the hell did Logan think he was fooling?

"That's cold, man," Logan sighed. "So cold." His eyes twinkled in laughter. "But so fucking true."

"And this weather is fucking cold." Crowe couldn't feel the cold; the Thinsulate he wore was military issue and would keep him warm at far colder temperatures.

Where he felt the chill was in his spine, a sure sign that things were going to go from sugar to shit soon. And that chill had the power to send ice coursing through his veins. The last damned thing they needed, no sooner than they returned to Corbin County, was trouble. Especially when women were a part of that trouble.

"Think we should disturb the little lovebirds?" Logan suggested. Anticipation filled his voice, as did amusement. Logan sometimes seemed years younger than his age.

"I think someone should," Crowe said as he turned his gaze back to the house. "This will be over soon, and when it is, the whole town of Sweetrock will converge on him once they learn where Miss Flannigan had been forced to stay during the storm. I think Rafe could probably use the backup if that happens." Especially considering the fact Cami's uncle was a part of that road crew.

"Protection is more like it," Logan retorted. "Talk about a man with his dick and his heart tied up in knots. Our little cuz is there, I believe."

But then Crowe had a feeling Rafe had been there for a while; he just hadn't been aware of it. There had been too many chance meetings between Rafe and Cambria over the years. Too many near misses. And in the past few years there were too many times Rafe had obviously been watching, waiting, for someone who hadn't shown. His anger then had gone soul deep.

"Well, the road crew isn't far from finding the car, or making their way to our little cousin's love nest. I guess the kindest thing we could do is warn him, don't you think?" Crowe drawled.

Logan's curse sizzled through the line, seconding Crowe's thoughts and sending a wave of tension to clench his jaw and tighten his muscles.

Breathing out roughly, Crowe twisted the handle grip of the powerful machine he'd ridden down from the mountain, listening to the low, carefully muffled power that vibrated through the machine. He'd modified the machines himself, his as well as his cousins', to ensure the power that vibrated and throbbed through the motors was silenced as much as possible. Worst-case scenario, he would bank the power and speed and run at near silence if absolutely necessary.

There were times that more power and more sound could be a life-threatening hindrance. And times that any sound could mean certain death.

"Let's go see if we can help him unknot his dick then," Crowe said as he gave a hard twist of the opposite grip and shot down the mountain, carefully balancing his weight, watching the terrain and landmarks for known hazards beneath the snow, aware Logan was riding in his tracks.

Exactly where Crowe needed him to ride.

Crowe had done this all their lives, going first to clear the way for the other two. All but once. Rafe had managed to race ahead of Crowe just one time, and they hadn't been the only ones who had paid for Crowe's lack of speed. Jaymi Flannigan Kramer had paid with her life, and her death had left a mark on their souls ever since.

"He's not going to be happy with us," Logan promised, the wry humor coming through the earpiece he wore as Crowe navigated around the heavy trunks of the sheltering trees.

"But he'll live, and that's the point." Actually, that was really all that mattered to Crowe. That Rafe and Logan lived, stayed free, and managed to find some small portion of happiness.

Crowe hadn't been certain that returning to Corbin County was the best way to achieve that, but he knew it would never stop haunting them, that the nightmares wouldn't cease until they faced what had happened there and the consequences of it.

And if he was lucky, very lucky, then Crowe himself intended to face whoever or whatever had begun the events that had destroyed all their lives twelve years before.

Rafe paused the coffee cup halfway to his lips as a low muted sound reached his ears.

He knew that sound. There were two snowmobiles approaching the house, and he knew the sound of the muffled motors, barely discernible above the sound of the wind howling outside the house.

The storm was over, the sun rising to a crisp, icy-cold morning and reports of crews beginning to move out in force to dig out drivers and houses alike from the massive amount of snow that had fallen.

That had been hours ago. He was living on borrowed time where his time with Cami was involved. That borrowed time could run out at any time. Any moment. But he'd expected his time to run out with the road crews slowly making their way from the road to the ranch house, with only one purpose in mind, and digging him out wasn't it.

He knew of plenty of times that those same road crews had refused to do more than pile more snow at the mouth of the graveled road that led to the house.

He hadn't expected his time to run out in the form of his cousins' arrival, though. Especially Crowe's.

Grimacing, Rafe pulled extra coffee cups from the cupboard, set sugar and creamer in the middle of the table, and glanced toward the stairs that led to the second floor.

Cami was showering.

She had borrowed a razor, and the water in the shower had only just begun running. He might get lucky and his cousins would be gone before she finished.

He had a feeling it would be the other way around. His cousins would arrive and wouldn't leave until after she did. That was more the way things ended up working for him.

His fist clenched at the thought of her leaving. At the thought of not holding her in his arms when he climbed into his bed. Of not being there to share that first cup of coffee, even if she was madder than hell at him.

And he sure couldn't use the kitchen table properly if she wasn't there, he thought with amusement as the snowmobiles moved quickly toward the house. *Damn, Crowe and his tinkering with the vehicles' motors.* They were now twice as fast and twice as powerful as they had been when the cousins first bought them. That meant if Crowe were of a mind to, he could easily get Cami back to town. Just as Rafe could have.

It wasn't long before the steady, hard throb of power eased into the yard, pulling up to the small area of shoveled show that Rafe had worked on as Cami slept that morning.

He opened the door, standing behind the glass of the storm door as his cousins stepped off the low-built machines and looked up at him.

He almost frowned. They were dressed in the lightweight, ultra-cold-weather gear that Crowe had managed to procure in the military as he worked in some of the coldest climates in the world. A ride from Crowe Mountain to the house wasn't long enough and the weather really not cold enough—was it?—for the snow camo outerwear.

Rafe stepped back as Logan reached the porch and watched him grip the door handle and lazily pull it open.

Even his eyes were hidden behind the dark goggles until he stepped inside, stripped off his gloves, then eased the goggles from his face.

He would have to make certain he thanked Logan nicely for slipping out, obviously well before dawn, to inform their cousin Crowe of Rafe's houseguest.

Logan's dark pine-green eyes were filled with laughter as he stripped the cold-weather gear and hung it carefully on the specially made hanger at the side of the door. Crowe was following suit, but unlike Logan, his eyes weren't filled with laughter. He was staring around the kitchen and living room carefully, no doubt noting even the slightest change to the rooms since he had been there the week before.

"You two are out early," Rafe stated as he moved back to the coffeepot, slid the decanter free, and set it in the center of the kitchen table, close to the cups, sugar, and cream.

"Not early enough, it would appear," Crowe grunted. "Where's your houseguest?"

Rafe slid Logan a look of promised retribution. "Had to run and tattle, didn't you, Logan?"

"I know; it's normally your job." Logan sighed mockingly. "But you appeared to be slacking this week, so I thought I'd help you out a bit."

Rafe almost rolled his eyes.

Logan could be the bane of his existence when he wanted to be. There were times that Rafe and Crowe wondered if Logan had ever matured past the age of sixteen.

As the middle cousin, he seemed to have inherited Rafe's father's sense of practical jokes and teasing games.

"'Preciate that, Logan," Rafe drawled. "I'll be sure to return the favor soon."

Logan chuckled as he followed Crowe to the kitchen table and the coffee.

The two men couldn't have been more different.

Logan had his mother's dark blond coloring rather than the dark Callahan hair. His skin was bronzed, a trait all Callahan men had, a reminder of their deep Irish roots. His eyes were the same the deep pine-green his mother's had been.

Mina Rafferty Callahan had been slender, delicate, and winsome. Thankfully, her son had only inherited her coloring. The rest of him was pure, tall Callahan. At six feet-two inches tall, powerful and broad, he could be a mean gutter fighter in the face of the enemy or project a charming, teasing familiarity with vulnerable children or frightened women.

Crowe on the other hand, was one hundred percent Callahan, from his midnight-black hair to his eagle-fierce golden-brown eyes. His harshly hewn features could never be called handsome, but women gravitated to him like bees to honey no matter where the Callahans went. At the very least, the women moved as close as possible, as though to draw in the aura of danger and the oddly shaped crescent birthmark they all carried on their right hip. He was an inch taller than Rafe, more than two years older than Rafe, and always seemed too determined to watch over and protect his younger cousins, whether they needed it at the time or not.

Rafe, on the other hand, was a plainer version. He had the black hair, but he had his mother's, Ann Roberts's sapphire-blue eyes rather than the Callahan brown eyes. In looks, the men were more like triplets than cousins, despite Logan's dark blond hair. Even as infants they had been almost impossible to tell apart until Logan's hair lightened.

Crowe was the image of the Callahan brothers, Samuel, Benjamin, and David. Rafe missed it only in the color of his eyes. They were as close as brothers and sometimes it seemed they shared the same bond triplets did as well.

Rafe leaned back against the counter with his own coffee as his cousins poured theirs. Strangely enough, Crowe sweetened and creamed his, while Logan took his straight and black. It always seemed as though it should have been the other way around.

It had always amazed Rafe that his eldest cousin could be found adding to the perfectly rich, aromatic taste of the specially grown coffee beans Rafe went to the trouble to buy and grind himself. It was almost a sacrilege, what Crowe did to his coffee.

It was the coffee that always seemed to tie them. Since Clyde Ramsey, Rafe's great-uncle, had taken then in, he had taught them the value of coffee, the kitchen table, and long discussions.

"So, to what do I owe the pleasure of your visit?" Rafe asked as he arched a brow and brought the cup to his lips, sipping at the coffee and preparing himself. He had a feeling he knew what was coming. Crowe was there because of Cami.

"I thought you might need some backup." Crowe shrugged as he leaned back in the chair, his oddly colored brown eyes sharp as Rafe met his gaze.

"What kind of backup do I need?" Rafe could almost feel the tension beginning to tighten at the back of his neck.

It was damned foreboding. That sense of coming danger or problems that would result in more trouble than anyone needed.

Hell, all he'd wanted to do was try to enjoy the few days fate had given him with Cami.

"They're clearing the snow blocking the road not far from here," Logan said then. "It won't be long before they find Ms. Flannigan's car. And her uncle is in the lead with the plow. Eddy Flannigan isn't known for his even temper."

Eddy Flannigan simply didn't suffer fools gladly, and he sure as hell didn't tolerate so much as an iota of danger where his niece was concerned. Eddy would know, though, that the last thing Rafe wanted would be to hurt Cami in any way.

Rafe's lips tightened in irritation at the thought as he moved to the refrigerator, reached up, and flipped on the police and emergency band radio he kept there. Turning the dials, he tuned into the channel he knew the road crew used whenever they were clearing snow and wanted to keep their conversations more private.

It wouldn't hurt to know ahead of time who else was on that crew and whatever they may have to say.

"Sheriff, I hope you brought that rifle of yours," a voice drawled over the radio. "Eddy may want to borrow it."

"Then why are you laughing, Martin?" Archer Tobias, sheriff of Corbin County, a man who had once, long ago, been a friend, came over the line.

"'Cause if that's Eddy's niece's car out there like he thinks it is, then we may get to have a Callahan killin' after all," Deputy Martin Eisner came back. "Don't worry, Eddy, I'll testify for it. Justifiable homicide."

Rafe glared at the radio.

"You want me to break your fucking legs, Eisner?" Eddy Flannigan came back, his voice entirely serious. "Because I can. And I will."

It was obvious the deputy was getting on the wrong side of the smart-assed, wisecracking uncle of Cami's.

"Hell, Eddy, I'm trying to do you a favor here," Martin snapped. "Those boys work fast, remember? We'll be lucky if she's not already dead."

"Let's not allow our imaginations to get out of control here Martin," Archer snapped.

"Yeah, that's what your daddy said when Jaymi went missing that night too," Martin snapped back as the sound of the plow's motor revved and geared higher. "You saw her car, Sheriff. That tire—"

"Martin, concentrate on clearing that snow and let me concentrate on what may or may not have happened," Archer snapped back, the heavy command in his voice working for a minute. "That's my job, remember?"

But no longer than a minute.

"We should call out the National Guard and have them bring the helicopter in. We maybe could use the help against the three of them boys now that they're back from the military." Eisner sounded worried, concerned. "Didn't we hear they were snipers or some shit?" He was obviously only worried about himself.

Rafe rubbed at the side of his face in frustration. Son of a bitch, Eisner sounded as though they were facing a full battalion of Callahans rather than just three of them.

Rafe knew the deputy well enough to know for a fact that it wasn't worry or concern he was feeling unless it was for himself. It was pure gleeful anticipation cloaked with a highly false, somber demeanor.

"Martin, we don't need a helicopter," Archer promised him patiently. "Eddy, take your plow up to the house and I'll drive your niece home, if she's ready to go."

"What do you think he means by that, Eddy?" Martin questioned with almost rabid curiosity. "What's he imply-in'?"

"That she might want to wait until the tow truck shows up to get her car out of the ditch, Martin?" the sheriff snapped, his patience obviously beginning to fray as the deputy continued to poke at Eddy's temper. That was never a good idea. Eddy's temper was short and his fists could be unpredictable. "And see if you can't manage to run that plow without taking out another fence, Martin." Eddy's tone was harsh and filled with disgust.

Logan sat up carefully as Crowe's face tightened, becoming stoney and emotionless at the order Eddy gave the deputy.

They'd spent more than a week replacing the old rotted and rusted fence. It was obviously a wasted effort where one fence was concerned.

"Sorry about that. I guess ole Rafe Callahan should have put those fences in better, huh?"

"I can hear the lawsuits now," Archer said, his sigh coming across the radio. "And trust me, Martin, I won't cover your ass on this one."

"Hey, I didn't see no fence," Martin's voice came back slyly. "Did you see a fence, Eddy?"

"Yeah, I did, and I'm going to be the one to tell the Callahans' lawyer what an asshole you are. Asshole." Eddy informed him, "It's no damned wonder the mayor put you on probation. If we're lucky, he'll get rid of your ass now."

Archer was silent, and that didn't surprise Rafe in the least. It did surprise him, though, that Eisner was so damned brave in destroying Callahan property.

"One of these days that girl is going to get herself in trouble taking up with the stray dogs in this county." Martin came back with an air of self-importance. "And if I ever seen a dog, those Callahan boys is three of them."

"I just hope for her daddy's sake she's okay," Martin radioed. "It's too bad how she doesn't help him much with her poor, sick mother. She's nothin' like her sister was, that's for damned sure. Jaymi would have been there helping her parents."

"Fuck you, Martin! You damned little son of a bitch!" Eddy was pissed now. Real pissed if the tone of his voice was anything to go by. "Get him the fuck out of here, Sheriff, because I'll show the little bastard exactly what justifiable homicide really is."

Rafe lifted his head and watched as Cami came to a shocked stop at the doorway of the kitchen.

Biting off a curse, he moved for the radio to flip it off and keep her from hearing any more of Martin Eisner's stupidity.

She beat Rafe to it. She moved in front of him, staring back at him in determination. "Let me hear what he has to say. That's one of Dad's best friends, and he's not saying anything I haven't already heard."

The radio crackled again. "Martin, shut the hell up." Archer's voice was rock hard and filled with command now. "You'll shut up or I can make sure you lose this nice cushy job of yours." It was that edge of worry that had suspicion rising inside him.

"Too late to shut him up, Arch," Eddy came back quietly. "Martin and I will discuss it later, though."

Martin's mocking laughter came back. "Your asshole

mayor didn't hire me, Archer, and neither did you. Neither one of you can fire me either."

"I guess you were right, Crowe." Rafe turned to his cousin, anger churning hard and deep inside him. "Selling out is the last fucking thing we need to do. They can just live with us."

He caught Cami's look of surprise, as well as the worry that edged it. His lips twisted sardonically. Yeah, if he stayed around, that just upped the chances that everyone might figure out she'd been doing the nasty with him, wouldn't it? *Fuck her.* Was she ashamed to admit that she allowed him to touch her? Of course she was. He'd suspected it before and now he was convinced of it.

He glared down at her. "Don't worry, Cami. No one will suspect for a second that we spent the weekend fucking like minks, and I'll damned well make sure of it. Now, if you'll excuse me, I'm going to try to attempt to make sure they don't destroy the fucking place while they're trying to rescue you."

Cami stared up at him, her lips thinning. She knew the same thing he, Logan, and Crowe knew now just as well Sherriff Tobias and Eddy Flannigan knew. Obviously one of the barons had hired Eisner.

Cami shook her head slowly. "Martin's James Corbin's second cousin," she said quietly as the radio seemed to go quiet.

"Well now, doesn't that just figure. Guess Grandpop is making sure he has his eyes and ears where he needs them," Crowe drawled mockingly.

"Martin is a pain in Archer's ass," she said softly. "Ignore it. Archer will take care of it."

Rafe gave a hard laugh. "Do you think he's going to destroy my property and get away with it?"

"Archer won't let him get away with," Cami argued.

"You're asking me to let it go?" he asked her coolly.

"Eisner isn't worth going after, Rafe," she told him firmly as she propped her hands on her hips in determination.

"Why?" he asked her again. "Afraid you'll have to testify?"

"I'm not afraid of anything," she assured him tightly, but he knew better. He could see the concern in her eyes, in her expression.

Pushing away from her, he stalked to the door, slamming out of the house and moving to the porch as he watched the plow slowly making its way up the lane.

Pulling one of the slim cigars from the pocket of his shirt, Rafe dug the lighter out of his jeans pocket and lit up before leaning casually against the porch post.

That was just fine, he thought as one of the plows took out another length of the new fence and barely missed taking out the corner of the old shed that housed Clyde Ramsey's pride and joy, his shiny dark-green tractor and all its attachments, still covered and looking all but new. No doubt that was the plow Deputy Eisner was operating.

Rafe could see the other man, in the glass-enclosed cab seconds later as he used the plow to carelessly push the snow from the driveway. It wasn't easy going for Eddy. The heavy, wet snow had the motor straining as Eddy pushed it harder than he should have, evidently simply intent on checking on his niece and getting out of there. Eisner, though, he was making it count. Amused mockery filled the deputy's face as another fence post met the force of the edge of the plow.

Rafe glanced to Eddy Flannigan again and watched as the older man shook his head and ran his hand over his face at the next post Eisner tore out. Fury tightened Eddy's expression as he shook his head angrily a second later.

Looking up, Eddy caught Rafe watching, grinned, and shot him the finger. That was Eddy Flannigan. Bastard.

Rafe was considerate, he returned the gesture.

Then a frown creased the man's face as Rafe heard the door open, then close behind him. All eyes were watching now. Her uncle's, Eisner's, and Sheriff Archer Tobias'. And Rafe knew why.

Cami.

He could feel her, smell the sweet, clean scent of her.

Rafe didn't move other than to lift the cigar to his lips and inhale slowly as he grinned back at the other man.

Eddy wasn't a Callahan fan, but neither was he an enemy. At least he didn't poke his nose in their business. At least he hadn't before now. And he sure as hell wouldn't be once Rafe filed his lawsuit. His lawyer would be contacting the town soon, Rafe promised himself, because that fence was too far from the center of the lane for it to have been an accident.

"I'm so sorry," Cami whispered behind him. "I'm so very sorry, Rafe."

And she was. He could hear it in her voice, in the low, husky tone of regret, and the echo of sadness.

"Sorry's not going to replace my fence." He shrugged as though he really didn't care about the fucking fence, and he didn't, it was the intent behind it that pissed him off. "Why don't you just get on out there and let her uncle and boyfriend know you're safe so that crew can get the hell off my land before they finish destroying it?"

"My boyfriend?" Outrage filled her voice. "Just to start with, Rafer Callahan, I do not do boys. And second of which, there's no one here that I'm seeing."

"And you haven't been going out with Archer?" He finally threw the accusation at her, amazed he had held it in this long.

Her eyes narrowed back at him, the soft gray of her eyes beginning to flicker in anger.

"Archer and I are friends, Rafe—"

"So were Jaymi and I," he reminded her harshly. "Or did you forget that?"

"Oh, trust me, I'm reminded of it often." The bitterness that flashed in her eyes surprised him.

"What do you mean by that?" he growled, careful to keep his tone of voice low, his demeanor controlled.

"Exactly what I said." She wasn't nearly as careful about

her demeanor. She was all but straight up in his face. The only thing that kept her from going nose to nose with him was the fact that she was half-pint-sized and not nearly tall enough. "Every time I turn around, every time I hear your name, I'm reminded in detail exactly how close you were."

It wasn't anger glittering in her gaze, it was pain. A sense of loss, and if he wasn't mistaken, guilt.

"Why would it matter, Cami?" he questioned her roughly. "You knew Jaymi and I were sleeping together at the time. I never lied to you."

She wanted to turn away from him, she wanted to rage at him, but she was far too aware of the fact that her uncle, Archer Tobias, and his deputy were still working their way to the driveway.

"At least Jaymi was honest enough to have her relationship in public," he continued as she glared up at him, her fists clenching at her sides.

"What the hell are you talking about? Are you trying to accuse me of something, Rafer?" she questioned through gritted teeth.

"Why, yes, kitten, I guess that's exactly what I'm doing," he informed her bitterly. "At least Jaymi wasn't ashamed of me. And she sure as hell wasn't ashamed of being my lover."

"You think I'm ashamed of you?" He could see the anger now, it was glittering in her eyes, flushing her cheeks. "You think I'm not agreeing to your demands because of shame?"

"What other reason could you have?" he demanded. "Come on, Cami, you acted as though we barely knew each other at Clyde's funeral and you cut me off three years ago. What else could it have been if not shame?"

"Oh, I don't know, perhaps it could have been the fact that there are other things I'm not willing to deal with besides whether or not anyone knows what the hell I'm doing?"

"Oh, yeah. What?" he snarled, feeling the anger and the lust suddenly rising, pounding through his veins, engorging his dick and burning through his veins.

She was almost shaking now. "Fuck you, Rafer!"

His lips twisted with mocking anger. "Go home, Cami. I have better things to do than deal with your shame or your fear."

"My anger or fear." She stepped closer. "Just let me show you my shame and fear."

Rafe didn't think he had ever been as surprised by a woman as he was by Cami in that moment. She was against him in a second, on her tiptoes, the fingers of one hand fisted in his hair as she pulled his head down, bringing his lips to hers.

In that second, he lost the anger, the accusations, and his common sense.

Rafe jerked her against him, his lips slanting over hers as he pulled her against him and poured every ounce of the hunger and need burning inside him, into her impulsive kiss. He took control of it. He stole it, and fought to bind whatever part of her that he could to him, whether it be shame, lust, or fear.

His tongue stroked against her lips, pushed forward and caressed her tongue, fought with it, and drew the hunger from whatever depths she pushed it to whenever she needed to hide it.

No, this wasn't shame, but he was damned if he knew what it was, or what she was trying to prove. He knew something raged inside her, something dark and angry that the pleasure he gave her seemed to tempt, even as pleasure seemed to burn through those emotions.

When he pulled back, releasing her slowly, he watched as her eyes fluttered open, and her gaze seemed rife with regret and a pain that went so deep he froze in shock.

"Cami-girl?" he whispered. Sweet Lord, who put that agony inside her?

"It's not shame, Rafer." She stepped away slowly. "But that doesn't mean it's anyone else's business either."

Turning, she moved quickly away from him and all but ran to where Archer's black, official SUV finally pulled into the small parking area close to the snowmobiles Logan and Crowe had driven earlier.

She jumped into the vehicle, slammed the door, then turned her head, obviously avoiding looking at him now. As though she had pulled a cloak of ice around her emotions, one that went clear to the core, Cami simply stared straight ahead as Archer Tobias drove her out of his life.

Cami was leaving again.

CHAPTER 9

Cami's chest was tight, her throat felt raw and scratchy. Her eyes ached, and it was all she could do to breathe without whimpering. The pain seemed to go all the way to the depths of her soul, and refused to return to that dark corner she had managed to push it to years ago.

What was wrong with her?

She stared straight ahead, determined to ignore Archer and the questions she could feel silently directed to her.

She hadn't been aware anyone had paid attention to the few dates she and Archer had had, or why anyone would have cared. Especially, why had Rafer cared enough to have dug up that information?

Focusing her attention on her surroundings rather than the emotions tempting her to come closer and peer in, Cami stared at the dash and center console of the sheriff's vehicle.

The backseat was enclosed from the front and the back cargo area with black steel bars and bullet-resistant glass—a laptop, radio, rearview and navigation screen, cell-phone holder, wireless radio, and several other electronic gadgets she wasn't certain the purpose for. She was in the middle of electronics paradise and she really didn't give a damn. All she wanted to do was demand he turn around and take her back to Rafe.

And that was the most foolish thing she could do. She

had been there too long already and had done nothing but add another scar to her heart.

Staring through the window beside her head, she watched as they turned from Rafer's driveway and passed her little aging sedan as it sat with its front tires buried in the snow that filled the ditch.

She couldn't believe she had actually found the strength to walk away from Rafer, because everything inside her had been demanding she stay. Just as she couldn't believe she had actually managed to walk past her uncle without throwing herself in his arms and sobbing as she had done as a child.

He had been defending her all her life, she thought, and she wondered if sometimes he didn't grow tired of the constant battles he and her father had gotten into since she was a child.

She didn't want him to have to defend her against her father's friends as well, such as Archer had been forced to do here.

She couldn't believe what she had heard from him. She had always thought he was so soft-spoken and kind. To learn he wasn't affected her far more deeply than she liked.

This was the same uncle who had defended her when her father wished she were dead rather than Jaymi, at Jaymi's funeral. The uncle Cami had always thought she could depend upon to care for her, no matter what choices she might make in life.

"You okay, Cami?" Archer asked, his voice gentle as she continued to stare into the snow-buried landscape they passed.

The gentleness in his voice had her throat tightening further, had emotions threatening to swamp her. He'd been one of Jaymi and Tye's best friends as well, and over the years had become one of hers.

"You know," he said when she didn't answer, "if there's something I need to know about, then now might be the best time to tell me, sweetheart."

She knew what he was asking, and the fact that he felt the need had the emotion tightening her throat instantly easing as frustration tightened her jaw instead. "He didn't rape me, nor did he attempt to murder me, if that's what you're asking," she informed Archer, as she turned and directed the full measure of anger churning in her on him instead.

"Well now, I didn't think he had been, but it's my job to ask."

"I was unaware that investigating stupid questions and obviously slanderous accusations was part of your job description."

"Normally it's not," he assured her. "But sometimes with some people it's better to deal with it and get it over with before moving on."

The Callahan cousins were accused often of all manner of crimes, he had once told her.

"At least they have one friend," she sighed. "I was beginning to wonder."

"I'm not the only one, Cami, but as you've probably learned by now, it doesn't do any good to argue with those who aren't their friends."

Of course it didn't. They were the fathers, the mothers, the aunts and uncles who had first followed the dictates the barons had first given where the cousins were concerned.

"Yeah, Jaymi learned that one," she sighed. She remembered those days far too clearly sometimes.

"Your sister was a fine woman, but she was more a rebel than anyone wanted to admit after her death. But, even more, she lived her life as she felt best, as she wanted to. That's really all you can do as well Cami. If Rafe is what you want, then that's what you should have. Don't let this town's pettiness affect that. And you and Rafe have plenty of us friends willing to stand by you if the barons decide there are other ways to make their grandsons' lives miserable."

She could hear a mild chastisement in his voice and she didn't understand where it had come from or what made him believe there was anything between her and Rafe that would warrant it.

"We're not lovers, Archer." She turned, glancing at his profile before staring through the windshield to avoid his gaze. As lies went, even she wasn't certain of the lie in that one.

"I never said you were. But, if I were you, I'd remember it was no one's business if you were. You're an adult, not a child to be ordered about."

Neither did she need anyone attempting to push her closer in Rafer's direction. She was going to feel like a bone between a gang of dogs very soon.

She suddenly remembered her sister Jaymi making a similar comment the summer she had died, while she and Rafer had been living together, or rather, sleeping together.

"Do you ever see the ignorance in this war against them?" she said as she turned to him. "I've never understood why his family disowned him, or why everyone made the decisions to either follow suit, or secretly befriend them."

Archer grimaced. "If you figure that one out, then why don't you let me know about it?"

"Do you have any idea why?" she asked.

Archer breathed out harshly. "You know, Cami, I've known those boys all my life. My father knew all their parents and worked for their grandparents, but I don't think I've ever heard why they disowned them. It might be interesting to know, though."

She hoped he had better luck than she had in finding out because so far she didn't have a clue. Even her sister hadn't been able to explain to Cami or to herself, why it had happened.

She knew the Callahan brothers Rafe, Logan, and Crowe's fathers had married three heiresses who had already been engaged to three men their fathers had chosen for them. Once those three women had met the Callahan brothers, their hearts had been lost forever, though.

Still, that wasn't reason enough to try to frame their only children more than twenty years later for the vicious rapes, torture, and murders of the six young women who had died twelve years ago. Nor was it reason enough to hate three children, as those young men had been hated in their youth.

"Why do it?" she murmured, almost to herself.

"Do what?" Archer was obviously paying close attention to everything she was saying.

"Why hate the sons so viciously for whatever their fathers had done?"

And that was what her sister had suspected was behind the animosity directed toward the cousins. Whoever had targeted the cousins' fathers had immediately turned their attention to the cousins once their parents had died.

"Did you know Jaymi and her boss were both threatened when she was seeing Rafe, just before she died?"

Cami turned to look at Archer, watching as he threw her a dark frown.

"No one mentioned that, even Rafe, and we've seen each other and discussed Jaymi's death a time or two since the charges were dropped."

"She was trying to keep Rafe from knowing about the harassment she was dealing with," she told him. "But she began getting calls after he would leave at night, or the next morning. Threats, filthy accusations. The Gillespies pulled the babysitting job she had watching their granddaughter, and someone called Dad and warned him that she would be 'punished' if she didn't sever the relationship."

Archer's gaze flicked back to her as he slowed down, obviously trying to make the drive longer as he grew more curious.

"Did she know who it was?"

Cami shook her head. "She never knew who was calling her. But she finally did break things off when her boss came to the apartment to talk to her the night before the last social she attended with me, Rafer, and his cousins. He was warned that if Jaymi didn't stop seeing Rafe and he didn't fire her, then they would burn down the pharmacy. He was so scared he was shaking."

"The man that killed Jaymi was linked to the other women's deaths as well," Archer mused. "Only a few of them had a connection to Rafe and his cousins."

"I'm not saying it wasn't him," she told Archer. "I don't know anything more than that. Two weeks after the pharmacy owner came to the house, Jaymi was dead and her killer was dead."

Archer was silent for long moments. "My dad was sheriff then," he said. "I asked him about it. He said there were no ties between the cousins and the killer at all. Nothing tied the six women together, and he couldn't remember seeing the Callahan cousins with any of the women that summer except Jaymi."

"And everyone wanted so desperately to believe they had killed Jaymi," Cami said softly. "Archer, didn't your father ever question any of this?" Archer gave a tight shake of his head. "I argued with him over that at the time. Not that it helped."

"None of it ties together, no matter how I try to find a way to understand it." And she needed to understand it.

Archer grunted. "And that's exactly how their lawyer managed to get the charges dropped," he reminded her. "The fact that the DNA that came back proved that Thomas Jones was the man Crowe stabbed that night managed to clear them."

"Yet they're still treated worse than rapists and murderers who admit to their crimes," she pointed out. "I thought it would get better for them, but in the past twelve years it seems to have only grown worse."

"It's easy to blame them," Archer suggested. "Thomas Jones is dead, and they're alive."

Could it possibly be that simple?

It wasn't enough to satisfy her though, just as she knew she had an ulterior motive. She wanted Rafe. She wanted back in his bed, she wanted to know why she couldn't forget him, why she ached for him, and that wasn't going to happen if she wanted to live and work in Sweetrock.

"Thanks for the ride home, Archer," she said dropping the subject and hoping she had given him enough for him to investigate it as he drew closer to where she lived in her two-story little ranch.

"I'll call Jack's Towing before heading back up the

mountain," Archer told her. "He can bring your car in some-time today."

She nodded slowly. "That's fine; thank you again."

She wasn't going to need it today anyway.

Archer sighed as he turned the car down Main Street and drove closer to the dark, probably cold, and definitely lonely house she had bought from her parents.

It was all she could do to keep from begging him to take her back to Rafer's. To beg Rafer to hold her just a little while longer. But the fear was like a padlock, locking the words and the ability to reach out to Rafer in such a way deep inside her.

"I don't know what's going on." She rubbed her temple with her fingers, finally glancing at Archer again as she breathed out a hard sigh. "Why did he have to come back, Archer? Why did he have to change everything?"

"He's not changing anything for you without your help," Archer said gently. "And from what you just said about Jaymi, you be damned careful. It might be a good idea to be a little cautious for a while." Archer knew about the nights they had spent together, though he didn't know about the child she had lost.

A sardonic smile twisted her lips. Hadn't that been the same advice she had given her sister twelve years before?

"I'll be sure to do that," Cami promised as she slid out of the sheriff's vehicle and closed the door before heading to the house.

She turned and waved good-bye as she stepped into the silent house.

Yes. It was cold. Lonely.

Closing and locking the door behind her, she turned the thermostat up, hoping to alleviate the chill inside her as well as the one that filled her home. She hadn't really been warm in years, until Rafer had held her again. Now the lack of that warmth was damned painful.

The cell phone rang out its strident ringtone to alert her she had a call. Caller ID was clearly blocked, and until now she didn't think she'd ever received a blocked call.

"Hello," she answered cautiously.

The voice, despite its gentle sadness, held a sinister, malicious edge.

"You better hope you spent your time with Rafer Callahan wisely. You should have chosen someone else to dirty yourself with if you needed a hard fuck," the voice warned her somberly. "If it happens again, you could meet the same end as your sister. Wouldn't that be a shame, Ms. Flannigan? Wouldn't it hurt your family, your friends, to find your body broken and discarded for fucking that bastard?"

Who the hell would call and say something so cruel? She and Jaymi had been close, much closer than most sisters with such an age difference between them.

But she remembered the calls Jaymi had received while sleeping with Rafe, and she had once told Cami that the caller's voice had sounded tearful and filled with regret.

"I'm always careful," Cami told him quietly, confidently. "And I don't do bullies. Or cowards." She disconnected the call quickly, then ignored the next several as she moved back to the kitchen and laid the device on the table. She stood back by the counter and simply watched it as though it were a snake, coiled and hissing as "*blocked number*" showed on the caller ID again.

As a third-grade teacher for the only elementary school in the county, she ended up meeting most people, whether they were parents or not, more than once. She recognized that voice, even as carefully disguised as it had been.

Still, she would remember whose voice it was, and when she did, unlike her sister, Cami would raise hell and make damned sure he paid for attempting to terrorize her, let alone threatening her.

She knew Jaymi had finally realized who had been calling her. The week before she had died she had attended one of the county-sponsored street dances in the town square, and when she had returned to the apartment she had been more than upset. She had been furious. She hadn't said she had known, but Cami had known her sister and she had known when the phone rang that night and the look on Jaymi's face when the caller ID had come up "blocked." Jaymi had taken the phone to the bedroom, but as she walked into the other room Cami could have sworn she heard Jaymi say, *Now I know why you hate him so bad*. But Jaymi had refused to tell Cami who it was or what was going on. The next week, Jaymi had been killed.

Cami drew in a hard, deep breath.

What was she going to do now? she wondered. The implications of the phone calls were frightening.

The phone rang again.

Eyes narrowed, she stalked back to the table, checked the number, and saw the "blocked" signal again. Pushing the call button, she brought it quickly to her ear. She would be damned if she was going to live in fear. "Fuck off, nutcase," she snapped.

There was silence for a moment. Long enough for Cami to realize it wasn't the unknown, threatening voice of moments before.

"I just wanted to make certain you got home okay," Rafe's voice came over the line carefully.

Cami's teeth snapped together. "Here's a piece of advice, Rafer Callahan. Unblock your number when you call; otherwise, I won't be answering."

She was not going to worry about missed calls and whether or not it was Rafe.

"You know, you're the only person that calls me Rafer," he growled, something in his tone warning her he was more angry than simply irritated. She didn't think it was because she was calling him by his full given name.

"Learn to live with it," she muttered as she began moving through the house, closing curtains and checking locks again.

The normal nightly ritual suddenly had a new, sinister meaning, and she didn't like it. Because it didn't matter she had already checked them once, she needed to check them again.

"Your cousin Martin took out close to a thousand feet of new fence on his way in and out," Rafe informed her. "I'm suing."

Yes, Eisner was her third cousin on her mother's side and Crowe's very, very distant cousin on his mother's side.

"And you're telling me why? I'm not his lawyer; that's his cousin Doug Atchinson. Give him a call." She had no sense of guilt because she rarely remembered Martin was related to her. Besides he should have known better.

"You're being awful accommodating all of a sudden." Suspicion laced Rafe's voice, and she could almost see him staring back at her. She could almost see herself drowning in those bottomless sapphire-blue eyes.

"So are you," she fired back. "How the hell am I supposed to pretend we haven't been occasional fucks if you start calling to check up on me?"

She needed to get over the past few days, the heated passion and the feel of his flesh against hers. She needed to let her body readjust to not having him inside her. To not having him pumping hard and deep and stretching her pussy with that delicious pleasure-pain she could have so easily become addicted to. She might have already become addicted, because she was dying for him. She needed her fix.

"What happened?" Suspicion laced his voice. "Was someone at the house when you got there? Has someone called?"

She tensed. How had he known she was feeling spooked?

"If there were, and they had, then I know how to use my Smith and Wesson to deal with it," she promised him as that craving for him began to pound through her blood veins. "And just to set you straight, Rafer, *you* happened. You're like some kind of damned catalyst or something, because every time you invade my damned space you completely fuck my life up. Stay on your own side of the county and let me deal with mine."

She disconnected the call. But she held the phone between her breasts, her eyes closed, her breathing rough, as she fought to hold back her tears and to contain her anger. She couldn't let this happen to her again. She could not allow herself to sink into that well of physical and emotional hunger as she had the last time.

She wanted to stomp her feet on the floor like a child and rage against fate, life and the unfairness of aching for a man she couldn't have. Because having him meant losing herself in him and she couldn't allow that to happen again, if she wanted to live in her hometown.

Other women could have affairs with married men, cheat on their husbands, or have more than one lover at the same time. She, on the other hand, couldn't even have the man she dreamed about the most. The one who kept her heart racing and her pussy so wet she was going to have to change panties. She couldn't do it because she didn't have the emotional distance to survive if anything happened to him.

A sigh fell from her lips as she closed her eyes briefly. Other women knew how to love and still retain their souls. She didn't know how to do that, it seemed. As for her panties, she realized she didn't have to worry about changing them because she had forgotten to put them back on after they had dried hanging over Rafer's shower.

"You're the only one who calls me Rafer." The remembered sound of the husky quality of his voice had her heart rate increasing, had it pounding fiercely. The sexual implications in the deep rasp of his voice had a burning, soul-deep response tearing through her system.

Yes, she was the only one who called him Rafer.

Even Jaymi had been amused by the habit Cami had of calling him by his full name.

It was more intimate. No one else called him Rafer, just her. It was a part of him that was only hers, because he refused to allow anyone else to use the name. And Cami allowed no other man to touch her.

Her experience at being a lover was confined to the few nights she had spent with Rafe over the past six years. so infrequent had been the times they had come together. She had been a virgin that first night, and she might as well have been a virgin the night she knocked on his front door.

The phone rang again.

Lifting it from between her breasts, she couldn't help but

smile despite the trembling of her lips and the tears that filled her eyes.

Rafer Samuel Callahan. The caller ID displayed his name clearly.

With fingers that shook more than her lips did she added the contact to the cell phone's address book the minute the ringing stopped. She was determined not to answer, not to hear his voice again, not to weaken and beg him to hold her again.

She was going to hear it enough in her dreams, and the torment of it would drive her insane for months.

Or longer.

He was living closer now, she thought. It wasn't as though he were half a world away and inaccessible. He was here, in Corbin County. And he wanted her.

She could go to him. She could take what she wanted if she could just be strong enough to forget her own past mistakes. That was the problem. It wasn't shame or fear of the county's condemnation. It was her own condemnation she had to worry about. And she should have proven that beyond a shadow of a doubt before she left the ranch.

Her family *would* turn their backs on her once they learned of that kiss or at least her father would. But he had turned his back on her years before. Her mother was dying, and if she learned of it, then she wouldn't exactly die hating her younger child. Her mother was able to process very little information now. Alzheimer's and a stroke had all but erased the loving, gentle mother Margaret Flannigan had tried to be whenever her husband wasn't around. She was the only person whose opinion Cami really cared about anyway, and her mother barely even recognized her anymore.

If Cami could only figure out why everyone hated Rafer and his cousins. She could show her father the injustice of what they had suffered—no, that wouldn't happen. There was no compassion left in her father after Jaymi's death.

Cami gave her head a hard shake. No, he wouldn't care because it would only be an excuse. What she hadn't considered while allowing Martin Eisner to see her kissing Rafer was the fact he would tell Mark Flannigan as soon as possible. When he did, Mark would use the excuse to ensure he never allowed Cami to see her mother again.

"Something's wrong," Rafe said quietly as he, Logan, and Crowe sat in the black SUV he had driven into town to check up on Cami and make certain she had gotten home. He hadn't been able to shake that foreboding or his need for her.

It was probably that returning hunger continuing to spark the warning he needed to check on her.

"No one's in there," Logan said from the seat as Cami closed the heavy curtains covering her bedroom window. "You can see straight through that house until she closes the curtains. Besides she's acting too calm."

It was the truth. The two-story home was open and inviting, and clearly visible through the pristine, sparkling windows.

Who had windows that clean? It was damned scary. And as he said, Cami appeared too calm and comfortable to be frightened of anything.

"I didn't say someone was in there; I said something is wrong," he reminded his cousin. "There's a difference, Crowe."

"Let it go, Rafe," Crowe stated softly. "Let's head back to the ranch and see about installing the last of those cameras before we head up the mountain tomorrow to take care of mine. Logan's is next and I'd like to have this finished and tied into the DVR on the master control before we head to that lawyers' meeting in Colorado Springs next week."

They had been installing the cameras at night, when it would be harder for anyone to watch what they were doing or to pinpoint the hiding places they had chosen for the electronics.

Rafe blew out a rough breath as he slid the vehicle into gear and pulled out onto the street. He should have gone to the door, but he knew that pushing Cami wasn't going to get him what he wanted. Besides, he wanted her to come to him for a change. Just once. Just a single instance where she accepted her need for him and made the first move. A move other than allowing her car to slide into a ditch at the entrance of his property.

He needed her, too—willingly, deliberately, without any excuses—to reach out for him. He wanted her to admit it to herself. Because he'd be damned if he would allow her to hide from it much longer. And he sure as hell wasn't going to allow her to return to a few stolen nights here and there because they couldn't fight the need any longer.

He had grown damned tired of having his lovers hide their relationship with him twelve years before. He'd had enough of it with Jaymi and the lovers he'd had before her in Sweetrock. And these stolen nights with Cami had eaten at him, because he was certain she had slipped out at dawn out of shame.

He'd be damned if he'd let himself be treated like a dirty little secret by Cami.

"Are we sure we want to go through with all this?" Logan asked lazily from his seat in the back. "You know if we go through with these plans it's going to cause a hell of a battle with the barons."

Rafer couldn't help but grin at the comment. How many times had some of the larger resorts attempted to come in and buy the land around Crowe's mountain? The deep white water that branched off from the Colorado River and ran through streams and tributaries until it began flowing through the deep boulder-strewn ravines through the mountains was perfect for white water rafting.

The mountain itself with its natural breaks and paths was perfect for skiing. The land was filled with wildlife and could easily support any hunting activities required.

That had been their parents' dream. The three couples had spent years planning for the day the wives came into their trusts at their thirtieth birthday. It was then Crowe's Mountain and the adjoining Breaker Valley and Rafferty River Run area would have become Callahan Holdings. From there Crowe Mountain Resort would have been born.

Just the thought of the pure rage the barons would have was enough to almost bring a grin to Rafe's lips. Damn, the explosion would be heard in China when they learned that the grandsons they had disowned would carry out their parents' dreams.

"Now's the time to back out if you don't want to be a part of it, Logan," Crowe warned him.

Logan snorted mockingly. "Are you dreaming, cuz? I just think we all need to be aware of what's going to happen when we file the papers. Because the shit is going to hit the fan." The anticipation in Logan's voice was contagious. That or just the sheer pleasure at the thought of yet another triumph against their grandparents.

The first had been the court battle for the land that Crowe's mother's trust left to him. The final appeal the barons had made would be heard in a month before the state supreme court. And Rafe had no doubt he and his cousins would win that one, too.

Breaker Valley, the land Rafer's mother had held, was now fully his. That land had once been the Callahan Ranch, and had belonged to his grandparents. Just as Crowe Mountain and part of the land called Rafferty River Run had. Crowe stated, "We're not going to have an easy time doing this, even after the property is out of the courts. I'd like to keep things as simple as possible."

And as quiet as possible to ensure the barons didn't guess what was coming.

"She'll mess your head up, I can already see it coming."

"And you need to get fucked." Rafe snorted as he slid his cousin a hard look. "That's not happening, so you may as well simply shut the hell up about it and let it go Crowe."

"She's going to get your ass killed," Crowe griped, his disapproval obvious.

"And you're going to get your ass kicked if you don't shut the hell up," Rafe growled as he headed the vehicle out of town. "I don't need the lectures and I sure as hell don't need your advice where Cami's concerned."

"No, you need to stay away from her," Crowe repeated between furiously clenched teeth. "Both of you need to re-member exactly how dangerous it is to fuck with Corbin County women."

Rafe ignored him. Crowe enjoyed playing the big brother, and he enjoyed trying to order Rafe and Logan around. Not that they ever let Crowe get away with it.

Especially now.

Rafe wasn't staying away from Cami.

She'd admitted to being his occasional fuck, and he was going to make damned sure the occasions became real fre-quent from here on out. Once he managed to convince her to make that first move, then she was his. Totally. Completely.

He had no intentions of allowing Cami off the hook or out of his bed for long. If Crowe thought he could convince him otherwise, then he might need to think again.

CHAPTER 10

The mid-April morning glistened across the Colorado mountains with a wave of warmth that gave rise to the hope that the snow would melt soon. Everyone in town was crossing their fingers that the weather would definitely cooperate in time for the Spring Fling Social, the first night of weekend socials hosted by the county every Friday through Sunday evening.

The first social, a more formal affair for the adults, was the highlight of the beginning of the spring and summer season. It was time to dust off dancing shoes and evening jackets and polish social smiles.

Cami had purchased her dress the month before while in Denver helping her father choose the rest home they would be placing her mother in.

She'd found the perfect strapless little number at one of the small exclusive stores there, and had bought it immediately, despite its hefty price tag.

That morning, the sun streaming through the skylight above her bed filled the room with heat, pulling her eyes open after a restless night and greeting her with the feel of its heated warmth.

The warming temperatures managed to give her an energy she hadn't had since the blizzard. Putting it to use after a quick shower, she found herself cleaning house, the back deck, and her front porch as the heat glistened off the land-scape and the snow slowly began to melt.

It wasn't a heat wave, but it was warm enough to allow the citizens of Sweetrock to begin clearing the fluff and the winter collection of dust and gloom that had accumulated.

Families were gathering in their yards along the block, working as a unit, parents overseeing and helping the younger children in many of the chores. The spurt of energy Cami felt was also infecting others it seemed.

For most of the day, laughter and generally good-natured comments could be heard echoing around the block, re-minding Cami why she had bought the home her parents had owned. All around the neighborhood there was a sense of the one thing she had never had.

That sense of family.

As she worked, both in the back yard that faced the wide alley and on the front porch, her gaze moved constantly to the vehicles driving by. She kept hoping, not expecting, she assured herself, Rafer to make an appearance.

She didn't want to admit to herself that there was a part of her that hoped Rafe would show up. The nights spent tossing and turning restlessly had given her too much time to think. Too much time to realize things she didn't want to realize.

She needed him. The ache that seemed to spread through her body, that need to touch and be touched that was driving her crazy, was all because of him.

When dusk began to close in and the temperature dropped once again, families began to retreat into the warmth of their homes. Quiet began to fill the street as Cami stepped out to the wide, covered front porch carrying the piece of porch furniture she'd pulled from the garage, and gazed around the darkness silently.

The street lights cast shadows along the bare limbs of the trees lining the sidewalk. The almost sinister cast of the long-reaching fingers of darkness had a chill chasing up Cami's spine.

She had never noticed it before. She had never paid

attention to how easy it would be for someone to watch her house, or even to find a secretive path to her home if they wanted to.

She had security, but security could be bypassed.

She had never realized the weaknesses in her protection until the phone calls had begun. But then, she remembered Jaymi too had become more diligent in her home security when she had been receiving the threatening calls.

There had been two blocked calls in the past two days. One each night, and they kept her nerves on edge as much as the restless hunger for Rafer did. If she left the house, she wondered if she was being followed. When she came home, she was a paranoid wreck until she realized no one had managed to breach her security, such as it was.

It would often take her hours to remind herself that Jaymi hadn't been taken while inside her home.

Still, the paranoia was there and strong enough that as the chill swept through her, Cami immediately retreated into the house and began locking up.

Windows and doors were checked, curtains were securely pulled closed. As she closed the last of the curtains, she stood in her bedroom for a moment and gazed around the room. It had been her mother's room. Not her parents' room, just her mother's.

The master suite with its small sitting area and inviting, king-sized bed she so loved. The cream-colored walls and ceiling were a perfect backdrop for the dark oak floors and furnishings, which the bedclothes, dripping with lace from the sheets to the comforter, lightened and feminized the room just enough to keep it from being ostentatiously girly.

The old-fashioned vanity table and lace-draped chair took care of that on its own.

It was hers, and the thought of losing it out of fear rather than choice just pissed her off. She hated fear. She was learning just how much she hated being frightened.

As she was coming back downstairs, the sound of the doorbell, unexpected and overly loud in the quiet house, had her jerking back so hard she nearly stumbled on the stairs.

"Ridiculous," she murmured as she took a deep breath, her eyes rolling at the sense of melodrama she realized she might be displaying.

She was letting those phone calls get to her way too much. And she wasn't even certain, she had only suspicions to go by that the phone calls had anything to do with Jaymi's death. After all, none of the other women who had died that summer had told anyone about any phone calls. And to the best of anyone's knowledge, the other women hadn't been one of the Callahan cousins' lovers.

Moving quickly down the stairs, she lifted herself to look through the peephole, then draw back with a frown.

That sense of unreality once again began to close in on her. It was rather hard to believe that particular person was actually standing on the other side of the door.

Lifting up, she checked again, and once again she saw the same, expensively dressed, arrogant-eyed individual she had seen the first time she had checked.

"Ms. Flannigan, I'm aware you're on the other side." Bored and heavy with impatience, the voice drifted through the heavy door. "I'll only take a moment of your time, if you don't mind?"

Only a moment of her time, huh?

She had a feeling he was about to take up a hell of a lot more than a moment of her time. This particular person could cause her life to go to hell in a handbasket, which would take up a hell of a lot more than a moment of her time.

Moving back, she quickly opened the door, stepped back, and allowed him in.

Considering who her visitor was, there wasn't a chance in hell he could kill her without at least someone telling someone who had been there. And once that happened, Rafe would learn who it was that had been at the house.

Then, blood would spill.

Hell, maybe she should have just pretended she wasn't home.

Pushing the door closed, he didn't even flinch as it smacked against the frame a little harder than needed.

She wanted to at least give the hint that she wasn't pleased to see him there.

Flipping the locks back in place, she prepared herself before turning back to him and crossing her arms over her breasts as she confronted him.

"And what can I do for you, Mr. Roberts?"

Rafer's grandfather.

She'd always thought Rafer looked more like his Callahan father than the Roberts' side of the family. Staring back at Rafer's grandfather, though, she realized there was no denying they were definitely related. Closely related.

Marshal Roberts had the same, intense blue eyes Rafer possessed. She'd heard his mother had had the same rich, mesmerizing color of eyes. The arch of the brow was the same, and that same arrogant line of the jaw.

Marshal Roberts's hair was now a shade of dark silver where it had once been a dark, dark brown. Rafer had that deep raven's black that all Callahan men had been known for, but he also had that same heavy wave at the front where the rest were ribbon-straight.

He wasn't as tall as his grandson either. He stood only six feet while Rafer stood a towering six two. But his shoulders were just as broad, and even nearing seventy, he was still an imposing figure of a man.

Marshal looked around, curiosity flickering in his gaze as he seemed to linger on the mantel of pictures over the fireplace.

"Your family?" He gestured to the pictures as he moved to them, reached out and picked up a frame that held an eight by ten of her father, mother, and Jaymi.

"Yes." As though he didn't already know.

"Strange," he murmured, glancing back at her. "I see very few of you here."

He indicated one or two of her and Jaymi alone. There were no pictures of her with her mother, and definitely none of her with her father.

"Rub the salt in the wound," she offered mockingly. "Then please be kind enough to tell me why you're here."

He turned back and replaced the picture before appearing to peruse the rest.

He was a member of the school board, which meant he held her job in the palm of his hand. He was a member of the city council, once again, a very heavy influence on her job. He was the president this year of the business leaders' association as well as the cattle ranchers' association. Okay, so that didn't have a lot of bearing, just a lot of influence over the other two.

He was a very busy man.

So what was he doing here wasting his time with her?

She could pretty much guess at this point. It was just so out of character for him to really care that she could only stare at him in bemusement.

And where was his driver? Because everyone knew Marshal Roberts didn't drive himself anywhere. But she hadn't seen anyone else in the unassuming pick-up truck sitting at her curb and no one was at the door with him before he came in.

Though she honestly couldn't say she had ever heard of Marshal Roberts visiting any of Rafer's past girlfriends, lovers, friends, or various associates. He'd always pretended his grandson didn't exist in any capacity or area of his consciousness. If one mentioned Rafer, she heard he turned away or stared back at them as though they hadn't spoken. He had his tricks and maneuvers that didn't quite match his presence here tonight.

"I hear you spent a few days at the Triple R ranch?" His head jerked around, his gaze piercing as he asked the question almost casually.

As though he would catch her doing something, or an expression on her face that would give him an answer of some sort.

She was tempted to simply roll her eyes again, just to show him she wasn't in the least intimidated. Though, actually, she might have been, just a little bit intimidated.

"I did," she admitted.

There was no denying it after all. Martin Eisner had seen

her kissing Rafer before she left. That spurt of reckless challenge that Rafer always awakened in her had ensured she didn't walk away from him without throwing caution to the winds. Caution and his belief that she could ever be ashamed of having a man like Rafer Callahan in her bed.

It wasn't shame that held her back. It was that debilitating fear. That overriding knowledge of the risk he could bring to her soul and her survival.

It wasn't one of her brightest moments, though, she admitted, but definitely one of her most honest.

He turned back to her, his hands pushing the edges of his silk business jacket back as he shoved them into the pockets of his nicely pressed blue jeans.

That was a rancher. Jeans and a silk business jacket.

It was standard for for this particular baron of Corbin County, as he and his two cohorts were called.

His head tilted to the side as he watched her carefully, a hint of curiosity in his gaze.

"What a contradiction of expressions on your face," he mused thoughtfully. "Tell me, Ms. Flannigan, is he aware you're in love with him?"

A frown jerked between her brows. "I'm not in love with, Rafer, Mr. Roberts. There are just—" She paused. Her teeth clenched as she fought for the reason. "There are just things between us. That's all."

"Things?" Arrogant and mocking, and fully aware of his own sense of knowledge, the arch of that dark brow assured her he believed otherwise.

"Exactly. Just things." She cocked her hip as her arms tightened over her breasts. "Do you mind telling me what you need? I'm rather busy with lesson plans and so forth tonight."

If he intended to threaten her with her job, then she would allow him the opportunity now rather than later.

He didn't speak immediately. He just continued to stare at her thoughtfully for long moments. Finally, he gave a small shake of his head as his lips quirked knowingly.

"I'm going to assume you're aware you could lose every

friend or acquaintance you have in this county," he said then, his voice soft. "Tell me, Ms. Flannigan, are you certain you want to continue in this relationship that seems to be developing between you and Rafer, considering the risks and losses you're looking at?"

Someone else who called him Rafer.

She could see the frown on Rafer's face now, especially considering the fact that there had been times it had seemed he was uncertain if he wanted her calling him by the full version of his name.

"He doesn't like being called Rafer," she stated. "He only tolerates it from me, you know."

And she was rather possessive of the privilege. Rafer had been known to get into fistfights over that name. But it seemed to suit him so very well.

"He's never tolerated it from anyone else, but his full given name is Marshal Rafer Callahan," he stated, and for a moment she saw something, sensed something she never had in her life. Pure, icy grief. "His mother loved her father," he said softly then.

And the rumor had been that the father had cherished his daughter.

"Your middle name is Rafer?"

"As is his," he inclined his head slowly. "But you're digressing, Ms. Flannigan, and being much too curious. I asked you a question."

"My friends won't walk away if they're my friends." She shrugged. "If they do walk away, then I don't need them in my life."

His lips quirked as an expression of insultingly sardonic amazement crossed his face. "How incredibly innocent. And stupid." He paused then, his jaw tightening before he said, "Haven't you already lost one friend because of the Callahans? I believe she even told my granddaughter that you were so besotted with him and the child you carried for such a short time that nothing else mattered to you."

She breathed in deeply, fighting the pain that wanted to tear at her soul. She couldn't believe Amelia had actually told anyone in that horrible family about the child she carried.

"Does anyone else know?" she whispered, wondering if Rafe knew, or if there was a possibility of any of the Callahans learning of it.

He snorted at the thought. "My granddaughter told only me, and Amelia hasn't even told her father as far as I know."

Cami rather doubted that. If she had told Marshal Roberts's granddaughter, supposedly her best friend and co-worker, then her father, Wayne Sorenson, knew as well.

She had prayed Amelia would keep that to herself.

"My granddaughter understands family loyalty," he assured her as though it were a question. "Trust me, it wasn't information we wanted bandied about."

Of course it wasn't. God forbid that the grandson he had disowned would dare to have children of his own. Or that any woman would desire to have his child.

"Did you have a drink to celebrate the loss of your great-grandchild, Mr. Roberts?" she asked painfully, certain he would have. "I hope you enjoyed it."

Her voice rasped, the inability to hold back her pain in front of this man was galling.

"No, Ms. Flannigan, I did not." The flash of some emotion she thought could have been regret flashed in his gaze. "I grieved, just as I grieved when I lost my daughter."

"You still had your grandson. Did you grieve when you disowned him?" Anger was beginning to churn inside her now. What the hell made him think he was wanted here? "You've had more than twenty years to show him you grieved and what have you done, Mr. Roberts? Better yet, why are you even here?"

She didn't want to deal with him. He had broken his grandson's heart. If his daughter had been living, he would have destroyed her if what he said was true, and she had loved him so dearly she had named her only child after him.

"I'm here to reason with you, because you carried my great-grandchild at one time," he said softly. "And because I know you grieved when you lost that child. I don't want to see you hurt further, Ms. Flannigan. And regardless of what you think, I don't want to see Rafer hurt anymore than he has already been. It may be in your best interests to consider severing the relationship now. Or convincing him to leave Colorado altogether. His chances at happiness would be greatly improved if he would do so."

She frowned back for a moment. "Isn't there some codicil in the inheritance his mother left him, and that was left to her, that states the heir can only be a resident of Corbin County? Not any other Colorado county or other state? And doesn't it only give certain reasons why he can be away for more than a year, with the military being one of those reasons?"

He stared back at her for long moments, his gaze icy before his lips quirked, though the ice in his eyes remained.

"Touché, Ms. Flannigan," he murmured. "Touché. And did Rafer give you these details?"

"He didn't have to. The details are a matter of public record for anyone who cares to check," she informed him.

"And of course, you cared enough about the man who fathered the child you lost to check," he said softly.

It hurt. The memory of the child was like a deep, burning wound that refused to stop bleeding with bitterness, or aching with an agony she couldn't dim whenever she allowed herself to think about it.

"Besides the point," she retorted. "What makes you think you have the right to steal what his mother wanted him to have?"

"Because his mother knew it wasn't hers to begin with," he suddenly snapped before quickly turning his back on her, his shoulders bunching with the obvious anger surging through him.

When he turned back seconds later, his expression lacked any emotion whatsoever. "Is that inheritance more important than his happiness?" he finally asked, his voice dripping with ice.

"Evidently, as Rafer is still in Corbin County, it appears the two go hand in hand," she retorted with mocking anger, her emphasis on the fact that he shouldn't have to choose apparent.

As his lips parted, another question pushed past her lips almost unbidden as the thought came to her. "Are you the son of a bitch behind the threatening phone calls I've been getting? Because if you are, you can inform whoever you've put up to making them that they aren't effective in the least. I will not be frightened away from something I want, Mr. Roberts. Or something I feel I deserve."

He seemed to freeze. For a second, she thought she might have seen fear flash in his eyes, but Marshal Roberts wasn't a man known for feeling fear. To the contrary, he was known for being rather fearless in the face of most situations.

"No," he finally said, his voice soft, his expression tightening and forming a hardened, emotionless cast. "I haven't put anyone up to calling you, Ms. Flannigan, and definitely not to threaten you. Have you told the sheriff of the calls?"

"Not yet." She'd had no intention of telling Archer. She preferred not to, suspecting the information might get back to Rafer.

She wasn't certain if she was ready for that.

Slowly, his hand lifted, and for a second, every one of his near seventy years was reflected clearly on his face as he covered it with his hand.

Weariness slumped his shoulders and the image of a man at the end of a particular rope had Cami pausing for a second. It was gone as quickly as it had flashed across his face, though. If it had even been there to begin with.

"I would highly suggest alerting the sheriff to these calls," he stated then. "And if I were you, I'd definitely tell Rafer. And then, it would be advisable, Ms. Flannigan, to sever the relationship building between the two of you."

He was once again the arrogant, coldly commanding Marshal Roberts. The man who had disowned his grandson. The one who had stood stony-eyed at his daughter's grave site, his son at his side, his granddaughter held in his arms as he deliberately separated himself from his only grandson.

"You can advise all you want, Mr. Roberts," she told him

with a sense of resignation. "Just as I advise Rafer on a constant basis, but it all comes down to him." She grimaced, admitting to the one person she knew would never tell her secret. "I have an incredibly hard time telling your grandson 'no'."

For a second, just a second, his expression seemed to soften. The image of an old man who knew his grandson well flashed across his face. And if she wasn't entirely mistaken, there was a glimmer of pride as well.

"My wife, God rest her soul, told me the same thing once when we were very young," he admitted, his gaze connecting with hers in a moment that seemed more connected than she would have liked with this man. "Take care of your yourself, Ms. Flannigan. And should Rafe not take no for an answer, then at least insist that he take careful measure of the security surrounding both of you."

There was an edge to the words, a deliberate warning that had her arms dropping from her breasts as she confronted him.

"Is that a threat?" she asked carefully.

His gaze was heavy with shadows, and she suspected, knowledge. But it was a knowledge he was refusing to admit to.

"Regardless of belief, I'm no threat to my grandson," he told her. "But that doesn't mean there isn't a threat that follows the Callahan family. A curse perhaps?" he suggested warily.

"You won't threaten him, but you won't save him either, is what you're saying?" she guessed.

"I didn't say that." Now the anger was back. "I would never stand idly by and allow my grandson to be harmed any more than I stood idly and allowed my granddaughter to die."

Cami could feel something in the air between them then, a tension that didn't make sense, as though he were trying to tell her something, warn her of something.

"But Sam and Mina Callahan's deaths were an accident," she posed carefully. "Weren't they?"

"Of course they were." Emotionless. There was no inflection in his voice. "And this conversation never occurred."

Her brow arched. "Do you think no one took notice of your pick-up, Mr. Robert?"

"It's one of my ranch hands'." He shrugged. "And think of this, Ms. Flannigan. To this point, I've actually been one of Rafer's most staunch allies. Don't make me his strongest enemy."

Replacing the western hat on his head, he tilted the brim to fully shade his face before moving past her and unlocking the door.

He paused once again as she watched him silently. "I'm rather good at choosing those I reach out to," he stated quietly. "You've hidden the loss of your child all these years, I suspect, to save Rafer from further pain."

Cami breathed in roughly, the fact that he had realized that somehow easing a wound she hadn't known she carried.

"What's your point?" she asked, unable to hide the evidence of the tears that would come later.

"My point?" He finally turned his head to stare back at her. "I rather suspect you'll tell no one of this visit. Unfortunately the one you need to hide it from the most will be the very one you ache to tell. Telling Rafer I was here could be a rather bad idea."

Cami pushed her fingers wearily through her hair and blew out a hard, irritated breath. "If you know Rafer anywhere near as well as I do, then you know damned good and well he's going to know exactly who it was, no matter the precautions you took. What the hell makes you think for a minute he can be fooled so easily?"

His eyes narrowed. "He doesn't read minds."

"He doesn't have to," she told him softly. "He has eyes and ears that no one suspects, Mr. Roberts. In forcing Rafer and his cousins to hide friendships and connections, you forced them to create bonds and spies. Have no doubt, for even a second, he'll know, eventually. And then, I guess we'll both have to deal with it."

Silent, almost moody, he glared back at her before nodding shortly. Pulling the door open, he stepped to the porch, the panel closing quietly behind him.

As Cami walked over and secured each lock, she heard the truck start, and a second later, the sound of it pulling away from the side of the street could be heard.

How very, very strange, she thought.

And like Marshal Roberts, she truly hoped Rafer never, ever learned he was there.

That wouldn't necessarily be a good thing.

CHAPTER 11

She was suffering.

Cami lay stretched out on the bed, a sheen of perspiration on her flesh several nights later her eyes closed. Need swamped her as she gritted her teeth and cursed Rafe until hell wouldn't have had him several days later.

Because she was miserable. Because no matter how hard she tried, she couldn't fight the burning arousal tormenting her.

The supple, firm vibrator lay pushed beneath her pillow, useless to her now. There had been a time when it had actually worked. When dragging it along the bare folds of her pussy had taken her close enough to the remembered feel of Rafe's fingers and tongue on her flesh to allow her to work it slowly inside her cunt and, long minutes later, to find the release she so desperately needed. There had been a time when she had known he wasn't close enough to go to, and her body had allowed a little alternate pleasure.

It simply didn't work anymore.

The feel of the battery-operated toy wasn't even close to the feel of his fingers and tongue, let alone the sensation of his cock working inside her. The heated stretch and burn of his iron-hard flesh was so much more extreme. It was thicker, hotter, throbbing inside her powerfully instead of the weak, pale imitation of the artificial vibrator. He had ruined her, that was all there was to it. No other man, no other touch would do.

She gritted her teeth and bit off a furious expulsion of breath. She was too scared it would turn into a scream of pure frustration. Because she was so damned horny she was on the verge of calling him and begging him to fuck her.

She could jump in her car; it wouldn't take that long to drive to his ranch. There were still some icy spots on the road, but most of the snow had actually been removed. She could knock on his door again and spend the night letting him fuck this need for him out of her system.

Sitting up in the bed, she propped her elbows on her knees and pushed her fingers through her hair, further ruffling the shortened strands as the hardened bud of her clit throbbed in misery.

If she could just get off a little bit, then it would help. Just take the damned pressure off or something. No matter how hard she tried, no matter how long she tried, it wasn't happening.

If she just hadn't been so insane as to take the mountain road that night and find herself snowbound with him. She wouldn't be in this position. She wouldn't be aching for him until she was certain it would drive her insane. Or was this why she had taken the longer, more mountainous route home from Aspen rather than the more direct drive along the interstate? Had that building need, that hunger she couldn't control, been working on her subconsciously? Creating a situation that left her with little choice? Because consciously she had known what would happen if she were to be stranded at the ranch. She had known the need pulling at her would have taken care of the rest.

The hunger was a craving that never seemed to completely dissipate. She was like an addict, strung out in desperation for that next hit. Her body demanding its fix.

That was how she felt. Addicted to Rafer Callahan. Now wasn't that a fine fix to find herself in.

As she cursed herself silently for the weakness, the low,

muted buzz of her phone on the bed stand had her reaching out quickly for it and pressing the call button.

It could be the nursing home calling about her mother. Cami hadn't heard from them all week. She could have checked the caller ID, but she didn't want to know it wasn't Rafer. She wanted to hope, to believe, until the last possible second—

"Hello?"

"I'm at the back door; let me in."

Rafe.

Her eyes closed as her heart immediately began racing in a hard, excited rhythm. Her body immediately sensitized further. She could feel her heart racing, demanding as though the need had somehow summoned him. He was there, a dark male hunger rasping his already deep voice.

Hunger flooded her system, stronger, hotter than ever as she felt her juices flooding the flushed, heated tissue of her pussy.

"You shouldn't be here, Rafer. Go home." It was all she could do to push the words past her lips and make the demand.

"Do you have company, Cambria?" The silky menace in his tone assured her it was a damn good thing she did not have company. The dominance in it had her breathing increasing; the sense of possession and determination rolling across the line shouldn't have been so erotic.

"No, I don't have company." Pushing her fingers through the shortened strands of her hair, she clenched her thighs against the increased ache. "I'm sleeping."

"Open the back door or I'm coming to the front. And I'll knock until you answer baby or until your neighbors call the sheriff. Take your pick.

"I can promise the gossip will be as juicy as that lush little pussy of yours." The words were an erotic warning. An explicit, completely arousing promise. Because her pussy was wet.

"Damn you, Rafe." She disconnected the call, tossed the phone across the bed and jumped from it, to race from the bedroom to the backdoor.

He would do it too. He would let everyone hear him knocking and demanding to be let in. He would probably let everyone hear the erotic promises. The warnings of spankings. Oh God, she was going to come before he ever touched her.

As she moved quickly down the steps and through the hall to the other side of the house, she told herself she should hate him for doing this to her. She should blast him herself for blackmailing her. It really wasn't fair. She should never let him get away with manipulating her like this.

Instead, she could feel the excitement pouring through her, tearing at her senses and sensitizing her body until the brush of her short, silky nightgown was like a stroke of sensual pleasure against her flesh.

She ran for the door barefoot, the folds of her pussy slick and heated, her nipples hard. Her womb was tight with the need for orgasm, her flesh, aching for his touch. Cami rushed into the kitchen and to the back door and threw it open with every intention of giving him her opinion of his high-handed arrogance.

Her lips were parted to let the insults fly. to berate, she was prepared to chastise. She had every intention of relieving some of the frustration that had built inside her all week.

He gave her another way to vent it instead.

Before she could get the first word out he gripped her hips and jerked her against him. Lifting her from the floor he pressed her against the wall.

The door slammed closed, the click of the locks sounding overly loud as his lips covered hers in a kiss so heated she was certain he was melting her toenails as they dangled above the floor.

His tongue was rapacious, as it thrust into her mouth. Licking and stroking, tasting her, and pulling every ounce of sexual need from the very core of her body to a full, blazing inferno.

With her back to the wall, one hand in her hair, the other beneath her rear to hold her in place, he held her easily, one hard thigh pushed dominantly between hers allowing her to ride the hard muscle. Rough denim rasped the bare folds of her pussy, exciting her beyond belief as the dominant thrusts of his tongue reminded her of the pleasure to come. Reminded her of the hard thrust of his cock impaling her, worked deep inside the clenched, sensitized core of her sex.

It wasn't enough.

Her nerve endings were screaming in need, pulsating with the rising hunger for this man. Her flesh ached with a need she had never been able to assuage in any way except with him. She craved him.

Lifting her legs, she gripped his hard hips with her knees. Aligning the powerful wedge of his erection against the overly sensitive area between her thighs, her hips shifted and rocked against him.

All she cared about was being closer to him, feeling him, taking him and being taken.

Cami whimpered with the erotic pleasure pouring through her.

It had been two weeks since she had known any relief for the heat and hunger for him that tormented her.

Two weeks of aching need, of brutally erotic dreams. Fourteen days of the tormenting flush of lust that kept her pussy wet, swollen, and aching for him.

With her hips under his, Cami felt his hands cupping her ass, steadying her. She tightened her arms around his shoulders and held on tight as he turned and began moving through the house.

She knew where he was going. She knew better than to question how he knew how to get her there. He'd never been in her house that she knew of. But she had a feeling she wouldn't have known of it unless he wanted her to.

Each step he took stroked his cock against the wet heat of her pussy, and even between the layer of denim that separated them Cami could feel the strength of the erection he was doing nothing to hide.

Then, he pulled his lips back from hers.

His kiss was gone as she was left panting, fighting to draw in air. He simply pulled back, then bent and eased her back to the bed.

"Rafer," she whispered his name as she felt the comforter against her back, then her shoulders. "This isn't a good idea."

She had to force the words past her lips, the objection pulled from the worry, the fear that haunted her not quite as deeply as the arousal did.

Standing, his gaze narrowed on her as he unbuttoned his shirt then stripped it from his body. And he was ignoring her objection.

Thank God!

"Rafer," she tried again anyway. "You know it isn't. It's just going to make things worse once reality returns."

Had she somehow lost her mind?

He sat down on the bed and began pulling off his boots, obviously deaf to her objections.

Clear reason was finally beginning to intrude. She was all too aware of what she could possibly be risking. Her heart reminded her of all she had already lost. Her career.

But her body, like her lover, was ignoring every objection and was deaf to every argument. All her body wanted was the feel of him, the heat of the power of his body invading hers.

It was going to be up to her to find the strength to stop this. But that meant getting the hell away from him.

She tensed, preparing to roll from the bed.

"Move from this bed and I won't give you that spanking I was considering."

Cami stilled instantly, incredulity surging through her at the threat.

That and the sudden acceleration of her pulse thundering through her veins. The excitement she could feel making her nerve endings scream out of each sensation.

"That threat is just *wrong*, Rafer," she protested weakly, hearing the hunger, the anticipation, building inside her.

"No, a hard dick pounding in my jeans all week is what's wrong," he retorted. "Craving the taste of your pussy while I should be sleeping is wrong. Jacking off and never coming hard enough to get a minute's rest is *really* wrong." Rising to his feet, he turned to her, his fingers flipping open the metal button fly of his jeans. Pushing them over his hips with a careless motion of his hands, his cock slipped free and stood imperatively out from his body. Like an arrow ready to fire.

Her mouth dried then watered.

Flicking her tongue over her lips hungrily, she was still amazed that she was able to take him as she did each time they had come together. Pleasure and burning resistance at once sensations that mixed to create an overpowering ecstasy she was becoming addicted to.

"We can't keep doing this." She could barely speak past the excitement suddenly pouring through her.

If this kept up then she would never find a way to live without his touch again. She would never survive without him.

"What? Sneaking around?" he growled, his expression hard and flashing with irritation. "I agree. Sooner or later I'll get really sick of it and begin retaliating."

A groan of exasperation and hunger slipped past her lips. "No, Rafer. This." She waved her hand at his naked body.

"Well, baby, the occasional fuck never hurt anyone." His smile was tight and hard. "Now take that pretty gown off before I tear it from you. Then, I want to watch as I fuck those pretty lips."

Dominant, powerful. So sexy it sent a rush of clenching sensation to attack her womb. The tone of voice, the arrogance in his expression, and the lust filling his sapphire eyes had her so close to climaxing from just the sound of his explicit words that she trembled.

He *would* tear the gown from her. She could see it in his face.

And she would let him. She would love it.

Gripping the knee-length black silk as she sat up and wiggled it up to her hips, she pulled it off slowly and tossed it to the side of the bed. It slid over the edge slowly.

"Son of a fucking bitch," he growled harshly.

Rafe would never get used to what the sight of her body did to him. The proof of her need for him was in the flushed, swollen mounds of her breasts, topped with candy-pink perfect nipples.

Her breathing was accelerated, her face flushed. The sassy cut of her hair messed around her head as small, sharp little ribbons of it lay over her forehead and cheeks.

She looked like a pixie, just as mischievous as hell and so damned sexy a man could lose his soul in her.

Forcing himself to hold back, to control the need to simply pound into her, Rafe slid his fingers into the short strands of her hair.

"Open your lips," he demanded, watching as the kiss-swollen curves parted.

With the fingers of his other hand, he gripped the base of his dick and drew her forward.

He watched her eyes darken. Her lips parted further as he pressed his cock head against them. Thighs tightening, he groaned as the silken heat of her lips began to stretch around the width and her hot little mouth drew him in.

"Fuck, Cami," he growled her name. "That's my love. Suck my dick. Make me crazy for you."

And she did just that.

Her tongue flicked and clicked.

Her lips tightened and the lush heat of her mouth sucked the width with tantalizing hunger.

Watching each shallow thrust past her lips and each flex of her cheeks had his balls tightening, the need for release pounding through them. The need to spill his come, to feel her sucking hungrily at each heated spurt had him forcing himself to pull back. To ignore the dazed hunger in her objection, he pushed her back on the bed.

Placing one knee on the bed, Rafe came down to her, forcing her to recline slowly, the dark gray of her eyes staring up at him with almost-bemused fascination as he almost touched her lips with his.

He was a second from tasting her lips again when his hand slid beneath the pillow at her side and they both froze.

Her eyes widened as she seemed to stop breathing as he

stared down at her. His fingers curled around the base of a device he hadn't expected to find.

A device she had no doubt been using that very night.

"What do we have here, kitten?" he crooned, the glow in his sapphire eyes intensifying with a lust that stole her breath.

"Rafer, please—" she whispered, wishing he would just ignore what he had found. Wishing he would just thrust into her and fill her with the throbbing heat of his dick.

"Oh, baby," he whispered as he rose to his knees, the device he had found gripped in his hand.

He looked from the sexual toy back to her, his lips curving with a smile of pure male anticipation.

"Kitten, my dick is bigger than yours," he stated silkily as he held the vibrating dildo up and looked at it before turning his gaze back to her.

Cami felt the tremor of excitement, arousal, and the edge of trepidation that began to rush through her system.

His expression was suddenly filled with more heat and with more lust than ever before.

And yes, his dick *was* bigger than hers.

Thank God!

And it was *so* much better than hers.

And she needed it. Now.

"My adventurous little kitten." He smiled with slow, sensual anticipation. "How dirty could you get with me, Cami, versus without me?"

Her gaze flicked from him to the dildo and then back again.

He looked like the warrior everyone suspected the Callahans had come from. Tall and fierce, conquering and savage.

"Spread your legs, Cami." He moved between them, pressing her knees apart as she locked her fingers in the blankets beneath her body.

Holding her legs apart with his knees, the hard, muscular body resting on his knees in front of her, he intended to conquer her.

Savage lust and brutal hunger reflected in his expression

as he moved the toy between her thighs. She could feel the dampness against the bare folds of her sex; the slick, heated warmth triggered a sensual, sexual response she hadn't expected.

She could barely breathe. Pleasure was tearing through her, anticipation racing through her veins as she felt the firm, supple tip of the dildo press between the swollen, slick folds of her sex.

"Touch your breasts," he demanded as he thumbed the switch at the base of the artificial cock and sent a pulse of near-electrifying sensation circling her clit. Why was it so much better with him?

"Don't do this, Rafer, please—" She didn't know if she could keep her heart intact, if she would survive never having him again, if she gave herself fully to him. And he was demanding everything from her. He was determined to have all of her.

"Just say no!" Dominance tightened his expression, glowed in his eyes, as he locked his gaze with hers. "If you want to stop, at any time, then don't play word games with me, Cami. Don't throw that ball in my court. If you don't want me, then you just fucking say no."

She knew what he meant. She could protest until hell froze over, but if she didn't say no, then he wouldn't stop.

"Why are you doing this to me?" The cry, rife with the needs racing through her, slipped past her lips.

He knew she didn't have the strength or the will to tell him no. That had already been established during the blizzard. Her body was too weak and her mind, her senses, filled with too many fantasies of them together.

"Because I'm starving for you." Part anger and part rising need strengthened and rasped through his voice.

"I won't survive when you walk away." The thought of that happening already had her chest clenching with pain. "And you know it won't last past tomorrow, Rafer. You know there's no future in this."

"Who says I'm asking for a future, or walking away?" The hard line of his lips assured her he had far more in mind than what he was letting on, and she knew Rafer. This wasn't just sex, it was a claiming.

"You know you will." She was weakening, her juices flooding her pussy, lubricating the swollen, sensitive folds and the hard, throbbing bud of her clit as it met the rounded crest of the vibrator.

The vibrating toy was driving her to distraction, making her crazy just to touch him, to feel the hard, thick flesh of cock pushing its way inside her, fucking her, taking her, possessing her.

"Oh God, Rafer." She jerked; pleasure blazing across her nerve endings as he pressed the vibrating head of the toy just beneath her clit and flooded her senses with the near ectasy of it.

"You were fucking yourself with it tonight, weren't you, kitten?" he crooned.

Cami felt a blush rushing through her cheeks despite the passion that eradicated any semblance of good sense or shame where Rafer was concerned.

"Did you cry out my name? Did you cry out for me, Cami, when you came? All you had to do was call me. I would have come to you, baby, I would have helped."

A whimper passed her lips as her hips lifted, rising and falling against the vibrating sensations in desperate pleasure and the quest for more.

She remembered what was awaiting her. She remembered how intense, powerful, and overwhelming her release could be.

"Would you have fucked yourself for me? Let me hear your little moans while I told you how tight and hot your pussy was?"

"Oh God, Rafer, yes!" Her hips rolled against the sensations.

He wove a spell of sensual power that she felt helpless against. One that wrapped around her senses and heightened the pleasure building inside her.

She couldn't fight against it. She wanted to. God knew she wanted to. But as the vibrating caress of the dildo eased lower once again, tucking against the clenched entrance of her pussy, she knew there was no way she could deny herself. She needed him too much.

"Please Rafer, now," she whispered desperately.

"Touch your breasts for me, baby," he crooned as he applied just enough pressure to lodge the broad head of the vibrator just inside her clenched sex. "Do it for me, Cami. Finger your nipples," he urged her as she hesitated, staring back at him as fear of the unknown clashed with the desperate, aching need for more pleasure.

Releasing her grip on the sheets Cami moved her fingers slowly up her body first to her hips, starting slowly to become accustomed to touching herself as he watched.

With just her fingertips she stroked slowly up her torso, watching his face, his eyes as they darkened, his jaw as the muscle there flexed furiously with the tension invading his body.

The feel of her own touch was more sensual than it had ever been before.

Threads of electric sensation sizzled over her nerve endings, washing through her body in a clash of sensation she couldn't fight. Didn't want to fight.

As she reached her breasts, her hands flattened, moving over her flesh until she was cupping both mounds, fingers and thumb gripping a nipple, and moaning at the pleasure flooding her. It was sharp, extreme, stealing her breath as he watched and pulling a tumultuous cry from her lips.

"Play with your nipples." He pulled the toy back before working it in again, moving it deeper, stretching her further as he let her thumbs rake over the stiff peaks.

Pleasure shattered through her. It was so blinding, so bright, that she nearly orgasmed from the erotic intensity alone.

She couldn't keep her eyes open. An incredible, overriding pleasure raced through her. It burned burning hot and bright as the vibration increased and the thrusts pushed deeper inside her. The feel of the fake cock, the arousing buzz, and Rafer's touch threw her into a world of pure sensation.

As her fingers began to play over her nipples, her hips

rising and falling to the thrusts moving inside her, Cami could feel herself becoming a creature of primal eroticism.

Through slitted eyes she watched as he came over her, his powerful body covering hers as his wrist continued to flex and tilt, fucking the dildo deeper, harder, faster inside the gripping, tormented depths of her pussy.

"Lift your nipple to me," he suddenly bit out in demand, the sound of his voice a hard, primitive rasp.

Cupping a mound, she did as she was bid, then cried out at the incredible heat of his mouth surrounding the desperately sensitive peak. His tongue began to thrash against it, erotically licking and tasting with rising hunger.

"Rafe." The sound of her own voice, so dark, so locked in complete sexual surrender, shocked her.

"Damn, Cami," he suddenly groaned. "It's not enough, sweetheart. I have to have you myself."

The vibrator pulled free of her body, only to have Rafer move in closer, his hips dipping, his cock lodging against her entrance. The heavy, thick crest was hotter than any toy created by man or by woman.

"Lift your legs, knees at my hips," he growled, those hips working, twisting, pushing forward to work his cock deeper inside the clenched muscles of her pussy.

Her hands were at his shoulders, nails biting into his flesh. She gripped his hips with her knees and tilted her pussy up to take more, to take him deeper. To facilitate each heavy thrust.

"Yes, fuck me, Rafer," she whispered as the coarse mat of hair on his chest raked across her tender nipples, sensitizing them further.

His pelvis stroked over her clit, his cock worked inside her, stretching her with such incredible pleasure she could only whimper with the sensations raking across her nerve endings.

His head lowered, his lips against her shoulder, his tongue licking over her flesh. With a final, hard thrust he buried into the hilt, the stroke forceful, powering through the clenched, slickened muscles of her pussy and spearing to the depths of it.

Buried deep inside her, pulsing, throbbing.

"So fucking tight," he groaned as his lips moved to her neck, his teeth raking against the tender nerve endings. "I couldn't forget how tight you were after you left, how hot and slick your pussy is. How it grips me and sucks at my dick until it's all I can do to keep from losing my mind with the need to fuck you."

Explicit. Demanding.

His hips were moving harder, faster.

Lifting one hand, he speared his fingers in her hair, clenching the short strands before pulling her head back, his lips covering hers, his tongue filling her mouth as the heavy, engorged flesh of his erection pumped inside her with ever-increasing strokes.

His lips rubbed against hers, parting them, his tongue licking against hers, tasting her as she tasted him, holding her to him, moving against her. Waves of heat and incredible bliss began to roll through her. Her muscles tightened, her pussy clamping down on his cock, rippling around it as he moved harder and faster inside her.

The bite of pleasure-pain began to burn hotter. It began to tighten further in impending ecstasy. It was a pleasure she couldn't resist, one she couldn't deny.

Holding on to him as his lips tore from hers, his head tilting back and a grimace contorting his face, Cami jumped headlong into the ecstasy of release and the pleasure that could only be found in Rafer's arms.

As she cried out his name, shudders began to race through her, tremors that shook her body, shudders that began to quake through her womb. Above her, Rafer buried his face against her neck, pushed in hard, deep, and with a ragged growl filled her with the hard, heated release that had been locked inside his balls.

Cami felt the flesh buried inside her as it seemed to thicken, to throb, then the heavy, fierce spurts of his semen pulsed inside her, searing her.

She could only hold onto him and gasp in brilliant ecstasy. It seemed never-ending, exploding through her again and again as Rafer continued to thrust against her.

His arms were around her, holding her close as he kept his weight from falling to her completely. As his chest met her breasts, Cami fought for breath, the ecstasy so intense she didn't know if she would ever learn how to breathe properly again.

God, what was she going to do if the time came when there was no chance at all of ever having him hold her? If she forever lost the fiery heat of his possession and his kiss again?

If something happened to him.

Was it truly better to have loved and lost than to have never loved at all?

Would she have wanted to miss the pleasure she'd found in his arms?

"I hear you became very curious and began asking questions about the Callahans this week," he murmured as his heart still raced. "You should have come to the ranch, darlin'. I would have answered any question you had about any of us."

Would he have known the answers to her questions, though?

She gave a deceptively unconcerned shrug of her shoulders. "They weren't questions about you or your cousins in particular," she told him. "I just wanted to know a few things."

"No, the questions were about our parents and about us in particular. Don't lie to me, Cami, and I'll say again, you could have asked me. You told me my bastard of a grandfather made his first visit to one of my lovers. Now I want to know why."

Even as she lay against him she could hear the warning in his voice. He wanted answers now. If she had any further questions, then she had better ask him rather than anyone else.

"I just wanted to know what happened," she said softly. "Nearly a whole community turns against three children and it seems no one has questioned why? Perhaps I thought it was time someone asked those questions."

"Let me give you the answer there, kitten," he offered as though the why didn't matter to him any longer. "Our fathers not only married three of Sweetrock's favorite daughters, but they married into the three richest families from here to Denver and past Aspen. Three supposedly shiftless, no-account brothers stepped in shit and came out smelling like a rose, as they say. Those families didn't appreciate the defection of their daughters, they didn't care for the bad blood that had been injected into their grandsons, and they sure as hell wanted to make certain that bad blood didn't go any further. And there you have it, the reason why a whole community turned against three young boys. To ensure they learned their place and never aspired to step above it." And there was the bitterness, just the thinnest vein of it, as he gave her the explanation everyone else accepted as well. "Now what the hell did Marshal Roberts want? Don't make me ask again, Cami." He rolled from her as he made the demand.

She sat up slowly, pulling the sheet around her breasts as she turned to stare down at him watching as he lounged back on her pillows, unashamedly naked. He didn't even bother to pull the sheet around his hips as he watched her closely.

She hadn't noticed his lashes before, she realized. They were thick, lush lashes women cried over because they didn't have, surrounding the deep sapphire blue of his eyes.

And she had picked a hell of a time to notice it.

"I'm not certain what Marshal Roberts was after," she finally said, trembling at the icy look in his sapphire eyes. "He made me very curious though about everything that's happened."

"Such as?" If possible, his voice and his expression were harder. Colder.

Cami swallowed with a hint of nervousness that she couldn't hide. "Your parents' deaths. Your uncles'." She had to fight to hold back her tears at the next thought. "My sister's."

Pulling her knees up, she rested her chin on them as Rafe sat up slowly.

"Cami, you know those deaths were unrelated."

She shook her head, her heart pounding in fear. "Your parents and uncle died on the same mountain road, on the same curve. God, Rafer," her voice dropped further. "Do you realize it was the exact place your grandparents, JR and Eileen Callahan died?"

It was too much. There were too many Callahans to die in the same place, the same way, and nearly the same excuse used across three generations. And no one seemed to want to question it, or to see the trail of suspicion.

"Cami, stop this, baby." His expression gentled slowly. "You're letting that old bastard fuck with your head. You can't do that."

He wasn't hearing her.

She could feel the danger that swirled around him. She had always felt it. As though some shadow haunted him and his cousins and refused to dissipate.

"Rafer, listen to me," she whispered, almost terrified that someone else would hear her. "There are too many coincidences. You say you don't believe in them, yet you're just accepting three generations dying in the same place, as well as your uncle Clyde. Do you realize no one else has ever died in that same place in the history of that mountain road?"

"Cami . . ." She could see his refusal to listen to her in his expression, hear it in his voice.

"No." She pushed her fingers through her hair with an edge of desperation. "You have to listen to me, Rafer." She clenched at the strands of hair she held as she fought and failed to fight back her fear for him.

"Cami, he's fucking with you, dammit!"

Rafer could feel the need to confront Marshal Roberts rising inside him with a wave of fury. He couldn't believe that old bastard had finally figured out that Cami was more important to him than any other woman in his life had been. And to actually have the sheer nerve to come to her house and frighten her this way was unforgivable.

"He's not fucking with me." She lifted her gaze to him as he pushed her back to the pillows, propping himself up to stare down at her. "What about Jaymi?"

He could see the fear flashing in her eyes now.

"Cami, Jaymi was killed by a fucking lunatic, you know

that." He ached for her. Jaymi's death had destroyed her, he knew that, but she had to realize—

"Did she tell you about the phone calls?"

He could feel his stomach clench with trepidation then. "What phone calls? Jaymi never mentioned any phone calls, Cami, neither did you."

He watched her lips tremble, watched the misery that darkened her eyes.

"I'm getting them now."

Fear tore a hole through his soul.

"What phone calls, Cami?" He could feel the rage beginning to burn in his stomach.

"The ones that warned her that if she didn't stay away from you, that something would happen to her. She knew who it was. She knew the voice, but she didn't put it together until the last social we attended with you, Logan, and Crowe. I heard her that night, telling him that she knew something. Then she went into her room where I couldn't hear her. She wouldn't tell me what it was, or who it was." Her breathing hitched with tears, the sound of them breaking his heart. "Two days later, she was dead." Her breath caught, and Rafe watched as she fought back her tears.

That wasn't a coincidence, because Jaymi hadn't been the only one of the young women who died that summer who had received such phone calls. And now, Cami was getting them?

"You were called?" he questioned her.

She nodded quickly. "I recognize the voice, Rafer, just as Jaymi did. I know that voice, but I can't put a face to it. When I do—"

"When you do, you'll tell me and I'll fucking deal with it," he informed her harshly, his hands moving to grip her shoulders imperatively as he made the order. "Do you understand me, Cami?"

"And if he decides to just kill you, Logan, and Crowe instead?" she asked tearfully, though she held the tears back. "What then?"

Rafe moved from her slowly, sitting up on the side of the bed and pushing his hands through his hair in irritation.

"That bastard is playing with both of us," he finally gritted out as he gave his head a hard shake.

Marshal Roberts was a master at manipulation. He had known it all his life.

How many times had Clyde been lured away from the ranch because Marshal had called for some reason or another, and convinced him to meet him somewhere? How many times had the ranch been vandalized each time, and Roberts hadn't made the meeting with Clyde?

It was a cycle. It had taken Clyde a few times to realize what his brother-in-law was doing. A few years to realize that the core of decency he thought Marshal had didn't exist.

When Marshal couldn't lure him away on his own, he'd found other means to pull Clyde, Rafe, Logan, and Crowe from the ranch.

It hadn't been to protect them as Clyde had once mused. Fuck, no, Marshal had done it out of a vindictive desire to destroy the ranch and make them completely paranoid. If it had been to protect them, then the attacks would have come the times they had sat in the ranch dark, silent ranch house and waited, weapons ready, for the vandals to strike again.

"I want to know everything he said, Cami," he finally told her. "And don't leave anything out."

He watched as she stared up at the ceiling.

"I can't do a play-by-play," she told him wearily as she turned her head to gaze back at him. "You don't believe me, do you, Rafer?"

"I don't disbelieve you," he finally sighed. "But, Cami, you don't know him as I do." He shook his head at the lifetime of memories he had where Marshal Roberts and his deceptions were concerned.

"Rafer, he was trying to tell me something," she whispered, and Rafer knew she truly believed that. "What else could it be?"

"Because he's a son of a bitch?" he sighed wearily.

"That's not a good enough reason, Rafer," she said, saddened not just because of the life she knew he and his cousins had lived but also because he seemed to have accepted it as deeply as everyone else in Corbin County. "Coincidences like this don't happen. There has to be more to it."

"The reason doesn't matter, Cami," he assured her with an edge of mockery. "And coincidences are called that for a reason, I've learned. Sometimes, it truly is a coincidence. Now I'm not concerned with the past, with grandparents or with Marshal Roberts. I want to know about those phone calls."

"I told you about the phone calls, Rafer," she argued with a surge of anger. The fear was being overshadowed now. Overshadowed by the anger that Rafer refused to even consider the fact that danger could be haunting him. "Why aren't you willing to listen to me?"

He gave a heavy sigh.

"Did you know the Corbins began this little campaign?" he asked her softly. "Crowe's granddaddy stood at the entrance to the funeral home when Logan, Crowe, and myself arrived at the funeral home with Clyde. He barred our way. The Callahans had no place there, he said. They murdered his daughter and he refused to have one attend her funeral, and Saul Rafferty, Logan's grandfather, and Marshal Roberts backed him on it. We weren't welcome there."

Cami had heard that story more than once, and each time she'd seen the conflict most people still had over it. She had also seen the knowledge that James Corbin had drawn the line that day and over the years and he'd enforced it. Marshal Roberts and Saul Rafferty hadn't, though, if she remembered the Callahan history correct. And she was pretty certain she did.

"James Corbin enforced it," she repeated. "Not the others."

"The other's backed him, Cami," he growled, frustration filling his voice now. "Mine and Logan's grandfathers were just as much a part of it as James Corbin was."

"I don't think Marshal Roberts was," she argued. "I don't know about Saul Rafferty, but I do know he moved from Corbin County just after his daughter's funeral. He only returns to oversee certain aspects of the ranch, other than that his manager handles everything. He's separated himself from the entire situation, hasn't he?" She knew he had. She had made it her business in the past few days to find out.

"Let it go, Cami," Rafe warned her. "This isn't your fight, and it's a fight you'll lose. For God's sake, if any part of what you suspect is true, then can you imagine the danger it would place *you* in?"

"You already suspected it?" she whispered, shocked that he was fighting her if he had already suspected something wasn't right about the past.

"No, Cami, I don't," he told her, his tone short now as he denied the charge. "Do you think we haven't thought of every question you've come up with?" He reached out, his fingertips caressing down the side of her face before he pulled back and watched her quietly for long moments. "Honey, this time, coincidence is coincidence."

"You're just accepting it?" She couldn't believe it. That Rafe wouldn't fight against the suspected murders of his family? Especially his parents and his uncle?

"It's not a question of accepting it or not accepting it," he informed her brusquely. "It's the way things are, plain and simple. The only reason you want to change it at this point is so you can fuck me without having to worry about the fine citizens of this county looking down at you for sharing a bed with a Callahan."

Could she blame him for believing it? How many people had ever questioned how the Callahan cousins had been treated over the years?

How many had ever stood up for them?

Or had they, like her, been torn by the fear of losing someone they would love with all their hearts and the three men who only sneered in the face of their unacceptance and flaunted the fact that they didn't give a damn? Men who dared their enemies to strike out at them or anyone who loved them.

"Why did you even come here tonight if all you wanted was to know about your grandfather's visit?" She was angry at herself, but a part of her was even angrier at him. "What did it accomplish, Rafer? You should have just called."

He chuckled at her question then, a dark, sexy sound of male amusement as the frustration and anger eased from his gaze.

"What did it accomplish?" he asked arched his brow, and gave her a heavy-lidded look of complete male satisfaction. "Other than eliminating your need for that fake dick tonight? It accomplished a hell of a lot of pleasure and the best come I've had since the last time I had my cock buried in your sweet little pussy."

"It's last time it's going to be buried," she retorted, knowing it was an empty threat, but growing so furious now that her pride kicked in. "You should have stayed home, Rafe." She pushed away from him, sliding from the bed as she acknowledged she wasn't going to walk away from him unscathed. Not now, and not in the future. "You're not willing to fight for anything, are you, but I'm supposed to risk every part of my heart and soul for the pleasure of having you in my bed? Does this seem a little skewed to you somehow? Tell me, Rafe Callahan, do you even care what a woman would go through in this fucking county for you? Would it even make a difference if you knew you had broken her heart after she had already placed herself on the firing line?"

Rafe grunted behind her, watching the slender, graceful curve of her back as she moved from the bed.

She was just damned determined to piss him off, and if he was honest with himself then he admitted she was getting close to that edge.

It wouldn't be pretty once he let that anger build inside him. He'd pushed those emotions back in his teens, determined to never let them free again. He'd fought his last battle when his Clyde had died and Rafe had realized how many friends the man had lost when he had taken in the three orphan cousins when no one else would have them.

"You know, kitten, you amaze me," Rafe drawled. "You lay in this bed with that little toy of yours, fighting to get off, knowing damned good and well that it's my dick you're fantasizing about, and still, you're determined to run my ass off. I'd like to understand the logic behind that one."

There it was. The anger was beginning to simmer inside his chest.

"You know the logic behind it, Rafer." Soft, filled with an anger he couldn't help but acknowledge.

She kept her back to him, drew the silky robe over her naked body before quickly belting it. "You simply refuse to accept it. Why should I fight this alone when you refuse to even acknowledge it? When you don't even give a damn about what's happening around you or why?"

"Acknowledge what? That you need everyone else to approve of who you're sleeping with?" He slid her a hard look, determined to hold back the years of resentment and anger that had once been buried. He refused to allow her to resurrect them.

He stared up at the ceiling for a long moment before rolling from the bed himself and jerking his clothes off the floor. He'd be damned if he was going to fight with her over this. It simply wasn't worth it and reminded him far too much of the arguments he had with her sister the summer she had been killed.

Why the hell did they insist on attempting to tie together events that even he and his contacts couldn't prove had a connection? And they were the ones who had fought that battle all their lives.

No matter how hard they had tried, they couldn't find a single piece of evidence to link their parents' or their grandparents' deaths. And God knew they would have loved to.

Socks and jeans were pulled on quickly before he sat on the bed and shoved his feet into his boots. Rafe straightened again, collected his shirt from the chair where it had fallen and pulled it over his shoulders as well.

All the while, he was aware of her watching him, her eyes sheening with tears every few minutes before she blinked them back.

"You're a coward, Cami," he finally told her as he secured the buttons of his shirt. "A damned little coward that would cut her own nose off to spite her face if it meant her daddy wouldn't get mad at her. If it meant he would love her."

She turned away from him, hiding the truth from him, he thought, knowing that was exactly why she wanted him out of her bed after he fucked the want out of her.

God forbid her daddy should find out about it, Rafe thought furiously.

"You won't even try to fight against the Corbins or to understand why they want you and your cousins out of this county so badly," she argued fiercely.

"Oh hell, yes, I do know why." He gave a bark of mocking laughter. "The inheritances our mothers left us were far more important to those bastards than the grandchildren those daughters left. Especially grandsons that looked too much like their hated Callahan fathers."

"Then tell me why Marshal Roberts grieved for you?" she asked him, burying the knife that was the past deeper inside his soul and twisting it cruelly. "Why, Rafer, did he show up on my doorstep at a time he would be least noticed to attempt to warn me of something more than his wrath if I continued to see you?"

"Because he's a smart, manipulative, evil old bastard, and if he died tomorrow I wouldn't shed a tear for him," he growled, wondering himself if that were even true.

"Or is it because you're too damned scared to know the truth? All three of you are," she accused.

She didn't know the effect that accusation had on him. She couldn't have known the bitterness that filled him, Logan, and Crowe, or the questions that haunted them as well. Questions they had no hope of finding because those with the answers were dead.

"There's not a damned thing I'm scared of in this county, Cami," he informed her furiously as he stared at her back, watching as her shoulders tightened, as she refused to turn back to him.

"I really don't want to discuss this with you any longer," she informed him, her voice low as he stood watching her, the fact that she had her back to him bothering him more than he wanted to admit. "I have things to do in the morning, Rafer, and I don't have time to deal with you before I leave."

And she sure as hell didn't want anyone to know he was here, he thought mockingly. God forbid someone on her street would actually realize she was screwing one of the Callahan cousins.

Son of a bitch if he wasn't sick and damned tired of dealing with this bullshit with every lover he'd had. He'd thought Cami, with her fire, her restless courage, and warmth would have cared more about whatever they could feel growing between them than whether or not her daddy approved of her lover.

"Do you think I don't get damned tired of this, Cami? Why don't you just admit to the fact that you're so damned scared of daddy finding out you're fucking his daughter's killer that you'll come up with any excuse to put a wedge between us?" he snapped furiously. "And the least you could do is turn around and face me, damn you!"

She shook her head furiously, her hand lifting in rejection, and in that moment, he knew she was crying.

Damn her. He didn't want to see her tears. He didn't want to see the hurt in her eyes, or the pain that drifted down her cheeks.

His Cami should never cry. And especially not because of him.

The knowledge of those years was like a dagger shoving inside his gut. Why would she care? For God's sake, nothing was going to change the past, nothing would ever affect the barons until he, Logan, and Crowe established the vengeance they'd returned home to put in place.

Striding across the room, he gripped her shoulders, pulling her around as he gripped her chin with one hand and lifted her face to see it in the low light on her bedside table.

And she *was* crying.

Silent, miserable tears washed over her cheeks and dripped down her face to her neck. Her gray eyes were dark, filled with pain, and silently begging him for something he didn't know how to give her.

"You need—" Her voice hitched. "You need to leave."

She tried to pull away from him, to hide her tears from him again.

"And you'd rather stand here with your back to me and cry than fight for a damned thing you want. And you have the nerve to berate me?"

He released her slowly.

"You don't know what the hell you're talking about," she cried out roughly. "I haven't cared what *Daddy* thought since the day I realized he was moving the family to Aspen the summer I graduated. And I wasn't invited," she sneered tearfully. "You know Rafer; you should give your grandfather more credit. Because the two of you are more alike than you could ever know."

"Oh, baby, trust me, I've heard that accusation more times than you could ever throw it at me."

He released her quickly before striding a few steps away from her. "At least I'm willing to admit to it. I know damned good and well that I could be a clone of that old bastard. But you, Cami?" He flicked her an angry look. "You won't even admit to the fact that the only reason you've slipped out of my bed at dawn and run like a scared cat over the years is because you didn't want that son of a bitch father of yours to know who you were screwing."

He couldn't get around her. He couldn't touch her because he didn't trust himself. Because he was getting hard. He was so damned ready to fuck her again he couldn't stand it. And how much sense did that make? She had him so mad he could probably bite nails in half, and what was his response? A fucking hard dick and a need to push her over the bed and fill the liquid heat of her pussy with every throbbing inch of it.

"You think you just know it all," she bit out, the anger suddenly pouring through her, filling her voice, roughening it as her gaze flickered with the same aroused rage.

God, she was getting just as hot, filling with the same fiery blast of lust that he could feel striking at him.

"That son of a bitch father as you call him probably couldn't care less who I was fucking," she suddenly yelled back at him. "I'm so low on his fucking radar these days that he only calls me when he needs my signature at the nursing home to authorize payment for medical care. To see her, I have to pay for the expenses her medical insurance doesn't. Other than that, I'm lucky if I get to see my mother at all, and I sure as hell don't care what my so-called father thinks."

Hell, he hadn't known that. He couldn't imagine the anger Jaymi would have felt if she had known how their father was using his youngest daughter.

"He didn't even care when—"

He watched her face suddenly pale.

Her lips clamped closed as she turned quickly away from him once again and pushed her fingers through her hair before clenching the strands in a gesture of pain and rage.

Rafe's eyes narrowed on her.

"When what, Cami?" he asked softly. "What happened that he didn't care?"

He could feel a hard, tight ball of suspicion forming in his gut that Cami was hiding something from him. He'd always known when she was hiding something. It seemed even when she was a teenager, before Jaymi's death, he'd known how to read her much easier than any other female he'd known.

She had been a bright, curious teenager with what he had believed was no more than a strong crush. He'd never imagined in those days that he would end up wanting her more than he wanted air to breathe at times. Or that she would become as vital to him as he could sense her becoming.

Watching her, touching her, seeing her laugh and even cry were experiences he hungered for when it came to Cami.

"I don't want to talk about this any further," she told him, her expression closed and tight as she all but glared back at him over her shoulder. "It'll be dawn soon, Rafer, and you really need to leave. There's nothing going on, and there's nothing wrong except the fact that I really don't want to deal with the aggravation for a man who even refuses to see the danger that's chasing him. Not to mention the danger chasing his lovers. I have enough problems."

She had enough problems?

And she was lying to him. What the hell was going on besides those fucking phone calls?

Whatever it was, she had no intentions of telling him. He could see it in her closed expression, in her eyes, which despite the tears were filled with steely determination.

Damn her, he hated it when she lied to him.

His lips tightened as his head jerked up, nostrils flaring in anger.

As if he were going to just walk away after learning some bastard was calling her, threatening her. If he'd known Jaymi had been receiving such calls, he would have ensured she was protected better. But he hadn't. He couldn't bring her sister back for her, but he could do everything in his power to make damned sure that no one dared to hurt her as they had hurt her sister.

He would leave now. Not because she didn't want anyone to see him, because he was suddenly aware if he was seen, then catching the mysterious caller could become that much harder.

"Yeah, just let me get my ass out of here before someone sees who's slipping out of your house at night and most likely fucking your brains out every chance he gets," he snorted, his pride still smarting at the fact that she wanted him to leave, despite the fact that he needed to go. "And when you decide to be a woman willing to face me with the truth of whatever you're hiding, why don't you just let me know? Because I'll be damned if I'm going to get down on my knees and beg you for it, Cami. You're going to have to be woman enough to admit you want it."

He turned, grabbed the jacket that had fallen to the floor earlier, and stalked from the bedroom.

He hadn't really believed she would be so stubborn as long as he attempted to ensure no one saw him coming and going. He'd thought he could have her, tease her, and charm her. That there was something burning between them, unresolved and waiting to blossom into something they could have both found some peace within.

It seemed he would never learn. There was no peace to be found in Corbin County. And there was no love, no respect, and no hunger strong enough to combat whatever Cami suddenly found herself frightened of or fighting against. Or was there?

He'd damned sure be finding out what that "something" was, though. Who was calling Cami and threatening her over the relationship developing with Rafe? Or any of the other women who had been involved with the Callahan brothers? What was going on that none of them was aware of?

Perhaps he should have questioned it sooner. Even more, perhaps Cami was right. Because Jaymi wasn't the only woman who had died that summer who had been involved with the Callahan brothers. There had been one other. And that one had been planning to meet with Crowe to give him something, a picture she thought he would want to see.

The next time Crowe had seen her, though, she had been a picture in the paper, the latest victim of the Sweetrock Rapist.

As he slipped from the house, Rafe decided it was time to start questioning the past himself.

CHAPTER 12

Three weeks. Cami waited three weeks for Rafer to return. For him to come back to the house, demand entrance into both her home as well as her body. Twenty-one days later, he still hadn't arrived.

The waiting was destroying her nerves. She swore she had lost five of that extra ten pounds she carried pacing the darkened house each night.

She didn't bother turning on lights. What was the use?

The waiting had so stretched her nerves that she found herself unable to stand one more night of it.

She wasn't waiting another minute.

She was horny, she was pissed, she was bored, and she was ready to socialize. For at least a few hours.

Thankfully, the county's only bar and local nightspot was only a few blocks from her home, on the north side of the city square.

Bartlette's Bar and Grill also hosted the county's meals and drinks for the weekend socials. Throughout the rest of the year, customers could count on a band every weekend and, weather permitting, the wide sidewalk to spill out to when the crush of the crowd became overpowering.

Dressed in jeans, a soft blue sweater, and low-heeled boots, Cami made the walk to the establishment as quickly as possible without running.

There hadn't been phone calls in the past three weeks from her less-than-admiring "blocked" caller. Evidently he'd either considered her a lost cause, or he hadn't realized Rafer had been at the house for that last one. Whichever it was, there had been relative silence where the calls were concerned.

That didn't ease her nerves, if anything, it made them worse. It also made the walk to the bar one filled with trepidation and the knowledge that Jaymi hadn't been taken from her home the night she had been killed. She had been caught on the street going after Cami's medicine.

That fact was something her father reminded her of often. That if it hadn't been for her, Jaymi would have never been killed.

Cami knew better. The killer had been focused on Jaymi, because she knew something about him. She had finally realized his identity.

Unfortunately, she hadn't told anyone else her secret, neither had she written it in the journal she kept.

Turning the corner to the city square, it was to the sight of a larger than normal crowd.

Customers were definitely spilling out of the bar, sitting on the cement benches across the street in the well-lit square, or at the bistro tables that sat scattered around the wide sidewalk, and in the well-manicured area of the festively lit inner courtyard that sat inside the four sidewalks that comprised the city square.

"Cami!" Loud and boisterous, a feminine voice lifted amid the music and the chatter as a slender figure detached herself and all but skipped across the street to meet her. "It's about time your fine ass showed up."

Green eyes sparkling, her freckled face filled with laughter, the kindergarten teacher, Emma Walker, threw her arms around Cami's shoulders for a boisterous hug.

"Geeze, Emma, you'd think it's been years since you've seen me instead of days," Cami laughed as she hugged the shorter girl back.

"It's been forever since you've come out to play." Emma

stepped back, almost bouncing, laughter bubbling from her lips and gleaming in the gem-bright green of her eyes.

"Well, I'm definitely coming out to play tonight," she informed the other girl.

"And just in time for some juicy, juicy gossip." Emma rolled her eyes expressively as she linked her arm with Cami and began pulling her down the block. "Tell me you were not at the Ramsey Ranch just after the blizzard wrapped around Rafe Callahan like a vine?"

"Like a vine?" Her brows arched as she glanced over at her friend. "I don't remember being wrapped at all. Locked against that wide manly chest, definitely."

Regardless of what Rafer thought, there was no shame in what she had done, or in having others know she had done it. What terrified her was losing him.

Emma came to a hard stop, staring up at her in shock.

The chill evening air almost brought a chill to Cami's spine. That, or the fact that Emma was staring at her as though she had just admitted she had the plague, or was some alien creature from another planet.

"Close your mouth, Em," Cami advised her ruefully. "I didn't kill anyone, I just kissed him."

"Oh my God, and wasn't it just so good?" Emma breathed out in awe now. "Tell me all about it. No one in this county will even admit to speaking to one of the Forbidden Triplets."

"Forbidden Triplets?" Cami didn't know about that one. "They're cousins, not triplets."

"But they look enough alike to be triplets," Emma protested. "And don't change the subject. Tell me about that kiss. It had to have been simply divine."

It was all Cami could do to hold back her laughter. Strawberry-red curls fell to Emma's shoulders and framed a delicate, heart-shaped face.

"Why did it have to be? It could have been wet and slobbery," she suggested as they began walking toward the crowd once again.

Emma snorted. "I rather doubt it. But if it was, then I still want to know. Now tell me."

"It was okay." She shrugged. "It wasn't slobbery or anything."

"Just okay?" Disappointment rang in the other woman's voice. "It wasn't earth-shattering or ground-shaking, or made your toes delicious?"

It was all those things and so very much more.

Cami assumed a thoughtful look to her expression. "It was okay." She nodded decisively as though that were the final word on the Callahan kiss.

"Oh, wow." There was a definite pout on Emma's lips now. "I think I've just been crushed."

Cami laughed again as they joined the crowd gathered on the sidewalk just outside the bar.

The waitress, a young woman Cami had gone to school with, took her drink order, as well as an order for hot wings.

She wasn't particularly hungry, but neither had she eaten that day. She was more nervous than anything and eating wasn't any higher on her list of priorities than it had been the day before.

As the first drink hit her system though, Cami felt the softening haze of relaxation begin to ease through her. At the first offer to dance, she was in the middle of the street with Dean Meyers, the Phys. Ed. teacher at the high school, and several dozen other couples, as a rousing beat filled the night.

The music faded and a round of applause for the band filled the street. Turning away from her dance partner, she was unaware of the large body that had eased in behind her.

She became more than aware of it though as his hard arms wrapped around her, and the once-rousing music turned slow and seductive as the bar lights strung across the streets dimmed to match the slower beat.

"Rafer," she whispered, her finger clenching on the hard biceps that tensed beneath her touch.

She was aware of not just the couples in the street, but also those along the sidewalk watching. She could feel all eyes on her, watching, dissecting the dance.

"You can slap me and stalk away if you want," he suggested, his expression hard, lashes lowered over the sapphire of his eyes.

"I told you, Rafer, I wasn't ashamed of you," she told him. "It's not shame."

"In three weeks you haven't called," he told her coolly.

"Neither have you."

"You don't answer the phone when I call," he growled, his head lowering until he was nearly nose to nose with her.

"You would have to actually call to find out, now, wouldn't you?" she said with a heavy, false sweetness.

His gaze narrowed on her as his hands dropped from her waist to her hips, drawing her closer to him as he placed his hand at the back of her head and pressed it to his chest.

She couldn't resist letting him hold her.

It had been three weeks. Three long, lonely weeks.

"Any more phone calls?" he asked her as they moved and swayed to the seductive rhythm of the music.

She shook her head, loathe to allow anything to intrude on the magical moment they were sharing.

She expected him to say something more. Some kind of I-told-you-so. A reminder that he had warned her there was nothing to it. Marshal Roberts messing with her head and nothing more.

When he said nothing, she relaxed against him, luxuriating in the warmth of his body wrapping around her, filling her, drawing her closer to him.

The dance was a moment out of time. It was a slow, unconsciously binding moment, one she didn't know how to fight.

As it drew to a close, he pulled back and stared down at her for a long, unbroken moment.

Just when she thought his head would lower that last inch and his lips would touch hers where God and everyone could see the intimacies they shared, he pulled back instead.

"Rafer?" she questioned, wondering why he suddenly seemed so distant.

"Later," he said softly. "I'll call later."

She stepped to the curb as he pulled from her completely, then turned and walked away.

She watched as he crossed the street, the self confidence in his walk, the strength of his shoulders, and the lift of his head drawing more than one feminine gaze.

What the hell was he up to?

"And the gossip ensues," Emma drawled behind her. "Not only does Rafer Callahan show up, but so does his cousin, Miss Anna Corbin."

Cami turned to her friend, then followed the direction of her look.

Another bitter loss of her past, Cami thought, as she saw the young woman entering the bar with another familiar face.

Amelia Sorenson.

She and Cami had once been as close as sisters. Collaborators, conspirators, and cohorts, they used to say.

Until that final year in college when Amelia had broken all ties with her and that friendship has disappeared.

And people wondered why she avoided commitment like the plague.

"Her daddy let her out to play?" Cami questioned quietly in amusement. The fact that Anna Corbin rarely came to Sweetrock was no secret.

"Oh, sweetie, that so is not the end of it," Emma drawled.

The most interesting bit of gossip was the fact that the Corbin son, and heir William, Crowe's uncle, and James Corbin, the patriarch, were given a fierce, heated dressing-down by Miss Anna. The first of the week when he and daddy Willy were arguing with Saul Rafferty over the fact that they couldn't run the Callahan cousins out of town.

Said to be the spitting image of her deceased aunt, Kimberly Corbin, and named for her, Anna Corbin insisted that the Corbin, Rafferty, and Roberts families were rumored to be temperamental and a pain in the ass when it came to authority. Of course, how anyone could be certain, Cami didn't know. Her parents had hired tutors when she was young, then sent her to private schools in California and Texas until college. She was currently attending a very exclusive Eastern college and vacations were always spent in some exotic location with her family.

"Oh, really?" Cami asked, silently prodding Emma for information.

"Definitely, really," Emma assured her. "She insisted that the Corbin family was turning into monsters where her cousins were concerned, and if they weren't all careful, she was going to return to fix the situation herself. I hear she dropped her little bomb, then lifted that pert little nose of hers and stalked right out of the house and headed to Amelia's. The Sorensons are rather close with the Corbins I hear."

The last Cami had heard of Amelia, she had detested the Corbins, but that had been years ago, Cami admitted silently.

"And who was sharing all this interesting information?" Cami arched her brows as she sat on the low cement wall behind her and watched as Amelia and Anna stepped from the bar and found an empty table.

The blowup was recounted by a maid who was promptly fired, paid off, and forced to leave the county, I hear. No one said the Corbins don't know how to move quickly or live with enough drama to create their own soap opera," the other woman said, laughing.

"I hadn't heard any of it," Cami admitted.

"Because you've stayed locked in your room rather than joining us in the teachers' lounge," Emma pointed out. "But dearest, that's just the tip of the iceberg, if the gossip I'm hearing is true. Teachers, administrators, and entire families are now discussing the past, resurrecting it, dissecting it, and coming closer by the day to rejudging the Callahan cousins." Emma tossed her head with amused mockery. "Bastards. They should have done that, what? Twelve years ago?"

Emma wasn't a native of Sweetrock or Corbin County. She well understood school and county politics, but that didn't mean she agreed with any of them.

"Twelve years ago," Cami agreed softly.

Emma's expression morphed swiftly to regret. "Oh hell, Cami, I'm sorry. I forgot that was the same summer—"

Cami gave her head a quick shake to silence her friend. She didn't want to hear the rest of it.

"It's okay, Emma," she promised her. "But the time line is right. And I agree with you. They should have thought of this then, rather than now."

Emma sat down beside her, her hands braced on the edge of the seat as she breathed out heavily. "My parents would have had a stroke had a child been treated so cruelly in school as I heard they were. Your barons, as they're called, have a lot to answer for, my dear."

"They're not my anything," Cami sighed. "And the influence they had then was strong, Emma. It still is, though it's diluted a bit over the years."

"Damned good thing," Emma sighed. "I would have been fired had another child been treated that way. I would have had to have my say, you know."

"That red hair," Cami agreed softly. "But I know what you mean. I had a few rather heated fights myself with several individuals, despite the fact that they were out of school."

They were silent then, staring at the dancers, occasionally glancing at Anna Corbin and Amelia Sorenson as they seemed deep in conversation.

"Tell me," Emma's voice lowered. "Was there ever a connection proven between the grandparents', parents', and Clyde Ramsey's deaths?"

Cami's head swung around to stare at the other girl in surprise. "Excuse me?"

Emma frowned. "There was no connection?"

"Not as far as the cousins believe. And if they had believed it, we would have heard about it," Cami answered without answering the underlying question regarding the connection.

"Damn, I was hoping for more county-wide conspiracy and mystery," Emma sighed ruefully.

Cami gave a light, forced laugh, hoping Emma didn't catch the fact that she was uncomfortable with the subject.

It took a few moments, but she was able to steer the conversation back to the school, the teachers, and the upcoming socials.

She didn't want to talk about Rafe, and unless there was more information than simply gossip, then she didn't want to talk about any other Corbin either.

After a final drink, Cami rose and wished her friend a good night before turning and crossing the street to head home.

As she rounded the first block and the lights became a bit dimmer and the streets much quieter, she could feel a distinct tingle along the back of her shoulders.

Once, long ago, she and Jaymi used to play a game. Jaymi would follow her, or Cami would follow her sister, and the one who caught sight of the other the quickest was the winner.

Even Tye, Jaymi's husband, had joined in the game while he and Jaymi had dated.

Cami had developed a feeling, a tension at her back that let her know whenever Jaymi was stalking her. She could feel that tingle now, but she knew it wasn't her sister following her.

Her steps quickened.

Gripping her keys tightly in her fist, the longest key extending between two of her clenched fingers, she watched the shadows suspiciously. She wasn't panicking yet, but she knew someone was out there. Waiting. Watching.

For a moment, she was drawn back to her childhood.

Jaymi and Tye laughing as Cami had managed to evade them the last day before he shipped off to Iraq.

The Navajo her sister had married had taught her how to move much more quietly than she ever had over those months. She'd gotten good enough to evade Jaymi, but not Tye himself.

"She'll be hell to catch if some bastard ever decides to chase her in the dark," Tye had bragged on her that night. *"Little sister will know how to evade, and when I come back, she'll learn how to fight."*

But Tye hadn't come back. Six weeks before he was due to ship out, he'd been caught in an explosion and killed instantly.

She hadn't just lost her own best friend that day, but she had also lost her sister. A vital part of Jaymi had died the day the Army officer and chaplain had arrived to tell her the news.

As the memory dissipated, she realized she was doing as Tye had taught her, weaving in and out of the shadows, never taking a straight path, using the trees as cover.

She never walked beneath the street lights, and didn't hesitate to walk on someone's lawn rather than venturing too closely to the pooled light beneath the tall posts.

It wasn't long before the sensation eased, though that feeling of tension that still gathered inside her assured her someone was still out there.

She entered the house by the back door, stepped in, and locked the door back quickly.

She didn't turn the lights on.

She didn't turn on the television.

Slipping up to her bedroom, she spent most of the night staring at the locked bedroom door and wondering who the hell was following her.

CHAPTER 13

The next morning Cami awoke as the sun poured into the sky-light over her bed, still dressed in the jeans and sweater and sneakers she'd put on after returning home the night before.

The boots would have been impractical if she'd had to slip out her bedroom window and make her way along the roof to where she could drop to the ground more safely.

The knowledge, or the feeling, someone had been following her had spooked her. She was on edge, restless, and that Saturday morning she was just plain pissed.

That was not Marshal Roberts playing with her head, no matter what Rafer believed.

As she poured another cup of the fragrant brew, the sound of the cell ringing had her quickly reaching for it and checking the caller ID. She prayed it was Rafer.

She'd actually swallowed her pride and called him the night before, but it had gone instantly to voicemail, an indication the phone was either turned off, or in a dead zone.

A frown pulled at her as she activated the call and brought the phone to her ear.

"Good afternoon, Jack?" she greeted him, a question in her voice.

"Hey, Cami, I'm pulling onto your street," Jack Townsend answered back. "Do you have a few minutes to talk? I have something I want to tell you."

"Sure. I'll be waiting at the door."

Disconnecting, she moved through the house to the door and opened it as Jack's tow truck pulled into the driveway. She couldn't imagine why he was at her house that early, or what he could want. She hadn't taken her car in since he'd returned it after the blizzard, more than a month ago. Well, actually, she thought, closer to two months.

He wasn't alone, though; his wife, Jeannie, was with him. The petite blond lifted her hand in a wave as she practically jumped from the truck and joined her husband as he came around the front, glaring at her.

"I keep telling her I'll help her out," he groused as they reach the front porch. "But Short Stuff insists on jumping. One of these days she's going to break a leg."

Jeannie punched him in the shoulder lightly with her fist as she laughed back at him. The love between them was apparent, though. It was actually so apparent that the gossip-mongers loved attempting to cast suspicion on it.

"Come on in," Cami invited, still confused at the visit. "There's fresh coffee and store bought cinnamon rolls."

Cami led the way into the kitchen after closing and locking the door securely behind them.

She admitted she had become paranoid in the past weeks. The phone calls might have stopped, but that feeling of being watched had her wary. Perhaps her caller had grown tired of calling and decided to act.

She couldn't tell if the caller knew about the last night Rafe had been at the house or not. The suspense was making her as nervous as hell, though.

"I thought it best to stop in and talk to you, versus the phone," Jack stated as she poured the coffee and set cups in front of both Jack and his wife at the kitchen table. "Some conversations you simply don't trust to normal channels of communication."

The last comment had her tensing.

"Jack's paranoid," Jeannie admitted. "We've received a few calls warning him about consorting with Callahans." She rolled her eyes. "I swear, you'd think we were involved in political intrigue or something. Or perhaps a return to the Middle Ages? Tell me, Cami, are the Callahans traitors perhaps? Did they steal national secrets? Attempt to assassinate the president?"

Consorting with Callahans. "No," Cami said softly, her gaze meeting Jack's. "But I've been getting similar phone calls."

Cami quickly related news of the calls she had been receiving to Jack and watched the couple exchange a worried look. She omitted the visit by Marshal Roberts, but over the weeks she had been surprised that no one else had mentioned it. Whoever had seen Rafe's grandfather here evidently wasn't telling anyone else.

"Hell." Jack plowed his fingers through his dark hair as he sat back in the chair slowly. "Did you tell the sheriff?"

Cami shook her head.

"I'd suggest it," Jack warned her. "I called Archer first thing, not that we've been able to trace the calls; they don't last long enough. But at least I have a paper trail if I have to cap someone's ass for messing with what's mine." He shot his wife a quick look, the possessiveness and concern touching.

"The thing is," he continued, "I was worried enough I called Dad and Taggert. Dad acted so damned strange that Jeannie and I went to Denver over the weekend to talk to him. They had some very interesting information. Some things I had forgotten over the years and a few things I didn't know about."

As Jack continued talking, with Jeannie injecting information where she remembered a few things, Cami began remembering things she had forgotten as a girl as well.

The Corbins' attempts to take Crowe Mountain just after Crowe's parents' deaths were well known. What Cami hadn't heard was the Corbins' attempts to destroy the Ramsey ranch after Clyde Ramsey, Rafe's uncle, had taken all three boys in.

Corbin hadn't managed to destroy the property, but he had managed to affect it financially for several years.

Then there had been the acts of vandalism, cattle missing or poisoned, equipment sabotaged, and several pastures salted.

As the Corbins were targeting Crowe, Logan's grandparents, Saul and Tandy, had gone after Logan's inheritance: the two-story house in town that was listed as one of the first houses built in the county, as well as a cash inheritance that at the time had come to more than a million dollars.

Crowe's trust fund was larger, the inherited account coming from the trust his mother had inherited from her grandparents as well as the property and cash her parents had added to it. She had died only days after coming into the inheritance and within hours of signing the will that made her only son her beneficiary.

Then there were the bits of information that seemed more sinister. The night the three couples had been killed, the sheriff had closed the accident site completely off. Only the coroner and a young attorney Wayne Sorenson had been allowed onto the site for hours.

Even Clyde Ramsey, Marshal Roberts's brother-in-law, had been barred from the site. In those early-morning hours he received a call from a ranch hand in the area who suspected Clyde's niece and her husband had been in the accident along with the Raffertys' daughter and son-in-law, and in the Corbins' case, their daughter and son-in-law as well as the newborn infant daughter—the only child her parents had taken with them to Denver that day while supposedly visiting friends.

It had been learned later that it hadn't been friends they were visiting. Rather, it had been a lawyer and a well-known resort developer. The sons of JR and Eileen Callahan, the first Callahans to have considered turning their property into a resort, had passed that dream on to their sons.

Nothing had been mentioned about the sons passing the legacy on to their sons. Or why the daughters of the barons who had married the Callahan sons would have considered something their families would have found so heinous.

The bodies had been burned beyond recognition, and only DNA had confirmed the identities of the dead. The coroner had quickly identified the three couples and the infant before the burials had been hastily arranged.

That was when the campaign to ostracize the cousins

began, Jack told Cami, though it had been there even before the parents' deaths. So much so that the three couples were looking at selling Crowe Mountain and the Rafferty house in town and gathering together the inheritances of the three women and buying a ranch farther west. There had even been talk that Clyde Ramsey had discussed selling his property as well and following them.

Kimberly Anna Corbin Callahan had been so enraged with her parents and brother that she had told several people that despite her brother's affection for her daughter, she would never allow any of them around her. Anna was done with her parents as well as the brother she had once idolized. She had even had them removed as secondary beneficiaries on her will. The papers had actually been signed with an attorney in Denver that day. Clyde had been named as that beneficiary barring any children Crowe or her daughter might have had.

Her daughter hadn't had a chance to see her first birthday, let alone reach maturity and the chance to conceive. She had barely been three months old at her death.

Then there had been the confrontation at the funerals. With only one funeral home, the three couples had been there together. Shockingly, the wives had been placed in another room and separated from their husbands. At first. Until Clyde had threatened to sue the funeral home, the director, and the families involved. Then, when Crowe and Logan had attempted to go in to attend their parents' funerals, their way had been blocked by their grandfathers and, in Crowe's case, by his uncle as well.

The entire county had attended those funerals and had seen the families' treatment of the cousins. Most of the county worked the Corbin and Rafferty ranches or in some other way benefited from their business. They hadn't been able to afford backing the boys and hurting their own finances or positions.

The result had been the steady unearned condemnation of an entire community toward three young, grief-stricken boys.

Clyde Ramsey had done the best he could by taking not just his own nephew in but also the others and raising them himself. His own grief at losing his treasured niece, and his inability to understand the hatred directed at their children had nearly destroyed him.

Clyde had suffered from the decision, though. Ranch hands quit on him, accidents happened around the ranch, and he was constantly warned to leave the county. But stubbornness had been set in his bones and he had refused to go, even as he advised the boys to fight against them. That this was their parents' home, they owned part of it, and they should never forget that fact.

As Cami fixed more coffee, Jack broached another subject she hadn't expected.

"Did you know about the phone calls Jaymi got before she was killed?" he asked gently.

Cami remained silent for long moments, finished the coffee, then turned back with the pot to refill the cups. She needed time to gather the strength to talk about Jaymi. No one mentioned her anymore, and Cami found it hurt more with each passing year.

She gave a brief nod as she sat down again. "I was here when she got a few of them. They were similar to the ones I'm receiving, except Jaymi figured out who her caller was a few nights before Thomas Jones—" She couldn't say it. She had relived that part of the past too much in the last few weeks the way it was. "I know that voice, too though," she said fiercely. "I know it; I just haven't been able to place it."

She described the voice. The regret. The hint of tears.

Jack nodded. "I remember that though Jaymi didn't say anything about realizing who the caller was, she left the social early that night, and she appeared angry."

"She was angry when she came back to the apartment too." Cami swallowed tightly. "When she answered the call that night she went to the bedroom. I'm not sure, but I think I heard her say something about her knowing why her caller hated 'him' so bad. Though I don't know who the 'him' was, and she wouldn't tell me. I always suspected it was Rafe they were discussing."

Jack and Jeannie exchanged a frown, though Cami didn't see a sense of recognition in their gazes either.

When Jack turned back to her, he leaned forward intently, his gaze somber. "Dad was managing the garage then. But do you remember the accident Jaymi had about a month before she was killed?"

Cami nodded warily. "She nearly went over one of the mountain cliffs that day."

It had terrified her, and Cami knew Jaymi had been shaken by it. Her brakes had failed on one of the long mountain roads. Though it hadn't been the one the Callahans, their parents, or Clyde Ramsey had gone over.

"I'd rather you didn't mention this to anyone who doesn't need to know. The sheriff knows, but Dad swears her brake lines had been messed with," Jack told Cami as he rubbed at his jaw in frustration. "He remembers it as clear as day, and there's not a lot Dad remembers real clear these days. But he remembers Jaymi, because he swears that when he saw those brake lines after he towed the car in he told Mother Jaymi would be dead before the summer was out. He knew someone had tried to kill her and the sheriff, Archer's father, didn't seem interested in believing him when he went to talk to him. The lines were clean-cut, not frayed. Someone sabotaged those lines and they hadn't meant for her to survive her drive back from Aspen."

Cami's chest tightened. She could feel the fear rising inside her at the knowledge that someone had tried to kill her sister before Thomas Jones had taken her.

That affirmation that she wasn't just paranoid, that there was definitely more going on than Rafer wanted to admit to, actually terrified her.

Jack's eyes were somber, filled with regret. But Cami knew she wasn't able to hide that fear or the shock in her own gaze. "Jaymi never said anything about the break lines being cut. Just that the brakes must have been bad."

She should have remembered that. She should have questioned it herself.

"Because she didn't know," Jack admitted, his voice hoarse

as his expression twisted painfully. "Dad didn't tell her, and trust me, Cami, neither myself nor my brother knew either. Dad says he received several anonymous phone calls that week warning him that it would be a shame if something happened to his wife and sons because he didn't know how to keep his mouth shut about things that didn't concern him. So he warned Jaymi, several times, to be careful. And he lived in fear of another accident."

It wasn't Jack's fault. She couldn't blame him. She wouldn't. But she could feel the rage that no one had warned Jaymi, and the knowledge that the threat against her sister had existed months before her death was heart-rending.

Cami shook her head as she fought back her tears. To know Jaymi's life was in danger even before she became the target of a serial killer, and hadn't known it, terrified Cami and broke her heart at once.

Even worse, to know that someone Jaymi had trusted, someone she had called a friend, hadn't given her a clearer warning tore at the foundations of friendship that Cami had always believed in.

But no matter who had wanted to kill her or who hadn't warned her, still, it had been a serial killer who had stolen Jaymi's chance to live. And that part confused her more each time she learned something new.

If Jack's father had warned her, though, maybe Jaymi would have been more careful. At least for a few more days. A few more hours. Long enough that Cami was certain she could have convinced Jaymi to tell her who the caller was. Perhaps long enough that Thomas Jones could have been caught before he killed his last victim. Long enough that maybe Jaymi would have trusted Rafer enough to tell him the truth.

A warning of danger and a few more days could have made a difference between Jaymi living and dying.

"It was Thomas Jones that killed her, Jack, not a mechanical failure that your father didn't warn her of," Cami finally whispered, more for his benefit than because she believed it. Because she knew in her heart that Jaymi had been so confident, so determined, that she would have never listened.

Or perhaps she had simply been that determined to join her husband in whatever afterlife he inhabited, no matter the cost.

"Let's say the coincidence is too fortuitous to suit me, just as it was for my father. Jaymi's death is why he left Sweetrock and it's why he's continually begging me and Jeannie to move to Denver with him and Taggert. He says there's something evil in this county, Cami, and I wonder if he's not right," Jack stated, his voice rough, his gaze filled with misery. "And remember, the FBI profile on those murders said there were two or more men working together. If that's true, then Jones had a partner, if not two."

"And serial killers don't just stop killing," she told Jack even as a chill raced up her spine and his declaration that there was an evil in Corbin County echoed in her head. "But I will be careful, Jack. I'm not Jaymi. I promise you, I won't ignore the bastard when I realize who he is, nor will I keep my mouth shut about his identity."

Because she had been warned now. Warned that whoever was watching her, calling her, had targeted her sister for the same reason. Because of Rafer. Because they were terrified the Callahans would develop ties to the county that would keep them there, no matter the cost.

They should have already realized that ties or no ties, the Callahan cousins weren't going anywhere.

"Does Rafe know any of this?" Cami asked.

Jack shook his head. "I tried to call him a few times this morning as we drove back from Denver, but the call went to voice mail." Just as hers had. Now she was beginning to worry about Rafer and his cousins.

"I'm assuming he's out of town, because the ranch looked deserted when we drove by."

"I tried to call as well," she whispered. "He didn't answer my call, either."

Jeannie chose that moment to lean forward, her gaze dark with pain.

"Cami, the thing is, whatever's going on has been going on for years," Jeannie said then. "They need to just leave; they'll never have any peace as long as they're in Corbin County, nor will anyone who's loyal to them." She flashed her husband a speaking look as she made the last comment.

Cami knew that wasn't about to happen. The Callahans, were back to stay. Their inheritance had demanded they stay, and in receiving it, if she had heard the rumors correctly, they had to stay at least five more years before they could leave.

"And they'll never have any pride if they give in that easily and run," Cami sighed, a part of her understanding why Rafe and his cousins refused to sell out and leave. "Their roots are here, Jeannie. They're not going to destroy that last tie to their parents."

It wasn't her place to mention the inheritance or the terms of it. That was Rafer and his cousins' business. And anyone who made the effort to read the court records in detail.

"Have you told the sheriff about all of this?" Cami asked the couple then.

Jack shook his head. "Phone calls, yes, the rest no. I think you should tell Rafe first, Cami. Tell him and then trust him and his cousins to take care of the rest of it."

She pushed her fingers through her hair as she tried to think of another alternative. Going to Rafer with this right now would only end up in the inability to keep her hands off him. She would end up in his bed so fast it would make both their heads spin. Besides, he hadn't believed her when she had tried to tell him her suspicions once before.

"Do you think Archer can be trusted?" she asked Jack then, remembering that Archer's father had been the one who had ignored the signs that someone had targeted Jaymi.

Jack sighed heavily. "I'd trust him with my life, but I wouldn't trust anyone with Jeannie's, so I can't answer that question for you, Cami. If you're going to continue seeing Rafe, then you have to tell him what's going on."

"I'm not seeing him," she objected as she leaned back in her chair and crossed her arms over her breasts defensively. "Just ask him, he'll tell you." She was, in his words, his occasional fuck, right? "I just want to know what's going on and why the grandparents hate him and his cousins so much."

"And someone doesn't want you to know why," Jack reminded her. "You be careful, and you watch your back. It hurt to lose your sister, Cami, but she left us in spirit the day she learned her Tye was dead. Losing you, Cami, would break too many hearts, because you've always been a part of the community, and a part of your friends, Cami."

Cami stared back at them for a second before lowering her arms to the table and giving them a bitter smile. "No, Jack, everyone loved Jaymi. They tolerate me."

"Jaymi was distant," Jack sighed. "She was just counting the days until she could be with her Tye again. Even moving from Sweetrock didn't interest her, despite your dad's insistence. Everyone knew that was his plan. He wanted her to be where there were more opportunities for her. Where her friendship with the Callahans wouldn't affect her so much."

Everyone knew but Cami. Why didn't it surprise her to know that her father had plans to leave Sweetrock and hadn't even thought to tell her about it?

"What had they been waiting on?" she asked, wondering why Jaymi hadn't told her. "They could have left at any time."

"They were waiting for you to get out of high school from what Jaymi said," Jack related. "Your parents didn't want you to have to deal with changing schools."

No, her parents hadn't wanted her to be with them, period, she guessed. If they had, they would have told her their plans rather than remaining silent.

Even her mother.

God, that hurt. Even Cami's mother had remained silent about the move. Had they been that determined to escape her?

At least she knew Jaymi hadn't intended to leave. Tye was buried closer to Sweetrock than to Aspen. She would have never left him.

"We have to go." Jack glanced at his wife before they rose from the table. "I'm sorry, Cami; I know what Dad did was wrong—"

"It wasn't you, Jack." She shook her head at the apology

as she rose from her own seat. "And thank you for coming to tell me what you had learned."

He gave a sharp nod before glancing at his wife and wrapping his arm around her. "You know, Dad might be right. Maybe it is time we leave Corbin County. The lock certain families have on this place sickens my gut, and to learn how they use their influence only makes me ashamed to be a part of this place."

"I can't blame you for feeling that way," she said as she faced them, knowing that wasn't an option she was willing to choose yet.

Once everyone who disagreed with those families was gone, who would be left to teach the children differently?

She couldn't help but consider the kids she taught. Third graders were sharp as hell; they saw so much more than people realized and were so much more influenced that it was frightening.

As Jack and his wife left, Cami glanced around the kitchen and breathed out heavily.

Tonight was the Spring Fling Social, the first night of the year's social activities. For all its undercurrents of intrigue, Corbin County and its residents had made inroads to protect their children that she hadn't heard of in other towns.

The weekend social gathering that was held in the town square during clear weather had begun unofficially the night before. The crowd that had gathered had been part of the volunteers stringing lights and decorating for the first weekend to celebrate spring. And if the weather didn't cooperate, then they gathered in the large community center.

Every Saturday night beginning in April with the Spring Fling Social, one of the dressier, more formal events held, the socials kicked off. Cami doubted there was a single family that didn't attend, and very few children that didn't spend the entire weekend at the community center.

The town square would be lit up like Christmas, the businesses surrounding it closed early, except the town's single bar, located in the town square which would remain open through most of the night and well past the last call.

The socials were open to all, but they were heavily monitored and the alcohol strictly watched. Through the years, the event had had its ups and downs, but the dedication of the city council and the parents involved with the project kept it going.

The Spring Fling Social itself was highly anticipated. The winter months closed down the socials to allow for skiing activities and the influx of tourism for the skiing season in the surrounding counties. Several outlying ranches in those surrounding counties had turned into resorts with a focus on winter activities, making participation in the socials much lower during the skiing months. April saw the winter activities tapering off, though. The snow began to slack and finally melt. Frozen streams and icy rivers melted and began to run with an abundance of fish and wildlife as the trees began to green and their tiny buds made their debut.

And for the third year in a row, Cami didn't have a date. She could have had one. If Rafe had returned her phone call, she might have had one.

She had her dress, her shoes, and all her accessories, and she was driving herself to the social, unless she wanted to walk it the second night in a row. Of course, driving meant finding a parking spot which would be impossible. Vehicles were already backing up along her street. On the other hand, finding company to walk home with wouldn't be a problem.

It would be decidedly harder for anyone to follow her, and not be noticed than it was the night before.

For a moment, she wondered if Rafe would have attended if she had asked him or even if she had simply left him a message.

What did he look like in dress black or a tux? Would he have danced with her? Would the women at the social watch her with envy and longing as Rafer danced with her, as they had the night before?

And why the hell had he left so abruptly come to think of it? This spring was definitely beginning rather oddly, and Cami wasn't entirely certain she was comfortable with it.

On second thought, hell, no, she wasn't comfortable with it.

And yes, she thought, Rafer would have danced with her again. He would have held her close as she laid her head against his shoulder, swaying to the music and counting the time until they could leave and find a bed.

She shook her head quickly, trying to chase away the images running through her mind and the needs that rose inside her from those images.

Three weeks. Too damned long.

As she headed to the shower she couldn't stop the visions of sexual satiation from dancing through her head. Long, hot kisses, the sight of his lips at her breasts, covering a hard, sensitive nipple, his cheeks hollowing as he sucked at the hardened tip, flicking it with the tip of his tongue.

The feel of those lips kissing their way down her torso, running over her belly, moving between her thighs. The feel of his tongue fucking her.

She wanted to moan in need. She was on the verge of screaming in frustration and making a decision she knew she would end up regretting.

Of course, he hadn't even tried to follow her home, otherwise he would have caught sight of her shadow the night before. If he'd had satisfying that hunger in mind, then he wouldn't have left her for a second.

She had told him to stay away from her; he was only doing what she had demanded. But even then she had been honest with herself, albeit silently.

She didn't want him out of her life. She wanted to change the past. She wanted to make things different. She wanted to be able to go to that damned social and dance in his arms before coming home to sleep in them.

She wanted everything she had dreamed of having, everything she had fantasized about having. She wanted Rafe until she was ready to cry with the frustration building inside her.

And Rafe was the one thing she couldn't have. The one man denied herself. The only man who could destroy her soul.

She wished it was only shame that held her from him. Shame would have been so very easy for her to conquer. The pleasure she found in his arms had shame beat all to hell. The ecstasy that surged bright and hot through her body as her release swept over her would have had such an edge on shame that it wouldn't have stood a chance.

No matter how much she wished differently though, it wasn't shame.

And she couldn't even say in all honesty that it had anything to do with the fact that the county refused to accept the Callahans. She knew it didn't.

The county had changed a lot in the twenty years since the Callahan cousins' parents had died. The school board wasn't from the same deeply rooted families that it had once been. Their ties to the community were new, their influence by the Corbins not the same as it had been with past board members despite Marshal Roberts's presence there.

The principal at the school where Cami worked lived in Aspen rather than Corbin County or Sweetrock. The mayor had been in the military for years before returning to the county and had run his election on the fact that such political cronyism would come to an end.

Not that she expected it to happen, but it wasn't as pervasive as it had been when Cami had been a teenager.

Corbin County was changing, and it had been changing for several years. But for all the changes that had occurred, it was still mired in the past and the wealth of the barons.

The barons were old now, though. Each man was nearing his seventies, and though they might yet have several years left in them, still their strength was waning, and with it, their power.

And they knew it.

She had seen it in Marshal Roberts's eyes, that knowledge that he wasn't the man he had been thirty-two years ago, and Corbin County wasn't the county it was thirty-two years ago either.

If they had killed Rafer's grandparents, parents, and uncle, and if they had been behind the deaths that had swept the county twenty-two years ago, then it wouldn't happen as easily now. The mayor hadn't been just a part of the military; he had been rather high-ranking as well. Such tactics, despite his ability to adopt them, didn't seem to be his style.

They were still dangerous, though, and she believed that was part of the message Marshal Roberts had tried to get across to her that night.

Their power was waning, but it was by no means gone. They would still make very formidable enemies.

CHAPTER 14

The dress was rich black and gold velvet with silver thread trimming the scalloped bodice and emphasizing her full breasts.

The empire waist of the design gave her such a delicate, fragile appearance that Rafe wondered that he hadn't managed to break her each time he'd fucked her as though he were dying for her.

The short, sassy cut of her hair framed her fine-boned face in a multitude of browns, the natural highlights almost fascinating to him each time he'd concentrated on them.

And her gray eyes. She watched the dancing with a sense of hunger, the slow, sensual sway of the bodies holding her attention as though she was imagining herself on the floor as well: What would it feel like? How would it be to be held against his body, to feel him moving against her?

At least, it damned well better be him she was fantasizing about. And how the hell was he supposed to ensure it when so much distance separated them? When the past and the whole of Corbin County stood between them?

What was he doing here? He should have never let Crowe and Logan convince him to accompany them here. What was Crowe doing even wanting to attend this crap? Hell, they'd even avoided it as teenagers, so why were they here now?

Had Crowe lost his mind as he'd matured? Perhaps taken

a bullet to the head? Had he somehow lost his mind? Crowe was sure making some odd-assed decisions lately.

Attending the Spring Fling Social was just one of those decisions.

Everyone in Corbin County seemed to attend the more important socials, as City Hall liked to call them. Through the spring, summer, and early fall, every Saturday the county paid for either a band or DJ and the guests partied, sometimes until the next day's dawn.

The bar facing the town square remained open even past last call, though alcohol wasn't sold past a certain time. That didn't mean many of the partygoers didn't bring their own. The community center, also facing the square, remained open the full weekend. From Friday afternoon through Sunday evening teenagers as well as young children joined the weekend slumber parties.

If Rafe remembered correctly, the teenagers brought their own sleeping bags or pillows, supplies were donated for pizza making, chips and drinks were brought by the sponsors and chaperones. In holding the weekend events a place was provided to keep the kids off the streets and entertained through the summer months, keeping them from running wild.

It was a pretty cool little setup. And to give the county credit, there hadn't been a single time that he and his cousins had been turned away when they were younger. Despite the fact that Clyde Ramsey used the weekend activity as a babysitter while he went to Aspen for what he called his adult fun.

Never had the Callahans been turned away from a weekend social or ostracized during one, unless it was their peers ostracizing them. Which it usually was.

And that was enough for the cousins. As soon as they were old enough, Rafe, Logan, and Crowe had begun camping out on the weekends Clyde was gone. He hadn't totally trusted any of them. *Blood will tell,* he was known to mutter as he locked up the house and drove them into town. He didn't want anything stolen out of his house.

Not that the cousins had ever stolen a damned thing in

their lives. They hadn't. And they hadn't been able to find a single time when anyone had been certain their fathers had stolen anything. It was all supposition and suspicion.

The cousins might not have been ostracized from the socials as teenagers, but as adults it was another story. Standing together in their dress blacks, combed and polished, they were well aware of the looks they were receiving and from which direction.

The citizens of the county who had been there when the Callahan cousins were growing up watched them suspiciously while the new residents, those who had come in since, watched them curiously. And more of the single women than not at least glanced their way in appreciation.

There had been a time Rafe and his cousins would have shown this county exactly how their fathers had managed to catch and marry the boys' mothers, heiresses though they were. There were several Corbin County moneyed daughters as well as a few he recognized from the social pages from Denver, Grand Junction, and Aspen. And if he wasn't mistaken— He allowed his lips quirk into a grin as one of those moneyed daughters arched her brow in invitation.

At any other time he would have taken her up on the silent invitation, especially here, in front of every bastard who had ever turned his nose up at a Callahan.

But then Cami had happened.

He was damned if he would mess up a chance to experience the pleasure he found in the sleek, hot depths of the sweetest pussy he'd ever known. And he knew beyond a shadow of a doubt, if he so much as considered taking another woman to his bed, then he would never so much as glimpse Cami's bed again.

Rafe's gaze slid to her once again, watched as she stood talking to one of the other teachers at the elementary school where she taught.

The bouncy little redhead was full of vivacious laughter, and her gaze kept straying to him, then back to Cami. As though she knew more than she had seen the night before. More than Martin Eisner had told.

Though, honestly, Eisner hadn't told near as much as Rafe had expected him to. For a damned gossip, he'd been amazingly reticent so far.

"Tell me why we're here again?" Logan muttered behind Rafe, just loud enough to reach both his and Crowe's ears.

Logan wasn't happy to be here either, evidently. But, just as he had done when they were younger, Crowe had all but forced them out of the house and into town.

"Because we're not hiding anymore," Crowe answered firmly, not bothering to lower his tone any more than necessary. He wasn't trying to keep anyone from hearing him, but neither was he trying to tell everyone around them either.

"I wasn't aware we were hiding before," Rafe snorted. "Simply uninterested. I'm still not interested."

And that was a lie of major proportions. The more he watched Cami, the more interested he became in the Sweetrock Saturday night social. He could see where and why the event could come in handy. At least he had a legitimate excuse for being in the same vicinity she was in. If he had his way, he'd have a hell of an excuse for holding her in his arms and staking a silent, though very clear claim on the woman he was considered his own. That sense of possession was growing stronger by the day.

"Well, I am," Crowe drawled. "If you two want to leave, then find your own ride. Personally, I intend to have a little fun."

Rafe looked back at him wryly. "I knew riding in with you was a bad decision."

And it had been all Crowe's idea. Hell, he should have just brought the Harley, but the mountain air was still colder than hell.

Crowe shrugged, the perfect fit of the black silk evening jacket he wore barely shifting over the broad width of his shoulders. "Sucks to be you boys, then don't it?"

His cousin was scanning the crowd again, as though searching for someone. As though he knew why he was there and who he was there to see.

Just why was Crowe so interested in being there?

There had to be more to this than simply wanting to force Corbin County to accept them. Because none of them really gave a damn if Corbin County accepted them or not. If they followed through with their plans, then the county would have to accept them anyway. Attending a damned social wasn't going to make a difference.

Rafe glanced over at Logan. He was staring above them at the brightly strung lights in the newly budding trees overhead.

The white- and peach-colored lights weren't that interesting. Rafe had always considered them rather bland and boring himself. Peach wasn't exactly his favorite color.

"You boys are boring me," Rafe muttered as he lifted the glass of beer he had bought earlier and took a hard drink of the warming liquid as he kept his eyes on Cami.

It was a damned good thing he liked the taste of beer, because it wasn't at its best after it warmed.

"Well, by all means, don't let us hold you back," Crowe grunted. "You're not chained to us, you know."

"Hmm." He all but ignored his cousin as he watched Cami lift her hand, her graceful fingers pushing back a strand of gold-and-walnut-streaked hair back from her cheek as a man, *another man*, walked up to her, smiled, and handed her a flute of champagne.

And she dared to smile at him?

Her lips curved with charm and graciousness, and was she flirting with the bastard? Were her lashes lowering over her eyes deliberately, giving that son of a bitch a sleepy, sexy, take-me-to-bed look?

Rafe straightened slowly from where he'd been leaning against the post of the pergola he and his cousins were standing beneath.

This wasn't going to happen.

He glared over at her, as though the force of his look alone would send the son of a bitch running.

Cami's admirer leaned closer and whispered something in her ear as she leaned in to him.

Fucker! Whoever the hell he was, he was risking his life.

Then, the other man's hand reached up, his fingers curling around her upper arm.

Another man was touching what was Rafe's? He could feel his jaw clenching.

Were those his teeth grinding?

He'd be damned if he would have this.

He set the empty beer glass down slowly, unaware of even having finished the warming brew before shoving his hands in the pockets of his slacks and clenching his fists.

Mine!

"Did you say something, Rafe?" Crowe asked behind him.

He didn't say a damned thing. Not out loud at least.

Had he?

Then the man standing with her gestured to the dance floor, where another slow song was beginning to fill the night air.

It was an invitation, and it was an invitation that just might get the bastard into more trouble than he could have imagined.

"Ah fuck, don't do it, Cami," he muttered.

He practically felt the blood beginning to boil in his veins as a surge of some impossibly possessive urge tore through his senses.

He felt like an animal.

He wanted nothing more than to snarl in primal rage that some son of a bitch thought he could claim, for even a moment, what Rafe had already tried to mark as his own.

Oh, if he hadn't marked her yet, then he would.

Tonight.

Tonight, he'd show her exactly how he could mark her. How he could take that collection of erotic toys in her bedside drawer and turn her little world inside out. She would be convinced he lived under her skin when he was finished with her.

She would know who that lush, graceful little body belonged to.

She would know exactly who claimed not just her kisses and her juicy little pussy but also every fucking dance she was willing to give away.

He took a step forward.

"Ah, Rafe, wait just a minute." Logan caught Rafe's arm, bringing him to a stop only because of the warning in his cousin's voice. "Are you sure you want to do this here?"

He turned to the other man slowly, his head lowered, his gaze boring into his cousin's with a fury Logan didn't know how to handle.

"Do what?" he asked between clenched teeth. "Dance? Why, I'm quite certain I do."

And he knew exactly who he intended to dance with. Exactly who he intended to show this entire fucking town belonged to him. Rafer Callahan wasn't just a kid they considered as from the wrong side of the tracks. He wasn't just the son of the bastard who had stolen Ann Ramsey from the marriage pool and impregnated her. Hell no, Rafe was also Cambria Flannigan's lover and before the night was over the world would fucking know it whether she liked it or not.

"Hold up there, Rafe," Logan protested again as Rafe attempted to move forward. "Not a good idea. Man, show some common sense here."

Rafe turned his head until he was glaring over his shoulder at his cousin. "Let me go, Logan, before I put you flat on your ass."

And Rafe could do it. Maybe not for long, but he could do it.

"Hey, man, he's walking away from her. See, you don't have to play the big bad wolf after all." There was more than an edge of amusement to Logan's voice; he was practically laughing out loud. "Let's not make a scene now."

Rafe's gaze flicked to where his cousin held on to his arm.

"Take your hand off me, Logan, or we'll fight."

They hadn't fought in a lot of years, but nothing or no one was going to stand between Rafe and what he had already claimed as his own.

That was his woman standing over there, her gaze once again locked on the dancers, that hunger still glowing in her eyes, eating at his control.

It was a dance. All she wanted was a dance, and she deserved that dance, in his arms.

He'd never danced with her before last night.

He hadn't been able to do anything but fuck her mindless every time he touched her. And he wanted more. More touches, more kisses, more fucking them both silly, and more dances.

Logan released him slowly. "Come on, Rafe; we don't want to fight before we leave here, tonight. Archer would have to lock us up again. You know we wouldn't like that."

"Archer wouldn't dare!" Rafe growled. "Aren't you fucking tired of being stuck on the sidelines of these damned things, Logan? Not good enough to dance with their women because they're fucking terrified we'll marry into their money again or claim one of their prettiest women?"

Logan grimaced. "Since when did we give a damn? This little event isn't an end-all or be-all, dammit. Stand your ground some other time, when you have something to back you besides just our fists."

He knew what Logan was trying to say. When they had a financial hold on the town that couldn't be refuted or denied. Once the financial benefits of the resort they had planned were felt, the county would change their tune fast. Damned fast. But Rafe would be damned if he would see another man take the opportunity to touch his woman while he was waiting.

He swung around, intent on stalking across the brick and tile square to where his woman stood and claiming her in front of God and Corbin County.

He came to a stop before he took his first step, his eyes canvasing the square slowly, moving over the chatting groups, the laughter-filled guests and flirting couples.

She wasn't there.

Where the hell had she gone?

"She took one look at your face and ran." Crowe's golden-brown eagle's eyes were lit with laughter. "My best guess is the little bird just flew away home."

Flew away home, did she?

Rafe rather doubted it. She knew he would follow her

home. She knew there wasn't a chance in hell she was going to get off that damned easy tonight.

Two weeks.

He'd waited two fucking weeks for her, and he was tired of waiting.

He'd never waited for a woman in his life.

He'd never chased one down in his life, but he was doing it now.

Striding across the square, his gaze moving over the area, searching the shadows, knowing she was there, feeling her there, he became the hunter the military had taught him to be. The hunter pure primal lust was turning him into.

He slipped into the darkness, knowing how to blend into the edges of the party and how to canvas each section of the town square until he found her.

Did she really think she could show up here and get away without dealing with him?

She hadn't called until last night and he'd been in a damned dead zone. She hadn't driven by the ranch; she hadn't indicated in any way, shape, or form that she even remembered a single moment they'd spent screwing each other's brains out. Well, he was of a mind to remind her of it tonight. And tomorrow night. And the night after.

He'd seen her face, he'd seen her eyes, and he knew she was just as hungry as he was. She was having just as hard a time keeping her eyes off him as he was having keeping his eyes off her.

He moved slowly around the couples that had sought out the privacy of the shadows as well. He ignored the whispers in the shadowed little coves and private seating areas. Not private enough to engage in anything illicit, at least not until later, once everyone was a little freer due to drink. Just private enough to afford a bit of intimacy.

She was here.

He swore he could feel her, like a warmth, a comfort that went beyond the physical.

The physical was there, though.

His cock was so damned hard he swore he could pound nails with it. The head was engorged, flared and aching, throbbing in need.

The remembered feel of her pussy gripping it, milking it, was burning him alive. The need to feel it again was making him fucking crazy.

To sink inside her, inch by slow inch, as her pussy flexed and rippled around the sensitive crown.

He paused.

He'd moved farther into the shadows, closer to the parking lot, a soft mountain breeze playing through the trees when he caught a subtle, elusive scent.

"You're hunting me," she accused me. "I can feel you."

He turned slowly, his gaze zeroing in on the small private seating area. This one was more private than the others, closer to the parking lot, more heavily shadowed by the unlit trees around it.

Turning, Rafe moved slowly through the night, moving into the unlit, sheltered area until he was standing in front of her, staring down at her as he lifted his hands and gripped her slender, rounded hips.

"Are you hidden well enough?" he asked, fighting to keep his voice calm, indulgent. "By all means, we can't allow anyone here to see us together, can we?"

Her hands lifted to his chest, her fingers flattening against it, just beneath the edges of his jacket. He could feel the warmth of her palms through the thin cotton shirt he wore beneath the black evening jacket.

Like a stroke of sensual fire against his chest. Damn her, that tentative, shaky touch and the sound of her accelerated breathing had his balls tightening violently.

She stared up at him with those hungry eyes, her expression almost dazed as her lips parted to breathe.

"I don't want anyone to see me like this," she whispered. "To see me shaking and barely able to breathe because you're too close to me."

"Can I get too close to you, kitten?"

He jerked her fully against him, the height of the heels she wore lining up her sensitive little clit to the hard wedge of his cock through their clothing.

She breathed in roughly.

Her nails curled, rasping over the fabric of his shirt as her lashes fluttered almost closed.

"Yes, in public you can get too close to me," she admitted. "And when you do, I lose my mind."

She lost her mind and forgot her resolve. When he was anywhere close to her she forgot what she had promised herself and wanted nothing more than to touch him.

She'd seen him several times in the past two weeks and forced herself to run in the opposite direction. A few times literally.

"And losing your mind is such a bad thing, is it?"

The indulgent though subtly angry tone of his voice had a flinch jerking through her. "You ask so much of me," she whispered, staring up at him as she fought to keep from laying her head against his chest. "I've watched for you every night, Rafer." The words felt torn from her.

They *were* torn from her, because they were words she would have held in if she could control herself whenever he was around.

"It goes two ways, baby," he assured her. "You have my number. You know where I live."

She shook her head slowly, her lashes feeling sensually heavy as his fingers began to stroke her hips through the light velvet of her dress.

The nights were still a bit chilly in the higher elevations of the mountains. In this area, surrounded by the trees and snow-topped mountains, the nights were never hot and balmy, even in the summer.

The dress that had been perfectly comfortable before she saw Rafer was now too hot, too heavy. She wanted it off; she wanted his clothes off. She wanted to be as close to him as skin would allow.

"I called last night," she whispered. "You didn't answer."

"Dead zone," he said.

"What are you doing to me, Rafer?" she whispered. "Why are you doing this me?"

His hands tightened on her hips, lifting her, wedging his cock tighter against her lower stomach.

"Because I can't get you out of my fantasies," he growled as his head lowered, his lips at her ear, caressing the sensitive shell. "Because all I have to do is think of you and my dick is so hard I've sworn it was pure iron. Because I can't get you out of my fucking system and I think I'm going to end up hating you because evidently you can get me out of yours."

"Oh, can I?" she asked hoarsely, her breathing rough. "Is that why I'm not sleeping every night? Is that why I lay and watch my door, praying you'll walk through it, or every time my phone rings at night feel my body sensitize and prepare for you and then see it's not even you?"

She could hear the desperation in her voice even as she felt it in her body.

Her head tilted to the side as his lips moved over her ear, his tongue probing at the outer shell, his teeth nipping at the lobe as she fought back a moan.

She could feel the echo of the pleasure washing through the rest of her body, rasping over her nipples, sending fingers of agonizing pleasure raking over her clit.

Her womb clenched, an involuntary spasm shuddering through it as sensual hunger tore through her with fiery desperation as his lips moved to a violently sensitive area just below her ear.

His lips touched her, parted, delivered a stinging little kiss that had her hands sliding to his shoulders as she tried to get closer, tried to burrow beneath his flesh.

"You haven't come to me, Rafer," she panted roughly. "I waited."

"I waited for you, baby," he whispered. "You didn't call. I won't beg you every time we come together."

"Do you want me to beg?" She was so ready to beg.

She could beg so easily if that was that he wanted her to do.

"No, I want you to dance with me, Cami."

Her hands tightened on his shoulders.

He wasn't going to make this easier for her, was he? It would be all or nothing. And didn't he deserve it?

All his life he'd been pushed to the back, told he didn't deserve the same things other men deserved, and each time he entered Corbin County he became a secondary citizen.

And he wasn't.

In so many ways, Rafer deserved so much more than others in this county could ever deserve.

He drew back to stare down at her, his eyes meeting hers, demand darkening them and tightening the fingers that clenched her hips.

She laid her head on his chest, feeling one broad hand move from her hip to the back of her head, his fingers threading through the short strands of her hair. Closing her eyes, she tried to soak in the warmth and confidence that was so much a part of him.

"Let you claim me," she whispered, knowing what he was demanding.

"Deny you belong to me, Cami." He sounded uncompromising yet incredibly gentle, even understanding. He knew what he was asking of her, knew what it could possibly result in, and still he was demanding it.

She fought the emotions rising inside her, her face tightening, clenching with the effort it took to hold back the instinctive objection to everything he wanted.

She swallowed tightly. "I can't belong—" But she wanted to. She wanted to so badly that the need throbbed through her veins and pulsed through her clit. It wasn't just a sexual need or a sensual pleasure. "I can dance with you," she dragged in a harsh breath.

The need was a hunger to be close to him, to allow the intimacy of a dance to pull them together. It would hold them and allow them to claim each other in public. He would do it in full view of not just their enemies but also the threatening caller that who finally called that evening as she made her way to the town square.

And this time, the threat had been more explicit.

Rafe tensed against her.

Oh, she wasn't going to do this.

Rafe stared down at her, calculating the best way to stake his claim. To impress upon her, and every man who would lust after her, that she was his. Convince her clear to her soul, that she was his. That no other man would touch her, no matter what, no matter where.

And there was only one way to effectively do that. To claim her, to mark her in a way everyone would damned well understand.

She was a stubborn woman and she had it in her head that she wasn't going to allow any kind of public claim. That she was either not risking her heart, or not risking her pride by being publicly claimed by a Callahan. He had to admit, at this point, he wasn't certain which it was. But he did know what he had seen moments before. Another man trying to touch her, to take her, to claim her.

Cami's reputation as a woman without a claim was coming to an end, and it was coming to an end tonight.

Lowering his head, nearly nose to nose with her, Rafe felt his teeth pull back in a primal snarl.

"Be very, very careful," he warned her, his voice rough, hoarse. "I saw that bastard touching you, Cami. I saw his hand on you and I saw his invitation to you, to dance."

Her eyes widened, her lips parted.

"Don't." He laid his finger against her lips. "No objections. Don't even bother arguing. Trust me, Cami. To the bottom of your soul trust this: If I see another man touch you, see him lay his hand on you, then I swear to you I'll break his hand. And God help us all if you agree to dance with any man other than me!"

Shock resounded through her.

The sound of his voice, the warning, the fury that glittered in his eyes, had trepidation surging through her even as he jerked her closer. His fingers tangled in the hair at the back of her head, pulled her head back, and his lips covered hers.

It was like pouring gasoline on fire.

Barely banked on a good day, the hunger suddenly flamed, raged through her, and stole her control. Her hands buried themselves in his overly long hair, tangled in it, and pulled him closer. Like roughened velvet his lips rubbed over hers, slanted, his tongue meeting hers desperately.

She tasted him. Male heat and flaming hunger. There was a hint of the beer he must have drunk earlier, and that smokey wine taste of his cigar. Just a hint of it. Just enough to make her long for more, to have her reaching to get closer, to taste the kiss deeper.

What was she doing?

She moaned in need. She was aching for him. The ache was becoming more intense by the night, the hunger to just have him near tearing at her.

His fingers clenched at her hip and in her hair as a male groan muted and filled Rafer with a need for her that was nearly intoxicating by itself.

She had never been wanted as Rafer wanted her. She had never been kissed, tasted, and touched as Rafer touched her.

And she had never ached for another man as she ached for Rafer.

She was shocked as he pulled back, but she didn't fight as he wrapped his arm around her back and led her the short distance to the edge of the dance area.

She didn't care at that point who watched, who saw. She didn't care what they saw.

She could feel the hard, thick wedge of his cock pressing against her lower belly between their clothes. Suddenly, she wasn't chilled any longer, she was warm. No, she wasn't warm, she was hot. Blazing. Fiery.

She could have melted ice as she stared up at him.

The flame of hunger in his gaze sank inside her. It washed over the places in her soul that she wanted to remain hidden, that she wanted to remain chilled.

She didn't want to thaw. She didn't want to feel the additional ache, the loss, the hungry need that went so far beyond the sexual.

But that was exactly what she felt.

As he moved her across the dance floor, held her in his arms, and claimed her to everyone willing to see, Cami felt that part of her soul open and come alive.

Rafe watched the crowd.

With his head bent over Cami's, one hand tangled in her hair, the other gripping her hip, he felt her melt against him.

She was accepting him. He could feel that acceptance to the bottom of his soul. And in doing so, she was accepting the claim he made on her.

With his gaze locked across the dance floor on Marshal Roberts, he stared back at his supposed grandfather with a fiery rage and unbidden fury he'd never been able to quench.

Until the old man turned away, replaced the western hat he invariably wore, and walked away.

He didn't know what the old bastard was up to, but he would find out. There were a lot of things he intended to have answers to very, very soon.

Until then, he had Cami in his arms. Slow dancing, swaying, holding her as close to him as two people could get.

Until the music ended.

Cami found herself back where they had started, sheltered within the small grotto, staring up at Rafer as he stepped away from her.

A second later, she was free.

Trembling, struggling to stand upright on the five-inch heels as he steadied her, but only for a second, before letting her go and stepping back.

"Rafer," she whispered.

She needed more. She was dying for more.

"Let me know when I can come through the front door, Cami," he bit out furiously. "Until then, you damned well better remember every word of warning I just gave you."

Before she could protest or argue, he was gone. Sliding through the shadows and disappearing, leaving her feeling suddenly deflated, lost.

She sat down slowly on the lovers' bench behind her and covered her face with her hands.

She should have told him why.

She should have told him about the phone calls and that the last threat wasn't just against her. The last time the caller had contacted her, he had threatened Rafe as well.

"You're not being a good girl, Cambria. Don't you know I'll punish you even more than I did your sister? This time, your lover will feel my anger as well.

You're not being a good girl.

In other words she wasn't staying away from Rafe or keeping him away from her.

Maybe she should have told him—

CHAPTER 15

Cami forced herself to go home that night.

The streets, as she suspected, were far from empty, which would make it much easier for anyone to follow her.

She walked back to the house with friends she worked with who had parked farther down the street and gave her a reliable excuse for walking with someone. She didn't have to ask anyone to walk with her, which would have required explanations.

But once she reach her home and stepped inside it, she almost wished she had stayed just a little longer at the outdoor party. Perhaps until daylight.

Because the house was too quiet.

It was too lonely.

The home she had grown up in, the one she had bought from her father when he and her mother made the decision to move to Aspen, seemed to close in on Cami. For the first time in her life she didn't feel comfortable, warm, and protected, and she wondered that she ever had.

There had been something about her mother's presence in it, Cami admitted. Her mother had made the difference. Before Cami's parents had sold the house and moved to Aspen, it had been a warm, inviting home. Sometimes. If her father wasn't there.

But still, it was the home she had been raised in. It was

the home where she had gotten to know her older sister until Cami had turned eight and Jaymi had moved out.

And even then, Jaymi hadn't forgotten about her. Jaymi had taken Cami to her new home regularly, and when her husband had been killed in the military it had been Cami who Jaymi had wanted to stay with her for a while.

And her father had never seemed to understand why Jaymi wanted Cami with her. He had never understood why her older sister seemed to love her. If her mother had felt the same way, Cami had never sensed it. But neither could she discount the suspicion. Because there was no way her father could have resented her and her mother not know it.

There were times Cami and Jaymi swore Margaret Flannigan had eyes in the back of her head, because they couldn't seem to get anything past her when they were children. She would have known, despite the sedatives she took. Margaret would have seen that her husband cared nothing for his younger daughter.

So why hadn't Margaret Flannery done something about it? Why hadn't her mother left Mark Flannigan, or at least made the effort to let Cami know that she accepted her?

Was she so unlovable to the father she had adored as a child that loving her was impossible? She wondered as she stared around the house for long minutes. Was she truly so bad that as her father said, he had been forced to take her mother away to Aspen to alleviate Cami's influence?

Or had he simply found the only way to punish her for not being the daughter who had died? Because taking her mother away from Cami truly was the only way he could have hurt her at that point.

She stood silently for a moment, staring around the shadowed house, feeling the loneliness that wrapped around her. That sense of suddenly having nothing to hold on to and no one to warm her. There were no parents, no siblings, where once there had at least been a sister and a mother.

Now there was simply no one but her aunt and uncle.

And Rafe.

When Cami allowed herself to have him.

Yet even he hadn't come back to the house with her. He hadn't followed her, and he wasn't at her back door now.

He had given her a choice, and now he was sticking to it. She could call him. She could come to him. But he wasn't going to allow her to excuse her choice with the excuse that he hadn't given her a choice.

With a hard jerk of her head she forced that thought, that need, back. Moving through the house, she checked the locks on the doors, checked the windows, and double-checked the alarm.

She felt restless, on edge. As though a foreboding followed her, an instinctive warning to beware that she couldn't seem to shake. The feeling had begun at the social, tingled around her on her way home, and now it had settled into her senses like a subtle scent she couldn't shake and yet couldn't identify.

She wished she hadn't danced with Rafe. Wished she had asked him to follow her home. She wished he were there with her, and she should know by now the folly of wishing for things that weren't meant to be hers.

Rafe hadn't followed her home, though; he hadn't spoken to her after he had left her back in that little grotto. And he hadn't mentioned that claim on her.

Even though Cami knew he had made it.

Even though Rafe was very well aware of the fact that he had a claim on her and they both knew it it was a claim she couldn't shake or deny.

And as his gaze had followed her throughout the night, she had felt that knowledge. Just as everyone else at the dance had. Even Emma had been reticent to say anything about it, or to tease Cami over it. And normally, Emma was the one to joke about anything.

She had felt his eyes on her nearly every second, especially if another man had dared to approach her.

As though Rafe's warning had kept her from dancing with anyone else. That had nothing to do with her decision, because she realized he wouldn't have really made a scene.

He would be madder than hell. He would hate every second of it. He would have most likely waylaid her in private again at first chance. But there wouldn't have been a confrontation. Rafer Callahan had more pride than that.

The truth was, she hadn't wanted to dance with anyone else. She hadn't danced with another man, slept with another man, or engaged in a serious flirtation with another man since the first night she had slept with Rafer. Well, they hadn't done much sleeping that night.

The most she had done in the past was to go out to dinner a few times with other men, hoping each time that there would be at least the faintest spark of attraction.

But there hadn't been.

Breathing out roughly, she trailed her fingers over the banister of the stairs as she moved to the the master suite.

The room that somehow hadn't had even the faintest mark of her parents on it when she had bought it.

She'd redecorated after buying the house from her parents anyway.

She almost smiled at the thought of that purchase. Her father had actually priced the house at the highest appraisal given, and that was the price she had had to pay for it. At twenty two, that hadn't been easy.

Thankfully, tourism hadn't really kicked off in Sweetrock yet, so housing prices weren't as high as they could have been otherwise. And her uncle had co-signed

She had bought the house the week after she had lost their child.

She hadn't been prepared for such loss, in more ways than one. When her period had been late, she had been certain—and she had been wrong.

Perhaps she had made her mistake in attempting to forget that night and every other time she had met him or deliberately run into him over the years until the miscarriage. It hadn't been hard to learn where he would be or when until his uncle Clyde Ramsey had died.

After that, Cami hadn't heard anything else about Rafer until his arrival in town more than three years later.

Reaching the second floor, she turned at the landing and took the several steps to the suite she'd completely redecorated. Merging the master bedroom with the guest room, she'd created a sanctuary within her home.

All of the rooms, in some ways, were an oasis, a sanctuary that fulfilled whatever varied mood she could have without reminding her of her father in any way.

But tonight, tonight her mood was unlike any she had had before.

It was interesting.

Stepping into her bedroom, she closed the door behind her, her hand still gripping the doorknob as she leaned back against the door. Staring up at the ceiling, she inhaled slowly, deeply, and blinked back the tears.

She didn't want to be here alone—

A shadow moved in the corner of the room. Quick, fast, like a blur of darkness it barreled toward her.

"Oh God!" Terror washed through her at the sight, at the instinctive knowledge of what it was.

Dressed in black from head to toe, a dark hood pulled over his face, nothing showing but dark, malevolent eyes.

Screaming, Cami jerked open the door and raced out of it, thanking God she had taken off the high heels, as she tore down the stairs to the front door and the security alarm control.

She knew she didn't have a chance of releasing the locks before her attacker caught her. She couldn't chance the back door, where there was no alarm control.

She was just there. Her hand slapped it, her fingers reaching for the panic button, when a hard, violent blow was delivered to the side of her head.

Her cheek slammed into the wall. Bells seemed to clamor in her head as her stomach pitched sickeningly with the pain and dizziness that suddenly attacked her.

Vicious, hard fingers suddenly caught at her hair, jerking her back and throwing her into the stairs. As though in slow motion, she felt herself hurtling across the space, unable to stop the fall she knew was coming.

She caught herself against the banister as she stumbled back, hitting a step with her hip as her head cracked against

the banister railing. For a second, dizziness washed over her
as a wave of raw pain swept through her head again.

Another blow cracked the side of her face.

His fist?

The agony was like nothing she had ever known before.
It resounded through her skull, sliced through her brain, and
seemed to rip her senses from their moorings. She was trying to scream, but she didn't know if she was. The wailing
clash of sound in her head was so loud.

"You fucking whore!" Snarling, furious, the harsh male
voice cracked around her a second before he jerked her up
by the hair on her head.

Her hands pulled his wrists, her nails digging at them,
searching for bare flesh as she fought to be free.

A second later he threw her against the door as she
screamed again, her fingers curling into claws as she aimed
for his face.

She was inches from his eyes when harsh hands grabbed
her wrists, jerked them over her head, and ripped her gown
down the front.

Bucking, her screams mixing with the piercing wail of
the siren echoing through the head, Cami fought desperately
to be free. Hard, cruel fingers wrapped around the mound of
one breast, squeezing harshly as she felt the screaming pain
of merciless fingers twisting her nipple.

"I'll fuck you first, then cut your fucking throat like I
should have cut your diseased sister's."

Low, vicious laughter sounded at Cami's ear as she fought,
kicking, screaming, until finally her knee struck its target and
slammed into the vulnerable balls between his thighs as he
moved to shift his weight.

The high, piercing cry tore from him. His suddenly lax
grip gave her the chance she needed to throw herself away
from him, reaching for the umbrella holder and jerking one
of the folded instruments from the opening.

As a weapon it was pitiful, but her dazed mind could
only comprehend the point, the curved handle, and the distance it would put between her and her attacker.

She whirled around in just enough time to see the front door jerking open and the black-clad figure disappearing as she heard the sounds of something crashing, yelling, cursing, and the pounding of feet running through her hall like a stampede of elephants.

"You bastard!" she sobbed, her legs collapsing, throwing her to the hardwood floor as she braced herself against the side of the steps. Cami felt her legs folding beneath her as the blows to her head, the terror, and the sudden, overwhelming relief stole her last bit of strength.

With one hand braced around the spindle of the banister, her fingers locked desperately around the smooth wooden support as she laid her head against her arm and screamed out in rage.

Tears filled her eyes, and one even escaped before she could battle it back. Breathing harshly and fighting back what could easily turn into desperate, agonizing cries, she whispered Rafe's name.

Her dress was ruined. The silk underslip was still intact; her stockings were probably ruined. And if she had just told Rafer about that call during the afternoon, then she wouldn't have been alone. And no one would have ever gotten the jump on Rafer as he had on her.

Oh God, where was Rafe?

She was cold and so scared. The entire world was spinning much too fast, and all she wanted to do was make the twisting, spinning motions cease before she began retching all over her pristine wooden floor.

"Cambria?" She heard Archer's yell as he rushed through the opened front door.

She tried to lift her head as he came to a hard, shocked stop. It wobbled on her shoulders, though, causing her sight to careen wildly once again, dragging a moan from her lips. Instantly he was kneeling in front of her, his hands and his gaze going over her quickly.

"Are you okay?" He touched her forehead. The brief touch sent a wave of pain tearing through her, causing her to flinch and jerk her head back a second before she began gagging from the revolving room.

She could taste blood in her mouth. The taste of it added to the sickening, retching sensation gripping her stomach. If everything would just slow down. If it would just stop spinning for more than a second or two, then she could find her balance.

Dizziness rushed over her again, forcing her to put her head down, to swallow desperately and fight the sickness threatening to overwhelm her.

"Did you get him?" she finally gasped weakly when she could lift her head to try to focus on Archer. He looked like he was wavering, slithering from side to side like a cobra attempting to mesmerize her.

Rather than mesmerizing her, it only made her feel sicker, more confused.

Frowning, she knew something was wrong but was having a hell of a time concentrating on what. She knew she was ill, that the blows to her head hadn't been a good thing.

"How many, Cami?" he was yelling at her, holding up his hand. Or something. He was holding something up in front of her face.

She tried to focus, blinking, almost whimpering at the disorientation and the pain surging through her head once again.

Oh God, she hated not being able to concentrate, unable to think or to rationalize.

"How many?" Archer yelled at her again.

How many?

"Two Archers," she whispered, dazed as she laid her head against her arm once again, wondering why she kept seeing two of him when she knew there was only one. Archer didn't even have a brother, let alone a twin.

"Archer, I don't feel well," she whispered, suddenly terribly frightened of the disorientation she couldn't seem to shake.

"Ambulance is on its way, Cami." His hands clasped her

face, forcing her to tilt her head back as the room swam
around her and pure agony raced through her temples, her
eyes, shooting to the back of her neck.

She tried to swat at his hand, to scream, but all that came
out was a weak whimper. "Rafer."

"It's Archer, Cami. Fuck, where is that ambulance?"

Who was he talking to? Please, not Martin Eisner. Martin would tell her uncle, and her uncle and Aunt Ella would
rush over.

Ella would fuss over her.

Her mother used to fuss over her.

Uncle Eddy would threaten to kill the bastard, and he
would mean it.

She needed Rafer.

"Archer." She couldn't hold her head up, could barely
breathe enough to force out a single word: "Rafer."

She could see the darkness edging in on her vision.

"Did Rafer do this, Cami?" Shock, fury, it all filled his
voice.

Why was he so angry? Rafer had slipped into her bedroom. She had tried to tell him they couldn't do this. They
couldn't slip around, and he didn't listen to her any more
than her own body did.

She could hear someone else beyond her vision, yelling
about Rafer.

She tried to shake her head.

"Get Rafer," she whispered. "Have to tell—"

She had to tell Rafer. She had to warn him.

"Cami, answer me, damn you!" Archer was yelling at her.
Archer had never yelled at her. "Cami, did Rafer do this?"

She needed Rafer. There were too many voices screaming in her head. Or was that around her head?

The darkness was coming closer, closer. And she had to
warn Rafer.

"Warn Rafer—," she could barely whisper. It was a breath
of a sound, the last of her energy before she faced nothingness.

Oh God, was this how Jaymi had felt when she died?
Could Cami feel that complete absence of being before she

left the world? She sobbed, crying out for the hell her sister must have endured and terrified of facing it herself. Of being unable to avoid it and unable to force herself away from it.

That dark, icy nothingness closed over her, like a freezing, merciless veil of ice. There was nothing comforting, nothing gentle, about it. It was terribly frightening, dragging her into it as she fought helplessly to retain consciousness, to warn Rafer.

Someone needed to warn Rafer.

Dawn was rolling over the mountains when Rafer finally gave up the battle to sleep, rose, showered, and dressed for the day. He was putting on coffee when Logan and Crowe made their way from their rooms, their distinctly irritated looks directed straight at him.

"I didn't wake you," he informed them both as he set out enough cups for the three of them.

"We didn't say you had," Logan growled, definitely testy. He never had cared much for early mornings.

"Then what are you doing awake?" Rafe poured the coffee.

"Hell if I know, probably because you're awake," Crowe grunted as he hitched the loose cotton pants he wore a little closer to his hips and scratched at his bare, scarred chest.

God, Rafe wished Crowe would wear a shirt. The sight of those scars on his chest and back was too much for Rafe to bear to look at. But saying anything to Crowe, pointing it out, or reminding him of it wasn't always a good idea. Though how he could forget about it Rafe had never understood.

Logan plopped down in the seat across from Rafe, the gray running shorts he wore riding almost as low as Crowe's pants as he yawned and scratched at the side of his rough jaw. The closely cropped beard, a shade or two darker than his hair, was never completely shaved free of his face. Unlike Crowe, Logan preferred to hide his scars.

The mementos they had from their teenage years sucked. Rafer didn't carry physical scars; he instead carried the mental scars. None of them had escaped unscathed from the hatred and merciless need for revenge that had been exacted on each of them in one form or another.

"We have two investors coming in day after tomorrow," Crowe reminded them both as he sipped at the coffee. "Do you think we could get a cook out here or something?" He looked around the kitchen with a look of hope.

Poor Crowe, he'd gotten used to breakfast the short time he'd been in Boston with Ryan's family.

Ryan Calvert, the lost Callahan brother, had been adopted by a family in Boston while his older brothers were in the military. He hadn't found the family forced to give him up until well after his brothers' deaths. But he'd been there in time to save the nephews he hadn't known he'd had.

"I doubt it," Rafe told Crowe, sipping at his coffee as he rose from the chair again and paced to the kitchen window.

"What the fuck are you looking for, Rafe?" Logan finally burst out. "You did that half the night, until we went to bed, and now you're starting that shit again. Are you on speed or something?"

Hell if Rafe knew what was wrong with him.

He kept expecting . . . something. Someone.

Cami. And the thought of Cami had a chill tearing up his spine. Son of a bitch, he couldn't figure out what the hell was wrong.

Rafe stared down the road again, his brows drawn into a frown as he tried to put together the pieces of what was making him so crazy.

Not that the nerve-wracking emotions made sense, but he'd learned a long time ago not to expect anything in Corbin County to actually make sense. Because it wasn't going to happen.

And nothing concerning Cami ever made sense.

One thing was for sure, though; he had to see her. Just as fast as he could get there, he suddenly thought. Back door, front door, slipping through the basement window, it didn't fucking matter. He should have gone last night. He should have turned around the second this feeling had hit him like a punch in the gut.

Hell, he should have never returned to the ranch last night. What he should have done was headed straight to her house, slipped in, crawled into that big bed beside her, and fucked her until they were both exhausted. Maybe then he could have slept. One thing was for damned certain, he wasn't sleeping now. And he wouldn't sleep until he got to her. Until he assured himself she was okay.

It was that thought. That feeling that suddenly had adrenaline surging through him and his body tensing to rush to dress and leave.

As he started to turn from the window he glimpsed a flash of black and orange amid the newly budding trees and paused until the vehicle came into view.

What the hell was going on? Why was Archer Tobias arriving in his official SUV. Whatever it was, it couldn't be a good thing. It never had been before when the sheriff had shown up. Though, Rafe had to admit, Archer was a damned sight better sheriff than his father had ever even considered being.

"Sheriff's here," he told his cousins quietly as that feeling of panicked need, that urge to hurry and get to Cami intensified.

Immediately Logan and Crowe were up and moving.

They didn't bother racing to their rooms to dress. They snagged the jeans, T-shirts, socks, boots, and jackets they kept in the boot room just for such times. Those times when they were too lazy to dress and could have regretted it.

By time Archer Tobias pulled into the drive and parked, they were dressed and ready for whatever the world, karma, or fate decided to throw at them. They were also waiting at the end of the drive for him.

The cameras were on and recording, audio was functioning, and everything set to record anything that might or might not affect the final outcome if Archer had arrived in any official capacity.

They were stepping through the gate as Archer stepped from the vehicle, his expression heavy enough that Rafe felt that first tight clench of his chest.

Moving from the vehicle, Archer faced the three of them, though his gaze was clearly focused on Rafe.

There was something in Archer's eyes that had a small, shadowed corner of Rafer's soul clenching in terror.

For the first time in his life, Rafe refused to allow the impulsive intuition he sometimes carried free.

"What are you doing here, Arch?" Rafe growled.

"I'm sorry about this, Rafe." Archer shook his head as he breathed out wearily. "I need to know where you were last night after you left the dance."

Rafe felt his jaw lock. Every damned time there was a robbery, an attempted rape, a stolen car, whatever, it seemed the sheriff headed to the ranch if they were in town.

First it had been Archer's father, and now it was Archer. The fucking past kept repeating itself, and each time it did so, it just pissed Rafe the hell off more.

He was damned sick of it too.

"We came back here, Archer," Crowe informed him when Rafe refused to answer.

"Did anyone see you?" Archer glanced above their heads to one of the few cameras that could possibly be detected. If a person was knowledgeable enough to know what to look for. "Do you have a time stamp on the recording the camera would have made?"

"I have a stamp," Crowe said. Rafe felt his lip curling in disgust that Archer was even here for the Corbin bastards.

And hell yes, Rafe's cameras were time-stamped. The cousins had learned early to protect themselves, and they'd learned to make damned sure to watch every step they made where this was concerned.

They didn't take chances. They'd learned young to watch their backs against circumstantial evidence.

Archer tilted his hat back and propped his hands on his hips as he stared back at them. "I just asked, Crowe." He turned back to Rafe.

"And I just answered you definitively," Crowe informed him. "That way, there's no misunderstanding."

"I didn't expect we would have a misunderstanding." Archer's gaze connected with Rafe's. "Would anyone know how to mess with your system? How to make certain your arrival wasn't recorded?"

Rafe glanced at his cousins as they shook their heads, their gazes sharpening on Archer's now. "We don't spread our business around, Arch," Rafe told him. "But to answer your question, no, no one should know anything about the system or even that it exists."

They had friends now, where they hadn't had before, security specialists who had assisted in the installation and programming of a security and surveillance system that would be almost impossible to crack.

But the questions Archer was asking had that cold, tight fist to Rafe's chest clenching again. He could feel it; something wasn't right. Something had happened.

Something had happened that Archer was hesitating to tell him.

That meant something that could potentially force Rafe or all three Callahan cousins to lose the control they had kept such a firm grip on in the past months.

There were few things that could or would threaten that control.

For Rafe, there was only danger or harm to his cousins or to—

Rafe felt his body tense.

The truth was there in Archer's eyes, in the somber cast of his expression. And there was only one connection they had that would put that look in the sheriff's eyes.

"Ah God," Rafe whispered, feeling as though he were choking, ready to gag from the implications of that look. "Fuck, is she okay?"

He could feel the world suddenly threatening to crash down on him. Not Cami. Ah God, please, please not his Cami.

Logan and Crowe jerked toward Rafe as Archer's hands dropped from his waist, one hand on his weapon.

Cami. Sweet God in heaven. Ah God, something had happened to Cami.

"How did you know?"

"Answer me, damn you." Rafe could himself begin to lose his control, fury building, burning.

Evidently Archer saw something in Rafe's eyes, that killing rage Rafe could feel beginning to burn inside him. It convinced the sheriff to start explaining fast.

"She's alive. Bruised, scared to damned death, and suffering a concussion, the doctor thinks, but she's alive. She was still unconscious the last I saw her, but before she passed out she was asking for you," he sighed.

"We'll follow you and the sheriff, Rafe," Crowe told him as he pulled his keys from his pocket, his attention focused on getting to Sweetrock, rather than the sheriff or any other questions he might have. "We'll bring her back to the ranch."

"Now, hold on," Archer began to protest.

"Argue on the way to the hospital," Rafe suggested as he strode to the sheriff's vehicle. "I don't have time for this; let's roll out."

He was jerking open the passenger side door and sliding into the passenger seat as he pushed aside a clipboard, a book of tickets, and several other packets that lay there.

"I didn't invite you to ride with me," Archer informed him, though he slid into the driver's seat and put the vehicle in gear.

Behind them, Crowe and Logan threw dirt and gravel as Crown's Denali tore from the drive and raced ahead of them.

"I'm going to give those bastards a ticket," Archer muttered.

"Wait until we get to the hospital," Rafe suggested. "But tell me what happened."

Archer pulled out onto the main road and laid his foot to the gas to catch up with Crowe and Logan.

"She was attacked last night just after arriving home from the social," Archer told him. "Her alarms went off, alerting her neighbors and calling nine-one-one. When I got there, she was leaning against the bottom of the staircase. It looks like he hit her in the head several times, and he has a hell of a fist if her head is anything to go by. She was displaying signs of a concussion, a severe one if my guess is right. Her dress was ripped down the front and she kept saying your name. It took me forever to figure out she was asking for you rather than accusing you. Just before she passed out, she said she had to 'warn Rafer.'"

She was asking for him. She was trying to warn him, of something.

His pride had done this. If he had gone with her as he'd intended, followed her home, and slipped in the back door, then he would have been there for her. She wouldn't have been hurt. He would have made certain of it. He would have never allowed some bastard to lay the first hand on her.

"You should have called me sooner." His fists were clenched at his knees, the need for blood pounding through his veins. "Waiting wasn't a good idea, Archer."

The sheriff should have called immediately. They'd be discussing that when Archer wasn't driving and Rafe wasn't desperate to get to Cami.

"I've been a bit busy, Rafer," Archer informed him mockingly. "There was a friend to get to the hospital for X-rays and MRI. There was a crime scene to process. All those sheriffy little things that take up so much damned time."

"You could have saved close to thirty minutes by simply calling me."

"I had to make sure you had the camera proof that you were here when she was attacked," Archer stated. "I wasn't certain and I had to be certain that the cameras on the outside of the house were cameras or really the birdhouses that were built around them. I'll need your permission to have the security consultants copy the digital and send it to me."

"Get a fucking warrant," Rafe snapped. "Fuck the bastards that don't want to believe what's right in front of your eyes. Do you think I'd fucking hurt Cami, Archer? I thought we knew each other better than that."

Archer's hands tightened around the steering wheel, his knuckles turning white as his jaw clenched, the muscle there flexing rapidly before he spoke.

"Rafe, there was a yellow ribbon tied around her bed pillow," Archer finally stated as he sliced a hard glare toward him. "I'm sure you know exactly what kind of response that news is going to raise when it gets out."

Rafe froze.

A yellow ribbon around her pillow. It could only mean one thing and that simply wasn't possible.

"He's dead. Crowe killed him twelve years ago, Archer. Thomas Jones can't be killing again."

"Yeah, I know he's supposed to be fucking dead," Archer burst out furiously. "Son of a bitch, he's a fucking nightmare for this town, Rafe. Do you think I wanted to see that god-damned ribbon and its perfect bow tied around the pillow on Cami's bed? The one opposite the one she slept on. The one a lover or a husband would use."

The yellow ribbon.

Thomas Jones had tied a yellow ribbon around a pillow of each of his victims' bed pillows. Never the pillow they used. Always the pillow a lover would use.

Though all his victims hadn't had lovers.

And only Jaymi's pillow hadn't had a ribbon tied around it.

There had been nothing that the FBI or local law enforcement could find to tie the women together or to explain why he had chosen the women he chose to kill twelve years before.

"We definitely have a problem," Archer admitted. "More so than you know. Did she tell you about the phone calls she's been getting? The ones threatening her if she's sleeping with you?"

He was going to paddle her ass. As God was his witness, he was going to paddle that creamy little ass until it glowed. "She told me. I thought Marshal Roberts was fucking with her. He used to do that. All three of the barons used to do that, Archer."

They would call suspected friends, lovers, associates, and threaten them anonymously.

Archer cursed under his breath. "Jack Townsend contacted me this morning as soon as he heard what happened. He talked to her yesterday. She told him she was getting phone calls similar to those her sister received before she was killed. Calls warning her to stay away from you or she would regret it."

Rafe looked over at Archer slowly, mechanically. "Jaymi didn't mention phone calls to me before she died. Cami was the only one who mentioned them."

"To no one else either except Jack apparently." Archer grimaced. "I checked. If Jack hadn't told me about it this morning, then I wouldn't have known. Evidently, though, Cami's been getting them for a while now. At least since she was snowbound at the ranch with you. The calls have been warning her to stay away from you, and the caller is threatening to hurt her and you if she doesn't keep you out of her bed. The same phone calls Jaymi was getting before she was killed."

Murder raged through Rafe's mind.

He couldn't accept that Jaymi had been in danger simply because she had been sleeping with him months before the serial killer Thomas Jones targeted her.

"I hadn't seen Jaymi for nearly two days before Jones killed her," Rafe stated. "We'd talked on the phone a few times, but that was all."

And she hadn't seemed the least bit worried or concerned.

"And you and your cousin had no connection to the other women," Archer asked as Rafe lied with the short shake of his head. "But here's a connection between Jaymi's and Cami's attacks. Those phone calls."

There was another woman who shared a connection to one of the Callahan cousins. One of the victims from twelve years back whom neither Archer nor any other law enforcement official was aware of.

Turning back to watch the road in front of them, Rafe remained silent.

Six women had died twelve years before. Each one had had a yellow ribbon tied around one of her pillows, except Jaymi. And Thomas Jones had raped, tortured, and stabbed each one of them to death during that bloody, horrendous summer that had nearly destroyed Rafe's and his cousins' lives.

For Jaymi, he, Logan, and Crowe had almost been there in time. They had almost heard her screams soon enough from their fishing spot to go racing for her.

Almost.

It didn't count when it came to a knife and a young woman's lifeblood.

Jaymi had taken her last breath in Rafe's arms, and hours later he and his cousins had been sitting in a jail cell. They had been arrested for her and five others' murders.

He would not allow that to happen to Cami now that he knew she was a target of what had to be a copycat killer. Someone determined to frame the Callahan cousins.

"She'll be safe," Rafe promised Archer. And he would make certain of it. Him, Logan, and Crowe. "Did you dust the house for prints?"

"Personally," Archer told him. "I wasn't trusting that to anyone else. I also called the FBI, Rafe. If Thomas had a partner, as the profile suggested twelve years ago, then he's getting in the game again, and I want help on this."

Rafe didn't care who Archer called in as long as Cami was protected. The more the merrier as far as her safety was concerned.

"Look, Rafe, you know how this county is," Archer began after a long moment's silence.

"Yeah, everyone and his brother is going to be looking at us, believing the Callahan cousins did it. Because after all, there was no crime before we returned," Rafe sneered.

He knew exactly how it worked.

"You're being targeted, Rafe," Archer snapped back at him. "The calls were a warning over you, and the attack was for the same reason, I believe. This isn't something we can keep under our hats while we search for him. And it's damned sure not because of whatever the hell you did in the military. This goes straight back to twelve years before."

"I'm a fucking Marine, Archer; what the hell do you think I did?" he snarled. "For God's sake, would you just pick up some speed here so I can get to her? Sometime this year would be exceptionally nice. You can question me later."

If he didn't get there soon, if he didn't see for himself that Cami was safe and breathing on her own, then he was going to end up losing his sanity.

Rage was like an animal inside him, twisting and clawing in its desperation for freedom.

He shouldn't have left her, he thought again. He should have heeded that warning itch at his back as he drove back to the ranch. The urge to turn back and slip into her house and into her bed had been nearly overwhelming.

He'd not ignore it again. Never again would he ignore that instinctive voice and blame it on his lust rather than that kernel of knowledge that something wasn't just right. That his instincts had picked up something his conscious mind had missed.

Better yet, she was coming to the ranch, where he could make certain she was protected, ensure that no one ever got to her again, ever harmed her again.

"You were just a Marine, huh?" Archer snorted as Rafe flicked him a brooding look. "You know, Rafe, for 'just a Marine' your records are all but inaccessible."

"And why would you want them to be accessible, Archer?" he asked smoothly.

"Let's say there was a time or two the mayor was curious about your whereabouts," Archer sighed. "I checked and all I could get was that you were a Marine. After that, forget it."

The mayor was curious, his ass. Most likely, there was another crime they'd wanted to pin on Crowe and his cousins and they wanted to be certain where the cousins were.

"And you can forget it now," Rafe assured the sheriff as he gripped the armrest of the door and all but tore it off in frustration. "Can't you drive any faster?"

Rafe could have driven these mountain roads faster with a blindfold for a handicap.

"Rafe, I'm going to tell you now, you, Logan, and Crowe stay out of this," Archer warned him as they neared the city limits and the hospital where Cami had been taken. "Take care of Cami and let me handle the rest."

Yeah, that was what Archer's father, Randal, had warned

them of twelve years before, as the sheriff, when the first girl had been found in Corbin County at the base of Crowe Mountain.

Rafe, Logan, and Crowe had just so happened to have been in Denver with Ryan Calvert that week meeting several recruiting officers and staying on the military base there with Ryan's family. If they hadn't been, they would have been arrested then and they would have never been able to clear themselves.

Archer wasn't stupid, though. The Callahan cousins weren't little more than boys anymore. They were adult men, military trained, and they didn't take orders worth shit from civilians.

It was one of their best traits, Crowe liked to say.

But even more, they knew how to protect themselves.

"Do you hear me, Rafe?" Archer snapped.

Rafe turned his head and stared back at Archer as determination flowed through him.

The determination to kill whoever had dared to touch Cami. Whoever had dared to bruise her, frighten her, or target her because of who her lover was.

Whoever did this would pay for it.

The bastard was a dead man walking; the Callahan cousins would see to it.

CHAPTER 16

Cami listened from her hospital bed, dry-eyed, resigned, to the sound of her father's high, shrill voice on the other end of her aunt's phone.

She'd warned Ella, Eddy's wife, not to call. Cami had warned Ella that Mark could be nasty and that since moving to Aspen he had rarely wanted to speak to his daughter, let alone see her. Unless he needed her for some reason, as he had the month before, to help get her mother settled in the nursing home.

That, or to pay her mother's bills.

She stared up at the pristine white ceiling and wondered why that searing pain was no longer there. Once, it had broken her heart that he hadn't cared, that he refused to allow her mother to care.

But perhaps, even more painful was the fact that her mother would opt to medicate rather than stand up for the child who needed her.

"I'll not have that damned Callahan trash dirtying my home or endangering her mother. Poor Jaymi, she'd be turning over in her grave to know the sister she thought so much of was still fucking the man that raped and murdered her."

Cami flinched.

There was such hatred, such bitterness in his voice. Did

he truly hate her so desperately for not being the child that died? For surviving when his favorite hadn't?

Parents weren't supposed to acknowledge favorites. If they preferred one child over the other, it was supposed to be a carefully hidden secret.

Mark had no remorse at all showing his preference for the child that died, and his belief that the wrong child had died. That he believed Cami didn't deserve to live when Jaymi had been taken away from him.

"Mark, you're a bastard," Ella snapped at that point. "How Margaret ever managed to stay with you all these years I don't know."

She flipped the phone closed.

Cami didn't lift her head; she couldn't. If she had to look at the pity in her aunt's gaze then she might not be able to bear it.

"He always was a fool, Cami-girl."

Her head did lift then. Eddy stood a few feet from the bed, his gaze gentle. She'd rarely seen Eddy with that expression. That was his funeral face and his new-baby face. And now, it was his feel-sorry-for-Cami face.

"Rafer didn't hurt Jaymi," Cami said, feeling numb, wooden. "He wouldn't have called her and warned her against himself. Just like the calls I'm getting."

Eddy sighed heavily as he shoved his large, scarred, and beaten hands into his pant pockets. "Well, a man gets suspicious and he gets paranoid," he said. "I'm not going to say he did do it anymore. But I won't say he didn't. You're our girl, Cam. Nothin' ain't gonna change that and nothin' ain't gonna make us stop worryin' 'bout you. Especially now." Somber and filled with brusque emotion, Eddy sniffed uncomfortably before glancing away from her.

"A benefit of a doubt then?" she asked wearily.

He nodded slowly. "For you, girl. I know you. I know you're damned smart, and you're a damned good girl. That's how Jaymi raised you but I ain't never called you a fool. And I never called Jaymi one. And she always defended those

Callahan boys. I'm not going to turn on my second-best girl just because no one else wants to agree with her."

His second-best girl. She glanced to her aunt, dressed in her nursing scrubs, her expression somber but her gaze loving as she watched her husband. Ella was his best girl, he always said, and bemoaned often the fact that she hadn't been able to conceive the daughter he wanted. A baby girl who looked just like his best girl.

Cami swallowed tightly. If she wasn't careful, she was going to end up crying. No, she wouldn't just cry, she would be sobbing, and she couldn't afford to sob. She hated crying. It pissed her off and made her eyes sore. And her head was sore enough. She felt overwhelmed by Eddy and Ella's anger at Mark, and the way they glanced at her, their sorrow for her aching inside them. She couldn't seem to make them understand that it really didn't matter anymore. She was used to her father's disregard, as well as his judgmental hatred where her past with Rafer was concerned.

She had actually needed him when she had lost her child. Him and her mother, but that had been years before. She had learned a long time ago not to let it hurt, not to let it bother her. That was just the way it was.

"It's okay, Uncle Eddy," she assured him, trying to smile, but her head just hurt too bad to attempt it.

At least her face wasn't too bruised. Thankfully, the bastard hadn't managed to hit her but once in the face. He'd split her lip, turned one side of her face a lovely shade of blue and red. No, the majority of the damage had been the bruises caused by those heavy fists at the side of the head and the concussion the doctor had diagnosed.

Her temple was so tender that any tug at the skin there sent pulses of pain radiating through her head.

"It's not okay." He shook his head. "But there's no changing him anyway."

"Has he ever been a father to you?" Ella asked knowing he hadn't been, as she turned away to secure the blood she had taken earlier in the small tote she carried.

Cami really didn't want to talk about this now, and she definitely didn't want to deal with it. She just shrugged.

"Cami knows he never was."

Cami's head jerked up, a whimper almost escaping as the movement sent a lance of agony twisting through her skull.

Rafe moved around her uncle, his leanly muscled, long-legged stride covering the distance until he was standing beside her, his fingers beneath her chin to lift her face.

She didn't fight him. She didn't have the strength. She just stared up at him, miserably aware of what he was seeing.

Her makeup was smeared, the right side of her head swollen, her face darkened with the bruise, and her lip split. She looked like she boxed for a living.

"School board contacted Archer as we drove into the hospital parking lot," Rafe told her. "Until this is resolved, and your attacker caught, you're on a medical leave of absence."

In other words, they didn't want the gossip or the small chance of danger that came with her attack.

She understood the concern, somewhat. But she hadn't been attacked at school. She knew her students, though; they were curious and full of questions at even the busiest time of the school day. Right now, she didn't need the questions or the knowledge that the answers would be spread among the general public.

It was the right decision for her, at this time. It just sucked to have the decision made for her.

"She needs to rest," her aunt Ella spoke up then, her tone confrontational as she glared from Rafe to her niece. "And she's refusing to stay here."

Rafe slid his fingers back, allowing Cami to turn her gaze from his, thankfully. She swore she was staring death in the eye. There was such latent violence swirling in his gaze that she had to suppress a shiver.

"I'll be fine, Aunt Ella," she assured her.

"You're not going home by yourself," Cami's uncle protested, though this time he had that tone normally reserved for his son.

"I'll be fine." She had no other place to run to, and she wasn't going to her aunt and uncle's. Cami loved them, but the thought of living with them terrified her.

"I'll take care of her." Rafe's tone brooked no refusal, and as she slid him a quick look beneath her lashes she realized she was hesitating to argue back as well.

The tension that rose in the room was unmistakable.

"I said I'll be fine—," she began to protest again.

"Like you were this time?" Rafe growled. "Because you were too damned stubborn and ashamed to let anyone know what was going on."

"Ashamed? Me?" She stared back at him in surprise. "I'm not ashamed, Rafe. I'm practical. Something you don't seem to be. And I did tell you."

"Really? You didn't adequately explain" he argued sardonically as he crossed his arms over his chest and stared down at her with irritating arrogance. "Practical is hiding the fact you're getting threatening phone calls until someone actually tried to rape and murder you in your own home. Right?"

She winced before glancing quickly at her aunt and uncle. Cami swore Eddy paled before he swallowed tightly to regain his equilibrium.

"That was uncalled for."

"It was the truth. Now, you can stay here, in this nice, sterile little room, or you can stop arguing with me and I'll take you home. Those are your choices. Now pick one before I pick it for you."

She so did not like being ordered around like this. If it weren't for the headache, as well as the exhaustion, she would have argued with him.

"I want to sleep in my own bed."

There was no way she was going to be able to sleep in a hospital bed. She loved her aunt Ella, but each time Cami had dozed off Ella had been there for blood or some other nursing reason.

Rafe gave a sharp nod of his head.

"She shouldn't be leaving, Rafe," Ella spoke up then. "The doctor wants her to remain until tomorrow morning for observation. A concussion is nothing to mess with, and he suspects she may have some cranial bruising."

"Don't listen to her," Cami told him mutinously. "She gets paranoid."

Ella rolled her eyes before turning back to Rafe. "Are you paying attention to me, Rafer Callahan?"

Rafe's brows arched as Cami glanced at him, though he seemed more amused than angry.

"Yes, ma'am, I am," he assured her. "In this case, you may have to settle for a Marine medic, though."

Ella propped one hand on her lush hip and stared back at him, suspicious. "You're a medic?"

"No, ma'am, but I have one." He grinned back at her. He had no intentions of telling them who the medic was or that Logan had had training that could have gotten him a job in any hospital as a physician's assistant.

"You two just are not going to listen to reason, are you?" Ella finally griped.

"Maybe it's a good thing, Ella," Eddy spoke up. "I just want her safe. And this is a public hospital. If her attacker's determined, he'll not have too hard a time getting to her."

Cami could see what he wasn't saying, though. What if they were wrong and Rafe and his cousins had been the ones to have killed Jaymi and, as many believed, framed Thomas Jones?

It was in Ella's and Eddy's eyes and in their voices each time they spoke and in their gazes as they shared one of those speaking looks that only true soul mates shared.

Eddy was rough talking, loud, and confrontational whenever his petite wife wasn't around. But once she was there, he went from growling lion to tame little house cat.

"Are you ready to go?" Rafe asked then. "Logan and Crowe are waiting in the hall for us."

Cami lifted her gaze to her aunt.

"Callahan, I wanna talk to you first. You and I can walk out in the hall while Ella helps her finish getting ready and gets her signed out." Her uncle wasn't growling, but he wasn't exactly the tame pussycat either.

Rafe stared across Cami's head at the older man, seeing more than simply the command in his gaze. Eddy Flannigan was pissed off, but he wasn't pissed off with Cami or even with Rafe this time.

Rafe gave a sharp nod before bending his head, his lips pressing the top of Cami's head. "Be good," he warned her. "Don't try to run on me."

"Rafe, if I had to run for my life right now then I think I'd probably have to just go ahead and die."

He doubted that. According to the doctor Rafe had talked to, she had put up one hell of a fight.

"I'll be right outside then." He let his fingertips caress down her back before he moved away and returned to the hall, the normally verbally abusive, smart-assed Eddy following behind him.

As the door closed behind them, Eddy held up his hand quickly as both Logan and Crowe straightened from their positions on each side of the door and glared at him fiercely.

"I'm not interested in fighting you boys, yet," he warned them.

Rafer crossed his arms over his chest and stared back at him curiously. "Then what do you want?"

"Did she tell you about the phone calls she was getting?"

Had she told Eddy? "The sheriff did," Rafe informed the other man. "Cami hadn't mentioned the full extent of it."

Eddy's shoulders sagged a little as he rubbed at the back of his neck in irritation. "Likely he heard it from the same place I did: Jack Townsend?"

Rafe nodded.

Eddy shook his head at the response or whatever thought Rafe could see darkening his gaze.

"Her aunt just got off the phone with her father," Eddy told them then. "Normally, this ain't no business but Flannigans', but I saw her face, and her daddy did nothing to keep his voice low enough that it didn't carry on the phone." He quickly went through the conversation, ending with the final insult to Cami when Mark had called her Callahan trash.

Rafe could feel the anger building inside him now.

"What the hell happened to him?" he sighed. "Mark Flannigan was a good man once."

Eddy snorted at that. "No, my brother, unlike me, likes to hide his faults and appear perfect in public. Me, now this is what you have." He held his arms out to his sides as anger filled his voice. "You're stuck with me exactly how I am. Mark, he likes to have all those pretty words said about him; he always did. And don't get me wrong; he loved Jaymi something fierce. Her death killed a part of him, I think. But Mark was never loving with Cami, Rafe. He was never a father to her. He resented her birth and he resented every time he had to balance buying for her with buying for Jaymi. Every time Jaymi had to share something, or couldn't have something, he blamed Cami's birth. The day of Jaymi's funeral he stated it was unfair that his Jaymi was gone, that she had suffered. If one of them had to die like that—" Eddy seemed to shudder as he blinked back a sudden moisture in his eyes. "He said it should have been Cami." Eddy lifted his gaze as Rafe fought to hide the horror that a father could ever say or do anything so atrocious. "And she overheard him." He cleared his throat uncomfortably. "Like I said, this should stay Flannigan business." He glared at Rafe as though it were his fault the story was coming out. "But that girl has enough on her shoulders right now; hearing her daddy call her trash wasn't something she needed. One of these days, she's going to accept to her soul that she doesn't have a daddy, and when she does, if you're there—" He broke off as though uncomfortable.

"There's no if about it," Rafe assured him. "I'll be there, and I'll take care of her."

Eddy nodded sharply.

"Tell me something, Eddy. All these years you've poked and prodded and sliced at us with that smart-assed mouth of yours, and not even for a minute did you believe we hurt Jaymi. Why did you do it?"

"Who says I didn't?" Eddy frowned, his gaze fierce and confrontational as he stared back at them.

"Because you would have never told me any of that if you

thought for a moment one of us hurt her sister," Rafe snarled back at, Eddy, his voice low but the fury raging in it loud and clear.

"And I would have never treated you any different even if your names hadn't come up in her death." Eddy was in Rafe's face, glaring, his entire demeanor one of defensive anger. "You were arrogant little shits as kids who slapped away every helping hand extended to you. You only slap my hand once, Callahan. And count yourself lucky, because of that girl in there." Eddy's finger stabbed toward the hospital room door. "Because of that girl, you're getting another chance. See if you can be appreciative this time."

The man had lost his mind. "When did you ever extend a hand to any of us?" Rafe bit out in disbelief. "You stood with the rest of this county every damned time they wanted to accuse us of something."

"And you made it so damned easy, didn't you?" Eddy settled back on his heels with a tough, mocking smile. Like a banty rooster standing in challenge. "You little shits. You were ten." He looked at Rafe. "Twelve." His gaze met Logan's. "And thirteen." He inclined his head to Crowe. "And that damned chip on your shoulder was bigger than each of you were. I offered you a ride to school one morning." He stared at Rafe expectantly, his look withering.

It was Crowe who nodded slowly. "It was snowing and damned cold," he murmured, his golden-brown eyes sharp, intent. "You were driving that beat-up old four-wheel drive of your brother's."

And Rafe remembered it then.

"You saw me, not Mark," Eddy growled, his gaze suddenly brooding rather than confrontational.

Crowe shook his head. "I saw Mark Flannigan, and I saw the day before as he came around that curve you drove around that morning. He came around it so fast that if Logan hadn't jumped for the ditch he would have run him over. And he didn't even stop to make sure he was okay."

"That was the winter after our parents died," Logan said quietly. "I don't remember much of that year. Except that lawyer Rafe's uncle got us to keep the Raffertys and the Corbins from stealing the inheritances our mothers left us."

For a second, abject regret filled Eddy's eyes. Remorse and shame flashed in his gaze before he hurriedly jerked his eyes away. When he turned back, it was with a sense of resignation and acceptance, though the remorse was still a heavy presence in his expression.

Eddy backed down. "Hell, I'm who I am," he stated, obviously making the connection that what he had seen as childish arrogance had been lingering shock and grief. "An asshole on a good day, but I'm not stupid." He turned to Rafe. "Jaymi and Cami both have defended you, against everything and everyone. When you were arrested for Jaymi's murder, Cami just about went crazy. She swore every day you didn't do it. She would sit up at night forming arguments for your lawyer, she said." He shook his head and sighed heavily. "God help me if I'm wrong." He turned his head, his gaze tormented now. "But that's mine and Ella's girl. We've done what we can to teach her to be smart, and to know her own mind. And she's damned certain you're a good man. And I'm damned certain I know every crime you've been accused of you weren't anywhere around when it happened, except Jaymi's death. And she wasn't the only innocent young woman that died that summer."

It didn't make up for the years of the man's confrontational insults and jeering attitude. But one thing Rafe could say in Eddy's defense: he was one of the few who hadn't called the cousins rapists and murderers to their faces, or behind their backs as far as Rafe knew.

Eddy was mocking, snide, sarcastic, and those were his good days, but he wasn't cruel, and he had never gone out of his way to be mocking, snide, and sarcastic either. It was simply what you found when you found Eddy.

The sound of the door opening drew all their attention, and Rafe had to force back a growl of fury at the timid, cautious pace of each step and the proof that the blows to Cami's body hadn't been made as a warning. The attack had been meant to be deadly.

"Get a wheelchair!" he snapped to Logan, turning, only to see Crowe jerking one from the nurses' station and wheeling it to her.

"Sit, baby." It was an order, cloaked in silk, she thought as she hid a smile and sat down gingerly in the chair.

The bruise on her hip from stumbling on the stairs was actually the worst of the it. Well, except for the bruise the doctor said her skull might have.

It wasn't so bruised that she wasn't well aware of the fact that Rafe was in command mode.

Which was really rather amusing. Why bother to hide it now with that dark, husky male tenderness? It was like throwing a tablecloth over the elephant in the living room, she thought, struggling not to grin.

"I see that grin tugging at your lips," he told her as he moved behind her and leaned close, his lips at her ear. "What's so funny?"

She wasn't touching that one with a ten-foot pole.

"So much for saving you from any more trouble," she sighed instead. "I was hoping to avoid this for you, Rafe."

"Trying to protect me, were you?" he asked as he knelt beside the chair, reached up, and brushed her hair back from her cheek.

Cami was tempted to close her eyes at the stroke of pleasure against her flesh, the warmth and calloused rasp of his fingertips against her skin.

"Maybe I was trying to protect us both."

"Cami, I'll be at the house this evening with your prescriptions and to check you out." Ella moved from the room, her voice brisk and no-nonsense, her expression fierce as she moved in front of Cami.

Ella was all but glaring at Rafe as he came to his feet. "I *will* be keeping a check on her, Rafe Callahan."

Cami watched her aunt in confusion. She had never known her aunt and uncle to be so protective. Well, perhaps that wasn't particularly true. Since her parents' move to Aspen four years ago, Cami's aunt and uncle had seemed to take more of an interest by the month in her.

"I understand, Aunt Ella," she promised.

Ella's gaze flicked to Rafe. "You take care of her, or you'll deal with me and Eddy, young man."

"Yes, ma'am." He nodded. "We should go now. I'd like to get her home and get her settled in."

Ella leaned down, hugged her gently. "Call me if you need me," she whispered.

"I will. I promise."

As Ella moved back, Cami's uncle took her place. He touched the side of her gently, a facsimile of his normal firm grip, and kissed the top of her head. "I'll be by with Ella," he promised. "Just let me know if you need me."

"I'm going to be fine. You two act like I'm going away forever or something," she chided them both softly.

They invited her to dinner, to the movies, to their Sunday drives when they were both off work together. And it was something Cami realized she sometimes forgot.

She wasn't totally alone; she never had been. She had always had Eddy and Ella.

But they weren't her parents; they had their own family. Cami always felt on the outside looking in, and that had made her feel even lonelier. She hadn't just felt as though she were on the outside looking in; she had been.

It wasn't their fault. It was hers and perhaps, in some ways, her parents'.

Giving her aunt and uncle a final quick hug, Cami allowed Rafe to wheel her to the elevator where he, Logan, and Crowe crowded around her. The doors were closing before she realized something.

"They never believed you hurt Jaymi," she murmured, frowning at the doors as the elevator moved slowly to the lobby floor. "They couldn't have, or they wouldn't have let you leave with me so easily."

She didn't look at Rafe, but she heard his grunt, mocking, disbelieving.

She shook her head. "You don't understand, Rafe." Eyes narrowed, she glanced up to where he stood at her side. "If they even suspected at the time that you had hurt Jaymi, they would have been going crazy over me leaving with you." It didn't make sense. "Why would Uncle act as though he believed it, if he didn't?"

"Because he's an ass," Rafe grunted.

"Because, like everyone else in Corbin County, he believed if our mothers hadn't married Callahans then they wouldn't have died," Crowe answered for him. "Kim Corbin, Mina Rafferty, and Ann Ramsey weren't just best friends and the daughters of the most financially successful families on this side of the mountain; they were also very well loved by everyone in the county. So much so that during those years before they they died in that wreck those who did love them were actually giving the Callahan brothers a chance."

"What chance?" Cami asked as the elevator door slid to a stop. "The last I heard they were reviled before and after they married their wives."

Crowe shook his head as Rafe stopped at the passenger side of the truck and she stared up at him in confusion.

"You don't know?" he asked as he stared down at her.

"Know what?"

"Because of Kim Corbin, Ann Ramsey, and Mina Rafferty they were beginning a future, Cami. In those few short years, the Callahans were doing something no one else had accomplished. They had actually found an investor for a resort in Corbin County that had all the earmarks of success. They were doing something the Raffertys and Corbins had nearly bankrupted themselves attempting to accomplish more than once. When they died, everyone in this county who was counting on that resort lost that dream. And they had only one way to punish the men who failed them."

"Through their children."

He inclined his head slowly, resigned. "Their children."

CHAPTER 17

"It isn't necessary that you stay here," Cami informed Rafe as he moved from the bathroom into the bedroom, his damp hair tasseled around his face, his bare chest and shoulders looking a mile wide as he strode across the shadowed room toward the bed. Cotton pants hung low on his hips, emphasizing the lean, muscled hips, the tight, hard, rippled abs.

She could feel her stomach tightening, her thighs softening, tensing, her heart rate increasing.

"I know it's not necessary," he assured her as he padded barefoot to the bed and pulled the blanket and sheet back before sliding into her bed as though he was supposed to be there.

Cami turned her gaze to the ceiling, swallowing tightly as she fought the edge of panic that seemed to be building inside her. How was she supposed to handle this? He wasn't supposed to be here. He wasn't supposed to be in her house and in her bed as though he were suddenly some fantasy come true.

This wasn't how it worked.

This wasn't how it was supposed to work. Not yet. Not until she had found a way to handle it. Right?

Her head jerked in his direction just in time to see him standing and pushing the pants from the tight, well-rounded, muscled contours of his ass.

Naked. He was naked.

Sliding into her bed.

As though he hadn't been there before, a part of her scoffed. But still, it was different. There was something about this that had her entire system going crazy with the implications of it.

She had never shared her space with a man, and only in her fantasies had she shared it with Rafe

"Okay?" he asked as he lay back and pulled the sheet just over his hips.

Just barely over the hard, engorged flesh of his cock.

He was aroused and so clearly very interested in assuaging the need she could feel beginning to burn inside her despite the bruises on her body.

"Fine." Clearing her throat, she fought to keep from sounding as though she had just swallowed a golf ball. Even if that was what it felt like was lodged in her throat.

He turned to her, his expression dark and brooding.

"Are you having a problem with it, Cami?" he asked silkily.

"A problem with what?"

"With me being in your bed with you," he explained.

"Well, it's not as though it's the first time we've shared a bed, right?" She could see his expression, and there was something there, something in his gaze, that warned her he wasn't nearly as calm as he appeared to be.

"No, it's not," he agreed. "Though I have to admit, it did feel rather strange walking in the front door. Do you think anyone saw us?"

What the hell was he getting at?

She watched him carefully. "I'm certain they did," she said. "I believe half the neighbors came out to view the event."

And it wasn't a joke, despite the mockery in her tone. There had been plenty of interest in their arrival. As the vehicles had pulled into her drive and Rafe had carried her into the house, several of her neighbors had stepped outside to view the event.

She could just imagine how hot the telephone lines were this evening. Gossip was probably raging like a fire burning out of control. Which was only slightly cooler than the hunger burning through her body.

The need was like a craving that couldn't be assuaged.

"Why didn't you tell me about the phone calls, Cami?"

She stilled. The breath seemed to stop in her chest.

Her tongue swiped over her lips in what she knew was a terrible mistake. It was a sign of nervousness, and they both knew it.

His gaze tracked it, his eyes narrowing on the movement before returning to hers.

"What phone calls?" She fought to come up with an explanation, a glib response, or some way to throw him off.

It was obvious he had to have talked to Jack. Only Jack and his wife knew about the phone calls.

Rafe's brow arched, slowly, with mocking emphasis, as his expression tightened with brooding irritation.

"Don't play games with me, Cami," he warned her, his voice dangerously soft. "And don't lie to me, kitten. I would be very, very displeased if I caught you lying to me."

"And that displeasure should affect me?" She only barely managed to keep her voice from squeaking.

She might not be frightened of him, but she had a very healthy respect for the fact that there definitely were ways he could make her regret anything she did to piss him off and still maintain the emotional abyss she was slipping into.

His arm lifted from where it had lain along his side as he stared at her, his head propped on his hand, his long, lean body spooned against her side.

His fingertips stroked down her bare arms, raising goose bumps and reminding her, forcibly, that he thought perhaps she should be concerned with his displeasure.

The pleasure was impossibly erotic. A touch that simple yet combined with the look in those sapphire eyes sent her senses reeling.

Against her hip, the heavy proof of his erection was cushioned between their flesh only by the thin silk of her short gown. Heated and heavy, the feel of it sent the blood thundering through her veins as she drew in a hard, deep breath.

"I want to know about those phone calls," he warned her. "And now is a very good time to tell me, Cami. Before I become frustrated with your attempts to distract me. And that frustration could lead to all kinds of punishments."

And did he truly believe such an erotic dare would go unanswered?

Oh, she knew she would have to tell him about the phone calls. He was already aware of them, likely already knew the full story; he only wanted her to tell him. He wanted to know why she hadn't told him. He wanted to delve into all the reasons why, on a totally deeper level, she hadn't come to him.

And ultimately, he wanted to ensure he had created a tie between them that she couldn't break.

The fact that she hadn't told him about those calls assured him that the tie he wanted in place wasn't as tight as he would have liked.

And he thought that was going to come easy?

She almost smiled at the thought.

She wasn't easy, even for him. Especially for him, the emotional ties he was determined to build were not going to be given without an assurance of ties in return. And there was no assurance. Not yet. And neither was there a confidence that she could handle the man he had become.

It wasn't, she had realized over the past days, a fear, shame, or embarrassment of the town. It wasn't that she didn't want to face fighting everyone around her for what she wanted. It was the fear that fighting everyone else would prove fruitless when he walked away.

"Cami, you're not making much effort to help me out here," he drawled, his tone velvet rough as it rumbled from his chest.

As he spoke, the blanket that covered her to beneath her arms was slowly pulled away from her, leaving her beneath his gaze clad only in the short, silky plum-colored nightgown she had donned after her shower.

"Am I supposed to be helping you out?" she asked him. "It seems you're only asking rhetorical questions, Rafe. You already know the answers."

"Let's say I know of the subject at hand, but the details have eluded me. And you will give me those details."

Would she?

She had no intentions of allowing him to order her to do anything. Just as she had absolutely no intention of bowing down to the dominance that gleamed in his eyes.

Submissive she truly wasn't. She would call no man master, nor would she ever give in to that dominance without a very sensual struggle.

"There were no details to give, Rafe," she assured him quietly as he pushed the comforter to her knees as she felt her womb flex and her pussy pulse erotically. The soft slide of her juices from the intimate recess of her body had her fighting not to arch her hips and bring attention to the needy flesh between her thighs.

She ached for him. There was no denying the fact that she wanted him more than she had ever wanted anything or anyone in her life. Just as there was no denying the sensual and emotional abyss that opened within her each time she had to deal with the conflicting pleasure and hungers that attacked her with each touch he gave her.

What the hell was she supposed to do with all this need? With the hunger for his touch, for his kiss, mixing with the overwhelming, overriding desire to challenge *his* arousal and his hunger.

It was like playing tug-of-war with herself.

His fingertips stroked against her knee before caressing above it, then back. Delicate velvet-soft touches before they went higher, petting and stroking as he stared down at her until the caresses were at her thighs and she was fighting to keep from parting her thighs.

"Did you recognize anything about the voice?" he asked her.

She cleared her throat. "It sounded very mechanical."

It was all she could do to concentrate on the fact that when he spoke it wasn't anything sexy. Still, though, the dark rumble of his voice had her entire body sensitizing when combined with the dark dominance that filled Rafe.

"No. Nothing. It just sounded like a robot." Her hips did arch this time as his fingers delved beneath her gown.

Her thighs parted, her senses becoming entangled in the insidious pleasure stroking closer to the swollen bud of her clitoris and the weeping center of her body.

Her nipples, though excruciatingly tender, ached with more than the pain of the callous treatment that had been inflicted on them by her attacker. They were hardened, throbbing with both arousal as well as the tenderness. It was an interesting, confusing pleasure-pain that she fought to make sense of.

Rafe's gaze moved from his fingers playing at her thighs, moving ever closer to the aching flesh there as his gaze centered on the hard buds of her nipples beneath the silk of the gown.

"Let me take your gown off."

Her breathing seemed to constrict in her chest.

She'd seen the bruises after her shower, and they were horrendous. Long, thick finger marks marred the flesh in shades of black, blue, and abraded red. Her nipples were swollen and a cherry red, rather than the pink they had once been.

"I don't want—"

He laid his fingers to her lips, stopping the flow of words.

"Do I make you feel good when I touch you, Cami?"

She could feel her breathing accelerate at the very thought of the pleasure he could give her. Instantly heat flooded her body, like flames burning out of control.

"That's not the point," she whispered, her fingers digging into the sheet beneath her as she fought to control her breathing.

She didn't dare touch him. Touching him would be the height of insanity. There was no way she could hold back then. No way she could pull back from that pit of dark, hidden emotions that swirled within her.

"You won't answer my questions, and you won't let me love your sweet body?" He reached over, picked up her hand from her side, and forced her fingers from their grip on the sheet. "Cami, love, is it so hard to be my lover?"

"We're not lovers." She had to deny it; she couldn't let herself accept that they were. Accepting it meant giving in, and giving in was something she couldn't allow herself to do. Not yet.

He only chuckled at the denial, though, his lips curving, his blue eyes filling with knowing amusement as she stared up at him.

"Ahh, so, Cami, what does 'a lover' mean beyond the fact that when we're together we're fucking like minks in mating season?"

She had to force her lips from a smile at the phrasing, as well as the fact that he was right.

He lifted her hand, forcing her fingers to curl around his as he brought them to the warmth of his chest.

"Lovers do more than fuck," she reminded him. "They spend more time together than that which is spent in the bed."

"We didn't spend the whole weekend in the bed when you were snowbound," he reminded her. "We cooked."

"I cooked while you shoveled out the sidewalk." And she had watched him through the window over the sink, and she had fought the intimacy of something so simple, so homey, as the fact that she was cooking and he was shoveling the snow.

"But we did more than fuck."

There was no denying that fact.

"Those were very unusual circumstances," she reminded him.

"Only because you made them unusual." He unfolded her fingers until her hand lay, palm flat, against the crisp, light mat of curls that spread across his chest.

Cami felt herself trembling, her fingers shaking against his chest, the urge to whimper with the need rising in her chest.

"I will have the answers to my questions." The hem of her gown began to rise. "And I'll see this very sweet body every night I lie in bed with it." There was a demand in his voice that brooked no refusal. "Tell me you're not mine, Cami. Tell me I don't own every response, every heated second of arousal." The hem cleared her thighs, revealing the tiny scrap of silk she wore as panties.

"Arrogant, aren't you?" But he was right, so very right, about the fact that she responded to no one else. That she wanted, ached for, and needed no other man except Rafe.

"Right."

His head lowered as his lips touched hers. Just touched. It wasn't a hard, hungry kiss. It was a tease, a temptation, the threat of that raw, erotic hunger flaring between them as he stared down at her.

The silk moved higher, over her hips, and she lifted for it.

She was insane, because she couldn't refuse him. She couldn't say no. She couldn't pull away from him. She didn't have the will to fight herself, let alone the will to fight him.

Within seconds, he pulled back and lifted her arms, pulling the gown over her head.

Cami closed her eyes.

She didn't want to see the damage herself; she had already seen it. She had already seen the damage to her skin, the proof that another man had touched her. No matter the fact that it was forced, or rather especially because it was forced, her attacker had left the proof of that force on her flesh.

"Oh God." Her eyes flew open at the feel of the violently intense pleasure that lashed through her system at the incredibly soft stroke of Rafe's tongue over the abused flesh.

His expression was mesmerizing. Drowsy male lust, brooding sensuality, and absorbed hunger.

His cock lay against her thigh, heated and thick, rubbing against her flesh as his hips moved imperceptibly. The feel of the hard flesh against her, his tongue rubbing over her tender nipple as his hand stroked her other thigh, had her moving against him, her thighs parting further.

She needed him inside her.

"It's been so long," she whispered as her hands moved to grip his shoulders, her hands sliding over his skin, loving the warm, rougher texture of his skin against her softer hands.

"You're a stubborn woman, Cami," he crooned as his lips stroked against the vivid bruises. "You're my woman."

A soft cry left her lips as a sensation akin to a punch of

exquisite pleasure lanced her womb and had her arching closer to him.

It couldn't have been the possessive ring in his voice or the proclamation that she was his woman.

"Rafe, please don't—" Don't make promises he couldn't keep. Don't lie to her. To make her hope for something, dream for things that couldn't be hers.

"Have you given another man what you've given me?" He breathed over the straining tip of her nipple before licking it again.

His tongue covered the brutally sensitive tip with a wash of such incredible pinching pleasure that living fingers of it shot straight to her clit, clenching her pussy and her womb as she gasped in response.

"You don't give me a chance to think," she whispered as her nails bit against the skin of his shoulders as she fought to hold on to him. To hold on to something. She felt as though she was perched on a free fall into a whirlpool of ecstasy so vivid it was nearly terrifying.

This was what he did to her. He made her want to believe. He made her want to dream, to hope, and to hold on to the illusion that he would be there tomorrow, next week, next year, and next lifetime.

"You've had weeks to think," he told her, his voice roughening as his hands stroked down her thighs and he began kissing his way down her body.

Pleasure attacked her nerve endings, pulling her deeper into the morass of erotic sensations building around her.

It was a roller coaster of pleasure. A thrill ride of extremes as each touch threw her ever deeper into the brilliant, heated rush of pleasure that she had only ever found in his arms.

As his lips and tongue painted a path of heated strokes and erotic caresses from her breasts to her hips, there was no pain, no remembered fear. There was nothing but the ever-increasing pleasure she could never get enough of.

The years in between his touch could be measured in the nights she had spent dreaming of his touch, dreaming of this.

Rafer in her bed, touching her, his lips feathering over the bare, silken flesh between her thighs, his tongue licking at the spill of juices that glazed her flesh.

"Have I ever told you that I've dreamed of the taste of your pussy?" There was no shame in him, no holding back.

Cami's hips arched with a cry as his tongue delved between the swollen lips of her pussy.

Her leg lifted, knee bending, as his palm eased along the curve of her rear. She could feel the heated, aching flesh of her vagina, the clench of her muscles. She felt so empty, so empty and so in need of his touch.

The need to touch him had her hands delving into the long strands of his hair. Once they were there, her fingers tangled into it, hips lifting as she directed the path of his lips.

The swollen, desperate bud of her clit throbbed in need as he blew a wisp of his breath over the bundle of nerves.

"Rafe, please," she gasped, the need for the touch of his lips against her clit flooding her senses with a pleasure she reached for with every part of her.

His lips surrounded it, but only for a second. Long enough to deliver a deep, quick kiss, the stroke of his lips too brief, too intense, to bear without crying out in ragged pleasure.

"Rafe," the whimper rose unbidden from her lips. "I need more."

"Tell me what you need, baby," he urged, his voice rough, echoing with hunger. "Tell me what you want, Cami. Anything you want."

Anything she wanted?

Her head thrashed against the pillows, a desperate effort to hold back the needs, to hold back the erotic, exotic fantasies she'd had for so many years.

The need for a touch she'd never had.

A need for a hunger she had resisted every step of the way.

His finger touched the lower curves of the swollen folds between her thighs, gathering her juices and easing lower.

Thrusting upward, she sobbed in need as his touch glanced over the clenched entrance of her pussy, then lifted again. Once again it stroked down, past the flexing entrance, then back.

On the next pass, it continued its journey until the heavy, slick juices were being eased along the forbidden entrance that flexed and echoed with aching pleasure at his touch. The press of his fingertip against her rear entrance had her moaning pleadingly as it slowly, gently, began to pierce the tender, nerve-laden area. Slowly, easily, the tightened entrance began to part, to open to steady impalement of his finger pressing inside.

His tongue circled her straining clit as his thumb caressed and stroked the entrance to her pussy. The sensations delivered to the three most sensitive areas of her body were doing more than throwing her toward ecstasy. They were tossing her about, flinging her closer, jerking her back, playing a devilish, agonizing game with her that had her arching, twisting, and sobbing out her need.

Fingers of pulsing pleasure were racing through her. Every cell of her body had sensitized to the point that she swore she could feel even the stroke of the air against her flesh. She was overwhelmed with sensation and begging for more, desperate for more.

As his lips joined his stroking tongue, surrounding her swollen clit as his thumb pressed into her pussy and his fingertip eased deeper into her anal entrance, Cami fought desperately for a release that teased at the edges of pleasure.

She could feel Rafe beginning to lose himself in the taste of her, in the act of pleasuring her. She had never understood it. She had never heard her friends discuss their own lovers placing such emphasis on their pleasure. She had never known Rafe to touch her any other way.

His earthy male groan echoed around her as her hips writhed beneath him. His fingers fucked her with even, shallow thrusts as his thumb sank into her pussy, possessing it and rasping against the tender inner tissue with rapid strokes of intense sensation.

With each caress, each stroke of his tongue, his lips, his

fingers, she flew higher, hurtling faster toward the center of an ecstasy she hadn't expected.

It shouldn't be this intense.

The bruising of her flesh, the memory of the night before, should have somehow affected her ability to reach so high, to strain so desperately toward the sensations building inside her. But she should have expected, should have known, Rafe could possess every part of her even to the point that nothing existed but pleasure. To the point that pain merged with the building ecstasy, erasing itself as it became part of the sensations Rafe stroked through her system.

Her fingers clenched in his hair as it continued to build. The sensations wrapped around her, flew through her, pulsed in her veins, and beat through her senses until they exploded through her with a surge of such incredible, blazing ecstasy that Cami swore she could feel herself melting. From the inside out she was dissolving with pleasure, exploding, imploding, and surging through a starburst of pure, erotic rapture.

It seemed never ending.

As she clenched, tightening over and again, the sensations arched her body, locking it in place as he continued to suckle at her exploding clit as his thumb fucked into her pussy and the tip of his finger worked itself rapidly into the clenched entrance of her rear.

As the exploding blaze of sensation reached its pinnacle, she felt each stroke, each touch, each caress begin to ease. As the aftershocks and waves of intensity began to shudder through her, he prolonged each one, using his lips and tongue to draw each sensation to its height.

When she finally collapsed, exhausted, to the bed, her body damp with perspiration, her senses ragged and laid to waste from the explosions that had torn through her, it was to feel the tender, soothing kisses at her thighs and lower belly as he eased his fingers from her body.

They were both breathing heavily, just as she realized he hadn't possessed her in a way that would have given him the same release.

As his head lifted, his gaze dark with drowsy satisfaction, she stared back at him in confusion.

"You didn't . . ." She wasn't as adapt with the words as he was, she realized as she struggled to finish the statement.

"I didn't come?" His voice was a deep, dark growl. "Sweetheart, you're the only woman I know that has the power to cause me to come in the sheets because I'm so damned excited over your climax."

Amusement gleamed in his eyes as confusion edged at her mind.

No, her friends had definitely never mentioned this when it came to their lovers, husbands, or one-night stands.

She swallowed tightly. "I could—"

"Shh." He moved up her body, his lips brushing against hers. "Your sweet body can handle only so much, baby. I found my release and, even more important to me, you've found yours."

With a quick kiss to her lips he eased from the bed before padding quickly to the bathroom.

Cami was too exhausted to move. Breathing out deeply, she let her eyes close and was almost easing into sleep when she felt the touch of a warm cloth against her thighs.

Opening her eyes, she watched him, so confident, so completely male, despite the fact that he was cleaning her and drying the sheets between her thighs and legs so thoroughly.

"Sleep, baby." When he finished, he laid a kiss at the top of her mound, just above her clit, then moved to her lips and kissed them gently as she stared up at him. "I'll watch over you. I promise."

How had he known? How could he have known that she had worried about coming home before he arrived at the hospital? That even after he had tucked her into her bed and gone to shower she'd been too tense to sleep? Until the moment he promised to watch over her, there had been a fear she hadn't realized she had.

That fear eased from her almost immediately.

Her lashes were suddenly heavier, lassitude invading her

limbs as he slid into bed beside her and drew her against him, his arms sheltering her.

"Sleep, baby," he growled against her ear. "We'll work the rest out tomorrow."

As Rafe felt her drift into sleep he stared across the room, his expression hardening. The marks on her breasts, the swollen flesh of her nipple, and the deep bruising at her hip and her head had rage building inside him.

The son of a bitch had thought he could rape, torture, and kill Rafe's Cami in her own home. Thought that she was too weak, that she would be too frightened to attempt to fight back.

She had fought back. But her attacker had given them all a heads-up. They knew he was out there now, no longer a piece of the past. Someone was trying to resurrect the past instead.

The man who had raped, tortured, and killed Jaymi and the other women twelve years before was dead. Crowe had killed him as Rafe had held Jaymi's dying body.

Now he was holding her sister, loving her sister. He and Jaymi had truly been more friends than lovers. She claimed he was her best friend, her last tie to the husband she had lost in a war so far away.

Rafe and Tye Kramer had been best friends. Tye had been from Aspen, born and raised there, and it was there he and Jaymi had lived before he had been called from the Reserves to go overseas.

When he had died, it had destroyed Jaymi, and Rafe had wondered how she would survive it. She had survived by holding on to everything Tye had claimed. Including his best friend.

And now someone thought he could resurrect the horror of the past and take something else from Rafe? From the Callahan cousins?

Cami was his, that meant Logan and Crowe would give their lives for her if needed. Definitely they would help Rafe protect her with everything inside them.

Because she belonged to him and that meant she belonged to the Callahans.

Cami didn't know it yet, but she *was* a Callahan.

Because he had no intentions whatsoever of ever letting her go.

CHAPTER 18

Having three men in her small house wasn't Cami's idea of peace and relaxation. Two days later, as she moved down the stairs, pushing back the memory of her desperate flight the night she was attacked, she came to a slow stop at the bottom of the stairs.

Leaning against the curved banister, she stared at the floor of her living room where, sleeping-bag-encased, Logan and Crowe slept in positions that would block all access to the stairs.

There was no way in hell to get from the kitchen to the stairs or from the stairs to the kitchen, where her coffeepot awaited.

"Just tell them to move their sorry asses," Rafe said lightly as he bounded down the stairs behind her rather than walking softly as she had.

"They're sleeping." She frowned up at him, not entirely agreeing with the command.

"They were, until Lard Ass stomped down the stairs," Crowe groused as he rolled over in the sleeping bag and jerked the extra-down-filled material over his head.

It wasn't exactly cold, but a fire would have been nice. Before she'd acquired three grown male bodyguards, she would have had the fire ready to light and the coffee set to have already been made.

She held back the sigh that would have slipped past her lips and looked at the clock.

Before she had acquired her bodyguards, she would have had a job to go to. The fire would have waited until evening, and then it would have been a nice glass of wine rather than coffee as she graded papers.

She was going to have to call the principal, though her Uncle Eddy had promised to talk to his other niece himself. Serena Carlyle was Ella's sister's daughter and had taken the post of principal the year before when the previous principal had retired.

A resident of Aspen, Serena wasn't influenced by the barons though. Thank God!

"Someone needs to make coffee," Logan grumbled from somewhere inside his sleeping bag.

"Get your lazy ass up," Rafe ordered as he stepped into the living room and began stepping over the bodies. "We have a busy day ahead of us."

"And what is ahead of you that's going to be so busy?" Cami asked as she followed behind him, albeit picking her way through the living room more slowly.

She was still incredibly tender, her hip was still one large bruise, and though the headaches weren't as severe or as often as they had been at first, they were still prone to hit and last for hours at a time.

The bruising to her skull could have resulted in much, much more serious complications. Thankfully, the initial concussion and disorientation was the worst she had suffered.

She could have returned to work, though she admitted it wouldn't have been easy. Cami was guessing she could look forward to spending the rest of the school year out on leave and when the new fall season began she doubted she would have a job.

Moving to Aspen was out of the question, she thought as she stepped into the kitchen, greeted by the tempting scent of coffee beginning.

"And what are you doing today that's going to be so busy?"

she asked as she pulled the edges of the gray sweater she wore snugly around the white cotton shirt she had tucked into her jeans.

"We have a few errands to run," Rafe told her as he moved to the cabinets and, as he had the day before, began preparing breakfast.

They never asked her to fix breakfast, though Rafe had acted like a kid in a candy store the morning she had cooked during their snowbound adventure.

"Logan and I have to check the ranch and my house before meeting you and Rafe at the courthouse," Crowe finished as he too stepped into the kitchen.

"Meeting us at the courthouse?" She arched a brow as she looked over to where Rafe was loading one of her larger skillets with bacon. "And why are we going to the courthouse?"

"My lawyer and I have a meeting with the county attorney to discuss Deputy Eisner and his lack of talent in navigating private drives with a piece of county equipment."

She almost winced. "You've sued the county?"

"Not yet." Rafe flashed her a grin over his shoulder before turning back to the two pounds of bacon Logan had brought in the day before. "That's what we're discussing."

Cami lowered her head, shaking it at the impossible sense of fun that seemed to fill Rafe's face.

"You know this is insane, right?" she accused him. "Rafe, suing the county is only going to piss more people off."

"Fuck 'em," Logan drawled as he moved plates from the cabinet and handed them to Rafe before taking Cami's cup from her hand and filling it with coffee. "You're probably the only one in this county that likes us anyway."

"Who says I like you?" She arched her brow, hiding the fact that she did like him.

She had always liked the Callahan cousins, even when she was younger. Especially when she was younger, when the cousins had been like fables, larger than life and used as a bogeyman threat against little children who refused to behave.

Logan pouted good-naturedly as Crowe grunted at the

response. She noticed he did that a lot. He didn't talk much, but he watched, listened, and he waited. There was always a sense of waiting where Crowe was concerned, as though he knew something was about to happen and was determined to be prepared.

"So I have to go to this meeting why?" She turned back to Rafe as he moved to the refrigerator and pulled a dozen eggs from the inside.

He flicked her a look that assured her he meant for her to go, one way or the other.

She crossed her arms over her breasts, cocked a hip, and tapped her toe against the floor twice as she waited.

"Ignoring me isn't going to get you your way automatically," she assured him as he returned to the sizzling bacon. "I have things to do today myself."

"And I have no intentions of leaving you here alone," he informed her, his tone hardening. "And I can't miss this meeting. Eisner deliberately took that fence out, and he was too damned gleeful about the results to suit me; now he's going to pay for it."

"And you don't think it would be a good time to take the high road and let it go?" she asked him. "Give it a rest, Rafe. No one is going to care if Deputy Eisner is fired or not, except Eisner. But what they will do is come together against you, rather than for him."

Rafe shrugged. "Good luck to them."

She turned to Crowe, wondering if, as the oldest cousin, he would at least show a bit more maturity.

"You should stay out of this one," he told her instead, his darker voice rumbling more than usual. "Let Eisner pay for his sins. He's quick enough to attempt to make others pay for sins that aren't theirs."

"Stay out of it?" She let her brows arch in amused disbelief. "There's not the first one of you that could possibly keep your nose out of my business at this point, and you have the nerve to tell me to keep mine out of a part of yours? Or his?" She nodded to Rafe. "Not as long as he's sleeping in my bed I won't."

Rafe had to turn back to the sizzling bacon to hide the grin tugging at his lips as Cami turned that teacher's attitude on Crowe without a thought.

There were very few people Rafe had ever known who were willing to stand and stare at his older cousin as though he were a mischievous schoolboy stepping out of line.

"I'm not sleeping in your bed, though," he pointed out.

"No, you're sleeping on my living room floor," she retorted with false sweetness. "If you don't like my opinion, then you're more than welcome to sleep in the backyard."

Logan's snort of laughter was followed by another of Crowe's less than impressed male grunts.

"The backyard is probably more comfortable," Crowe informed her. "Unfortunately, not as secure."

"Yeah, like someone's going to get past Rafe while he's pacing the bedroom floor," she stated.

Rafe arched his brows at the acidic little comment. He had no idea she was aware of the fact that sleep was often a long time coming for him.

He wasn't exactly pacing the bedroom floor, though. That would have been counterproductive. More often than not he was standing by the bedroom window, silent, still, and watching the shadowed edge of her back garden carefully.

Crowe had managed to pinpoint the location where her attacker had come into her yard and slipped into the window well that hadn't been as secure as it should have been.

There had been no prints, just as Archer said there hadn't been. But what Crowe had found was that the back door lock had been broken from the inside, not the outside. Someone hadn't wanted it known that the basement had been used for the entrance point into the house. That window had been opened from the inside as well, not from the outside.

Someone she had trusted had opened that window.

Crowe had locked it back, and now the cousins were going to see about giving that someone a chance to slip in and unlock it again.

That meant getting her out of the house without it appearing

as though he had deliberately gotten her out of the house.
The meeting was the perfect opportunity for that.

Besides that, he knew for a fact that the county attorney,
Wayne Sorenson, would have a much harder time playing
the bastard with Cami sitting there watching him.

Cami and Wayne Sorenson's daughter, Amelia, had been
best friends. They had practically grown up in the same
house. Amelia's mother had been best friends with Cami's
mother, and the two girls had been inseparable as children
and young adults.

Wayne and Mark hadn't associated with each other much,
though. Wayne had been younger and hadn't seemed to connect with Mark's aloof bigotry.

"It may not be a good idea to take me to that meeting
with you, Rafe," Cami advised him as the last of the breakfast dishes were cleared away more than an hour later.

She was still limping a bit, the bruise on her hip obviously bothering her as she shifted in her chair again, accepting the cup of coffee Logan reached to her as Crowe finished
loading the dishwasher.

She had watched them as though they were aliens as they
cleaned her kitchen. Or as though she had expected them to
leave the mess for her.

"And why is that?" Rafe asked as he rinsed the skillet he'd
used to prepare the meal and turned back to her.

Drying his hands, he watched her as she nibbled at her
thumbnail, a concerned expression on her face as she watched
him.

"Wayne's not exactly enamored of me any longer," she
finally sighed. "And Amelia and I haven't spoken in ages."

There was a shadow of hurt in Cami's gaze before she
looked down at her coffee, but there was also a shadow of
deception in her eyes. She was hiding more half-truths and
shadows of lies than Rafe could have ever guessed.

What the hell had happened to her since he had been
gone?

Rafe glanced at his cousins in a silent exchange that had
the other two men making their excuses and leaving the

kitchen. Several minutes later the sound of the front door clicking shut had her head lifting once again. She was obviously surprised that the other two had left the room and she was now alone with Rafe.

And she didn't look comfortable with him.

What the hell did it take, he wondered, for her to get a clue that she was stuck with him?

"Why haven't you and Amelia spoken for the past few years?" he finally asked Cami.

She breathed out heavily as her shoulders lifted in an uncomfortable, defensive little gesture more telling than words.

"Things happen." She shrugged. "It began before we graduated college. That last year actually. I started work as a substitute and Amelia already had an offer for her own classroom in Aspen for a while." Cami smiled at something that she obviously still found to be a pleasant memory before rubbing at the side of her neck a bit nervously. "Something changed that year, I guess. No matter what I did, I couldn't stop her from disassociating herself from me."

Rafe knew she had been twenty-two that year. She and Amelia had roomed together at college and watched out for each other as they navigated the much larger city after being raised in near isolation in Sweetrock. It didn't make sense that they would have just grown apart.

"There's more to it, Cami," he probed. "The half-truths are only going to piss me off. Now tell me what the hell happened before I have to begin questioning others. You don't want to push this much further."

Her lips thinned as a flash of anger clouded her eyes. She glanced away from him for a second, obviously searching for some other way to get out of answering the question.

Rafe stalked to the table, planted his hand on the top of it, and leaned close as she stared back at him in surprise, her eyes widening as he leaned in, nearly nose to nose with her.

"I asked you a question," he growled furiously as he felt that primal instinct itching between his shoulder blades again.

The secrets she was keeping had somehow contributed to the isolated, near-friendless life she was living at the moment.

"Lie to me and I'll paddle your ass."

Delicate little nostrils flared. "Perhaps I'll like it," she snapped back. "Go ahead and try it, Rafer."

"Oh, you'll like it," he promised her as he came in closer. "You'll love it, Cami. You'll beg for it. Your pussy will become so hot, so wet, so desperate for release that you'll beg me to fuck you. You'll beg for my cock as deep and as hard as you can take me."

Her face flushed, her eyes darkened.

"And I'll even give it to you," he promised, dropping his voice until he knew the lower, rougher tone would take on a brooding, rasping quality that never failed to affect her.

And it did.

Her face flushed, arousal heating her cheeks at the very sensual promise.

"And that's supposed to convince me—"

"Do you know what that does to a woman, Cami?" he whispered. "You don't see yourself as submissive. You're an independent, freethinking woman. But once you've come until you can come no more, once you think it's all you can do to breathe, once you think it's over." His voice dropped further. "I'll do it again, Cami. And I'll do it again. And when it's over, when it's all you can do just to breathe, what you'll realize is what will sear you to your very soul. You'll realize I didn't just spill my come inside you so many times, pumping it as deep inside you as possible. You'll realize I own you. Heart and soul. You'll be completely mine, Cami, and you'll love being mine. You'll ache for more of it. You'll come to me when I so much as whisper your name, because I'll be buried so deeply inside your soul that you won't be able to cut me out. There will be no forcing me out. Is that what you want now? Is that a step you think you're ready to take at this moment?"

It was a step she had already taken and one she that had nearly destroyed her. Those horrible, bleak days were still a part of her, still a part of her memories, and the scars were still a part of her soul.

It would destroy her to belong to him so completely again. And she couldn't risk his attempt to do just as he said he would, because he could. She was too weak where his touch, his kiss, was concerned. Too weak, too hungry. He was already too much a part of her.

"Now, I'm going to ask you again, kitten. What happened?"

She swallowed tightly. "Amelia used to keep a diary," she whispered, her gaze lifting to him as the anger faded from her gray eyes and they darkened in pain instead.

He eased back slowly. "And someone found it?"

Cami drew in a slow, deep breath. "It wouldn't be hard to guess. Her father did while helping Amelia move the year we graduated. He learned both our secrets."

"And what were those secrets?" It was worth a try.

Cami shook her head, stubborn determination smoothing all but the final, last vestiges of emotion. "It's her secret," Cami whispered. "I'll never betray her, not in any way."

"She betrayed you, evidently."

Cami only shrugged.

"And what did he learn of your secrets?" Rafe asked her instead.

"He learned of the night we had spent together and how I felt about it." She licked her lips nervously. "How I felt about you. And while he was being nosy, he learned something Amelia had fought to hide from him. After that night, she never spoke to me again."

That secret must have been a huge one. If Rafe remembered correctly, there was some sort of gossip surrounding her return and the hasty marriage that took place weeks later.

"She's married now, isn't she?" he asked to be certain.

"She's married," Cami agreed.

"And how did Wayne handle these secrets?"

Her lips quirked bitterly. "He was very disappointed in both of us, he said. And he was, but I really didn't give a damn. Shame wasn't the reason I didn't tell anyone, and shame has never been the reason I didn't want anyone to know we were lovers."

She rose slowly from her chair.

She felt as though she had aged ten years. As though exhaustion were so much a part of her now that there would never be any shaking it off.

"Cami." He moved to touch her, to draw her into his arms, to give her what little comfort he could.

Her hand lifted imperatively, a demand that he stop as he watched a hard shudder shake her body.

"I don't have friends for a reason," she whispered. "I don't have my parents for a reason." She lifted her gaze to him and it didn't take a frigging diary to see the pain that filled her eyes. "Because you never had to fuck me all night long, spank me, or make yourself so much a part of me that I couldn't exist without you, or without that part that I'll suddenly be living and breathing for."

He heard the tears then. They didn't fall. They didn't fill her eyes. They were stuck in her soul, a wound that never healed, that never eased. And it broke his heart.

"Cami?" What could have happened? How could he have hurt her in such a way without ever knowing he had done so? Fear lanced through him then. Fear that somehow he had damaged her, taken from her something she hadn't willingly given because his hunger had been so strong, so wild.

"You did the night we spent together." He froze at the statement. "You left a part of yourself inside me that I never wanted to be free of. That I never wanted to live without." Her voice was ragged now, torn, until he moved for her, desperate to hold her as she jerked back from him, leaving him staring at her in shock as her expression twisted in rage. "And I lost it anyway, Rafe. I lost the baby I already loved until it felt as though my soul had been seared and then ripped from my very spirit. But I was still living, I was still breathing, and I was alone. And I've stayed alone. That way, I didn't lose again. I didn't suffer again. And I sure as hell didn't ever take that risk again until I decided to see if rumors were true and drive by the ranch." Her breathing hitched as she held her hands to her stomach, the rage and anger in her voice ripping his soul apart. The image of complete aloneness that surrounded her, tearing into his soul. Cami should have never been alone. "Until I walked to your house during a blizzard, instead of the Phillipses', which was closer. Until I realized I had to see you." And there were the tears; they gleamed in her eyes, but they didn't fall. "I had to see you; I had to know if you were really home. If you were really here. And I swore I wouldn't touch you." Throwing her head back, she blinked desperately as she drew in ragged breaths. "I just had to see you," she whispered hoarsely. "Now what else do you want to know, Rafe? Tell me!" she screamed then, the pain suddenly overflowing, penned up for five years, locked in a dark part of her soul where she had refused to let it escape, and now it was exploding like a volcano of rage and pain. "What the fuck else do you need to know?"

She turned to run.

Cami had never meant to let it go, to let it rise inside her until it spewed from her soul like an erupting volcano that couldn't be stemmed.

When he had threatened to leave a part of himself that she would never be free of, he had triggered that inner helpless rage she had been able to control in the past.

"The hell you will!" Rafe jumped for her as she turned to run, to escape. "Damn you, you're not going anywhere. You will not run from me again, Cambria. Not this time. Not now."

He had seen the intent in her eyes, wild with the agony of a loss he had never known.

Catching her around the waist, he was only distantly aware of Logan and Crowe rushing back into the house from the front porch. Coming to a stop in the hall, they watched, surprised, not prepared as a desperate cry of agony tore from her and her arm swung with all the force in her small, delicate body.

Rafe caught her fist a bare inch from his face, staring back at her in surprise, in anger. She dared to try to strike him, even in her pain, in her rage against fate, when she hadn't told him that together they had created a life? That she had lost that baby and suffered that loss alone and had never given him the chance to share it with her?

"You never told me," he snarled down at her. "You were pregnant and you never told me? Why?" As he gripped her upper arms it was all he could do not to shake her, to demand, to rage along with her for the tiny unborn life he had never had the chance to know about.

The tears fell now. Staring back at him, her eyes were nearly black with the emotions, the secrets she had kept for far too long, and the tears he wondered if she had ever shed.

Jaymi had remarked several times that Cami held too much inside, even as a child. That Jaymi never knew what her sister was thinking or what Cami was doing until it was already done.

"Dad said I deserved it," she whispered as those tears fell from her eyes, her lips trembling violently as she stared up at Rafe beseechingly. "Mom said it was for the best. That I wouldn't want my child to suffer as you and your cousins did." Her fingers clutched at his arms now with the same desperation that her fist had aimed for his face with. "It wasn't for the best, Rafe. I wouldn't have let my baby suffer. I would never, ever let anyone be cruel to my child." Hoarse, rough with the tears that fell but the sobs she held back, her voice grated with pain and tore a hole in his soul.

"Cami. I would have been here." How had it happened? He had used a condom. He remembered using a condom. Had it broken? Had he only thought he had rolled the latex over the violently hard flesh that was so eager to sink inside her?

She shook her head as though she had read his thoughts. "It was my fault." She swallowed tightly. "You had drunk so much that night. After I fell asleep you woke me. You asked if it was okay. You asked if you could have me bare." Her breathing hitched, those sobs fighting to be free. "I told you it was," her voice lowered. "I told you it was, and I knew it could happen. I knew, and I wanted—"

She gave a hard shake of her head, lowering it and fighting to be free again.

"You wanted my baby?" he asked, baffled, as she struggled to escape. "No, Cami." A small shake was acceptable, he told himself. Just enough to get her attention. Just enough to make her look up at him, those tears still falling, her lips trembling with such vulnerable pain it was destroying him. "You wanted my baby?"

Every woman he had ever been with in Corbin County had been damned vigilant about condoms and birth control. Not that he had been any less so. He had been determined no child of his would be raised away from his protection, and he knew no woman in that county would want to claim him as the father.

Except Cami.

"I wanted our baby," she whispered. "I wanted a part of you to hold forever, because you were always leaving, Rafe. You couldn't stay and I wanted to hold on to you forever because leaving before you awoke, so I wouldn't have to watch you leave, nearly killed me."

She couldn't let the sobs free. She hadn't allowed herself to cry, to release the rage and pain building inside her, because she feared the price.

If she shattered, she might not know how to put herself back together again.

"Let me go." If he kept holding her, kept staring at her with that naked hunger, then she might not survive it. "Don't tear at me anymore, Rafe, please. Please don't ask any more from me. Please God, don't ask me for more."

Let her go? It wasn't happening and now wasn't the time to tell her that was something he would never do. What she definitely didn't know was that he had never let her go.

"I won't leave you alone." He had to force himself to speak past the lump in his throat.

As he stared down at her he was only barely aware of the doorbell ringing.

The door opened before Logan or Crowe could reach it and check for danger. Cami wished they had made it.

The danger wasn't physical, it was so much more dangerous than that.

Stepping into the small den her father had once used,
Cami could feel her insides tightening in trepidation as she
faced her father.

She really looked nothing like him.

She remembered so many times, staring at him and wondering how she had acquired traits and a sense of decency
that she knew he didn't have.

"Is Mother doing well?" she asked as he moved naturally
to the large desk she had taken as her own.

He sat down in the large padded chair comfortably and
stared back at her.

Cami knew this wasn't going to go well.

It never had whenever she had faced him across the table
in the past.

His lips were curled into a sneer, his brown eyes filled
with disgust.

I see the rumors are true," he mocked her, his tone low.
"You've not only insisted in fucking the murderers but you
have them living with you." His gaze flicked over her. "Are
you fucking all of them?"

"Is it any of your business?" she asked him.

His lip curled tighter. "You've managed to get my Jaymi
killed and now you've also turned my brother against me."

"I had nothing to do with Jaymi's murder." She was already too raw, too shredded inside to take the blame for it.

He leaned forward against the desk. "She died for you,"
he accused her. "To collect medicine you begged her for."
He raked her with a look filled with bitter hatred. "You could
have waited until the next morning."

She couldn't deal with this.

She was savaged from the secrets she had revealed to Rafe,
the memories raking her soul as the hatred in his gaze seemed
to increase. "You lost your child, Cami, and I thought it only
fitting punishment."

Vicious, cruel, the sound of the satisfaction in his tone
shocked her.

"Why?" she whispered painfully, shocked. "Why would you say something like that to me?"

"Because you deserved it." He rose from the chair then, glaring back at her. "You took Jaymi from the parents who loved her, and you thought your presence would help with that loss?"

"I thought you had a spark of decency was what I believed," she whispered painfully. "I learned you didn't a long time ago, though. And it was no more than the truth."

The cold hard smile he directed her way should have hurt her. It should have at least hurt for the simple fact that he was her father.

"Why should I?" he asked, his voice dropping further to ensure Rafe didn't hear them, she suspected. "You weren't my child, Cami. You're nothing to me. So why should I care?"

It didn't hurt, that was the first thing she noticed. The bitterness was there. The pain was there, but Cami found herself unable to care about that either.

She stared back at him, wondering though if Jami had known . . .

"That's enough."

Cami swung around as Rafe pushed the door opened and stepped inside.

He stood tall, broad, strong.

And Cami could feel the emotions tearing free inside her then.

"Bastard," Mark Flannigan growled insultingly. "You have no say here."

"No, I do." Cami swung around then and this time, she let her gaze rake over him in satisfaction. "You haven't hurt me, Mark. You didn't even surprise me. You have no idea how proud I am that you are no father of mine."

His brows lowered furiously as his hands fisted at his side.

"It's time you left," she told him. "Leave now, and don't bother coming back. Because you're not wanted any more than you ever wanted me."

CHAPTER 19

Cami stalked into the bedroom.

She'd intended to retreat to her room alone. To hide, lick her wounds, and find a way to repair the shattering of her defenses.

Rafe wasn't allowing her to rebuild anything, though. He was behind her, surrounding her as the door closed behind him, and she felt him watching her silently.

"Could I please have some privacy?" she asked, aware of the belligerence in her tone as she turned back to him, her insides shaking with the emotions flooding her.

"So you can turn into that pretty little robot you were before you broke down and told me about our child?" He arched his brows in surprise that she would ask. "I doubt it, kitten. But you can try to convince me if you want."

Try to convince him?

"And how am I supposed to do that?" Then his words sank in, and she felt her expression tighten in anger. "I was never a robot."

Rafe could feel himself breaking apart inside. Chunks of his soul being shredded as he stared in her eyes and saw the pain, the depth of it, and the years she had all but carried it alone.

"Do you know what amazes me, Cami?" His voice softened.

"What?" She was breathing roughly, her breasts rising hard and fast as she glared back at him.

"That you wanted my baby."

Her eyes darkened.

She'd just learned the man she had called Father all her life hadn't been. That he thought, at fifteen, she should have suffered her sister's fate, and that his hatred for her, that she hadn't, went soul-deep, and that hadn't seemed to faze her.

What had fazed her was revealing to Rafe that she had lost their child.

"Why didn't you tell me before now?"

She shook her head.

"Cami, answer me." Moving to her, he gripped her chin gently, aware of the bruising of her flesh, and turned her gaze to him. "Why?"

Her lips trembled. "You were safe. If I had told you, you would have come back here. They might have tried to hurt you again."

Nothing could have shocked him more.

"What?" He could hear the confusion in his own voice.

"The barons, this town." Swallowing tightly, she was obviously fighting her tears, her pain as she continued. "They wanted to destroy you and Logan and Crowe. I wasn't going to help them, Rafe. I couldn't."

A single tear slipped free.

"But, Cami, that was my child, too," he said softly.

"And if I hadn't lost our child, I would have told you." That intriguing ring of blue around the soft gray seemed to darken. "I would have told you then, Rafer. I would never have taken something so precious away from you."

And she wouldn't have.

He framed her face with his hands. "Cami, I would have still held our child as precious," he whispered.

"And everyone here would still be waiting to find a way to destroy everything you were fighting for. They would have convicted you for Jaymi's murder, Rafe, and for the other girls'. They would have stolen your life if they had the chance."

"Instead, you let Mark Flannigan steal yours." Lowering his head, he touched her forehead with his.

"He hasn't had that power since he refused to allow me to talk to Mom when I lost our child," she revealed. "Probably a lot sooner."

God, how alone had she been?

He hadn't been here for her. He hadn't protected her as he had sworn to, not just to Cami, but also to himself when he'd realized how much she cared for him so long ago.

"Sweet Cami," he whispered as his lips lowered to hers.

He meant to only brush them, to comfort her, to hopefully ease the pain both of them had endured over the years. A pain that could have been eased, that could have healed if stubbornness and pride hadn't held them apart.

But her hands lifted to his chest, small, delicate and warm, lying against it with a tentative, almost hesitant caress as her lips parted beneath his.

Gentle, heated, the need that rose between them was unlike any he had felt, even with her, in his life. As though something had come together that morning. Something he couldn't fight or deny, something that slipped free of his soul and began to fill his heart as their kiss deepened, grew hotter, and began to meld them together.

He had dreamed of finding her soft heart, of feeling her kiss infused with that "something" that only her acceptance of that emotion could bring.

And she was accepting it. Accepting it and holding it close to her as she was pulling him close to her.

Disposing of their clothing was easy.

Her hands pushed at the material of his clothing as his hands removed hers, his fingers brushing against her flesh and feeling the softness of her flesh and the hunger rising between them both.

It had been there since she had been sixteen. It had only grown through the years.

Drawing her to the nearest piece of furniture in the room, Rafe sat back in the chair behind him, drew her forward, parted her thighs, then drew her to him.

He watched.

Hell, he couldn't help but watch as the tight, saturated flesh of her pussy eased over his cock head, drawing it inside, sucking it into her body with slow, sweet milking motions of the tight muscles and silken tissue.

Pleasure whipped every cell of his body as he held her hips and watched as she shifted hers, rolled them, and slowly took him.

Her hands were braced on his chest, her head thrown back, pleasure suffusing her expression as she began to thrust against him, above him.

"God, yes, baby," he groaned as she finally slid down, taking his full length as her pussy began to flex and clench on his flesh. "Ride my dick, baby. Take it up that tight little pussy."

He was dying for her.

He hadn't expected this. Not this hunger that surged so hot and fast, searing over his nerve endings and burning through his senses. And he sure as hell hadn't expected her head to lower, her eyes to meet his. "I love you," she whispered as she began to move harder, faster.

Though still tender and bruised, she took him, her pleasure obvious, her need rising.

His hips rose, thrusting up, shafting her with the thick width of his cock as he felt her tighten, watched her eyes open wide, then watched her orgasm wash through every particle of her being.

Just as Rafe felt his own release explode in his balls, surge through his cock, and in hard, powerful jets, spill inside the giving depths of her body.

Son of a bitch, she had slipped out of the bed on him again.

Rafe came awake hours later, the knowledge that Cami wasn't by his side surging through him.

It took him a moment to remember where he was, what had happened, and to know his cousins would never allow her to leave the house.

After showering and dressing, he went in search of her.

She was in the kitchen, staring in the cabinets with a frown.

"Dinner," she mumbled. "I don't know if I have enough for three mountains pretending to be men."

The teasing edge of amusement in her gaze had his lips twitching.

"Yeah, especially after you helped us build a hell of an appetite."

He moved to her, kissed her neck, then wrapped his arms around her and pulled her to him.

He kissed her gently at first, and would have gone for more if his own stomach hadn't decided to begin growling.

Cami laughed at the sound before pulling away from him and moving back to the ingredients she had laid out.

Just then, Crowe's cell phone rang and they heard his cousin walk down the hall to take the call.

It wasn't long before Crowe came back.

His expression was a hardened demand that spurred Rafe and Logan both into action.

"What's happened?" Rafe questioned harshly as Cami moved to his side, her face etched with concern.

"It's Archer on the phone," Crowe growled. "Jack Townsend's garage outside of town just exploded. Jack's tow truck and Jeannie's car were both in the parking lot and no one saw them leave." He glanced at Cami as a small, unconscious sob finally tore from her, only to quiet just as quickly. "It looks like they were killed in the explosion."

CHAPTER 20

Cami felt numb inside as Rafe pulled the Denali SUV into the parking lot of Jack's Towing and Repair just outside Sweetrock city limits no less than fifteen minutes later. Staring at the burned, charred mess of the building, she couldn't imagine how anyone could have survived such an explosion. Especially if they had been in the apartment overhead where Jack and Jeannie had lived.

More than half of the garage was just gone, with the debris scattered through the parking lot, vehicles lying in a tangled mess here and there. One lay in the field across from the garage. There were more than half a dozen that had been parked in the waiting lot, ready for needed repairs.

There was no repairing the damaged messes they were now. Cinder blocks, mortar, and metal had been slammed onto the vehicles. The wreckage defied any sense of logic or attempts to make sense of what had happened.

Cami stepped out of the truck, aware of being surrounded by Callahans and all the eyes that turned to them as three hard-cored, hard-muscled, steel-eyed Callahan men wrapped themselves around her and defied anyone to attempt to get close to her.

As she stared up at the garage, her heart in her chest, she tried to blink back the tears she couldn't hold back any longer. She couldn't believe this had happened.

"This wasn't an accident," Crowe muttered from behind her and Rafe as she felt his arm tighten around her back, his hand falling to her hip, his fingers gripping it firmly, as though she would attempt to tear herself away from him.

At the moment, her emotions were so torn, conflicted, and thrown into chaos that she couldn't imagine moving away from the only person who seemed to ground them.

"No," Rafe growled. "It wasn't an accident."

"How can you be so certain?" she asked faintly. "Why would anyone want to hurt Jack and Jeannie?"

"We'll find out," Rafe promised as Cami glimpsed Archer amid a group of volunteer firefighters and several state police officers.

Catching sight of the Rafe and Cami, Archer lifted his hand in acknowledgment before excusing himself and moving quickly across the debris-strewn parking lot. "The fire marshal is refusing to allow anyone onto the premises." Archer's voice was low as he reached them, his gaze filled with somber anger. "I can't check for the bodies, Rafe."

Cami wanted to close her eyes; she wanted to deny that this could have happened. That there was a chance that Jack and or Jeannie could have been in that building. But Jack's tow truck was there, as was Jeannie's little gray car. Was there even the smallest chance that they weren't in the building?

"Neighbors saw Jack going in maybe half an hour before the explosion," Archer sighed. "They didn't see anyone else."

"He was at the house the other day," Cami told Archer softly. "He remembered the accident Jaymi was in just before she was killed; his father towed the car in and repaired it. The brake lines had been deliberately cut."

As the four men stared at her, their expressions cast in hard, brooding lines, Cami detailed the meeting and the information Jack had given her.

"You're getting the same phone calls," Rafe stated when she finished. "You're getting them and you didn't tell me. Someone else had to tell me."

He was furious.

Cami could see the pure rage burning in his eyes now, as

well as the silent promise that it was a subject they would discuss in detail later.

She could feel the regret then, that feeling that had hidden inside her for the past weeks, teasing her, brooding in her mind. It was regret, and the knowledge that when Rafe did learn what she had been holding back from him, everything she had been holding back for him, the time to pay would come.

That time was growing closer by the second, and she was suddenly very aware of what she could lose.

His trust.

Whatever emotion burned in his gaze for her.

She could lose Rafe, and she suddenly realized that despite the distance she had placed between them, she didn't want to lose him. She couldn't bear to lose him.

For the past five years she had lived for the rare times they had come together. She had waited for him, watched for him, and she longed for him with a strength that had kept her from settling for any other lover.

And in that second, gazing in his eyes, she realized that was what she would do if she wasn't very careful. She was going to damage whatever it was between them that had kept them coming to each other over the years. That bond of hunger, and something, something she simply couldn't define, that kept the hunger growing ever stronger.

"I'm so sorry," she whispered. "I should have told you, Rafe. I should have told you so many things."

She should have never kept the secrets she had kept. Not just about the phone calls but about most especially about the child she had lost. That part of Rafe, that part of the soul-deep need she had for him that she had so longed to give birth to, that had been taken from her.

She should have told him. And now, it just may have come too late.

CHAPTER 21

The past was like a ghost, a haunting spectre he couldn't escape no matter his attempts. No matter the attempts his cousins made. From their births, they had faced the hatred and controversy of their well-loved mothers marrying the town's least-loved citizens.

The Callahan brothers had been more than the town had known and yet less than it would have taken for Corbin County citizens to ever make the move to ignore the call to ostracize anything Callahan.

Before Rafe's, Logan's, and Crowe's fathers had married the three heiresses, they hadn't been ostracized. They had been liked, not always trusted but always able to charm their way into the hearts and minds of those they knew. Once their relationships with the Corbin, Rafferty, and Ramsey daughters were known, all that had changed.

James Corbin and Saul Rafferty had been certain that public condemnation would destroy those relationships. They hadn't realized how stubborn and how deeply their daughters had loved the men they had chosen.

As Rafe stared down at Cami, he was reminded, not for the first time, of the legacy his, Logan's, and Crowe's parents had left them. A legacy that made the lives of the women they might love potentially dangerous. A legacy that those women might not be able to adapt to as easily as they had, because they had lived it every day of their lives. Perhaps, in a way, they had grown used to it.

Cami wasn't a woman known to apologize. Jaymi had once told her that even when Cami had been no more than a teenager, she never apologized. When Jaymi asked her why, Cami had stared back at her with what she described as grim determination and said because she made certain she meant everything she said and everything she did.

She had just been a child then, her life a series of disappointments and chastisements. What Jaymi had said was a teenager's habit of rebelling, Eddy had described as a result of a young girl constantly being berated instead.

"We'll talk later," Rafe promised as he fought to push back the rage that still burned from their earlier confrontation.

It wasn't a rage directed at her, at least not entirely.

It was directed at life, at the circumstances, at the loss of a life that hadn't had the chance to even live.

She turned away quickly, the sharp inhalation of breath drawing his attention. Hurting her was the last thing he wanted to do. The last thing he intended to do. But neither would he lie to her.

He wasn't about to tell her to not worry about it, and he sure as hell wasn't going to tell her it was okay. Because it wasn't. What he did intend to do was teach her to never fucking hide anything else from him.

She hadn't exactly lied to him, but the lie of omission could be just as destructive. And if there was a chance in hell of a future with her, then she would have to learn the value of never keeping secrets from him.

Catching her wrist as she moved to turn away from him, Rafe threaded his fingers with hers, gripping her hand and holding her close as the sheriff discussed the explosion with Crowe.

Rafe could see Archer was having problems with the information Cami had given him and the fact that the garage had obviously been deliberately blown to fucking hell.

"Sheriff, we can't find any bodies," the fire marshal, Drew

Jacoby, stated in a rasping growl. Jacoby, a transplant from Denver whom the city had hired when they moved from the volunteer fire department to a paid force, was a tall, rough-talking Texan who rarely put up with any crap at all. Especially the gossiping kind.

Archer turned from the Callahans as he whipped his hat from his head and pushed his fingers through the short strands of his thick, dark hair.

"Maybe they weren't there," he suggested, hope filling his voice.

Jacoby gave a heavy shrug of his shoulders as he turned back to the charred remains of the garage, his expression brooding.

"We can hope—"

"Hey, Sheriff, it's Townsend!" Deputy Eisner announced, his voice high, excited, as a black sedan raced into the parking lot to come to a bone-jarring stop.

Jeannie was out of the car first, with Jack stepping out more slowly, his expression bemused as he stared at the garage as though he was certain he had to be seeing things.

Cami ran for the couple, aware of Rafe's hand still gripping hers as he all but pulled her along, his long, powerful legs outdistancing hers.

"Jeannie." Cami pulled away from Rafe, her arms going around the other woman as Jeannie suddenly began sobbing.

"Oh my God," she cried, holding on to Cami desperately. "What happened? Cami, what happened?"

"We were so scared you and Jack were in there." Cami pulled back to glance back at the garage, then to Jeannie and Jack once again. "Thank God you're all right."

"But what happened?" Confusion and fear filled her gaze.

"Bastard!" Jack suddenly cursed. "That fucking bastard. He called last night." Jack turned to Cami, his eyes blazing with fury. "He told me I should've kept my nose out of Callahan business and I'd learn the hard way I should have gone to Denver with the rest of the family."

Cami drew back from Jeannie slowly.

She could feel the guilt moving in, slowly, surely. This was her fault. Jack had been trying to help her. If he hadn't been the one she had questioned after leaving Rafe's, if he hadn't become curious because of her questions, then this would have never happened.

"Cami, this wasn't your fault." Jeannie suddenly caught her arm as Rafe, distracted by Jack's announcement, turned away from her. "You didn't cause any of this, I swear. Jack has been bothered by too many things lately where his friends are concerned. And pretending the Callahans weren't his friends when they returned wasn't happening."

Cami shook her head. She didn't believe Jack would have begun questioning his father over the Callahans, though, or learned about the brake lines to Jaymi's car with the wreck twelve years ago if it hadn't been for her.

Those particular questions were the ones that had made Jack a target. Just as they had made her a target.

"Let me find the son of a bitch and I'll kill him," Jack snarled as Cami turned to see him staring at the bulding with naked pain.

"Jack, think of Jeannie," Archer warned him, his voice low. "If you're out chasing the bad guys, who's going to protect her? Leave this to me. I promise you, I'm not my father. I'll find out who's behind it."

"Dammit, Archer, you think I'm just going to sit around and wait for that son of a bitch to just find me and Jeannie and announce his presence again?" A tight, savage smile curled his lips. "Hell no, I won't. You better hope you find him before I do. Because when I get my hands on him there won't be anything to prosecute."

He was enraged, but at least he was alive, Cami thought as she felt Rafe's arm curl around her back, his fingers gripping her hip to pull her closer to him.

He was making a statement. As the crowd grew around the destroyed garage he was making it a point to show everyone who bothered to look exactly whom she was with there.

And there was plenty of looking. She could feel the gazes,

some antagonistic, others curious, and still others calculating.

She met those gazes defiantly. She'd spent too many years running from what she wanted, running from the only man who did anything to fire her blood or to make her feel more than friendship.

These people's opinions should have never mattered for even a second, but she had pretended as though they had, to save her own heart. To keep her emotions shielded and her secrets closely guarded.

There were no secrets any longer. Rafe knew the past, and he would either accept it or walk away. She wouldn't demand anything from him either way.

"You're staring at Eisner's back as though you're going to send a dagger through it," Rafe murmured beside her as she realized she was indeed staring at Eisner, wishing she could kick him, scream at him, hurt him as he had tried to hurt the Callahans so many times for the very people he was now talking to.

James Corbin and his son, William.

But standing with them and glaring at Eisner as well was William's young daughter, Kimberly Ann Corbin.

Ann Corbin at nineteen favored her father's side of the family. Long auburn hair fell nearly to her waist in a riot of curls while sea-green eyes stared at Eisner, her expression creased in anger.

Her father, Will, kept trying to shoo her back. The more he tried to shoo her, the closer she got until she was standing at his elbow.

Both Corbin men would glare at her; they would cut Eisner off at some points. William rubbed at the back of his neck in frustration as he shot her several irate looks. She was the darling of the Corbin family, though. The spitting image of her dead aunt, Crowe's mother, in both looks as well as temper. And if her expression was anything to go by, an explosion could be imminent.

"Eisner deserves the dagger more than most," Cami muttered. "The two men he's talking to even more so."

"That's the first time I've seen the girl out in years," Logan commented. "They usually keep her away from town."

"She and Jeannie are good friends," Archer interjected before blowing out a hard breath and staring around in frustration. "It's going to take this crowd hours to disperse, and Jack's not in a good frame of mind if anyone decides to get ignorant with their mouths."

Cami almost grinned at the saying "get ignorant." The fine art of the smart-assed remark that could be delivered mockingly, snidely, sarcastically, or in a rage. It went along with having done something "for a minute," which usually indicated more than a few days, and asking a person if they had taken their "smart pills" or if they were mixed up with the "stupid pills." The locally grown little sayings had always amused her, and she had found herself missing them when she had been away at college.

"Yeah, well, getting ignorant is what some of them do best," Rafe breathed out roughly. "Get your fire marshal to take him over the damage, then drive him to the hotel outside of town. Keeping him away from the homegrown yokels is your best bet unless you want to see blood shed."

Cami looked around again, her gaze caught by the flash of a red Mercedes as it pulled in next to the Corbins' black four-door Jaguar.

Wayne Sorenson, Corbin County's attorney, stepped from the car accompanied by his daughter, Amelia.

After Amelia had taken the teaching position in Aspen, Cami rarely saw her and they never spoke. Amelia had never forgiven Cami for revealing the secret Sorenson had learned when he read the journal she had so carelessly left lying in her dorm room that day.

Amelia had changed.

Once, she had dressed in fashions that highlighted her unique temperament and sense of adventure. Now, she was dressed in a dark peacoat, black slacks, a gray sweater, and staid, low-heeled black pumps. The very type of clothes she had once sworn no one would ever catch her dead wearing.

Was this maturity? Cami wondered. Or was it a confor-
mation aimed at attempting to gain Amelia's father's love as
well?

It seemed to be working for her, just as easily as it had
worked for Cami over the years.

Which was not in the least.

How long would it take Amelia to realize that no amount
of conforming would gain the acceptance and the love she
needed from her father?

"Cami?" Rafe's hand at her back and the questioning
tone of his voice had her head lifting. "Are you ready to
leave?"

Was she ready to leave?

Did she really want to stay and watch the girl who had
once been as close to her as a sister pretend to be something
and someone she wasn't?

"I'm ready." She'd rather face Rafe's wrath than watch
the Amelia doll pose with tense expectation next to the father who didn't even know she was there.

As Cami began to turn away, Amelia's head lifted and
Cami couldn't help but be drawn to a stop.

For the briefest second it seemed as though misery and a
plea were reflected in the emerald depths of Amelia's eyes
before she quickly turned away.

"We still have that meeting to make," Crowe reminded
Rafe as they headed to the car.

At that moment, Wayne detached himself from the
Corbins, his expression dark with irritated anger as his fingers curled around his daughter's upper arm and pulled her
along after him.

Rafe and Cami drew to a stop, watching as Wayne neared
them. As he drew closer, Rafe carefully slid her between his
back and the cousins behind him.

She nearly rolled her eyes as she pushed from between the
three men, her elbow pushing warningly into Rafe's stomach as Wayne and Amelia stopped in front of them.

"Rafe." Wayne nodded to the men in general.

"Wayne," Rafe drawled.

The fact that Rafe hadn't addressed him more formerly had Wayne's lips tightening for a second as Amelia pushed her hands into the dark peacoat she wore and looked down at the ground. If Cami wasn't mistaken, Amelia might have been hiding a smile.

"We're going to have to reschedule the meeting we had this afternoon." Wayne lifted his head, his nostrils tightening as though he smelled something rotten. "I'll have my secretary contact you to reschedule."

Rafe's arms crossed over his chest.

Narrowing his eyes, Rafe watched Wayne suspiciously. Cami could feel the tension that began to radiate in his body and the sense of distrust that filled the air around the three men where the county attorney was concerned.

Amelia was aware of it as well.

How strange, Cami thought, that even after all these years she could read Amelia as though they had never spent the past three years as all but enemies.

"I'll see you later then." Rafe gave a short nod of his head as his arm once again curled around Cami's back, his fingers lying close at her hip.

Wayne didn't acknowledge the agreement; he merely turned on his heel and stalked away as though the simple courtesy of saying, *Good-bye, See you later,* or, *Fuck you, Callahan,* didn't apply in the least.

Amelia moved more slowly, and as she turned she pulled her hand from the pocket of her coat and a piece of paper dropped free.

Rafe's foot immediately covered it, and just in time.

"Amelia?" Wayne turned back to her, his gaze going past her to Rafe, Logan, Crowe, and then Cami, as though searching for something, as though he had expected Amelia to try to stop and talk or, perhaps, to attempt to warn them of something.

"I'm coming, Father." Her hands were back in her coat, as though they had never slipped free.

God, what was going on?

Cami couldn't take much more. She couldn't handle the

hell that Corbin County was turning into any longer or the haunting agony the past and the present merging was creating.

It was her fault her best friend, the one person she had had who believed in her, who loved her, whom she could trust, had turned into this unemotional robot that Amelia had turned into.

It was all Cami's fault, because she had allowed Wayne Sorenson to learn the secret that Amelia had held close to her heart and had never told anyone but Cami.

The fact that Crowe Callahan had kissed Amelia. That he had held her and made her want more. That he had filled her with such a hunger for him that she had told Cami she understood why the loss of the child Cami and Rafe had created had nearly destroyed her.

She could feel her hands shaking. She could feel something inside her stomach trembling, as though the tremors attacking her fingers had begun in her stomach and refused to dissipate.

As several firefighters, Archer, Jack, and Jeannie moved between Rafe, Cami, the Corbins, and Wayne Sorenson, Rafe quickly bent and retrieved the folded note from beneath his shoe.

Turning his back on the group, he held it between his fingers as he watched Cami expectantly.

Allowing Rafe, Logan, and Crowe to shield her, she took the note and slowly unfolded it.

The house is being watched. Trying to get there. Kick some ass. Love you. Your twin.

Cami felt her lips tremble. Why, after all this time, was Amelia making contact?

"She's going to try to slip to the house." Cami frowned, confused. "Why would she have to slip over to see me?"

This was going beyond fear of gossip or of Amelia's father being angry. It was going beyond the fact that the Corbins rewarded anyone who stood against the Callahans and punished those who stood with them.

And Amelia had signed the note: *Your twin.* They had always sworn they were somehow kidnapped at birth and taken from loving parents to be forced to exist with those they suffered through. They called each other twin when they were afraid of being caught passing messages during the frequent groundings they both had suffered as young girls and as teenagers.

Amelia was afraid of someone finding the note or learning she had written it.

Her twin. If anyone had ever been meant to be Cami's twin, then it was Amelia. And to learn that at least something had survived the past three years and the horrible mistake Cami had made had tears wanting to fill her eyes again.

She hadn't been this emotional since the first six weeks of her pregnancy. She had cried at everything then, and that was what she felt like doing now. Sobbing, because there was nothing that made sense anymore except the thought that she had to find an alternative to leaving her home if it was truly bugged. She wasn't ready to leave. She wasn't ready to leave the security and the memories of her mother yet.

"Crowe, get Tank out here," Rafe muttered. "Get the house checked over for bugs, and until he gets here we need something that will generate a cover for anything said there."

"She'll be at the house tonight," Crowe said quietly. "She's going to end up endangering herself if she does that."

Cami shook her head. "The fact that I was attacked in my own home and that whoever it was is trying to mimic Thomas Jones will keep her in. She wouldn't risk herself like that."

"You did," Crowe pointed out.

She stared back at him, his expression and the somber tone of his voice instantly registering with her.

Amelia would be there to see him if she could find a way to slip past whoever was watching.

"Keep an eye out for her," Rafe told him. "Unlock the back door and see if you can spot whoever's watching."

"If they're watching, I'll find them." It was Logan's voice, pitched low and filled with danger that had a chill racing up Cami's spine.

There were rumors he, along with Rafe and Crowe, had trained as snipers in the Marines. That they were three of the military's sharpest, coldest killers.

She could believe it. The lives they had lived hadn't exactly been easy in Corbin County. That dark bitterness could have easily transferred into a rage that would see Rafe going after more than one target.

"Let's go," Rafe said, his voice carefully low. "I want to give Crowe time to meet the agent from our security company in Aspen to pick up some equipment we need."

"And I want to make damned sure if she slips into the house that I'm there to greet her." There was nothing welcoming in Crowe's voice as he turned and began leading the way to the SUV they had driven to the ruined garage in.

"This is getting out of hand," Cami protested as the fear still crawled through her system like a potentially killing virus. "What are they hoping to accomplish? Why do you and your cousins' presence threaten them to the extent that they would go to these lengths?"

"We remind them of the past," Crowe stated quietly. "And of a loss they don't want to accept."

"And you accept that?" she asked, more surprised than she would have thought she would be. "That's not a good enough reason, Crowe, and it's gone far enough."

"Evidently it hasn't gone far enough," Rafe answered her, his voice cool. "They're still pushing, Cami, and I have no intentions of leaving this county again. They'll find out fast enough, they can't run us off now any more than they could do it twelve years ago. The Callahans are home to stay."

CHAPTER 22

Cami stood at the wide bay window of the breakfast nook just off the kitchen and stared into the backyard that night, her arms crossed over her breasts, her fingers curved over the balls of her shoulders.

And she waited.

Darkness had finally rolled in. That pure pitch dark that only came when winter was putting up its final battle before acceding to the coming spring warmth.

The back porch light was turned off. The house lights were out and Rafe, Logan, and Crowe were sitting at the breakfast table, their voices low, barely discernible amid the static pouring from the AM radio sitting in the center of the table.

Static, Rafe had explained, would cover their voices if they had somehow missed the bug that might have been placed within the house. Or not. Either way, he explained, it was insurance.

Her lips thinned. Insurance. Insurance against their conversation being overheard as they discussed the past and the possible reason why?

Why did the Corbins, the Raffertys, and the Robertses want the Callahans out of town so desperately?

Why did the citizens of Corbin County follow three families who had turned on their own grandchildren? Even more important, at the time they were the only grandchildren those families had.

Clyde Ramsey, Rafe's uncle, had taken all three boys in. He had called each of them his boy and would stand in any man's face, or woman's for that matter, red faced, his gray eyes bulging, his heavy nose twitching, as he defended each of "his boys" against the dictates of crazy old men—Saul Rafferty and James Corbin—who thought they had to attack children for the fact that their daughters had had minds of their own and hearts of their own.

Clyde had been known to say often that he hadn't approved of his sister's choice of husband, but by God, his wife's parents hadn't cared much for him either. But they sure as damned hell, he'd claimed several times, had not disowned their beautiful little baby girl.

Saul and Tandy Rafferty, Logan's grandparents, had doted on Logan, as long as his mother, Mina, had been alive. When she had died, Logan's grandparents had joined the Corbins in attempting to take the inheritance that went to Logan on her death, just as the Corbins attempted to do with Crowe and Dale and Laura Ramsey had done with Rafe.

It just didn't seem reason enough, though.

"Clyde knew something," Rafe murmured. "He called before the accident, but I was on an operation and didn't get back in time to return his call. At the time, I didn't think a lot of it, but it was rare for Clyde to try to get hold of me while I was out of the country."

Because he knew what Rafe did, Cami suspected, and knew it would do very little good to try to get hold of him.

"He could have called one of us," Crowe reminded Rafe.

"He didn't trust us enough to tell us what was going on," Logan sighed, the words barely decipherable above the noise of the generated static.

"Hell, he wouldn't even allow us to stay at the house when he wasn't there." Rafe's voice held a thread of amusement.

Cami could see both Logan's and Crowe's expressions as well as Rafe's. They all thought Clyde hadn't trusted them.

"Perhaps he thought we were going to steal the silver," Crowe stated with an irritable breath.

How three supposedly smart men could have such tunnel vision she wasn't certain.

"Maybe he didn't want any of you hurt." Cami turned away from the window, keeping her arms in place as she watched the three men in exasperation. "Did Clyde ever say he didn't trust you?"

The three men looked back at her, their expressions knowing and suspicious.

"He said blood would tell," Rafe stated somberly. "He obviously simply didn't trust Callahans."

Yet these three men had cared for Rafe's uncle, and even more, they'd respected him. But they were so wrong about Clyde.

"And you're certain he was talking about you?" she asked. "Or was he talking about the Corbins, Robertses, and Raffertys? Three families who have been known, for generations, to strike out in violence if needed. Perhaps he was more worried about his 'boys' than he was about his silver?"

"And you come up with this how?" Rafe sat back in the chair, arched his brow inquisitively, and stared back at her, his eyes so deep, such a dark blue, she wondered if she could drown in them.

But the question held her attention. She knew the answer to it, despite the doubt she saw in his eyes.

"Because the year my mother was the assistant principal when you were in the eighth grade, Rafer, just before she retired for medical reasons, Clyde Ramsey had occasion to pay her a visit, and during that visit he informed her quite frankly, and quite furiously, that there wasn't a single one of his 'boys' that would steal so much as a drink of water if they were dying of thirst."

Rafe's gaze narrowed on her.

"You remember that, don't you?" she asked him softly, careful to keep her voice low, just as she had from the first word she spoke.

"The principal, Todd Collingsworth, had accused us of

stealing brass from the science lab to sell," Rafe remembered, his expression thoughtful.

"I don't think Clyde ever believed you'd steal. I think he didn't want you there alone, because it was so far from town and anyone could have struck out at you with no one knowing. But at the town socials, if you stayed there, or later if you went camping on those weekends he was out of town, then you were much safer."

The three of them watched her. The doubt she had seen earlier was still there, but there was also the knowledge that it was possible she was right. They were considering her argument; that was what mattered.

"Anything's possible," Rafe finally admitted. "It doesn't change the fact that he never told us of any of those battles and there were only a few of the fights we were aware that he had with the Corbins."

The fights with the Corbins had been bad, but the ones he'd had with his father and mother, Rafe's grandparents, had been particularly brutal several times.

"Did you hear of the arguments he had with Dale and Laura Ramsey?" she asked.

She didn't call them Rafe's grandparents. The disrespect to Clyde and to Rafe was more than she could bear.

"Let's say, we caught wind of them," Rafe sighed. "Just as we noticed that neither of them were at the funeral when he died." Rafe's voice hardened as his eyes looked like chips of ice for just a second. "Clyde never told us about them, though, and he never admitted to them."

Of course he couldn't admit to them, Cami thought. If the stories her uncle had told over the years had been true, and Eddy wasn't prone to lie, then Clyde had nearly attempted murder the first time his father and mother showed up in court against Rafe to claim the inheritance Dale's daughter had left to her son.

"He did it to protect you. Jaymi told me of several times Clyde came to the high school after she began there as a substitute. The principal was known to run and hide when his truck was seen pulling into the parking area."

Jaymi had always believed Clyde Ramsey had loved each of his "boys" and had done his best by them. Cami had always argued that he could have done so much more.

"None of this answers the question on the table, though," Logan pointed out. "Why were you warned away from Rafe, then attacked when you didn't obey the demand carefully enough? And why was Jack Townsend's place just blown to hell and back this morning?"

"Are we sure it began here?" she asked them all. "Jaymi was receiving the same phone calls. Maybe we've been wrong all these years. Maybe she wasn't a random choice by a crazed serial killer. The FBI said there were two men committing those crimes, not just one. Maybe Jaymi was targeted for other reasons? Because she refused to do as she was told."

"Why would anyone care to kill the women we sleep with, Cami?" Crowe asked incredulously. "Why give a fuck? There are no heiresses left in Corbin County with the exception of William Corbin's daughter, and she's rarely in Corbin County, let alone around any of us."

At that point, Cami's hands fell from her shoulders to allow her to rake her fingers through her hair in frustration. "I didn't say I knew why," she admitted. "But as you said, why give a fuck who you fuck? Why call Jaymi and threaten her? Why do the same with me? And why resurrect a monster? Unless there were two killers and one of them has decided to start killing again."

Her gaze met Rafe's, and she saw the suspicion her questions had raised, but she also saw doubt. The cousins didn't want to accept that Jaymi could have died because of her tie to Rafe, but Cami had accepted it a long time ago. She had simply believed the past was dead.

Unfortunately, it wasn't dead.

She could feel it, like a chill racing across her flesh, like the whisper of unseen force at her ear.

There was so much more going on here than three families' disowning their grandsons because of who their fathers were and because the boys' mothers refused to love anyone else. No, there was something more sinister, and she had a feeling that finding the answers to the questions she had raised could be a long time coming. And asking those questions where other ears could hear would be more dangerous than she might have anticipated.

As she began to turn and move toward the counter and the coffee left in the pot, one of the cell phones in the center of the breakfast table began to vibrate imperatively.

Rafe's hand flashed out, gripping the phone and flipping it open before hitting the call button in a seamless move as he brought it to his ear.

"Yeah?" he answered quietly, and waited a second, a frown brewing between his brows.

"How long have you been there?" His voice seemed to harden, his sapphire eyes gem bright and just as hard as he listened.

Pulling her gaze from his, Cami moved to the coffeepot and refilled the empty cup she had set in front of it earlier.

"Stay in place until daylight, then head to Cami's," he said. "Crowe or Logan will have breakfast for you."

Rafe listened again before grunting mockingly. "Not in your dreams, Tank," he replied to whatever the other man said. "I'll be sleeping."

Perhaps Tank wanted Rafe to fix breakfast.

"We'll talk tomorrow," Rafe told him before flipping the phone closed and staring back at Cami. "Tank's at Amelia's. No one is moving in or out, but he saw Amelia in her upstairs bedroom window as she closed the curtains. She's not showing up tonight."

It was still early.

She would show, Cami knew, but it wouldn't be until late. Very late if Amelia followed the time line they'd had when they were younger.

Amelia had always been very adept at slipping out of her father's house and slipping into Cami's.

"She has the key to the basement door," Cami told Rafe quietly as she set the coffee cup back on the counter. "I never had the lock changed, just in case she needed someplace to run to."

Rafe leaned forward. "Cami, what was the secret you were keeping for Amelia?"

Closing her eyes, she lowered her head, her jaw clenching painfully.

Had it just been this morning? Had she told Rafe they had lost a child and in the next second been forced to face yet another emergency?

There had been no chance to rest, to find peace or a few moments to discuss much of anything that had happened three years before.

"Cami, the time to keep secrets is over," he warned her, his voice low yet hard. "Why did Amelia go from the rebel with a cause to that staid, silent wraith of a young woman we saw today? What did her father learn when he read your diary?"

She was careful to keep her gaze down, but from the corners of her eyes she watched Crowe. Closely. And he was consciously not looking in her direction.

"Cami, I have to agree with Rafe," Logan stated, his gaze compassionate but just as determined as his cousin's. "We need to know now. She's passing you notes that she can't sign in her own name, and coded with a message that only you would understand that she needs to meet with you. Something's wrong here, and it's affecting more than just those in this room at the moment."

But it affected one of them more than the other, and obviously, that one hadn't trusted his cousins with the information.

"Cami." Rafe's tone was warning. "I won't beg for the information. What I'll do is start asking questions around town; is that what you want?"

Cami flinched.

Crowe lifted his head then, his gaze slicing across the room to her, obviously aware she was watching him from the corners of her eyes.

She watched as he drew in a deep breath and gave a short shake of his head before he said, "She helped me break into the courthouse the month we were home on leave that year.

She stole her father's key, slipped inside with me, opened the safe, and I took the file he had been putting together on us. We wiped the computers, made certain there were no copies, and then I took her home."

Cami swallowed tightly.

Amelia had told her about it several nights later, after Crowe had disappeared into Crowe Mountain once again. Excited, nervous, her emerald eyes sparkling with what Cami knew was a surfeit of pure sexual arousal, Amelia had told her exactly what had happened before he took her home. Crowe was leaving quite a few details out of the story.

"Hell." Logan blew out a hard breath as frustration creased his face. "Now he's blackmailing her."

"And no one cared to tell us." Crowe directed the accusation at Cami.

"Perhaps someone thought you'd be man enough to at least pay attention to any changes in her after your little escapade," she shot back. "Tell me, Crowe, did you even bother to question why Amelia married so quickly? Or why she changed so drastically?"

His lips thinned. "I didn't know until today."

Cami's jaw tightened as her lips pursed for a second in an attempt to hold back her anger.

It didn't work.

"Why doesn't that surprise me?" she charged roughly. "Did you even give a damn after you charmed her out of what you wanted and left her watching for you every damned day?"

His eyes narrowed.

"Cami," Rafe warned, "let it go for now. We're all less than calm, and there's no sense in fighting among ourselves."

She let her gaze connect with Rafe's, the need to continue the accusation straining her patience. Because she knew how Amelia felt where Crowe was concerned.

Like Rafe for Cami, Crowe had lit a fire inside Amelia that even the knowledge of the repercussions if anyone learned what she had done couldn't cool. Amelia knew that

Crowe was even more forbidden to her than to any other woman in the county, with the exception of the current Corbin princess, Ann.

And someone had found out. The wrong person had found out, and it had destroyed Amelia's dreams.

Her father had somehow found the diary that Cami kept hidden in a box of letters and cards tucked in the back of her nightstand behind books, mementos, and a picture of her with her mother and Jaymi.

Cami had never learned how he had found it. What she learned, though, was the price she and Amelia both had paid for the discovery.

The price they were still paying.

"I hate this fucking county," Logan breathed out roughly as silence filled the room. "Wayne Sorenson always was a Corbin lapdog. It's a shame his daughter is paying for his lack of backbone."

Wayne Sorenson was particularly cruel. Amelia hadn't just betrayed him; she had broken the law. He had the proof of it in the journal Amelia's best friend had recorded the events of the night in. Amelia and Cami would stay away from each other, Amelia would marry the man Wayne had been shoving down her throat, and she would become the perfect daughter. If she didn't, he would ensure that she was arrested for breaking into the courthouse and interfering in an investigation against suspected criminal elements.

There was nothing he could do to Crowe, because for some reason Cami hadn't mentioned his name. It was a habit she had taken as a teenager. She never wrote their names. She called them instead by the predatory nicknames she had given them.

Rafe was the wolf, Logan was the tiger, and Crowe was the lion, the king of the jungle, simply because he seemed to be harder than the other two.

There was no way Amelia could deny Cami had written about her, though. Her name was there, written in bold black, and the act had been described in exacting detail.

"I'm getting a shower and heading to bed," Cami told the cousins. "This hasn't been my best day and I'd just as soon go to sleep and forget it happened for a while."

She could feel the heaviness weighing her soul down as guilt bit at her hard and deep.

She hadn't just lost everything she had held dear, but she had also managed to strip every shred of Amelia's freedom. Because if she hadn't returned home and done exactly what her daddy wanted, then he would make certain her prints were found inside the safe and the county attorney at the time would have arrested her and made certain she spent time in prison. Then her father had upped the ante. She would do what he wanted, or he would take Cami's journal and implicate her in the crime as well. He might not be able to arrest Crowe, but Wayne could destroy both her and Cami's life.

Wayne Sorenson had tied his daughter's hands, hobbled her, blindfolded her, then shoved a dagger so deep inside her heart that Cami knew her friend would never recover.

Moving through the house and up the stairs, Cami told herself she would make it up to Amelia one of these days. It was one of those promises Cami made almost daily and one she knew she couldn't fix. She'd lost so much simply because of the county she had been so determined to stay in. She hadn't wanted to move to Denver, but Aspen was just small enough that she could never live there without running into her parents.

If her mother ever recovered from the stroke she'd had, if she ever left the nursing home— Unfortunately, she had seemed more than content exactly where she was. Away from her husband.

Still, if not her parents, Cami would end up running into her father, and how painful would that be?

The heat of the shower only reminded her how cold she felt inside. How tired she had become. She'd kept her secrets as long as she could, and when they had come spilling out there had been no stopping them. Just as there had been no stopping the emotions tearing her apart.

There were times she felt she'd placed herself in deep

freeze after she had lost the only friend she had been able to depend upon, then lost her and Rafe's child.

That ice was chipping now. She could feel it inside, fracturing, trying to break apart, the seams melting and weakening as she fought to hold back the pain.

Laying her head against the shower wall, the heat of the water pouring over her, Cami fought to hold it inside, to keep the pain from breaking her apart.

The knowledge that she had carried Rafe's child had been like a ray of hope heating her from the inside out. The thought of that perfect little life, that part of Rafe that could never be taken away from her . . . Yet it had been taken.

Lifting her head, she hurriedly finished, knowing the cost of what she was doing. Standing there beneath the warmth of the water and letting herself remember, revisit that loss, was the most dangerous thing she could do.

She wasn't strong enough for this.

She was losing too much too fast and facing too many truths that were coming at her from too many different directions. She'd tried for years to harden herself, but all she'd managed to do was build the most fragile of defenses against the pain. And those defenses were weakening by the moment.

"Are you warm enough yet, kitten?"

She whirled around, her eyes blinking open against the sting of the shower to see Rafe leaning casually against the ceramic wall at the entrance to the shower.

He watched her as though he could see into the very heart of even those secrets she hid from herself.

"I just needed to relax before going to sleep." She had to turn her back on him.

Staring back at him, seeing the warmth in his gaze, the sensual hunger, and the sparks of anger that still sizzled in the sapphire blue was more than she could bear.

She pushed her face beneath the water once again, because she knew the warmth slipping down her face had nothing to do with the water spilling from the shower.

She'd been finished minutes after stepping beneath the

spray. The soft hint of almond milk soap still filled the heated warmth as she tried to force the water to soak beneath her skin.

To warm her.

To hold the nightmares she knew she would have tonight at bay.

"Poor Cami." Heated and warm, his arms went around her, his bare chest was suddenly at her back, and the feel of his nude body, so hot, so strong, sent a surge of lightning-fast, wicked-hot need erupting through her system.

She was forced to draw in a quick, hard breath.

The solid length of his cock nestled against her lower back, while his powerful thighs cushioned the rounded globes of her rear.

"Do you remember our first night together?" he asked as his lips lowered to her shoulder, brushing against the tender flesh there before nipping at it erotically.

"Yes." She was almost moaning now in pleasure.

"Do you remember what you begged me for more of?"

Her body felt weak, flushed.

She didn't want to be reminded of it. Her dreamworld was working out just fine, thank you very much.

Or was it?

It wasn't this warm.

It wasn't Rafe holding her against his body.

It wasn't the feel of him, so very prepared to send her system into a pleasure so extreme it tempted insanity.

"Poor Cami," he whispered. "Holding everything so tightly inside. Do you ever feel like a wind-up doll ready to blow apart all the mechanics that hold you so tightly bound, Cami?"

"Stop, Rafer." She didn't want this.

She didn't want to break apart into so many pieces it was impossible to put her together again.

He chuckled at her ear before his teeth raked against the sensitive flesh of her lower neck.

"I'm going to fuck you, baby. I'm going to ride us both into exhaustion, feel you beneath me, over me, in front of me," he whispered at her ear. "I'm going to paddle that pretty little bottom and hear you scream for me, hear you beg for more, as I ease inside your tight little ass and feel you go crazy beneath me."

No.

She didn't say the words, she couldn't force them past her lips, as she felt his fingers sliding between the curves of her rear.

"And I'm going to watch," he growled, the image of him watching his thick erection stretching her, easing inside her, flickering through her imagination, and sending her juices flooding the outer lips of her pussy.

The heated warmth surrounded her clit as Rafe moved behind her, shifting, his knees bending beside hers until she felt the thick silk-over-iron crest easing against the slick, bare lips of her cunt.

"Yes. Rafer, yes." Her legs parted farther as she leaned against the shower wall.

His hands gripped her hips, easing her back, positioning her hips as she felt the engorged cock head parting the folds of flesh.

A second later she cried out in such erotic shock she nearly lost her footing in the shower.

His hand landed in a gentle, sensation-igniting pat, just heavy enough that the sound of wet flesh coming in instant contact echoed around her.

It was the heat that bloomed against the soft rise of her pussy that held most of her attention, though. The sensation, so rich and lush with sensual eroticism, was almost too much to bear.

The heat blossomed around her clit, swelling it tighter as the head of his cock forged its way into the snug opening of her sex.

"There, baby," he groaned as he pulled her hips back a fraction farther and, with one foot, pressed her legs wider.

"I could fuck you for hours, Cami. Stay inside this hot little pussy and do nothing but relish the feel of you."

Her head twisted against the shower wall as cries spilled past her lips.

Then, with a tight, hard surge of his hips, half the heavy length of his cock buried inside her. Then the other half, until she was filled so deep, possessed so fully, she couldn't imagine ever being without him now.

"Fuck yeah," he growled as she felt the full, throbbing length of his dick thickening inside her.

"I dreamed of fucking you," he admitted as he began to move then. "Dreamed of watching my dick stretch your sweet pussy open as it milks my flesh inside it."

And her flesh was milking his cock. The inner muscles were flexing, rippling, tugging at his flesh as the nerve endings buried there became so sensitive she could barely breathe for the pleasure.

Each thrust filled her, stroked her, heated her.

She was dying for more, dying for him to fuck her harder, faster, to take her with all the pent-up hunger, need, and desperation that burned inside her.

Gripping both her hips now, his lips at her ear, his breath heated and warm, he began moving harder, faster, each stroke burning to the center of her core as she began to sway, to move. Pushing back, she took him harder, her back arching, her fingers curling into fists at the ceramic wall as she felt tightening of pleasure begin in her womb.

The sensations radiated through her. Burning, intense, they flowed through her system, drawing her to her tiptoes and causing her to cry for him again, to beg him to send her over that edge of oblivions.

When it came, she could only collapse again, shaking and shuddering in his grip as she felt the hard, heated spurts of his semen filling her, adding to a pleasure that had already stolen reason and common sense from her mind.

He was her weakness. He was the one person she couldn't say no to, the one man she couldn't resist.

Breathing heavily, her knees weak and shaky, she leaned against the wall, fighting to catch her breath. What he did to her should be illegal. She was certain it *was* illegal somewhere.

"I would have wanted our baby," he whispered at her ear, his own breathing heavy and rough. "But even more, Cami-love, I would have cherished his mother just as much as I cherish her now."

And the inner walls came crumbling down around her.

CHAPTER 23

Rafe was aware of the confusion in Cami's gaze as he pulled the detachable shower from the mount and carefully washed Cami from head to toe.

As he ran the soft, soapy cloth between her thighs to wash away his semen, his gaze flicked to her face. Her expression was somber, her soft gray eyes filled with conflict, with hunger, and with the saddened memories of all she had lost.

"I should have never let you run as I did," he whispered as he knelt in front of her, running the suds-filled cloth along her soft thighs, then across the gentle curves of her pussy.

He knew if he touched her flesh it would be softer than the rich lather covering it, silkier, warmer.

"You didn't let me do anything, Rafe," she assured him. "I do as I wish."

He let a grin tug at his lips. The fire inside her was often hidden, that temper that he knew she had often controlled and tempered with her compassion. But it was there, just waiting to flare free.

She was independent, but she'd had no choice in adapting to independence. What she didn't know was that all that lovely independence was perfect; it was fine. But he possessed her. She was his, from her very lithe, sexy body to the depths of her fragile feminine soul. She belonged to him.

She sensed it, though he doubted she had considered the consequences of it.

He wouldn't stand back and allow her to slip away in those hours before dawn any longer. He wouldn't allow her bed to be separate from his, and he sure as hell had no intentions of allowing her life to be separate from his.

Leaning forward, he laid a gentle kiss against her hip, his lips lingering against the almond-fragrant flesh as her fingers threaded hesitantly into his hair.

When he pulled back to stare up at her, it was to see the storm raging in her gaze and in her emotions as she watched him.

"What makes you think you could have changed any of the decisions I've made?" she asked him then. "It wasn't your choice, Rafe. It was mine."

If that was what she wanted to believe, then that was fine. He'd let her run scared, thinking she needed to realize things on her own, to live, to be certain of the future she wanted. He had never imagined that she would have seen it as his disinterest.

The fact that she hadn't told him about their child proved that was exactly how she had seen it.

"I let you run," he told her firmly. "I knew you were avoiding me. Just as I knew you were no longer letting your friends know your schedule when you came home from school."

Awareness flickered in her gaze then. "It wasn't a coincidence that you were always there."

"You've always said you don't believe in coincidence," he reminded her. "I thought you would have figured it out."

"You always knew when I was coming home and when and where to meet me," she whispered.

"I'm smart like that," he agreed. "Then you stopped informing your friends of your schedule or posting it to the Web journal you kept. You started avoiding me. I should have put a stop to it then. I would have, if I'd even considered the possibility that we would fall in that one percentile where the pill you were taking would fail."

"I had the dosage increased when I heard you were back in town," she admitted as he looked at her again. "I think I knew I couldn't stay away from you."

"I wouldn't have allowed you to stay away from me."

He'd been growing tired of waiting for her. If she hadn't shown up during that blizzard, then he would have shown up on her doorstep afterward, and he knew it.

Directing the spray at her thighs, he gently rinsed the soap from her flesh as he parted the delicate folds and watched as streams of water ribboned over her belly where he directed the spray, between her thighs, over the silken folds of her pussy.

Lather washed over her thighs, along her legs, and to the shower floor below. The thick suds caressed her flesh and were washed away as the scent of sweet almonds filled the air. He'd never thought almonds could be so damned sexy.

"What are you doing?" she whispered.

"I'm not finished yet," he told her, and he wasn't. "Do you think a quickie in the shower is enough for me? Was it enough for you?"

It wasn't enough for her. He could see the embers of need still glowing in her eyes and in the response of her body.

Tonight was theirs.

Tonight he would make up for everything he'd never been able to have with her. It was for all the nights they had been apart. It was for all the regret that had filled them both for so long.

It was for all the nights she had slipped out before dawn, all the nights he hadn't been certain if she was adventurous enough, experienced enough, for the hungers that swirled inside him. It was for all the years they had been apart whenever he had longed to touch her. Whenever she wasn't in the room with him. Whenever he thought about her. Ached for her. Dreamed of her.

Hell, for all the nights he simply hungered for her, and those hungers were often darker, more sexual and erotic, than he'd shown her thus far.

"Could it ever be enough then?" Confusion darkened her

eyes as he watched her face flush in response to the stream
of spray he directed over the soft pink bud of her clit.

"I doubt it, but we'll find out, love," he agreed, running
his fingers over the soft pad of flesh. "We have a few things
to clear up here, and tomorrow we'll talk, and we'll clear up
the rest."

He directed the spray to her clit again, teasing her with
the pulse of the water pounding around it. He was rewarded
by the quick, sharp intake of breath and the response flaring
in her gaze as he glanced up at her.

"What do we need to clear up?" Her legs parted farther,
just a fraction. It was an unconscious shift, a need rising inside her to get closer to the pleasure that was as much subconscious as it was conscious. A primal, instinctive need to
get closer to the ecstasy each touch promised.

Rafe couldn't blame her. He could feel it himself. It was
the reason why no other woman would do. Why he would
wait six months, a year, for sex with Cami rather than taking
another woman.

After that first time, it had nothing to do with the sex act
or just the physical sensations. It was about a pleasure that
went so much deeper than flesh and a release that burned
hotter, burned deeper, than simply emptying his tight balls.
It was something that couldn't be found anywhere but with
Cami.

Her pleasure was his. Touching her, stroking her, was as
exciting to him as it was to her. He could spend hours just
touching her, just making *her* come. Hell, he could come
with her without even being inside her, and that was something that had never happened with another woman.

"Why are you doing this?" she whispered as he bent
forward, laying a kiss against the gentle rise of her mound
at the crease of her thigh. "Why like this?" She indicated
him kneeling in front of her, touching her, just because he
could.

"Because I love touching you." Rising, he replaced the
shower head before kneeling in front of her again. "Because I've spent too many nights wondering what it would

be like, Cami. And regretting the fact that you always slipped out before I could."

The heated water washed over them, keeping her warm as he let his hands cup the rise of her buttocks and clench gently.

Her breath caught in another sharp intake that signaled her pleasure rising. His fingers eased between her thighs then, finding the soft fall of her juices beginning to build there.

Slick feminine heat met his touch as her lashes fluttered in surrender and in acceptance of whatever touch, whatever hunger, he gave her.

He chose that moment to move.

Straightening, he quickly turned off the steamy water before jerking a towel from the heated rack he'd turned on earlier and wrapping it quickly around her. Picking her up in his arms, he was surprised there were no objections as her arms looped around his shoulders.

She was staring at him suspiciously, perhaps uncertainly. She didn't know what to expect, but he knew what she sensed. She had to sense the intent rising inside him. The certainty that after tonight the rules would definitely change between them. If they didn't, then he might have to just lock her in his bedroom and keep her fucked into submission.

"So many secrets," he said as he laid her in the bed, took the extra towel he had grapped, and hurriedly dried himself. "I should have known you were hiding from me, Cami."

Then he returned his touch to the lover he should have fully claimed long before now. If he had, then there would have been no secrets between them.

"I should have never given you the time I thought you needed to be free," he told her as he used her towel to dry her gently from head to toe. "You've never been free, have you, Cami?"

Her tongue licked over her lips in a charming, nervous little gesture. "Whenever I was with you. I was always free with you, Rafe. I was always me."

Until she had lost their child. Until there were secrets she had to protect.

Allowing her freedom had been the point of staying away from her, though. He had believed that to be free she needed to be away from him. That his possessiveness, his dominance, would restrict her, would bind her to him rather than allowing her to be certain what she wanted.

The truth was, even with the possessiveness, she would have at least had someone to hold on to. Someone who loved Cami just for herself, just for the compassion, the kindness, and the laughter she gave. Those were gifts she never expected payment for. She hadn't even asked for the same compassion and kindness, let alone the laughter. And it was a good thing, because she damned sure hadn't had it.

Tossing the towel aside, he came over her, his lips covering hers as she met his kiss with a soft, whimpering little sigh.

He loved the sounds she made as she loved his touch, reached for it, pleaded for more. There was something more exciting, something more intense, about loving Cami than there had ever been with any other woman.

The pleasure was sharper, more intense, and more heated than anything he had ever known before.

As her fingers speared through his hair, gripping the thick strands, Rafe could feel her giving herself up to each sensation, allowing it to immerse her, to swamp her with the ecstasy.

She gave herself to him, completely, and he loved every second of it. There were no pretenses, no simulated moans, arches, or faked responses.

It was all completely natural, completely Cami. It was a woman reaching for the pleasure she was owed, willing to pay any price for it but, even more, willing to love in return for it.

As she arched to him, her thighs spreading as he came between them, Rafe let his lips wander from hers, to her jaw, to the sensitive flesh beneath and then along the side of her neck. She tilted her head in response, allowing him access to even the most tender skin just below her ear and shuddering with pleasure as he kissed it gently.

Kittenish little sighs and rumbling moans met each caress, assuring him he was drawing her deeper and deeper into the pleasure he wanted to create for her.

He wanted her completely immersed in his touch, reaching eagerly for the rising rapture beginning to spread around her. Through her.

With his lips, his tongue, the rasp of his teeth over her nipples, the feel of them against his tongue, he pushed her higher. His lips surrounded one tight peak, drawing it inside and working the engorged, sensitive tip against his tongue as he pleasured the other with his fingers.

Her nails bit into his shoulders as she fought to hold on to him. Hips lifting, her mound pressing against his hip as he lay between her thighs, she rubbed the silky, slick flesh against him.

Each touch, each stroke, each kiss designed for the ultimate pleasure for her, the ultimate surrender.

It was that surrender he needed. That complete feminine submission to every stroke, every caress, ever naughty act. Only in that submission would the subconscious trust, the bond he needed between them, come. He wanted her to trust, to know, to instinctively understand that he was more than just her lover; he was her other half. The one she told her secrets to. The one she made secrets with.

"Rafe," she whispered his name, the imperative hunger rising inside her as he continued to kiss his way down her body, stretching out between her thighs to taste the lush sweetness spilling from her sex.

Bright, wicked shards of sensation whipped through her senses as she felt Rafe's lips brush against the mound of her pussy as his hands pushed beneath her, lifting her to the caress.

His tongue licked over the silken folds, slid into the narrow slit hidden by the swollen, flushed lips of her cunt.

Knees lifting, she spread her thighs farther, her heels pressing into the bed to lift her closer to him.

She could feel his finger at her rear, parting the curves and sliding into the narrow cleft to caress her entrance gently with the tip of his finger, erotic, an edge of the forbidden. Cami felt her senses awakening further, reaching eagerly for each new sensation. Fingers of electric pleasure raced up her spine, wrapped around her senses, and spread through the erogenous points of her body.

Her nipples tightened further, aching with such sharp need that her fingers lifted to them, gripped them, tugging at them as her hips churned beneath each hungry swipe of his tongue over her clit, through the swollen folds, and lower to the entrance to her pussy.

There he rimmed the entrance with his tongue, flickered against it as he slid one hand back while the other caressed and played at the entrance there.

Cami felt her fingers clenching in his hair and fought to pull at it too sharply to remember that Rafe was attached to his hair and she really didn't want to cause any loss of the thick blue-black strands that framed his face.

But God, it was so hard to restrain herself. The pleasure was streaking through her. It tore through her senses, wiping away any thought but that of his pleasure. Of the incredible feel of his fingers, his lips and tongue, stretched between hers.

She was only distinctly aware of the fact that he was preparing her back entrance, lubricating it by slow degrees as he drew his fingers back, returned with the lubricant, then repeated the process.

She knew what was coming. She knew what he planned to do, and the conflict rising inside her in regards to it did nothing to halt her pleasure of it.

If she decided she didn't want it, then she would do something about it the moment she decided it. But not right now. Not yet. Not until she saw where the pleasure was taking her, how extreme it could become, and until she actually found the strength to make herself refuse him.

She couldn't do it.

The pleasure was too wild and much too intense.

"Oh God, Rafe." Her hips jerked as she felt the first finger press inside her, sliding past the tight ring of muscles that clenched almost violently, involuntarily, around his finger.

Cami gasped for breath, the alternation of pleasure and pain sensations exploding through her body with such quick progression that she couldn't keep up.

"That's it, baby," he groaned between her thighs as he laid another kiss over her clit. "Just let me have you. All of you, Cami. Give it all to me."

Give him everything? But hadn't she already done that years ago? Hadn't she already given him her deepest heart, the most vulnerable depths of her soul? Hadn't he owned that since the night she met him?

His finger began to move slowly, pulling back, leaving her body, returning, slicker than before, pressing back, and heating her further as the lubricant prepared her.

Cami could feel herself climbing that edge of sensation so sharp, so intense, as rapture teased the edges of her senses.

With each stroke of his fingers she wanted more. She wanted to feel that sharper, more exacting pleasure. She wanted each thrust to stretch and burn to push every limit of pleasure that could exist.

And God only knew why she was aching for it. Reaching for it.

"Rafe, please," she cried out as he returned again with only the same thrust, though it was slicker, wetter, than before.

"More, kitten?" he asked, his tone strained. "Tell me what you want, baby."

"You know what I want," she moaned desperately. She could feel the desperation rising inside her, sense it beginning to rise out of control.

His finger pulled back, but he added another, increasing the sensations with its return. "Oh God, yes," she demanded fiercely at that slightest edge of what she needed so bad. "More, Rafe. Please. You know what I need."

The thrust was followed by his fingers spreading, stretching the entrance. The unique burn racing through her. But still, it wasn't enough.

Her hips thrust back at him, writhing into the caress as she felt her breathing becoming heavy, restricted.

She could feel something wild and uncontrolled rising inside her with each thrust and stretch. It was like being locked, imprisoned, in a whirlwind of sensation so hot, so imperative, that fighting against it was impossible.

Her knees lifted further, her hips lifting and thrusting as the need for that sharper, burning sensation was tearing through her.

She felt on the verge of tears. She'd never been so desperate for a touch that she had no idea how to gain. For a caress she had never had yet sensed was awaiting her.

Perspiration gathered on her, burning, the hunger became so sharp, so intense, she felt on the verge of screaming.

When Rafe pulled back, his caress, his fingers, abandoning her, she reached for him desperately, a cry parting her lips as confusion laced her senses. She didn't understand what she needed. She sure as hell had no idea how to attain it.

A second later Rafe was rising above her, pulling her legs over his, lifting her hips until he could move into place.

Lifting her legs until her ankles lay against his shoulders, Cami watched, panting for air as he gripped the shaft of his cock, bent forward, and tucked the thick, engorged tip against that tender, unbreached entrance with dominant demand.

Then slowly, his hips began to press forward.

Cami felt the flames erupt first. The burning sensation of her flesh beginning to stretch tore through her. Untouched nerve endings were suddenly, shockingly revealed as the puckered entrance began to stretch to accept the heavy impalement of his cock.

She stared up at him, her gaze locked with his as he gripped her hips, held her still, and began to rock against her. The small thrusting motions began to work his flesh slowly inside her rear.

With her legs lifted and lying against his shoulders, the angle of penetration enabled him to move inside her as he watched her face, watched her eyes glaze in mesmerizing pleasure.

The ultrasnug tissue of her ass opened and spread around the wide crest of his dick as he eased inside to meet the tighter, more sensitive ring of muscles just inside the entrance.

Pressing into it, he watched as she strained against him, her fingers clenching into the blankets beneath her, her back arching as she seemed to flush from head to toe.

Cloudy gray eyes turned thunderous. Her lips parted; lashes fluttered over her eyes.

He tightened his thighs, held her hips tighter, and then, as he watched her face, began to press past that final, clenched ring of muscles that began to tighten and milk the head of his cock.

"Rafe. Oh yes, more," she moaned, her head thrashing against the mattress. "I can't stand it. Please, Rafer, I can't stand—" The erotic cry was both a protest and a plea as he felt the violently engorged crest pop through the tightened ring to sink inside the desperately flexing entrance of her anus.

Cami felt the sensations, wild and erotic, suddenly exploding through her. The excitement of the nerve-rich flesh combined with the erotic, forbidden classification of the act sent her senses careening.

She wasn't just rising; she was being propelled into a starburst of sensations and pleasure that she had no idea how to process, how to handle.

She wanted to scream, but first she would have to breathe. She wanted to breathe, but first she would have to find the ability to process more than just the rapid flood of sensations racing through her.

Then, he added to them.

His fingers moved between her thighs; two pushed inside her pussy, burning the sensitized flesh there, increasing the bursts of ecstatic pleasure as she began rocketing higher, reaching, crying out for that ultimate release.

His hips were moving fiercely now, his cock thrusting harder, faster, inside the tightening depths of her rear as his fingers moved in quick thrusts inside her pussy.

Each thrust, each burning stretch, each gasping moan increased the pleasure that became so much more than pleasure that there was no way to understand it, no way to process it.

And Rafe was controlling it. The measured thrusts were pushing her deeper into the starbursts, tiny explosions erupting through her system. She was reaching desperately for release. She could feel it, just out of reach, teasing her, there, and then moving back, coming closer only to retreat.

She could feel the insanity of that need clawing at her until she and Rafe bent closer, his fingers turning inside her pussy as he twisted his wrist to the side, thrust his fingers inside her, then ground his palm against the swollen, violently sensitive bud of her clit.

It tore through her then. Ecstasy exploded with a white-hot brilliance that tore at her mind, ripping it from its moorings as pleasure expanded, exploded, enraptured until she swore her spirit was torn from her own body and shot straight to Rafe's.

The emotions that swirled through the pleasure were a combination of so many things, so many hopes, needs, and dreams that she had never known she had.

The bond she had always sensed between them seemed to open up, to burn around her, as she stared into the rich brilliant blue of his eyes as he tightened before her, his expression tightening, his body tensing, his teeth baring a second before she watched his release flood his expression and the sensitive recess of her rear.

Hard, fiery spurts of semen blasted inside her, the sensation adding to the ecstasy, pushing it higher, increasing it, rocking the very foundations of her knowledge of herself and Rafe.

As though such pleasure could never be contained, it exploded again, imploded, tore through every particle of her body, then tossed her through the sensations until she found herself trembling beneath Rafe, shuddering at the extremity of the sensations as she fought to catch her breath.

She was wasted. Exhausted. She was so weak she could

only whimper helplessly as she felt him slowly pull free to collapse beside her.

She was used to Rafe cuddling her afterward, but when he wrapped his arms around her he pulled her close to his heart, holding her more firmly than he had before.

And she hadn't even realized how she had needed this each time they had been together. To be held so snugly, so close, that there would be no chance of slipping free of him, whether he was asleep or not.

Drowsiness gripped her, exhaustion settled inside her, as she felt the heavy lassitude of sleep slowly easing over her.

She roused only seconds later as she felt Rafe running a warm, wet cloth over and between her thighs, reaching back to the slick cleft of her rear. He cleaned her as though the thought of her comfort was uppermost. He had every time. Each time they had been together he had taken the time needed to rise from the bed, collect the cloth, then clean her gently.

Her lashes lifted drowsily, as she was uncertain whether she wanted to wake enough to watch him or not.

"Sleep, baby," he murmured tenderly as he dropped the cloth to the towels that lay beside the bed. "We'll talk in the morning."

About what?

She didn't ask the question, though. Instead, she let sleep overtake her, though she didn't slip into the deepest reaches of it until she felt Rafe return to the bed. When his arms went around her, he pulled her into his embrace and the heavy beat of his heart against her ear lulled her into a sleep more peaceful, more fulfilling, than any she had known before.

CHAPTER 24

She had expected Amelia to show up before dawn, to slip into the house as she had done when they were teenagers and grounded for some transgression.

What Cami didn't expect was to come sharply awake just after dawn to the heavy crack of her bedroom door against the frame.

Before her eyes were open Rafe was moving.

He rolled her from the bed, still naked, moving with a powerful surge of strength as he took her over the side of the bed to the floor, the weapon in his hand trained across the room.

She couldn't blame him for it. He'd been trained to react and to move at the slightest sign of danger.

After all that had happened in the past weeks, who could have blamed him for leveling that weapon on her father?

Her sperm donor, she liked to call him, because there was nothing fatherly about Mark Flannigan.

"What the hell are you doing here, Flannigan?" Rafe growled, even as he wondered where his cousins were.

"Now then, wouldn't it just surprise you to know I'm here to see my wife's daughter."

His wife's daughter, not his own. Rafe caught the mocking inference in Mark's tone, and from the flinch of her body he knew Cami had caught it as well.

"I need my robe," she whispered almost silently, more than uncomfortable at the thought of being naked in front of her father.

Rafe had no such problems, though.

Rising to his feet as he cast Mark a scowl, Rafe padded across the room to where the silken robe was draped over the lady's chair that sat in the corner.

Pulling it quickly over her arms, Cami kept her gaze on her father and wondered why he was there. In the time since she had bought the house from her parents, not once had either of them come by to see her home.

"There was no need," he assured her, his gaze scathing as it flickered over her and Rafe again.

Rafe still hadn't dressed. He was too busy sitting on the bed and watching her father warningly. She could have told Rafe that no amount of warning could stop whatever her father had in mind to say.

His gaze flicked back to her again.

"How disappointing," he told her, a sneer pulling at his lips. "I would have never expected such a betrayal of your family, even from you."

Even from her, as though betrayal were something he had grown to accept as a part of her.

"Your opinion of me or anything I do isn't anything I lose sleep over, Mark," she told him casually, knowing that the worst thing she could do was allow him to see how easily he could wound her.

She had learned better than that years before.

"What I'd like to know is how he managed to slip past Logan and Crowe," Rafe stated.

Mark snorted. "They were out back for some reason." He shrugged comfortably. "I have a key."

"I'd like that key back," she informed him. "Is Mom okay?"

"As if you care," he accused her. "You're too busy fucking her daughter's murderer to even check up on her."

Cami could only shake her head. She called the facility daily and went to visit whenever she could.

Her mother didn't even recognize her. Cami doubted her

mother even thought of her when she did have the presence of mind to remember her.

"What do you want, Mark?" Cami asked wearily as Rafe rose to his feet, pulled his jeans over his legs, and pulled the zipper up nonchalantly.

"I couldn't believe it when I heard how you were consorting with these bastards." Mark flicked his fingers to Rafe to indicate not just him but also his cousins, who weren't in the room at the moment.

"I don't want to hear this." Cami lifted her hand, seeing the rage in her father's face and wishing she had changed the locks to the house when she had the chance.

"You don't want to hear this," he sneered back at her. "This is how you repay the love and loyalty Jaymi felt for you, isn't it? They killed her, Cami—"

"They didn't kill her, and I won't deal with you at the moment. Leave, Mark."

His expression twisted in fury. "Give me the courtesy of calling me Father, you little whore."

The conversation was over as far as she was concerned. The accusations she could handle; the name-calling was much harder to overlook or to turn the other cheek on.

"Your mother heard what you were doing here, in her home, in the room where she once slept in her bed," he snarled back at Cami as he shoved his hands into the pockets of his slacks and watched her as though she were a foul odor he couldn't disperse.

"Then you told her," Cami accused him, feeling her chest tighten in pain and anger at the thought of what Mark would have said or could have done to torment her mother. "Tell me, Mark, don't you ever get tired of punishing Mother for having me, and me for living when Jaymi didn't?"

His expression darkened further. "I forgave her for giving birth to you," he informed her. "But no, Cami, after this." He nodded toward Rafe. "After this, I'll never forgive you for living. Jaymi wouldn't have betrayed you this way. She sure as hell would have never slept with the man who killed you."

"I would hope not." Cami shrugged. "You should leave now. If you really believe Rafe and his cousins are murderers, then it's hard telling how they'll react if you continue to stand here and throw their crimes in their faces."

She glanced at Rafe. The smile he gave her father was all teeth. "Yeah, only God knows how much fun we could have with that one," Rafe snorted.

"Leave the key before you go, Mark." It should have hurt. It should have broken her heart a thousand times over, but all she felt was regret.

He could have been a father to her.

He had been Jaymi's father. He had loved Jaymi with a father's devotion that Cami had envied.

A devotion she'd prayed for just a bit of. An ounce of. Hell, she would have settled for Mark to simply tolerate her.

The smile that curved his lips was one that echoed with relish. She knew that whatever was coming, he expected to cut her to the bone.

"Your mother will never know I told you the truth," he told Cami confidently. "She'll never know I finally found the chance to tell you how thankful I am that you're not my child."

Shouldn't she be shocked?

Cami stared back at him as Rafe cursed under his breath and moved to her. His arm went around her as he moved behind her, drawing her against him and providing a warmth, a security, she'd never had before. Facing Mark had never been easy. It had never been comfortable. But he'd never been so deliberately cruel either.

It wasn't shock that filled her, though, and it wasn't pain.

"I think I've known that for a very long time," she told him softly. "If you meant to hurt me, Mark, then you haven't succeeded."

That was exactly what he had expected.

He glowered back at her and Rafe. "You'll pay for this," Mark finally snapped. "You'll pay, Cami, when he kills you. When he tortures and rapes you—"

"And if you didn't notice the fact he was in my bed when

you so rudely barged in, then you'd realize he didn't have to rape me," she retorted. "No more than he would have had to rape Jaymi. Stop walking the Corbins' line, Mark, and think for yourself for a change. Jaymi tried to tell you he and his cousins weren't involved in any wrongdoings. But like everyone else, it's much easier to please James Corbin than it is to think for yourself, isn't it."

"Cami," Rafe said her name softly. "Go get ready, sweetheart. We have things to do today, remember?"

No, that wasn't what she remembered.

He'd told her last night they had things to clear up, and that was far different.

"I'm finished with the little tramp—"

Before Cami could process the fact that Rafe had moved, he had done just that.

His hand was wrapped around Mark's throat, holding him pinned to the wall he had thrown him into.

"Leave," Rafe said softly.

Anything else he said Cami missed while waiting for her brain to kick into gear once again.

She rushed to the two men, and her fingers curled around the arm that bulged with strength as he drew on that power to keep his fingers wrapped around Mark's throat.

"That's enough," she said softly. "I really don't want to have to deal with Archer later, Rafe. And you know Mark; he would definitely file a complaint if you leave so much as a single bruise."

"Oh, he won't be bruised," Rafe promised her, though he released Mark slowly. "But I bet you he remembers how little I like hearing that trash rolling out of his mouth to you."

"And I'm sure he really won't care once he gets away from you," she told him before turning her gaze back to the man who had thought he could destroy her.

"Who was my father?" she asked Mark.

"Dead." He seemed to relish the word. "The bastard was some cop in Denver when she left me one summer. She never made that mistake again. Again," he reminded Cami.

"Did you kill him?"

Mark chuckled at the question. "I only wish I'd had the chance. A drug dealer and his tramp did that for me when he thought he could poke his nose in their business. His stupidity got him killed."

If Mark could have set it up, then he would have, Cami thought.

She could see it in his eyes, in the hatred and regret that filled his expression.

"I'm going to shower and dress," she only partially lied. She'd showered the night before; she only intended to dress and face whatever issues Rafe thought they should iron out. Or clear up. He'd said they had things to clear up, and she had a feeling she knew exactly what a few of those things were. The fact that she'd kept secrets from him, that she hadn't contacted him when she needed him.

Turning her back on Mark, she moved to the dresser, collected her clothing, then moved into the bathroom.

Whatever Mark had thought he would accomplish by attempting to ambush her, he hadn't quite managed it. Had it been ten years before, even five, then he could have shattered her with that knowledge.

Perhaps a part of her had already accepted, over the years, that no father could be as cruel as he had been over the years. He hadn't laid a hand on her, but there were times that words could hurt much worse than a fist.

Moving into the bathroom, she wondered at how easily Mark had slipped in, though. He'd obviously been watching her, waiting, stalking her.

At this point, she didn't give a damn what Rafe said to Mark. She was beginning to wonder if she would even care what Rafe did to him. Mark had made her mother's life hell, and Cami knew it. A part of her acknowledged that he was the reason her mother had turned to the Valium and the wine. He was the reason she had closed herself off, even from the child she'd conceived, likely with a man who had loved her.

Cami dressed quickly, unwilling to leave Rafe with Mark long enough to actually hurt him. But when she stepped out into the bedroom, it was to find Rafe sitting in the large easy chair, lounging back, as he waited patiently for her.

His expression was slightly mocking, knowing.

"You know, he didn't come through the front door," Rafe told her. "There are several webcams scattered through the house now. He came through the basement window, just as your attacker did."

Cami paused and stared back at Rafe, confused at the statement.

"But you secured that window." And she knew he and his cousins would have done the job right.

"Yes, we did," he agreed. "And from what I saw on the camera, he's damned good at picking a lock, Cami."

She rubbed at her temple, uncertain what to make of that. "He wasn't the one that attacked me." *Was he?*

If he had been, then that meant he had also been the one behind Jaymi's death.

Cami shook her head. "He would have never hurt Jaymi. Whoever tried to hurt me was behind Thomas Jones attacking her as well. Mark was devoted to her."

"But she was sleeping with me," Rafe pointed out.

Cami shook her head again. "He truly loved her, Rafe. He loved her, and he loved Mother, despite any infidelity she may have committed. It was me he hated. It was me he made pay for it; that way he could could forgive her."

And Cami believed that to the bottom of her soul. "Mark's world began and ended with Mother and Jaymi. Losing a part of that world was more than he could bear."

Rafe watched her for long, considering moments. "Pack up." He surprised her with the command. "We'll move to the ranch until this is resolved."

"And what will that solve?" She breathed out with an edge of weariness. "Running won't make him move any faster; it will only delay the inevitable. And I'm not running. Not yet."

She hadn't run from her problems since she was a child. "That was one of the few lessons Mark has taught me.

Running shows weakness and fear. I'm not ready to give that impression quite yet."

"You're being too damned stubborn," Rafe muttered as he came out of the chair and stalked over to her. "Should I have that put on your gravestone? 'She Died Stubborn.'"

Her lips almost twitched. "Look at it this way," she suggested. "I may die stubborn, but I intend to make certain that he knows he didn't get the best of me in any other way. He'll know he failed."

"And that's so important to you?" Rafe asked incredulously.

"Important?" she whispered. "Not so much important, Rafe, as all I have left. Through the years it's all I've had, Rafe; Mark took everything else. And what he didn't take Thomas Jones did when he killed Jaymi. Besides, what will leaving accomplish?"

"I know my home turf. I can protect it," Rafe answered her instantly.

"And he doesn't. Whoever attacked me won't come after me there. He'll just wait, and he'll watch, and the Callahan cousins will have to blink eventually."

"If I lost you, Cami, it would destroy me."

She blinked back at him.

He said it so seriously, as though the words were torn from a place so deep inside himself that he wasn't certain where they came from either.

Cami swallowed tightly. "What do you want me to say?" She was suddenly terrified. Terrified of herself and the emotions she suddenly felt being torn from deep inside her.

She'd kept parts of her locked down for as long as she could remember, definitely since she had lost their child. But even before that, there were hopes, dreams, needs, and desires that she'd refused to allow herself.

"You seem so surprised," he murmured as he stopped in front of her. "Why do you think I arranged to meet you in Denver all those years ago? Why do you think I tried so hard to give you the time you needed to make that first move, to come to me, to be sure you wanted me, Cami? To be sure you'd tasted freedom and were ready to accept everything I felt for you? Everything I need to be with you?"

She shook her head, staring up at him, at the blaze of emotion in his eyes, at the truth of everything he was saying.

"We can talk about this later," she forced the words past her lips.

"Because you're terrified to hear the words? Tell me, kitten." His hands cupped her cheeks, forced her to keep her gaze locked with his. "Has anyone ever told you they loved you?"

Had they?

She'd known Jaymi had loved her, but had she ever said the words?

She hadn't, Cami realized.

"Mother," she whispered.

When she had been younger. Before Mark had decided she was such a threat.

"I love you, Cami."

She flinched.

Something seemed to shatter in her chest. A wash of fear, followed by a blaze of heat and an outpouring of emotion that dragged a sob from her chest and left her trembling in front of him.

"Don't lie to me," she burst out, her voice as shaky as her knees now. "Please, Rafe. Please don't lie to me. I couldn't survive it."

"Have I ever lied to you?"

He never had, but that didn't mean he wouldn't. It didn't mean he couldn't change his mind later.

"No, you haven't lied to me," she whispered as she felt that first tear ease from her eyes. "I couldn't bear it if you lied to me now, Rafe."

His head lowered, his eyes locked with hers.

"I love you, Cambria Flannigan," he whispered. "To the very depths of my soul. You've bound my heart since you were seventeen years old and didn't have a date for the prom, and I've only grown to love you more each year."

Her breathing hitched. Another sob shook her.

"Cami?" he questioned her gently as his lips touched hers. "We both know you feel it. Aren't you going to tell me you love me too?"

Her lips trembled.

"I love you," she suddenly cried, feeling the tears as they began to run down her face, the love as it finally broke free inside her, pouring into the light, refusing to allow her to ignore it any longer. "Oh God, Rafe, I love you so much."

His arms wrapped around her as he jerked her closer. His lips covered hers, his body surrounded her, and the warmth and strength that was so much a part of him encompassed her. She felt warm, heated.

For the first time in her life, Cami felt warm from the inside out.

CHAPTER 25

The day seemed to fly by.

For the first time in her life, Cami felt as though she were walking on air. There was no fear that dawn would come and force her to leave the man she loved. There was no fear that if she stared into his eyes too long, then she would see the same lack of emotion that she had seen in the eyes of the man who had called himself her father.

For the first time, Cami felt loved.

She felt wanted.

And for the first time the love she had carried so carefully inside her heart, kept wrapped and hidden away from harm, could emerge, be free, and she did not have to worry that the emotions that drew it free would turn on her and destroy her.

She'd lived her life in the shadow of Mark's hatred, her mother's inability to deal with reality, and her sister's death. Still, Cami had held that dream inside her, that hope, and an endless well of love for one man. That love had always remained steadfast, living, breathing, and waiting for the day it could emerge.

But there was also the knowledge that there was no true security, not yet.

There was still that unseen threat that made no sense and the shadow that haunted her, no matter how she trusted in

Rafe's ability to protect her. As she had said, even the Callahan cousins had to blink eventually. Returning from the grocery store that evening, she couldn't help but fear the day the other shoe would drop.

When that unseen threat would make its move and destroy the life she had dreamed of having.

If that threat hadn't reared its head, then neither had Amelia. That was another worry that followed Cami through the day, as she wondered why her friend hadn't slipped into the house yet and why she hadn't found a way to contact Cami and let her know what was going on.

It had to be important or Amelia wouldn't have taken the risk she took the day before.

"I'm going to go shower," Cami told Rafe as he put away the bacon, eggs, and other items his cousins seemed to thrive on.

It was growing dark, and Cami knew if she didn't try to keep her nerves at bay, and her fears from taking over, then she would end up going after Amelia herself.

Making her way up the stairs, Cami wished she'd been smarter, perhaps not so willing to ignore the fact that Sorenson was such an asshole.

She simply hadn't expected him to search through her things, though. Even more, she hadn't expected him to read that particular journal. It was almost as though he had known exactly where to look for it.

Sighing at the futility of her thoughts, she pushed her bedroom door open, stepped in, then as the door cracked closed whirled around in shock and fear.

Dark brown eyes that watched her carefully, short brown hair, a tattoo on the back of his hand, and extending from the grip he had on it a weapon lifted and aimed for her heart.

Lowry Berry.

"Didn't expect to see me, did you, Cami?"

That was the voice. Low, evil, rasping with dangerous intent as he stepped from the wall, reached over, and locked the door securely. Cami stared at the weapon.

"How did you get in?" She could feel terror rising inside her.

"I have my ways." His smile was soft, hesitant. That boyish, apologetic charm that had fooled so many for so long.

"Don't do this, Lowry," she whispered as the teacher stared back at her, the dark brown of his eyes heavy with remorse. "Why did you even come here? Whatever you're involved in, I didn't know anything about it and I don't care."

"And you wouldn't have recognized my voice either, would you?" he asked regretfully, the little Texas twang in his voice sounding dark and sinister now rather than friendly and a bit shy as it had the night he had asked her to dance at the Spring Fling Social.

"You were calling?" She knew it was him. The minute she had swung around and seen him, she had known.

"Your sister knew too." His voice dropped further as Cami felt her heart fall to her stomach.

She could see it in his eyes. That silent admission that he was the reason Thomas Jones had managed to take Jaymi.

"What did you say?" No, this couldn't be true. Lowry had been Jaymi's friend. She would have trusted him. She would have felt safe with him."I didn't have a choice, Cami, just as I don't have a choice now." He took a step toward her as she stepped back.

"You'll never get me out of this house, Lowry," she warned him roughly, tears thickening her voice. "Rafe will be up here any minute. And even if he isn't—"

"I got into the house, didn't I? I got in, and I slipped right up the stairs while y'all sat in the kitchen chitchattin' about your whys and your whens. And all these years, those boys never figured Jaymi was given to Thomas for the sole purpose of framin' them just enough to get their asses thrown in prison."

She was going to throw up.

She could feel it roiling in her stomach, thickening in her throat.

"How did you get in?" Her entire body was shaking, trembling in fear and in anger.

His smile was gentle as he looked around her bedroom.

"I like your room," he said, staring around. "The soft cream and smoke color of the walls with the heavy, dark brown winter curtains." He tilted his head and looked at the furnishings, the bedcovering. "Feminine softness without the prissiness," he sighed. "Jaymi wasn't like that, was she?"

Cami shook her head. The delay would give her more time, and it would give Rafe more time to get upstairs.

"She was girly to the bone." Lowry smiled in reminiscence.

"What did you do, Lowry?" Cami whispered tearfully.

She couldn't believe he had done something so cruel. That he could have been involved in Jaymi's death.

He had been her friend. She had dated him a few times. They had always laughed that he was the brother fate had taken from her.

"What do you think I did?" he asked Cami softly.

A sob jerked at her body, stealing her breath for a precious moment. "You helped Thomas Jones kill her, didn't you?"

There was no hiding from it. And there was no denying it.

He nodded slowly. "I picked her up. Jones was waiting for me. I was to take her to him, just like I did the other girl. The one Crowe was fucking. That lobbyist's daughter that he met at a party the week she died."

"I didn't know about her." Keep him talking. She had to keep him talking.

"Not many people did know about her. But once they were on trial for murder, then she would have been brought up."

"By who?" And why? There were so many questions, but she wanted to keep him talking, right here, right now. She was not leaving the house with him.

"Now see, I don't know that." He shook his head as he moved to the dresser next to the door and leaned casually against it, as though it were simply a casual conversation as he kept the weapon trained on her. "I get a picture and my orders and I do what I'm told."

"But why, Lowry?" she whispered again, this time desperation shadowing her voice. "Why would you betray your friends this way? Who could possibly make you hurt the people who care about you?"

"The person who knows that even though I can't kill my friends, I won't take the chance of going to prison if the cops find out that I'm the one that raped those three teenagers in Aspen the year Jaymi died, and at least two a year ever since. And I can tell you, Cami, I wouldn't survive prison." He straightened and waved the gun toward the door before coming back to her. "Now, you be quiet. Real quiet. There's this little bug in the kitchen, and I listen through here." He pulled an earbud free before tucking it back into his ear. "Your friends are still in there, but I'm not betting they'll stay for long and we need to get out of here."

"Why?" Her breathing hitched. "Where are you taking me, Lowry?"

"Because I don't have a choice," he sighed. "It's what I was ordered to do, and I can't ignore the order."

"Why?" she whispered desperately. "Who has such a hold on you that you would do something so evil?"

Sorrow darkened his eyes. "I don't know who he is," he said regretfully. "I just know he was Jones' partner. He's the man that's going to kill you, Cami."

Like hell he was.

Did he think she was going to give in without a fight? That she would just lie down and die for him with a warning like that?

"Was Jaymi that easy, Lowry?" Cami asked, confused by his demeanor and the fact that he had managed to kidnap her sister.

"She missed her husband an awful lot, you know," Lowry commented softly. "I think she knew. And I think preferred dying to living without him. But she didn't know who would kill her until we arrived at the clearing and I had to help Thomas tie her down."

He blinked quickly.

"Tears from a murderer?" Cami sneered suddenly. "From a child rapist without a conscience?"

His lips trembled. "I lose sleep." It was a whine. It was a childish attempt to make himself look better, though he knew that wasn't possible. "I feel guilt, Cami. I hear her telling me, though, that she was happier in his arms. In her husband's arms."

"You're hearing your own demented wishes," Cami cried out as he flinched, then looked around wildly as though expecting Rafe to suddenly materialize.

"Shut up," he hissed, fury blazing in his eyes.

"Shut up?" She laughed, a broken, hollow sound. "Why, Lowry? Why should I shut up? Why should I obey you when you're going to kill me anyway?"

Her lips parted to scream.

"Lowry?" Cami swung around as Amelia stepped from the bathroom.

There were tears on Amelia's cheeks; her emerald eyes were filled with pain and with betrayal.

Lowry hadn't been just Cami and Jaymi's friend. He had been Amelia's as well. He had helped her and Cami evade curfews when they were younger and slip out when they were grounded.

Since Jaymi's death, he had been too distant to aid in anything. He'd withdrawn, and now Cami knew why.

Lowry stepped back, shocked, as Cami watched the gun in his hand carefully.

He didn't know whether to aim it at Amelia or aim it at Cami. It swung wildly between the two of them as his dark brown eyes grew even wilder and a sense of helpless bafflement tightened his face.

"You're not supposed to be here," he hissed.

"But I am here."

Staid, buttoned-down. This was the Amelia who had broken Cami's heart for the past three years.

Amelia's long hair was bound at the back of her head, a thick bun that gave her a schoolmarmish appearance. Sensible shoes, no jewelry. Strangely, she wasn't even wearing her wedding band.

"You're not supposed to be here." Lowry gave his head a quick shake, his lips tightening as anger began to burn in his gaze.

No, that wasn't just anger. It was demented rage.

Cami stepped back farther, her intent to get to the door on the wall closest to her.

It looked like a closet, but the door led instead into another bedroom and then out into the hall.

"If you fire that gun, Rafe and his cousins will hear it," Amelia pointed out. "Is that what you want?"

"Do I have a choice?" he asked as something akin to resignation flashed in his eyes. "We could have done it the easy way." He turned his attention back to Cami now. "Now, we'll just have to do it my way."

His finger began to tighten.

Cami felt the scream that tore from her throat as the bedroom door crashed inward in that second and Rafe came hurtling into the other man. His body much taller, heavily muscled and controlled, Rafe took the other man down as the first shot rang out.

Cami looked around, desperate, terrified of where that bullet had gone and whom it had struck.

Amelia was thrown back against the wall, eyes wide, her palms flat against the wall. Logan and Crowe were running a second late behind Rafe.

It was as though hell had opened up and poured a crazed strength into Lowry. He should haven't been strong enough to resist Rafe's pure, possessive fury. Yet Lowry was. He fought back, kicking and screaming and pouring out his hatred of Cami as he fought the man determined to save her.

At first, it looked as though they had to pull Rafe off, that for whatever reason, he was unable to get to his feet on his own. Then, Cami saw the damage.

She stepped forward, one foot, one step, a sob tearing from her throat as Rafe rushed for her, pulling her into his arms as his hand went to the back of her head to hold her against his heart.

"Ah God, Cami."

"How did you know?" she cried, her arms locked around his neck as she fought to hold on as tight as possible, to pull him into her skin if there was any way she could do it.

"Crowe had a receiver up here, baby," Rafe answered, his voice raw, torn. "Thank God. He put the receiver up here earlier. The minute I saw the voice activation was blinking I knew—" His hold tightened on her. "Oh God. Baby. I was almost too late. I was almost too late."

She held on to him, certain that if she let him go, if she let her arms release him, let him out of her sight, then she would find out it was all a dream and once again she would be alone.

So alone.

Her hold tightened.

She couldn't be without him again.

She couldn't allow herself to waste so much as a single moment that they could be together.

She had lost so much time. She had nearly lost him.

"I love you," the words tore from her lips as the sobs finally escaped.

More than twelve years of holding them inside, of telling herself it didn't hurt so she could survive. Seven years of loving him, of aching for him, of realizing that nothing, that no one, could ever touch her, hold her, kiss her as Rafer did.

And she could never love anyone as she loved him.

"Ah, Cami." Pulling his head back, he rested his forehead against hers, staring down at her, his gaze so dark, so filled with emotion.

And that emotion had always bound them.

That bond she hadn't been able to decipher hadn't been so hard to figure out; she just had to allow herself to get past the denial. The denial that she had lost their child, that she had lost her dearest friend, and the knowledge that if she lost Rafe again, then like Jaymi, she wouldn't want to live.

She believed that. How many times had she heard Jaymi whisper that she didn't know if she could wake up another morning without her heart?

And now, Cami understood. She knew what her sister had felt, how she had loved, and knew that if she had nothing left of Rafe to hold on to, no reason to get up every morning, then she too would wonder just how much longer she had to wait.

"He's dead, Rafe." Crowe's voice drew their attention back to the scene in the middle of her bedroom floor.

Lowry Berry, the shy, socially reclusive teacher whom she and Jaymi both had called friend, had been a crazed child rapist and a killer.

"Who the hell was he working for, though?" Logan muttered as he propped his hands on his hips and stared down at the bloody corpse.

There was a single gunshot wound to Lowry's chest, directly into his heart. A self-inflicted wound. He had killed himself rather than face trial or have to face the fact that his crimes would be brought to light.

"What do we do now?" she asked as Crowe pulled his phone free of the holder at his hip.

"Now, we call Archer," Rafe breathed out roughly before turning to Amelia, then back to Crowe. "Let Logan call the sheriff. You get her the hell out of here and back home. We don't need her name in this."

Amelia still stood against the wall, watching, her face pale, her eyes locked on Lowry's lifeless form.

"He called me last night." She lifted her gaze to Cami, misery reflected in their depths. "He's never called me before, Cami. He said friends should say good-bye." Amelia gave her head a hard shake as her gaze lifted back to Cami. "I didn't know what he was talking about until I heard Jack's garage had blown up."

"Get her out of here, Logan," Crowe growled. "Now."

"I thought that was your job?" Logan muttered.

Crowe shot him a dangerous, brooding look. "I think she comes with more trouble than I need."

Cami's breath caught at the pain that suddenly flashed in her friend's eyes.

Amelia's shoulders straightened, though, her emerald eyes turning dark and emotionless.

"I didn't need any help getting here, and I don't need any help leaving," she informed them.

Then, steady and calm, she moved to Cami.

"It would kill me if anything happened to you," Amelia said evenly. "And I never blamed you for what Father found. He was looking for something and he found it." She shot Crowe a cold look. "It was my fault."

"Amelia—"

"I hear fucking sirens. Get her the hell out of here if she's going," Crowe rasped.

Amelia turned on her heel and, with Logan close on her heels, hurriedly left the bedroom.

Cami listened until the sound of Amelia's footsteps on the stairs faded away and nothing else was heard.

Rafe's arm slid around Cami once again, pulling her against him, the warmth of his body, the steady strength found there, a balm to what had been her shattered soul.

How had she managed to survive without him for the past three years?

"We don't know who was behind it," she said softly as the sound of the sirens grew closer.

"But now, we know he's out there," Rafe said, his hold on her tightening. "We know he's there, Cami, and we know to watch our backs."

Looking over her head to his cousin, Rafe made a vow to himself. Whoever it was. Whatever had made them a target for whatever reason. They would find him. They would find him, and they would make damned certain he paid with his life as well.

Rafe was thirty years old and he'd believed a single coincidence, Jaymi's death, had marked his life forever.

His life had been marked for far longer than the years after Cami's sister's death. It stretched back to his and his cousins' childhoods and possibly even to the deaths of their parents.

The question was why.

Laying his cheek against Cami's head, he swore to himself he'd find out why. Because he couldn't risk this, he couldn't risk his soul by losing this woman.

If he lost Cami, then he would lose everything he was and he would lose the only reason he had to fight another day.

"I love you, kitten," he whispered against her hair, his eyes clenching closed, his hand stroking down her back as his arms held her close.

She was his.

And in the darkest hours of midnight, when sin was in the eye of the beholder and secrets were guarded with the blood of others, Rafe knew he would no longer be alone.

Coming soon . . .

Look for the next novel in this exciting new series from
#1 *NEW YORK TIMES* BESTSELLING AUTHOR

LORA LEIGH

DEADLY SINS
ISBN: 978-0-312-38909-3

Available in March 2012 from St. Martin's Paperbacks